9112

DATE DUE

WITHDRAWN

4 STARS

Series: TORN BOOK 2.

Also by Erica O'Rourke

Torn

TANGLED

ERICA O'ROURKE

Teen

KENSINGTON PUBLISHING CORP.
www.kensingtonbooks.com

To Danny and my girls:
Home is wherever I'm with you.

ACKNOWLEDGMENTS

Once again, I am faced with the task of figuring out how to adequately thank all of the people who have helped bring this book into the world. The number is so great, and their contributions so huge, I'm not sure it's possible—but I will try.

Joanna Volpe has championed Mo and her story from the first time she read it. I am continually amazed by her brilliance, her heart, her dedication, and her willingness to forgo sleep for the sake of her authors. Sara Kendall has been incredibly generous with her time, attention, and advice, and I am eternally grateful for all three. Nancy Coffey, Kathleen Ortiz, and the rest of the NCLMR family have had my back every step of the way—words are inadequate, but I thank you nevertheless.

Alicia Condon gave me the chance to tell Mo's story and then pushed me to make it even stronger. I am so fortunate to work with someone as encouraging and supportive as her, and I appreciate her faith in me and this project more than I can say. The entire team at K Teen / Kensington has been wonderful, especially Megan Records, who wrote out Verity's postcards by hand to make sure they looked just right, Amy Maffei, copy editor extraordinaire, who triple-checks my math so I don't publicly humiliate myself, and Vida Engstrand, my publicist, who has worked tirelessly to get the word out.

As always, the members of Chicago-North RWA have been the support system every writer dreams about. They listen, they encourage, they prod, and every time we meet, I come away excited to go back to the page. Lynne Hartzer, Keiru Bakke, Clara Kensie, and Ryann Murphy have become friends as well as colleagues, and I am the richer for it. Blythe

Gifford and Margaret Watson are the epitome of graciousness, talent, and professionalism, and I am continually in awe of them. My other writerly groups—the Unsinkables, the Broken Writers, the MargaRITAs—are equally precious. They are smart, funny, gifted writers, and I love them all.

Some people get by with a little help from their friends—but the help my friends have given me is no small thing. Loretta Nyhan's intelligence is matched only by her talent and her kindness. Lisa and Laura Roecker have welcomed me without reservation. Lee Nichols is warm and generous and sends the nicest e-mails when I need them the very most. Kim MacCarron's sharp eye catches all the things I miss. KC Solano is always willing to bounce ideas and design postcards, even when she's sleep-deprived. Lexie Craig is the best long-distance neighbor I could ask for. Lisa Tonkery has saved my sanity—and my bacon—more times than I can count.

Hanna Martine is a brilliant writer and an even better friend. She never, ever lets me take the easy way out, and for that, I would follow her to the ends of the earth.

Eliza Evans reads every word I write. Even the bad ones. *Especially* the bad ones—and she sticks around regardless. I'm glad, because without her, I couldn't write a grocery list, much less a book. Best friends like her are a rare and beautiful thing. Her friendship is one of my greatest treasures.

I knew my family was awesome—but I didn't realize the depths of their awesomeness until I began this journey. My mom has shown me what it means to work hard and accomplish a goal—it was the most important lesson she could have taught me. My dad has demonstrated, every day of my life, what it means to have a moral code. He also taught me about money laundering, but it was strictly from a theoretical standpoint. My sister is brave and smart and makes me laugh until I cry, and is an amazing aunt to my girls. My mother-in-law cheerfully visits museums with my kids, and never complains when I disappear from family visits to write.

Writing these books has brought me great joy, but it pales in comparison to watching my three girls grow up. Smart and feisty and strong and beautiful, and I am so very, very lucky to be their mom. I hope I make them as proud as they make me.

And lastly, Danny, because he is the best person I have ever known. Because he is always pleased, but never surprised, when I do something clever. Because he is the heart of everything I write, and everything I do, and because thank you doesn't even begin to cover it.

CHAPTER 1

Truth is overrated. Lots of things are overrated: Oreos, the Christmas windows on State Street, classic rock, marriage. Everyone wants you to think that the truth is this beautiful shining gift that will set you free. They are lying.

The truth is scary, and usually painful, and it might set you free, but it can also leave you lonely. People say that truth hurts—and they're right, it does—but you can survive the truth. Lies, on the other hand, will kill you dead.

And here's the lie I told myself: I could get my old life back. I could let the nightmare that began my senior year fade away and be the girl I used to be. Ordinary Mo Fitzgerald.

Like I said: The truth might be overrated, but a lie will kill you.

"I don't believe you," Lena Santos said, leaning against a bank of lockers while I rummaged through mine, looking for a library book. "No. Sorry. Not possible."

I shoved aside loose papers, hair elastics, and SAT prep guides until I found it, stuffing the dusty volume into my already-overloaded bag. "Got it. I will not be sad to finish this presentation."

"Don't try changing the subject. I refuse to believe you are skipping the Sadie Hawkins dance."

"I don't have a date."

"So? Neither do I, but I'm still going. Have you even asked anyone?"

We trudged up the staircase, in no particular rush to get to the library. Other schools had lounge furniture and a welcoming staff. St. Brigid's had wooden chairs and Sister Agatha, with her thick black glasses and perpetual shushing. Our presentation on the 17th-century French monarchy was not an incentive to pick up the pace, either.

"Who would I ask?" I shrugged, adjusting my book bag.

Lena made a show of tapping her chin thoughtfully. "Oh, I don't know . . . Colin?"

"Trust me. Colin Donnelly is not the type to attend a high school dance."

"He would if you asked. Aren't you two kind of . . . together?"

"We're figuring it out." I stared at my shoes as we rounded the corner. There was a lot to figure out, like why Colin had put the brakes on—way, way on. Our relationship was like rush-hour traffic. A tiny bit of progress, accompanied by rapid, forceful application of said brakes. He had his reasons, he said, but I was losing patience.

"Besides, can you imagine what my mom would—ow!" I slammed into someone and went sprawling, books, binders, and pens spilling everywhere.

"My apologies," said the man I'd run into—an older gentleman in a black wool top coat and slightly outdated pinstriped suit. He looked like someone's well-off grandfather as he leaned heavily on an ivory-handled cane. "Are you all right?"

There was the faintest trace of an accent in his voice, but I couldn't quite place it. His hat, a black fur dress cap, the kind you usually saw in winter, had fallen nearby. "My fault," I said, handing it to him as I scrambled up.

"No, no. Let me help you." He bent and picked up my bag, then smiled approvingly at me. "One good turn deserves another, yes?"

Bowling him over didn't exactly seem like a good turn, but

I took the olive-drab bag and returned the smile. He wasn't wearing the stick-on ID badge that the office printed out for all visitors, which was strange. The security guards were pretty good about making sure people checked in.

Lena must have noticed something was off, too, because she said solicitously, "Are you looking for someone? Do you need directions?"

"No, thank you." He clamped his hat to his head. As he headed toward the stairs, swinging his cane jauntily, he called back, "I found who I was looking for."

My grip tightened on the strap of my bag and I stood, unmoving, until he was out of sight.

"Library," Lena said, nudging me.

As Sister Agatha shelved books and frowned at our whispered conversation, we grabbed a computer and pretended to review our presentation slides.

"What about the other guy? From this fall?" Lena asked when Sister Agatha had tottered into the stacks. "Ask him to the dance."

"He's gone." Saying the words out loud felt like a door slamming shut inside me. Gone was good, I reminded myself.

My tone must have been too harsh, though, because Lena drew back and inspected her notes for our history presentation with a lot more care than necessary.

I felt a pang of guilt. Lena was smart, and fun to hang out with, and pretty much the only person at St. Brigid's who didn't treat me like a leper. Since my best friend's murder, people had avoided me, like grief was contagious. I didn't want to drive Lena away, too.

"We could do something after the dance. You could crash at my place. If you don't have plans already," I said.

She thawed. "That sounds fun. You're sure you don't want to go?"

I shook my head, and she sighed. "Okay. Sleepover after. Hey, have you sent in your NYU app?"

I swallowed, careful to keep from sounding defensive. "Ummm . . . not yet."

"What?" She looked genuinely startled. "I know your interview was a disaster, but they'll understand."

Disaster was putting it mildly. I'd walked out midquestion. With good reason, but none that I could explain to the college rep I'd been trying to impress. It had ruined my shot at early admission, and maybe even getting into NYU at all.

"You haven't changed your mind about going, right? You've been talking about NYU since freshman year, you and . . ." She trailed off. "You and Verity. I get it now."

She really, really didn't. And there was no way I could explain it to her. Verity and I had always planned to go to college in New York, the two of us united, leaving behind my family's shady history and her picture-perfect one. Now Verity was dead, and I was the one left behind. Despite the rumors, I hadn't blown the interview to sabotage myself. I'd bailed because no matter how much I wanted to get into my dream school, revenge for Verity's death was more important. I'd gotten it, and now I needed to get my life back to normal.

It was nearly impossible to picture normal these days. I knew what it was *supposed* to look like: Verity and me, window-shopping at the funky Wicker Park boutiques she liked, scoping out college guys over sushi, poring over guidebooks for New York, and making plans for our great escape. But that world vanished the day Verity died. In its place was one of ancient magic, dangerously beautiful and full of secrets, with a boy to match. We'd saved his world, and I hadn't seen him since. Every day I reminded myself how little I missed him.

After the things I'd seen and done, I wasn't sure how to make a normal life again. I wasn't sure I wanted to.

But one thing was certain: Normal wasn't going to happen here in Chicago, in the shadow of my family. I needed to be in New York, where people reinvented themselves every day. It was what Verity and I had planned all along, and I owed it to both of us to make it happen.

I rubbed my temples, trying to dispel the headache that had been brewing all morning. "I tanked in the interview, and Jill McAllister was perfect. If they compared us during early admission, there's no way I'd get in. If I wait until regular admission, I might have a shot." Plus, I could show them I had recovered from Verity's death. Strength of character, triumph over adversity, all the things admissions counselors liked to see in an applicant. It felt like I was trading on my grief, but I'd learned that even when the world was falling to pieces, you had to carry on and make do with what you had.

Through the glass doors of the library, I could see someone coming down the hallway, weaving slightly, leaning against the wall for balance. Lena followed my glance. "Jesus," she said, voice low. "Speaking of missing Verity. That girl is going downhill fast, chica. Do you think she's wasted?"

"Constance?" I shook my head. Baby-faced Constance Grey, my best friend's sister. She was struggling, sure, but I couldn't see her filling a water bottle with vodka just to make it through Biology class. "Maybe she's sick."

Constance stumbled, lolling her head. Her caramel-colored hair, a few shades darker than Verity's, swung in a curtain across her back. My skin prickled, like I'd scuffed across shag carpeting in my socks.

"Cover for me with Sister?" I asked, standing up. Lena nodded, with a look mixing pity and exasperation.

"She won't want your help," she called.

The library doors swung shut behind me. Constance and I were alone in the deserted hallway. "You okay?"

Her head snapped up, and my heart squeezed. She looked so much like Verity. Lighter eyes, more freckles, features more rounded. But the same nose, the same cheekbones, the same slight wave to their hair. For a second, I wondered who she saw in the mirror each morning: Herself? Or Verity?

She scowled and turned away. "I'm fine. Go 'way." Her voice was strained, like she couldn't get the words out, and she banged into the lockers with a crash. Lena was right— she didn't want my help. I still had to try.

"Are you sick?"

"I said, go away!" She turned to glare at me, and I stepped

back at the sight of her pupils, so enormous they were barely ringed with blue.

"You're on something." She didn't smell like alcohol, though. The prickling feeling intensified, centered in my palms. I rubbed my hands together. "Constance, what did you take? If one of the teachers finds you . . ."

"No! Don't feel good. Itchy," she said, sounding fretful. "Skin's too tight."

"Somebody gave you something. What was it?" Glancing around, I guided her into the bathroom.

"Nothing!" Inside, she pressed her cheek against the tile wall and moaned, scrabbling at the sleeves of her navy sweater. Her nails scored thin red lines along her arms. "Too tight."

I reached for her hands, but she shrieked and twisted away. I had to talk her down. Someone would hear her soon, and we'd get caught, and it wouldn't matter how sorry people felt for her—a fact she'd been using to her advantage since the first day of school, blowing off homework and mouthing off to teachers, skipping chapel and coming in late every day. If they found her high as a kite in the bathroom during second period, she'd be starting school at a building with metal detectors and a visible police presence by the end of the week.

Constance hated me. She'd made that clear the day of Verity's funeral, and who could blame her? Verity and I both went for ice cream. I'd lived. Verity hadn't. What she didn't know—and what I couldn't tell her—was that her sister's death wasn't a random street crime. It was an assassination. Maybe if she'd known, things would be different between us. Maybe she'd let me take care of her. But I kind of doubted it, especially when her elbow caught me across the face and I staggered back, crying out.

"What the hell, Constance? Knock it off!" Blood poured out of my nose, and I clapped my hand over it, trying to staunch the flow. The tingling sensation spread from my hands to my arms and into my chest, uncomfortable but not painful. I glanced around the room, shoving back dread and the feeling that I was in over my head. Again.

"How long?" I asked.

She rapped her head against the tile, still clawing at her arms, the shrieks transforming to agonized moans.

I grabbed her wrists and dragged her away from the wall, blood dripping onto my shirt. "When did this start?"

"This weekend," she panted, the veins in her neck standing out. "It hurts so bad. What's wrong?"

"I don't know, honey. Hang on." The scar on my hand, a shiny, mottled pink, pulsed painfully, and Constance started to keen. Around us, the air thrashed and twisted, the caustic scent of ozone burning my nose. As I watched, her dark gold hair began to lift and kink into knots.

"Mo?"

"I'm here. It'll be okay."

I was lying. It was the last thing I said before my best friend's little sister went supernova in the second-floor girls' bathroom, taking me with her.

CHAPTER 2

I don't know how long we were out. Not long, probably, because Lena entered, her expression more mild concern than outright panic as I was waking up. "Everything all . . . holy shit."

Constance was sprawled near the sinks, pale as moonlight except for the crimson streaks dribbling from her nose. I knelt next to her, holding my hand an inch above her open mouth. "She's breathing."

She looked at me, did a double take. "You're bleeding! What happened?"

I shifted Constance's head onto my lap instead of the black and white tiles. "It was an accident."

"Her fist accidentally ran into your face?" Lena yanked a handful of paper towels out of the dispenser and ran cold water over them. "Use this."

"Thanks. She didn't mean it. She's . . . sick." Could magic make people sick? The instant before we'd been knocked out, I'd felt it. Raw magic, staggeringly powerful, sweeping through us both. It was gone now, but its appearance in that bathroom pretty much confirmed Constance was an Arc.

So much for getting back to normal life.

"Look, Mo. I know you worry about her, but maybe it's time for some tough love, you know? The girl is on something." She handed me another clutch of damp paper towels.

I brushed Constance's hair away from her face and dabbed

at the blood. A whisper of a breeze flittered through the room and vanished. "She's not waking up. Shouldn't she be waking up?"

"Hell if I know. We should get the nurse."

"The nurse can't do anything." We needed Luc. I'd promised him my help, if he needed it, but I wasn't looking forward to asking for his. Owing Lucien DeFoudre was never a good idea. I touched my wrist, trying to sense the faint, otherworldly chain connecting us. The last time I'd felt it had been a month ago, in the graveyard where Verity was buried. "I need more time."

Lena checked her watch. "You've got eight minutes until the bell rings. What if she's hurt?"

"I know somebody. He can help."

Lena squatted down, carefully tucking her skirt under her. "Mo, whatever the frosh is mixed up in, it's bad. Don't let her bring you down, too. Let someone else take care of this."

Constance convulsed once on the floor. The air thrummed while my scar burned white through the blood coating my hand. Last time the blood had been Verity's, and she'd died. I wouldn't let that happen again.

"Promise you won't get the nurse," I said.

"Tell me you are joking."

"I'll take care of her. You know I wouldn't let anything happen to her; she's Verity's sister, for God's sake. But I can't let anyone else see her like this."

"Mo, in five minutes, half the sophomore class will be in here."

"Go back to the library. Tell Sister Agatha I didn't feel well." Which was not a lie. My headache had bloomed into a migraine and my stomach clenched with nausea. My skin crawled as the magic built, turning the air oppressive and charged, like a lightning strike. The sensation made me nervous, for all of us. "Seriously. I will take care of Constance. But you need to go."

"I do not understand you."

"I know. Lena, please."

She bit her lip, hurt and indecision clouding her face. Lena was the kind of pretty that made people underestimate her. They saw big brown eyes in a heart-shaped face and immediately wanted to protect her. At first, anyway. Once they'd seen her in action—ferociously bloodthirsty on the soccer field, blunt and opinionated everywhere else—they reconsidered. But right now, she just looked wounded, like I'd betrayed her somehow.

"Later," she said, voice brittle. "You're going to explain all this later, right?"

I hesitated, not wanting to make a promise I couldn't keep. "I'll let you know how she's doing."

Constance convulsed again, eyes rolling back, her body slamming into the ground.

Lena shook her head and backed out of the bathroom.

"Constance, honey. It'll be okay." Another false promise, and the stall doors banged wildly, as if a tornado were ripping through the room. She gasped, trying to get a full breath as the pressure in the room ramped up. Why was the magic attacking her—attacking *us?*

I didn't want to see Luc again. I'd done what he and his people, the Arcs, had asked of me, stopping a prophecy that would have destroyed them. I'd even agreed to help if they needed me again. Something about the sharp slash of his smile, hinting at things I wasn't sure I was ready for and wanted all the same, had convinced me to say yes. But I'd barely recovered from the experience. Now my days were filled with school and work, trying to figure out how to live a normal life without my best friend. To invite Luc back would ruin all of that. He'd upend everything, he'd make Colin furious, he'd pull me back into a world where I was even more of an outcast than at St. Brigid's.

But Verity's sister was in danger, and Luc was the only one who could help us.

Keeping one arm around Constance's shuddering form, I touched my wrist again. The line where we'd been bound was blisteringly hot, probably reacting to the magic in the room. I closed my eyes, trying to envision the silver chain trailing off into a network of magical lines I knew existed yet couldn't see. I pictured my fingers gripping it and yanking, like someone in a church tower, ringing the bell for compline. "Please," I whispered to the wild, charged air around me. "Come on, Luc. You promised."

Constance writhed. Around us, the air began to hum again. I leaned over, trying to shield her from the rising magic as she clawed at her skin and caught my arm, too. My lungs squeezed shut. We wouldn't survive another surge. Distantly, I heard the bell ringing and the clamor of two hundred teenage girls spilling into the corridor outside.

And then, much closer, a noise like the world splitting open. I braced myself for what came next.

"Mouse," Luc drawled, unflappable and infuriating as always. "Next time, maybe just pick up the phone, hmn?"

CHAPTER 3

I sank back as Luc's dark green eyes darted around the room. Someone pulled on the door, and he waved his hand as if he was shooing a gnat. It slammed shut. On the other side, voices rose in outrage. He moved to Constance's side and checked her pupils and pulse, frowning.

While he looked over Constance, I watched him—never a chore. The keening of the magic ratcheted up, and the pounding on the door increased. He touched my chin gently and then pulled back. "Best we go," he said abruptly.

"Won't the door hold?" I asked, my fingers hovering over where he'd touched me, trying to focus. He always had that effect on me. It was one of the things I had not missed.

"Keeps them out. Won't keep the magic in. Hold tight," he said, lacing his fingers through mine with one hand and sliding the other arm around Constance. The awful, nauseating, familiar sensation of going Between jerked through me, everything black and bottomless.

When we came through, we were in a shack—the walls more gaps than boards, two chairs and a slanted table shoved against one wall, an ancient-looking twin bed under a window with a cracked pane of glass. I stumbled on the braided rug.

"Bed," he grunted, jerking his head in the right direction.

Constance was still seizing, but we managed to settle her down, even as the air began to charge again.

"Out," he said. "I got this."

"She's Verity's sister. I'm not leaving her."

He touched her shoulder and murmured indistinctly. I'd forgotten how he sounded when he was casting magic, the weirdly beautiful echo of it slipping over me. Constance seemed to relax a bit. I tried to move toward her, but Luc blocked my way.

"Happens this way, sometimes. You can't help."

"What's wrong with her?"

He ran a hand through his hair, jet black strands immediately falling back into place. "Her powers are comin' through. Nothing for you to do, Mouse. Out you go."

As the magic gathered strength, the room took a slow, sickening spin.

"I managed before," I said, grabbing on to the back of a chair and trying to sound confident. "I'm not leaving." But the distance across the tiny room seemed so far.

Luc glanced at Constance again, and then he reached out to steady me, his hand on my shoulder. "Can't watch you both," he said, his face so close to mine I was afraid he might kiss me. The thought terrified me and I didn't know why. We had bigger problems right now than our nonexistent relationship. "You want to help her, get clear. Now."

So I did, stumbling through the doorway into a patchy clearing. To one side, a dirt road left a faint trail through low, scrubby grass. My sweater, the same navy V-neck every girl at St. Brigid's wore October through April, was suffocatingly warm. I pulled it off, and my hair crackled with static. Or magic. Hard to tell which.

The press of the magic seemed to ease as I moved away, and I filled my lungs with humid air. The only sound was the whir of insects and, farther away, an occasional splash. The shack was silent, and a sudden fear enveloped me, my vision going dark again. What if Constance died? How would I explain it to the Greys, their only remaining child gone, months after their oldest had been slaughtered?

My knees buckled, and I stumbled to a giant tree stump,

sweater clutched in my hand. Despite the stabbing pain in my temples, I tried to reason through what I'd witnessed.

Constance's powers were coming through. By Arc standards, it was happening too early. Magic was hereditary, but they typically didn't develop their powers until sixteen or seventeen. Verity's powers had manifested junior year, though she'd kept it from me. Was Constance in danger because her powers appeared earlier?

Arcs didn't interact with raw magic; they drew their power from ley lines—currents of magical energy, rooted in one of the four elements. The lines crisscrossed the world, from the core of the earth to the stratosphere, conduits that tempered the corrosive raw magic and made it usable for Arcs. Flats, regular humans, were unaffected. They could pass through a line and never realize it. Most Flats went about their everyday life unaware that just beyond their seeing was a world with near-limitless power.

And then there was me. No one knew exactly how Verity's powers had been transferred to me or what the long-term repercussions would be. Everything about me was an anomaly to the Arcs—a Flat who could withstand raw magic but couldn't cast a spell. A month ago, I'd stepped into the very heart of the magic, dug my fingers into it, and remade the ley lines. I'd kept none of it for myself, except one small shard I'd used to kill the woman who had ordered my best friend's death. Constance and Verity's aunt. I didn't regret it. I'd sworn to get revenge for Verity's death, and in killing Evangeline, I'd gotten it. But if Constance died because Evangeline wasn't here to help her, it was my fault.

I sank onto the tree stump, knees wobbly, and stared at the battered shack.

The tiny building with its slanted porch and sagging roof seemed perfectly real. I'd seen firsthand how Arcs could spell a building, making it look disreputable and uninviting, to keep Flats out. But there was no one here to break the quiet or pay attention to the run-down little house. It truly was as sorry looking as it had seemed at first glance.

It totally didn't fit Luc. Luc, with his perfect, nonchalantly elegant clothing, so carelessly gorgeous you knew it must have cost a fortune. Luc, with his charming, luxurious townhouse in the French Quarter, filled with art from around the world and some very nice, very potent bourbon. Luc, who made me furious and made me want him, usually within the same minute.

Luc, who wanted the girl he believed me to be, not the girl I actually was.

I pulled my knees to my chest and watched the windows with their twisting, flapping gingham curtains. He couldn't expect me to sit out here forever. My teachers would mark me absent. The school would call my mom. Mom would run to my uncle. And then it was all over. Because I'd learned how to lie to my family in the last few months, keep secrets bigger and more dangerous than anything they'd ever held close. They'd taught me, after all. But when I turned up missing, my uncle would call the one person I couldn't lie to. The person who knew me so well, he practically had a road map of my soul. Colin, who would know immediately that whoever had taken me was more magic than Mafia.

And he would be pissed.

I tried to envision what to tell him: *Verity's sister was attacked by magic, so I called Luc, not you, and he took me someplace hot.* I glanced up, taking in the mossy vegetation and the damp, decaying scent of the air. Hot and swampy. Louisiana, I guessed. Luc's home, though he was more suited to the glamour of New Orleans than the bayou.

The peeling green shutters slammed against the walls. A splintering sound rent the air, and I expected to see the shack fall down, but in the silence that followed, a couple stepped around the edge of the shack. They strolled across the clearing, flames edging their path like an awards ceremony carpet, extinguishing harmlessly when they'd passed. Important people, I guessed, and the kind that wanted everyone to know it.

The woman wore a dress the color of wine, simple lines in beautifully rumpled linen with a gauzy scarf wound around her neck. Her fingertips rested lightly on the man's arm as he guided her across the scrubby terrain. Despite the oppressive heat, they both looked cool and fresh. The man doffed his hat as they approached, and I stood, trying to straighten my shirt. My filthy, bloodstained, slightly singed shirt. I discreetly tossed my ruined sweater behind the tree stump.

"You must be the Vessel," drawled the man. His skin was the color of pecans, dark and shiny, his features strong and aristocratic. "Yes?"

I was a lot more than the Vessel. It would be nice if one of the Arcs would notice. I didn't bother to keep the edge out of my voice. "I'm Mo Fitzgerald."

"The Vessel," he said again, his expression faintly amused but his tone expectant, a bit challenging. I had the sensation I was being tested for more than just my identity.

The woman, delicate and birdlike, with her dark hair in an elaborate chignon, tugged his arm. "Dominic," she chided. "Of course it's her. Who else would Luc bring here?"

Dominic. The name stirred a whisper of memory, and I followed it back through events I'd tried to forget. *Yes, Dominic cleaves to the old ways, doesn't he? It's certainly cost him enough,* Evangeline had said, mocking and triumphant.

I stared, mortified at the realization I'd just mouthed off to one of the most powerful people in the Arcs' world. It was like having the president of the United States drop in on a student council meeting. Dominic DeFoudre stopping by meant that something had gone very, very wrong. "You're Luc's dad? He called his *dad?*"

We were in bigger trouble than I thought.

CHAPTER 4

Fathers were an area I had almost no experience with. None good, anyway. Luc's father was a member of the Quartoren, the council that governed Arc society, and the Patriarch of his House, in charge of all Arcs that drew on the fire-based ley lines. And I was magically, permanently bound to his son.

"I'm Mo," I said, forcing myself to say the words. "I'm the Vessel."

"Glad to hear it," he said, cutting his eyes toward the shack. "Dominic DeFoudre. Been waiting on you for a while, Maura Fitzgerald. Didn't expect this was how we'd meet."

A hot, keening wind kicked up, making my hair lash around my face. The moss hanging from the trees twisted and swayed. "Constance!" I turned toward the house. Even at this distance, the magic stung my skin, but I forced myself to ignore it.

"Dominic," said the woman. Luc's mom? Luc had a mom? He'd never mentioned her before. She withdrew her fingers from his arm and made a delicate shooing motion. "Go on, now. This will be nice for you two."

Nice? Father–son golf outings were nice. Saving Constance from an onslaught of raw magic didn't qualify in my book. Even Dominic's expression was more grimace than smile, but he bowed to both of us. "Ladies."

He ambled toward the shack, one hand clamping down on

his hat in the increasingly violent wind. If I'd had any doubts that he was really Luc's dad, they were erased in that instant. The man walked cheerfully into disaster, like there was no place he'd rather be, like braving the raw magic was something he did every day, after his café au lait but before the crossword puzzle. No wonder Luc was always so easy in his skin.

"I'm sure your friend will be fine. Some of us take the transition harder than others," Luc's mother said when he'd gone inside. Her voice was soft, but it carried through the din. "I'm Marguerite," she added. "I'd been hoping to meet you, but perhaps not quite like this. Shall we sit?"

There were no chairs, but she held her hand up, palm out, and the weedy, dusty grass transformed to something resembling the grounds at Wrigley Field. Magic terrified me, but even I had to admit there were times it came in handy.

"After you," she said.

My legs were trembling, and I sank down gratefully into the lush grass. Marguerite followed, arranging her skirt with a delicate grace. "You're unwell."

I tugged at my shirt again, feeling grubby. "It was the magic, at school . . . I got caught in it."

Her eyes, a faded green, not half as vibrant as her son's, closed briefly. "No. It's more."

"I'm fine," I said. I'd felt lousy all morning, but it seemed wimpy to complain about it now. Marguerite gave me a reproving smile, like she could hear the lie in my voice. "It's more important to help Constance now. She doesn't have anyone else."

"She has you."

"I'm not her sister." She must know Evangeline was dead, and with Verity gone, there was no one to explain the Arcs to Constance. I was useless. Despite the Torrent, and the magic that had run through my veins like blood, I had no powers of my own. I knew more about quantum physics than I did magic.

"Luc spoke about her often." She rested a sympathetic

hand on my sleeve. "It's hard to fathom how she could be gone, isn't it?"

Something in her gentle question prompted my honesty. "I miss her. Still. All the time."

"And why wouldn't you? That kind of loss, so abrupt . . . There's no timetable for grief, Mo."

The words were an unexpected comfort. "That's not what most people say."

"Most people haven't experienced that kind of sadness." A shadow crossed her face. "I hope it's not my son telling you such tales. He should know better."

"Luc gets it, I think. He misses her, too." I remembered the bleakness on his face when he'd told me Verity was dead, the tender way he'd laid a bouquet of delphiniums at her grave. In a way, her loss united us.

"Yes." Delicately, she touched the corner of her eye. "He wears his grief differently than most. He holds it so close, I'm not sure he even knows what it does to him."

I tugged at a blade of grass, surprised at the tremor in her voice. It seemed odd that she would be so affected by talking about Verity when they'd never met. Across the clearing, Constance cried out, and a few shingles tore off the roof of the shack, landing nearby. Marguerite pressed her hand against my arm when I started to stand.

"Luc called his father here for a reason. I wouldn't always suggest leaving things to those two men," she added with a mischievous smile, reminiscent of Luc's, "but I promise, she couldn't be in more capable hands."

I studied the shack, how it seemed to sway in concert with the surges of power. "They'll help her? Luc is really as good as he says?"

"Better," Marguerite said, so promptly I had to believe her. "More than he thinks, in fact. I wouldn't want him to get a big head, so it's best not to bring it up. You understand."

I couldn't help the laugh that slipped out, and she joined me for a second, then sobered, not quite meeting my eyes. "He's destined for such great things, and he doesn't realize the half of it. Fate doesn't make mistakes, you know. It wouldn't call someone who wasn't capable."

"Fate." No wonder Luc was always going on about it, if Marguerite believed, too.

"It sounds so pompous when I put it that way, doesn't it? It's a hazard, of being married to a Patriarch, I suppose. Everything's always so somber and grand. I imagine Luc'll be different when it's his turn, but it'll all depend."

"On what?"

Before she could answer, a window exploded, the sound startling. Marguerite tipped her head to one side, listening, but didn't turn to look. Instead, she kept her face pointed to a spot just above my shoulder.

"You're . . . blind?" Oh, God. Could I be more rude? To Luc's mom? I should have noticed how she tracked the sound of my voice instead of my movements, the way Dominic had guided her across the yard.

She shrugged lightly. "As I said, some people take the transition harder than others."

"I'm sorry. Luc never said." He'd never told me anything about his family.

"When would he have had time?"

Valid point, but my insides curdled with embarrassment. How had I not noticed? And how had I never asked Luc about his family? He knew plenty about mine. Why had he stayed so quiet? Somehow I doubted his silence could be chalked up to absentmindedness.

"Don't pity me too much. I have other gifts." She paused. "It's quieter now. Do you feel it?"

The air seemed to be losing its charge, the wind cooling to a pleasant breeze. The crackling, ripping sounds from inside the shack gradually subsided.

I struggled to my feet. "Can I go in?"

Marguerite closed her eyes. "It should be safe. May I take your arm?"

Mortification flooded me. I'd been ready to dash off and leave Luc's mom sitting on the ground in the middle of the bayou. Way to make a first impression. I helped her up, and she rested her hand on my arm.

As we approached the shack, I looked back to see the verdant patch of green fade away. Nice trick. Marguerite would be a definite hit in my neighborhood.

Luc opened the door, one arm braced against the top of the door frame, and I nearly stumbled on the uneven ground. I'd forgotten how searingly gorgeous he was, his body all lean muscle and a face that looked like it had been carved from amber. The magic only sharpened the effect. The line around my wrist throbbed, and I stepped toward him without thinking. He grinned at me, a little more worn than usual but just as arrogant.

"*Maman,*" he said, never taking his gaze off mine, his eyes flashing with amusement and challenge and heat. "Thanks for taking care of Mouse. What do you think of my girl?"

Before I could remind him that I was absolutely not his girl, Marguerite stepped ahead of me, no hesitation, and rapped Luc on the shoulder with a loose fist.

"I think you need your head examined if you believe that's a proper introduction."

He laughed and hugged her, then turned toward me again. "Mouse, this is my *maman,* Marguerite DeFoudre. *Maman,* Maura Fitzgerald, but people call her Mo."

"You don't," she pointed out.

"I'm special."

She smacked him again, fondly. "You're *something,* son."

"Constance," I said. "I want to see her."

" 'Course you do." With a sweeping motion, he gestured me into the shack, past his father, to the rickety cot.

Constance lay on the bed, ghostly white, her hair sticking damply to her face. But her breathing was even, and the bleeding had stopped. "She's okay?"

"Right as rain," Luc said. "Or air. Guessin' air, anyway." Relief washed over me, and Luc's fingertips grazed my hand like butterfly wings.

"Come outside, please." Without waiting for a response,

Dominic stepped through the open doorway, his footsteps making the entire cabin shudder.

I glanced back at Constance, frowning, and Marguerite touched my arm. "I'll sit with her."

"Thank you," I said, and Luc pulled a chair over to the side of the bed, then guided Marguerite to it. She eased into the seat with a grace I'd never possess in a hundred years, and reached for Constance's hand.

I smoothed back Constance's hair and adjusted the thin blanket over her. Luc stood unmoving at the broken window.

"Patience has never been your father's strong suit," Marguerite said.

For a moment longer, he was motionless. Then he turned, holding out his hand. "Ready, Mouse?"

I hesitated, then slipped my fingers inside his and followed him onto the porch.

Near the spot where Marguerite and I had waited, Dominic was deep in conversation with two other people—an old woman leaning on a cane and an aging hippie with a receding hairline. None of them looked happy. A few feet beyond the group, three separate doors were cut into the air, each outlined with a different colored flame. The space inside was filled with endless black, icy air leaching out and flowing across the stubby grass.

"Who are they?"

"The Quartoren," he said with a grimace.

"That's a bad thing, isn't it?" I couldn't imagine why they would take an interest in Constance.

"Ain't good." But before I could ask more, Luc tugged me across the clearing.

CHAPTER 5

Luc's fingers tightened on mine as we approached the Quartoren. With my free hand, I brushed at the sweaty tendrils of hair clinging to my face. Dominic waited until we'd stopped, and Luc dipped his head, murmuring a greeting to the strangers.

"Pascal, Orla," said Dominic, nodding to the man and woman. "I'd like to present Maura Fitzgerald. The Vessel. Pascal and Orla are the Heads of Earth and Air, respectively."

"Nice to meet you," I said, the words sounding more like a question than a statement.

Pascal studied me, adjusting his wire-rimmed glasses, his lips moving silently. Orla gave a short, unfriendly nod and turned back to Dominic. "You're certain?"

"Of course I am. The girl belongs to your House. See for yourself, if you don't believe me."

Orla glanced over at the shack and pursed her lips, her orangy-red lipstick feathering into the wrinkles around her mouth. "That won't be necessary."

"Good. We should be getting this under way. You'll come with us," Dominic said, nodding at me.

Luc's hand urged me behind him with the very faintest pressure, but I stood my ground.

"Come with you? Where? For what?" I eyed the flickering doorway to Between. "I can't leave Constance."

"The girl is fine," said Orla. "Marguerite's with her."

"We need to return to New Orleans," Pascal said. "We've work to do."

"No offense, but the only place I'm going is back to Chicago. Constance needs a doctor, and I'm supposed to be in third period right now."

"I'm afraid that's not an option. Something's wrong with the magic," said Dominic. "It's not typical for an Arc's powers to come through this way. But we're seeing it more and more, with children much younger than the girl lyin' on that bed."

"Her name is Constance Grey." I gave the words a faint edge. "She's Verity's little sister."

"We know exactly who she is," snapped Orla.

"Point is, when you remade the lines, something changed. The magic is stronger. More wild, like it's lashing out. It's putting our people in danger." Dominic looked at me, clearly troubled.

"You think it's my fault?"

"Easy," Luc murmured. He'd been strangely silent, and now he was taking their side? I pulled my hand from his.

"Fault's a strong word," Dominic hedged. "We think you can fix whatever's gone wrong."

"I don't know what's wrong. I fixed the lines, like you wanted. That was the prophecy, right? Remake the lines, stop the Torrent, save the world. And I did." There had been a moment, caught up in the pandemonium of the Torrent, that I'd understood everything. I'd grasped the true nature of the magic, saw the underpinnings of the world. Once Luc had pulled me out, the knowledge had burned away like fog on a sunny morning. But one fact remained clear. "The lines were balanced. They were whole. Everything should be okay."

Pascal spoke. "The issue resides within the magic itself, not the lines. You're the only person we know of who has encountered raw magic and lived. It follows that you'd be the only one who could fix it."

Logical, sure. But there was no guarantee that I'd survive a second go-round.

"It's endangering everyone," Dominic added. "Spells and workings are turnin' destructive without warning. Children younger than Constance are getting their powers. You know what would have happened if Luc hadn't pulled you two out? That school would have fallen down around your ears. Darklings would have come. They're getting stronger, you know. Every time the raw magic overflows, the Darklings are on it like a hound after a fox."

I shuddered before I could stop myself. Darklings. The assassins who had killed Verity. Nightmare creatures, impossibly fast and strong, willing to devour anyone who stood between them and a feast of raw magic. I flashed back to the memory of a curving, bone white talon gleaming with blood, reaching for me.

"You caused this," Orla said. "Now you need to fix it. And we are wasting time by arguing."

Fear bloomed inside me, turning my skin slick, and I fought to keep the tremor out of my voice. "I have school. And work. I have . . . a life. You can't expect me to abandon it."

All three of the Quartoren stared at me. It was obvious that was exactly what they expected. I looked at Luc, waiting for him to tell his father it wouldn't work, that I couldn't help, that they had the wrong girl. Again. But he kept his eyes fixed on the patchy grass at our feet.

"We need your assistance," Pascal said eventually. "Without you, it's unlikely we can find a solution."

"Your solution sounds a lot like you're throwing me under the bus. And I'm sorry if there are problems now, but I didn't cause them. I fixed the magic. Now I need to fix my own life."

Orla scoffed. "You're so fond of your Flat life? You'd place it above the needs of our entire people? Then take the girl back with you." She raised her chin and addressed the others. "She is descended from Flats and a traitor, and my House wants no part of her."

"Let's not say things we don't mean," Dominic cut in.

"I mean every word," Orla said. "The House of Rafale will not claim the girl. I'll have no business with the Flat, no matter that she is the Vessel. We'll find another way."

She turned on her heel and stalked a short distance away, cane thumping into the ground. She was surprisingly fast for an old woman. Dominic jerked his head at Pascal, who gave me a long, searching look before following her. A moment later, there was a crack like a gunshot, and the pair of them went Between.

Dominic frowned at me. "She's wrong, you know. There is no other way. Pascal's looked at it from every angle—it's what he does. We need your help, and we don't exactly have an overabundance of time."

"You've waited a month," Luc said, speaking up at last. "Wouldn't hurt to give her a little breathing room."

Dominic inclined his head.

"The Darklings were coming? To St. Brigid's?" I wasn't ready for the magic to infringe on my world. Whatever problems I had in my real life were nothing compared to the trouble Darklings would bring.

"It's why I brought you here," Luc said. "The magic was centered on Constance, not the school. Pulled her out, there was nothing left to interest the Darklings. And here, there's no people, no major lines for miles around. Not as much magic for them to feed on."

"Good plan," I said, surprised to find my legs were shaking. "Great plan, actually."

He shrugged, but the smile playing across his lips told me he was pleased.

When we entered the cabin, Marguerite was humming softly as Constance slept. Her color was improved, her breathing regular. Orla had insinuated that was temporary. How long did Constance have?

Dominic helped Marguerite to her feet, the gesture unexpectedly sweet. "We'll be going now."

"We've only just met Mo," she protested. "Surely it won't hurt to stay a bit longer."

"Orla's feathers are ruffled. Best we go and soothe them," he said, slanting a look toward Luc that seemed to be both warning and reproach. "We'll talk. Soon."

Luc's hand reached for mine again, but I'd moved away to hover over Constance.

Marguerite gifted me with a smile. "It was so nice to finally meet you. Luc . . ." He bent down, and she brushed a kiss over his cheek. "Behave yourself."

I would have sworn he blushed. Dominic doffed his hat and drew Marguerite outside. In a moment, we heard the lightning-strike sound of their trip Between. Luc dropped into one of the rickety chairs, the cocky veneer he'd worn in front of the Quartoren falling away. My nerves prickled, the way they always seemed to when we were alone.

"Your parents seem . . ." I searched for a word that would fit both Marguerite and Dominic. Chalk and cheese, my uncle would say. "They seem nice."

He rolled his head from side to side, working out the kinks. "*Maman* is. My dad's more like you."

"Not nice?" From anyone else, it would have been an insult. From Luc, it was almost a compliment.

"He's got a big role to play. Not much room left over for nice."

Right. I was never just Mo, to Luc. I was always the Vessel, the one he was fated to be with. But I wasn't sure I believed in fate. And I wanted a guy who wanted me, not the prophecy I'd taken on.

I wanted to snap at him, but he looked so worn-out, features drawn, eyes shadowed. Dealing with raw magic was dangerous, exhausting work, and he'd done it solely because I'd asked. My frustration leached away. "Thanks for helping us."

His closed his eyes, exhaled slowly. "I helped you. She just happened to be in the room."

On the cot, Constance stirred. "We should probably go home. People are going to notice we're missing."

"Let her rest for a bit. You should, too."

I skirted the shards of glass scattered across the floor and sat down in the other chair. He waved a hand lazily, mouthing the words to a spell, and the pieces flew back into place, the cracks glowing red before melting together, creating a fresh pane before my eyes. It must be nice to fix things so easily. A talent like that, you wouldn't even care what you had broken.

"Been a month," he said. "How you been?"

"Good, I guess. Considering."

He nodded, and I figured he probably felt the same way. "Cujo still hangin' around?"

"Colin is still around, yes." It was the most comfortable explanation I could give, especially to Luc.

"That's a shame. No cause for it," he said. "Seraphim come after you, won't be anything he can do."

"He's not there to protect me from Arcs." If he were, you can bet he'd put Luc at the top of the "people to avoid" list. "Do you really think the Seraphim are still a problem? We stopped them."

"They turned a member of the Quartoren. They killed the Vessel." His mouth crooked. "Tried to, anyway. Not the mark of a group who gives up easily. If I had to guess, they're regrouping, figuring out their next move."

"You think they'll come after me." Something shadowed and slithery stirred inside me.

"Seems like a possibility." He eyed me. "You don't sound too worried."

I watched the moss-draped branches sway in the breeze, keeping my face blank. Luc would not be in favor of me going up against the Seraphim again. "Should I be?"

He seemed to consider the question. "Not yet. Maybe not at all. We're keeping an eye on it."

"Okay. I'll worry when you tell me to."

"Speakin' of bad guys, how's your uncle? Still playing errand boy for the Mob?"

"I don't ask." It was better not to. My family's relationship with organized crime had sent my father to federal prison, which made me less inclined to ask about things better kept secret. I wasn't lying to myself, exactly. There was no changing the truth of my family. I simply stayed as far away from it as possible. Except for Colin, of course. He was the exception—the very hot, very intimidating exception—to the rule.

Constance whimpered once and fell quiet. I started to get up and check on her, but Luc clamped a hand over my wrist. "She's fine, Mouse. For now, anyway. What were you thinking, running in after her?"

"I was thinking I should help Verity's sister."

He gave a harsh laugh. "Nearly forgot. Anything Vee would have done . . ."

"You didn't complain when I took her place in the prophecy," I said. "That's what she would have done, too."

He rubbed a hand over his face. "Too tired to go 'round with you on this. You took over as the Vessel. Nobody forced you. But now that you are, I'd appreciate if you'd stop divin' headfirst into raw magic like it's a damn swimming hole."

"I was trying to help."

"Getting yourself killed won't help anyone. Specially not Constance Grey." He glared at me. "And you're still bleedin'."

I touched my upper lip gingerly. My finger came away a deep, shiny red.

"You want me to . . ."

I wiped the blood away with the back of my hand. "It'll stop soon."

He frowned. "C'mon, Mouse. Let me kiss and make it all better."

I shivered despite the heat. "No, thanks."

"Because of Cujo?" He scraped at the peeling paint of the floorboards, carefully not looking at me.

"Is it so hard to believe I don't want to kiss you?"

He considered for a moment before turning his burning gaze back on me. "Yeah. Let me heal you. No kissin' involved."

The droplets were falling faster now, and I leaned forward, pinching the bridge of my nose. My head throbbed, and pain won out over pride. "Fine."

I expected a smirk, but his expression was more relieved than victorious. Gently, he cupped my face in his hands. My eyes drifted shut as he whispered, silvery words that dissolved before I could register them, and the pain in my head dissolved with them. When I opened my eyes, his fingertips still curved along my jaw, his mouth inches from mine.

"You're sure?" he asked, voice low and strained.

I wasn't, and the realization sent me stumbling out of the chair. "Orla said she won't claim Constance. What does that mean?"

He sighed. "Getting your powers isn't like flipping a switch. Most of the time, it comes on gradually. Lets a kid get some training in before they start handling all that power."

"You could train her," I said.

"I can give her pointers," he said. "But she's an Air; she needs someone from her own House if she's going to get this under control."

"And Orla just said the Air Arcs won't help. She's screwed, isn't she?"

Luc stood and crossed the room, taking my hand in his. "I'm sorry. For all of it."

"Pascal thinks I caused the problem with the magic. If he's right, this is my fault?"

He didn't answer, and I was grateful. Nothing he could say would make it better. If Pascal was right, the only way to help Constance was to go back into the magic. If he was wrong, there *was* no way to help her at all.

Instead, he rubbed a thumb over the scar across my palm. The magic that bound us together flared bright and true, and for an instant I felt less alone.

The bed creaked as Constance shifted. "She's waking up. We have to go home."

"Need you, Mouse." His tone was so stark it hurt.

"You need the Vessel."

The corner of his mouth twitched, in a grimace or a smile, I couldn't tell. "One and the same."

CHAPTER 6

We came Between in Constance's room, all cotton candy pink and lemon yellow. It didn't suit her anymore. Like me, she'd changed—once when Verity died and again, now that the magic was claiming her. The only way I could help was to send Luc out of the room, ease her into an old, clean T-shirt, and tuck her in bed. My entire body ached from the morning's events—even my bones felt bruised—and I carefully made my way out into the hall.

I hadn't been in Verity's home since her funeral. It was eerie, how nothing had moved but everything had changed. The door to Verity's room was shut, and I touched the cutglass doorknob as I passed. Normally, the Prairie-style house was light filled and warm, but today the shades were drawn, casting the hallway in chill shadows. It wasn't right—Verity's house had always been noisy and vibrant, just like her.

Midway down the stairs, Luc was studying family pictures of Verity, a half smile on his face. When I approached, trying hard not to look at them, he reached out and gave my hand a gentle squeeze.

We started down the stairs. "What do I tell her?" I asked.

"You're always going on about the truth," he said. "Try that."

"Will she remember what happened?"

"Parts, more'n likely. Don't get her riled."

"Why?"

"She shouldn't be able to use the lines without calling on them proper, but I wouldn't like to see what happens if she gets pissed off." He shook his head.

"She needs training." I sank down onto the bottom step and he sprawled next to me, his thigh brushing against mine. "Maybe your dad could talk to Orla. Convince her to change her mind."

"It's not that simple. Not for Orla and the rest, anyway."

Instinct made me go still. "Your dad's a member of the Quartoren."

"Not exactly news."

"He's got better things to do than bother with a girl who's not from his House. I get why Orla was there, but why Pascal? It wasn't because of me. They could have found me whenever they wanted. If this is happening to lots of kids, why was the Quartoren so interested in Constance?"

"Evangeline's dead, which makes Constance the only living blood relation of a Matriarch. There was a possibility she'd turn out to be a Water Arc. If that had been the case, she'd have been next in line to lead their House."

"But she's Air. Not Water."

"No," he said, and there was something like sadness in his voice. "Now she's just the descendent of a traitor. Quartoren's got no reason to help her, or to let anyone else try."

"If this happens again, and she doesn't have training. . . ." I closed my eyes and saw Constance laid out on the bathroom floor again. "They have to help her. They *have* to."

"They're the Quartoren. They don't have to do anything." He ran a hand through his hair, the dark locks falling haphazardly around his face. He met my eyes. "But they will. For a price."

And suddenly, my entire body felt leaden. *This* was the Luc I remembered. Everything was a deal, an exchange, a bargain struck.

"Me."

"Orla's not the type to change her mind. But I know these people." I heard the desperation in his voice. "I've spent more'n half my life training to be one of them. They'd never admit it, but they need you, and that means you've got lever-age."

Leverage, at least, was a concept I was familiar with. "So I could offer a trade. My help in exchange for someone to take care of Constance."

"It's called a Covenant. A contract, enforced with magic. It ain't something to take lightly."

"You're sure they'd agree?"

"Never entirely sure what the Quartoren'll do, but it's the best chance you have. Either of you."

I glanced up the stairs, past the family pictures, trying not to see the resemblance between Verity and Constance.

"I need to think about it."

"Quartoren won't wait for long. I'll talk to them." He stood and helped me to my feet. "Drop you at your fancy school?"

The idea of going Between again made me shudder, but I didn't want to look weak in front of Luc. "I need to call her mom. You go ahead."

"How will you get back?" he asked. When I didn't answer, he drummed his fingers on the banister. "Cujo."

"He'll cover for me." If he wasn't too angry. "You'll tell me what they say?"

" 'Course." He took a step toward me, and I backed up. "Month's a lot longer than I remembered. Missed you."

I felt my skin heat under his gaze, too flustered to respond.

He smiled again. "*À bientôt*," he said, and was gone.

While Constance slept, I called her mom at work, then took a deep breath—several, actually—and called Colin.

"Why aren't you in school?" No hello, I noticed. Not a good sign.

"How did you know?"

"Your friend came out. The hyper one."

I zipped the hoodie I'd borrowed from Constance. It would hide the bloodstains on my shirt, if you didn't look too closely. "Lena."

"She talks a lot."

"Compared to you, mimes talk a lot."

He humphed. "She dropped off your bag. Said you'd taken off, figured I might know where."

Smart thinking on Lena's part, to let Colin know something was going on without alerting the school. I owed her. Big. Again.

"I *don't* know where." His voice was tight, temper reined in. Probably not for long if I didn't start explaining.

"I'm at Verity's house. Her little sister . . . got sick. I brought her home." I knew he'd catch the hesitation in my response, but I couldn't seem to say the words. Once I did, everything would change again, more obstacles between us when there were too many already. I couldn't stop what was coming, but I wanted to slow it down, even if only for a moment.

He drew a breath, and I imagined him rubbing his forehead, bracing himself. "How?"

"How what?"

"How did you get home?" he asked, the words sharp edged. "Because I didn't drive you. You didn't take a bus. Your friend would have known if you'd gotten a ride with another student. Since your wallet's here, you didn't take a cab. So I have to wonder, how did you get Verity's sister home from school on your own?"

I closed my eyes. "Can you pick me up? Please?"

A car door slammed, and I opened my eyes to see Verity's mom hurrying up the steps. "I have to go."

"You told me it was done," he said, so softly I could barely make out the words.

I was about to apologize, but he'd already hung up the phone.

CHAPTER 7

I waited a few moments before following Mrs. Grey upstairs. "Mo said you got sick," she was saying as Constance propped herself up on her elbows, face wan. "Do you think it was something you ate?"

Over her mom's shoulder, Constance narrowed her eyes at me. Luc was right—she definitely remembered. "Mo said that? I guess she'd know."

I tried to laugh it off. "I never trust those breakfast burritos from the caf. Feel better," I added. "I'll check on you soon."

Mrs. Grey turned, and I waved her off. "I can let myself out."

She shot me a look of gratitude, but Constance's wasn't nearly so benign.

Growing up, I'd spent as much time at Verity's house as my own. I knew the way the third stair sighed when you stepped on it, the worn smoothness of the newel under my hand. I knew the path of the afternoon sun through the foyer. Now it highlighted the clutter on the hall table—unopened piles of mail threatening to tip over, a teacup left out so long that all the liquid had evaporated, leaving a rusty stain. I ran my finger over the edge of the table, and it came away furred with dust. Verity's house had always been messier than mine, more chaotic, more alive. Mine had been neat but not nearly as warm.

This was a different kind of messy. It felt lonely, as if when Verity had died, the other occupants had drifted away as well. I'd tried to watch out for Constance at school, but she'd made it clear she didn't want me around. At church, the Greys kept to themselves, rarely staying for coffee hour. My mom said Mrs. Grey had quit volunteering with the Altar Guild. They were struggling, even more so since Evangeline had supposedly headed back to New Orleans without a proper good-bye. Sometimes I wished I could tell them the truth, but it would only hurt them more.

Evangeline hadn't been working alone. I thought about that sometimes, at two AM, after another nightmare, when the scratching of a squirrel on the roof or the sudden roar of a bad muffler reminded me of the Darklings. I would lie in my bed and think about the Seraphim, all the victims of their crusade, and the justice I had meted out seemed insufficient. But I always tamped down on the hunger, afraid it could be more dangerous than the magic I'd touched.

Stepping outside, I hugged myself against the brisk November wind. The sky was still vividly blue, but winter was coming. The richly colored leaves would turn muddy and damp, the sun a pale glow in a steely sky. I'd always known what the next day, week, month would bring. Since Verity had died and I'd met Luc, I'd been fighting off vertigo, the awful cartwheeling sensation that nothing would go the way I'd planned, ever again.

With a rumbling sound, Colin's truck pulled up to the curb, under a large scarlet maple still clinging to most of its leaves. The ancient red Ford was liberally spotted with rust. The most valuable thing in it was the gleaming steel toolbox, bolted to the bed and secured with a padlock the size of my fist. Typical Colin. Keep the outside as anonymous as possible, keep your head down. Hide the important stuff away, like a treasure.

I wondered if that was how he saw me.

In the dappled shade, it was hard to see his features, but it didn't matter. I knew the expression he'd be wearing, and I wasn't looking forward to it.

I climbed inside, taking in the smell of fresh coffee and sawdust and soap, paying close attention to fastening my seat belt and tucking my skirt around my knees. He watched, taking in my disastrous hair and the bloodstains on my collar. It wasn't how I wanted him to look at me, cataloguing the damage done. Lately, what I wanted hadn't concerned Colin overmuch.

"I can still make my last couple of classes," I said. "But I need to change clothes first."

He pulled away, mouth grim and eyes flinty, taking side streets to my house. I lifted my hands, about to speak, and fell silent again. We stayed like that, anticipation roiling my stomach, the entire ride home.

He killed the ignition and we sat in the driveway, neither of us making a move to get out of the truck.

I pressed the heel of one hand hard into the scar slashed against my opposite palm, trying to keep from shaking.

"So," he said finally, tone caustic. "How was your day?"

My spine bowed under the weight of his anger, dark and palpable.

Then I straightened. I hadn't done anything so terribly wrong. Colin, more than anyone, should understand trying to help someone who was in danger. It was his job, as he liked to remind me, practically his whole reason for being. Just because the danger facing Constance was magic, not mundane, didn't mean I could ignore it.

"Constance's powers came through at school. They were out of control."

"So you stepped in."

"Should I have let her die? My best friend's sister?"

Slowly, he eased down the metal tab of my zipper, revealing the ruined blouse underneath. I watched, immobile.

"That's a lot of blood," he said.

I closed my hand over his. "I'm fine."

He turned his hand palm-up, lacing our fingers together. It felt solid and safe. "Where did you go?"

"With Luc." Colin knew enough of Luc's powers to know that we could have gone anywhere on the globe. "He sent me out of the room until it was over."

Instead of shutting down again, like I expected, the tension in his jaw eased a little. "So he's not a complete dumb-ass."

"Today, anyway."

He nodded and leaned back. "Verity's sister is all right?"

"She's . . . resting. She'll need help learning to use her powers."

"That's not your job, is it?"

"Nope. No experience."

"Good." He touched our joined hands to his lips. "They'll leave you alone now?"

The words caught in my throat. "Not exactly."

His expression hardened. "You're a mess," he said, reaching for the door. "Let's get you cleaned up."

I followed him into the house, waiting while he deactivated the alarm. "Colin . . ."

"You might as well burn that shirt," he said, filling two glasses with water from the tap and handing one to me.

I looked down. "You think?"

He drained half the glass. "Your mom might get suspicious, come laundry day."

I took a sip, suddenly aware of how dry my mouth was. "My mom's capacity for willful ignorance is impressive. You should know that by now."

"Good point."

He stood outside my room while I changed into a fresh uniform—a perfect gentleman, if perfect gentlemen worked for the Mob and carried a gun or two.

"So," he called through the closed door, a strange note in his voice, "Luc's dragging you back in."

"He's not dragging me," I said, peeling off my disgusting top and crumpling it up. It was cowardly, but talking to him like this, when I couldn't see the worry and frustration on his face, was easier. "Something is wrong with the magic. The Quartoren think it has to do with what I did. They think I changed things somehow."

"So? You saved their asses. They should be thanking you, not blaming you."

I pulled on a fresh shirt, trying to find the right words, ones that would explain without setting off too many alarms. "They're not blaming me, exactly. But they need to figure it out. Constance shouldn't have been in danger today."

"Not your problem."

"What if it is? What if I damaged the magic somehow, and that's why Constance got hurt? I can't walk away from that."

"You've got plenty on your plate right now," he said, exasperation in his voice. "The magic will have to wait."

I fastened the itchy plaid skirt and opened the door. "Better?"

He gave me a slow, appraising look, and I curled my toes into the carpet. Suddenly, I was very aware that Colin was, for only the second time ever, standing in the doorway of my bedroom. "Better," he agreed.

"You could come in, you know."

He leaned against the doorway, mouth quirking up on one side.

"I am in."

"Not really." I could feel the blush rising along my neck, up to my cheeks, but I pressed on. "You're . . ." I wobbled my hand. "Teetering. On the edge."

"And you think I should, what? Jump?" His eyes, obsidian dark, held mine.

"Would it be so awful?"

"No," he said after a long, considering moment. "Dangerous, though."

"I don't care."

"Yeah, I get that." His voice was easy, but there was nothing relaxed in the way he was looking at me. "There's too much at stake."

"This is about Billy?" The ache inside me was dull and painful, like a stone pressing on my chest. Nothing else made sense. My uncle had something on him. Some secret, some information. Leverage, to keep Colin loyal. He'd strayed a bit—*hands in my hair, mouth on my neck, my fingers tracing the scars crisscrossing his back*—but in the end, Billy still had something on him. I couldn't compete.

Colin switched his gaze to the carpet. "I told you. Your uncle's been good to me."

"How?"

"I'm not having this discussion."

"Why not? Why do you get to know everything about me—things I don't want to tell you, private things, embarrassing things—and I get to know nothing about you. Why is that?"

"There's a difference between knowing someone and knowing about them."

"What do you mean?"

"Lots of people know about you." He pushed off the wall. His steps into the room were slow and measured, punctuating his words. "Your dad's in prison. Your uncle's a mobster. You're a straight-A student at a school your mom can't afford. You're leaving for New York as soon as you can. Your best friend was murdered a few months ago and nobody knows why. You're a very nice, quiet girl, but since the summer, you haven't been quite right." He cocked his head, so close I could touch him if I was brave enough. "You keep blowing off your bodyguard."

"That's not . . ."

"You? No, it isn't. Not even close. Those people, they don't know how angry you are at your family. They have no clue how far you've gone to avenge Verity or what it's done to you."

I stared out the window as he kept going.

"They don't know how you take your coffee, or that you always fall asleep halfway through your Spanish homework, or the way you look when magic is burning through you.

They don't know," he said, fitting his hand around my hip and drawing me in, "how good you smell, like rain and apples."

His fingers brushed along my side, and I looked up into his face as he leaned over me. "I know you, Mo. And you know me. My past, who I was before . . . you don't need that. Not really."

But I did. How else could I break Billy's hold on Colin?

He kissed me, his mouth light and sweet. But I was tired of sweet. It had been a hell of a day, and it wasn't even half over, so I kissed him back, mouth open, pouring out all the frustration and want that had been building up in me since the Torrent.

He made a noise in the back of his throat like a growl, said my name through the kiss, and I thought for one crashingly awful moment he was going to pull away, berate me for pushing when he'd just told me not to.

And then his hand cupped the back of my head, the other one splaying wide against my back, and we stumbled toward the bed.

"We're not doing this," he murmured, his mouth drifting over my cheekbone, warm against my ear. The back of my knees hit the edge of the mattress and I fell onto the bed, pulling him with me.

"Sure." The weight of him was so lovely, and I wrapped one leg around his hip, as if that could stop his escape. He tasted like almonds, clean and warm. Finally, I thought. He'd wasted so much time being noble when this was obviously what was supposed to happen.

I slid a hand under his shirt, the muscles of his back like granite, the scars barely perceptible, one of those awful parts of his life he refused to share. He froze in the middle of brushing kisses along my temple, his fingers coaxing open the buttons of my shirt.

"We're not doing this," he repeated, voice ragged, eyes focused on the line of my bra.

"Not to argue, but . . ."

He propped himself up on one elbow. "Jesus," he said under his breath. "You're so freaking beautiful." His finger traced along the curve where lace met skin, and I closed my eyes at the sensation, losing my breath. He had the nicest hands, rough from his woodworking projects but still gentle.

And then he pulled back, leaving me cold and lonely on the narrow bed. "Don't," I said. "Don't say something like that and then stop."

He kissed me again, and I arched up, wanting something I couldn't quite name but knew I needed. Eyes squeezed shut, mouth turned down, he rolled away.

"I'm not going to be that guy," he said.

"What guy?" I tried to wriggle closer, but he put out a hand to stop me.

"The one who sleeps with you and then asks you to keep it a secret." He wound a lock of my hair around his finger. "Here's something else I know. You don't like secrets."

"This is different." It was. We weren't hiding our . . . whatever you'd call us . . . out of shame. It was my family's craziness forcing us to keep things quiet.

"You're sure? You've changed in the last few months, but you're still happier when people don't see you, when you can fade back. Harder to do if people know we're together."

A fluttering thrill ran through my veins when he used the word "together," making me bold. "There's this dance at school this weekend. Sadie Hawkins. The girls ask the guys."

"Mo . . ."

Bold and stupid, apparently, but I pressed on. "Go with me. I wasn't going, because there isn't anyone I want to ask, except you. So I'm asking."

"There's still Billy."

Three words, squashing the thrill like a boulder. "You could tell him you're chaperoning," I said, but it was weak and he knew it.

"You should go," he said, touching his forehead to mine. "Have an amazing time. Be with your friends. Be a kid."

I shoved him away. "A *kid?* Seriously? We're back to that

again?" I yanked my shirt closed, fingers fumbling on the buttons, torn between embarrassment and anger.

"I didn't mean it that way," he said. "You have the chance to be a regular girl for one night. Why not take it?"

"Because I don't like lies," I said. "Why pretend to be normal when everyone knows I'm not?"

He didn't answer, stretching out next to me on the faded patchwork quilt and pulling me against his chest. "We'll figure it out."

I pressed my face into his T-shirt, breathing in the scent of his skin, the only way to keep him close. "You always say that, but we never do."

I could feel the laughter rumbling through him, but there was no humor in it.

CHAPTER 8

After Colin dropped me off at school again, I had just enough time to stash my bag in my locker and sneak into Journalism, my last class of the day. I slipped into my seat as unobtrusively as possible, but Ms. Corelli lifted an eyebrow and tapped her watch. Only today's guest speaker prevented her from issuing a detention on the spot.

Nick Petros was a political reporter for the *Tribune*; he had a column on page two several times a week. The mayor was one of his favorite topics; organized crime and rampant corruption were others. My family's name wasn't mentioned much, these days. But when I'd Googled it, I'd found he'd taken quite an interest in my family thirteen years ago. Even now, my uncle would complain about him and his "libelous, muckraking, so-called journalism."

Up close, he seemed like a decent guy. He wore pleated khakis and a long-sleeve black polo shirt, both of them pulling a little tight across the belly. His salt-and-pepper hair was neatly combed back from a reddish face, sporting the broken vessels along his nose and cheeks I'd seen in the heavier drinkers at Morgan's. He didn't stop talking when I came in. Hands stuffed in pockets, he leaned against the podium and continued speaking, but I got the distinct impression he'd transferred his attention to me.

He asked a question, something about impartiality when

reporting a story, and as several underclassmen waved their hands wildly, Lena nudged me.

"Well?" she asked out of the corner of her mouth.

"I took her home," I murmured. "She's fine."

"Colin's not. He was furious when I told him you'd left. I don't care what you say. The guy is not indifferent."

Not indifferent, intractable. I wasn't sure which was worse.

Petros's voice cut into my thoughts. "There's always a disconnect between what you know and what you can prove. I write maybe a tenth of what I know, tops."

"Isn't that frustrating?" asked one girl.

He laughed. "Sure. I keep plugging away, digging up dirt, looking for the proof I need. Someday it'll all come together. Might take a while, but that just makes it even sweeter."

Lena whispered, "She's really okay?"

"Yeah. Food poisoning." I tried to sound vaguely repulsed, to discourage more questions.

Lena wasn't buying it. "Sure."

Petros ambled over to our table, and we both looked up guiltily. "Let's ask our editors-in-chief. Tell me, ladies, do *you* run into a lot of ethically challenging situations?"

"For the paper?" Lena asked. *The Clarion* wasn't really the type to print hard-hitting investigative pieces. We ran articles on the sports teams, service projects, the drama club.

"Paper, real life, wherever. I imagine things can get pretty murky sometimes." He watched me closely as he spoke, and I squirmed in my seat.

"We're a high school paper," Lena said, brown eyes widening. "We leave the murky stuff to people like you."

He swiveled toward Lena, who tilted her head to the side and gave him a bland smile. After a long, uncomfortable moment, he turned away, addressing the whole class again. "Remember, girls, if you want to print it, you have to prove it. If you dig deep enough, you'll find the truth."

Lena poked me lightly with her pen and wrinkled her nose, trying to break the tension. I smiled back gratefully.

Ms. C stood up, a little perplexed but still cheerful. No doubt this was not the career day speech she'd envisioned. "Ladies, how about a round of applause for Mr. Petros, and a thank-you for his offer to speak with us today?"

We applauded dutifully while he gathered his coat and briefcase. "I'll leave some business cards, in case you have more questions."

On his way out, he paused at our table again. "Here you go," he said, handing us each a card. "Seriously, any time you two want to come down to Tribune Tower—tour the newsroom, shoot the breeze, ask me questions—swing on by. Nice to meet you both, Lena and . . . Mo, right?"

"Yeah. Thanks." I set the card deliberately on the table.

"He was weird," Lena said once he was gone.

I'd had all the weird I could take for one day.

Once we were out in the hallway, she started in again. "What happened with Constance? How'd you guys get home?"

"I called a friend." Hard to say what Luc was, but friend would do for now. "He's good in situations like that."

She crossed her arms. "Mmn-hmn. Not Colin. Mystery guy? You said he was gone."

"I may have been wrong about that," I said cautiously. Telling her about Luc seemed dangerous. It was safer for everyone when the two halves of my life, Arc and Flat, didn't touch, but a part of me yearned to share. Instead, I shrugged a little, like it didn't matter. "What did I miss?"

"Mass, for starters." We ducked around a cluster of freshman. I heard Constance's name and kept my eyes down. "I told Sister Donna All Souls' Day was too much. You wanted privacy. I think she bought it."

All Souls' Day, when we remembered those loved ones who had died in the past year. Ironic I would have forgotten when I still longed for Verity every day.

"Thanks."

Lena grinned. "What are friends for?"

By the time Colin had dropped me at The Slice is Right,

my headache had subsided, even if my worries over Constance hadn't. In the cramped closet that served as Mom's office, I tossed my bag on the ground. As I dug out a pair of brown cords, a small card—four inches square, stiff cardstock—fell out. Drawn on it, with careful, detailed strokes, was a sunflower. It wasn't mine—my artistic abilities were limited to stick figures and photography. Whoever had drawn this had pressed hard enough to leave grooves in the paper. Probably it had fallen out of one of my library books, but it was too intricate and pretty to throw away. I slipped it into my pocket and headed out.

After wrestling my hair into a ponytail, I grabbed an apron from the stack by the office door. The Slice's aprons, the color of a granny smith apple with a ruffle *and* rickrack trim, were bad enough, but the matching kerchief was worse. It was constantly slipping to the side, squashing my hair, making me look like a deranged milkmaid. I picked up a pencil and order pad, waved to Tim, the cook, and readied myself for another day at The Slice.

The Slice is Right was home. In some ways, even more than our orange brick bungalow, because once my dad went to prison, The Slice was our only source of income. Back then, I didn't realize it. All I knew was that we spent long hours at the restaurant and that my mom was happier there than at our house. At home, my dad's absence was apparent in every room—two places set for dinner instead of three, unread stacks of *Sports Illustrated* and the *Wall Street Journal* piling up until the subscriptions ran out, quiet mornings where there used to be booming laughter and tickle fights. The Slice, on the other hand, was so crowded and busy you could go for an entire shift without realizing what was missing. And the regulars were always happy to see you, especially when you had a full pot of coffee and a warm piece of pie.

The restaurant had always been my mom's domain. She'd poured her heart and soul into making it work for twelve years. I was her daughter, but The Slice was her baby.

Framed in the rectangular pass-through between the kitchen and the counter area, Mom was talking to someone, animated and attentive. Curious, I craned my neck to see who was making her so cheerful.

Elsa Stratton? My former lawyer was here for a visit? Somehow I didn't think she was getting her Thanksgiving order in early. The clink of silverware on china and the other customers kept me from hearing anything but the last few words.

"I'll contact you when I hear more, of course," Elsa said.

Even from across the room, I could see the flushed excitement in my mom's cheeks as they shook hands. After Elsa had left, I pushed through the swinging doors.

"What was Elsa doing here? Is it Verity's case?" When the police had questioned me after Verity's death, she'd accompanied me at my uncle's request. She was the type of lawyer who inspired shark jokes, and her hourly rate was more than I earned in a month. I'd been very relieved she was on my side and not the opposition's.

"And good afternoon to you!" Mom trilled. She came behind the counter to give me a hug before taking off her apron. "Did you have a nice day?"

"Why was Elsa here?"

"Oh, it's a long story, and I've still got to go to the bank and make the Shady Acres delivery. Let's talk at home?"

"Right." I should have known she'd never talk about anything important in front of the customers. "Lena and I might stay late at school tomorrow, work on our history presentation."

"Why don't you invite her here? Take a back booth and study."

"She's pretty busy." And too observant. If she came to The Slice, there was a chance she'd meet my uncle. Knowing Lena, she'd ask about stuff I couldn't explain. Inviting her home seemed less tricky. "But she might sleep over on Friday, if it's okay."

Come to think of it, Lena had never invited me to her house, either. Maybe all her questions were a way of deflecting attention.

I refilled water glasses and coffee cups while Mom counted the register. "I wish you'd invite Colin in," she said, peering out the window. "It's not right to make him sit outside."

"He likes it. He says it's too noisy in here." Also, he had a better view, should trouble come calling.

She shook her head. "You should take him some coffee, at least. And something to eat. Brandied pear is the special today. Or a nice piece of mince pie. He'd like that."

I grimaced. "Mom, nobody likes mince pie except the crowd from Shady Acres." We did a steady business from the local retirement apartments just a few blocks away, both walk-in and delivery. I'd never seen anyone order mince pie who didn't qualify for the senior discount.

"Shush." She glanced around, worried she might be offending one of the Shady Acres crew, but the only person at the counter was a girl my age. "Take him some pie before we close up."

For a split-second, I considered arguing. Pie wasn't going to fix our problems. Instead, I asked, "Who sent the flowers?"

Next to the cash register was a vase filled with cheerful yellow-orange sunflowers, electric in the sleepy air of The Slice. She glanced over as she headed toward the kitchen. "You know, I'm not sure. They just got here. Aren't they charming?"

I wiped clammy hands on my apron. "Was there a card?"

"I didn't see one. I'll see you at home. Remember, Mass tonight."

Intent on the flowers, I didn't hear her leave. I dug past the glossy green filler and oversized blossoms, but she was right—no card. I fumbled in my back pocket, pulling out the drawing I'd found. Suddenly, neither the sketch nor the bouquet seemed even remotely charming. Had someone broken into my locker and put the card in my bag? I thought back to

Nick Petros, the oddly piercing look he'd given me during Journalism. Were they from him? He'd given me his business card, in plain view of the entire class. There was no reason for him to be cryptic.

And then it hit me. This morning. Running into the old guy by the library, dropping my bag, his insistence on handing it back to me. He could have hidden the drawing inside my bag then. *I found exactly who I was looking for,* he'd said.

He meant me. Somehow, the old man had slipped into St. Brigid's unnoticed and found me. He'd found me here, too, but why? Was he an Arc? One of Billy's associates? It wouldn't be the first time they'd tried to send me a message.

The plate glass windows in the front of The Slice turned threatening—the perfect way to put me on display—and I fought the urge to call Colin and beg him to come inside. If the old man was an Arc, I'd do better to tell Luc. Colin would notify Billy, and I'd lose what little freedom I had. Worse, Colin would launch into bodyguard mode, slipping even farther away from me. If the guy was trying to show me I was being watched, it was old news. I'd had people watching me since Verity died.

I jammed the drawing into my back pocket again and forced myself to act naturally. Arc or Flat, I didn't want to show any fear. Instead, I checked on my booths, refilling coffee and clearing plates. The girl at the counter was still there, picking at her apple pie. The ice cream had melted, and she pressed the fork into the crust, making a crust-apple-cream sludge.

"You want me to take that for you?"

The girl looked up at me, hazel eyes startled. "I guess I wasn't hungry."

"No problem. More coffee?" The sturdy white mug was empty, though I'd refilled it when I came in. Judging from the tremors in her hand . . . "I've got decaf."

"Was that your mom?" She tilted her head toward the kitchen.

"Yeah. Family business," I said, trying to smile as exhaustion crept up on me.

"You're Mo."

I looked closer. Chapped lips, light brown hair in a messy ponytail, and a challenging note in her voice. *Another message from the old guy? The Seraphim making a move?*

Warily, I brushed a finger over my wrist, wondering if she could sense my connection to Luc. If so, maybe she wouldn't attack straight-out, not when I could summon him so quickly.

I pointed to my plastic nametag. "Looks like it, huh?"

"Mo Fitzgerald."

I set the coffeepot down on the counter. "I didn't catch your name."

She brushed a wisp of hair out of her face. "Jenny Kowalski," she said, lifting her chin and trying for brave. "I think you knew my dad."

Oh, hell. Not magic, but trouble just the same.

CHAPTER 9

"You're Jenny?" I could see it now, in the shape of her nose, in her coloring. A little bit around the eyes, too. She had the taut, lean look of a distance runner. Maybe she got that from her mom, because Joseph Kowalski had been a big guy, muscle softened to fat over his twenty years with the Chicago Police Department.

I swallowed, looked down at the counter. "I'm really sorry about your dad. He was a good cop."

"He was a great cop. He was a great dad. Did you know he was retiring soon?"

"He mentioned it." He'd talked about sending his youngest daughter off to college, then taking his wife to Florida and doing some fishing in the Gulf. No fishing for Kowalski. No watching Jenny cross the stage for her diploma. He'd never do any of those things now.

Because Joseph Kowalski had died trying to save me.

And nobody knew it.

The official story was that he'd gone to investigate a report of a gas leak at the Chicago Water Tower. Nobody made mention of the fact it wasn't his district or that he'd been off duty for the night. He'd been nearby when the call came across the radio, and he'd checked it out. And been caught inside when the Water Tower exploded.

The real story was that he'd followed me there, trying to piece together the truth of Verity's death. Evangeline had tricked me into releasing the raw magic, triggering the Torrent. When Kowalski had seen me in danger, he'd braved the magic and the Darklings anyway, trying to bring me out safely. The magic had caught him. He'd never stood a chance.

"I'm sorry," I said again. "How are you doing? Your family?"

I'd seen them huddled together at the funeral, Kowalski's wife and four daughters, surrounded by a sea of navy blue dress uniforms. The story had been splashed all over the papers, but I was careful not to read the articles. There was nothing left for me to learn about that night.

"Pretty crappy. How's yours?"

"Mine?"

"Your family. My dad was really interested in your family, did you know that? He talked about you guys all the time."

"My family didn't have anything to do with what happened to Verity."

Elsa told me once that Kowalski had specifically asked for Verity's case. It must have seemed like a great way to gather evidence against the Chicago Mob. Everyone assumed Verity had been killed by a rival crime organization, probably Russians. They thought she'd been either a mistake—that they were actually supposed to come after me—or a warning, like, "Turn over your territory or your niece is next." So Kowalski had followed me, looked into Colin's history, harassed my uncle, and all for nothing. The Outfit wasn't responsible for Verity's death. It was magic, and in the end, it killed Kowalski, too.

"You think it was coincidence? A random twist of fate?"

I stared at her. Her hands were still trembling, and she pressed them against the counter. I knew that look in her eye, the bewildering grief and rage, the deafening need to make some sense of what had happened. She'd fixed on me as the key to it all.

"Not fate. Awful," I said. "And unfair. Like what happened to your dad, wrong place, wrong time."

"No!" Heads turned, and she lowered her voice. "My dad was there because of you. Because you went into that lineup and said you didn't recognize the perps."

"I didn't."

"They turned up dead a week later." I must have looked genuinely surprised, because she continued, a bitter twist to her mouth. "Didn't your uncle tell you? Both of them, execution style. Found in a Dumpster over in Back of the Yards. I saw the pictures."

My mouth tasted sour. "Pictures?"

She shrugged. "The detectives who caught that case used to play poker with my dad. They don't like sharing that stuff, but they can't say no, either."

"Jenny." I chose my words carefully. I knew from experience how much people lied to you when you were grieving, thinking they were doing you some sort of favor, protecting you from ugliness. "My family didn't have anything to do with what happened to your dad. Or Verity. I know he thought otherwise, but he was wrong."

"You're lying."

"I wouldn't. Not about this. My uncle didn't kill your dad."

"No," she said thoughtfully. "He wouldn't. Not himself, that's not his style. He always makes other people do the dirty work. Someone else takes the fall, pulls the trigger. Like your dad. And . . ." She spun around on the cracked vinyl stool, stopping to peer at Colin's truck. "Your bodyguard. Or is it boyfriend? Dad was never quite sure. Dangerous game, he said, for both of you."

I stepped back from the counter.

"You don't even realize, do you? The things your uncle's done, the things your family's done . . . don't you ever wonder about the cost? Don't you think it might be too high? Or are you so happy being ignorant, you don't even want to know?"

No wonder Luc had thought I was crazy when Verity died, raving about justice and revenge. I must have sounded like this. Except I'd been perfectly sane, and so was Jenny. Witnessing her grief was like falling through a mirror. "What do you want?"

I already knew.

She started to answer, and then her face transformed. In an instant, her eyes turned cheerful and a pleasant, impersonal smile rounded her cheeks. A second later, a hand clapped my shoulder. "Time for Mass. Who's this?"

Billy. Jenny must have known who he was. Did he know her? My brain scattered, unable to reply.

Jenny stood and slipped on her coat. "Jen," she said. "A friend, from school."

"Lovely to meet you, Jen. You'll have to excuse us, but we've got church. If we're late, my sister will have our heads." So charming, my uncle, with his snow white hair and neatly groomed beard, eyes creasing in amusement. Like a really deadly garden gnome. In church clothes. Looking at him, you could almost forget how quickly his cheery expression would fall away if you crossed him, replaced with something ruthless and steely.

Almost, but not quite. I'd seen firsthand how tightly Billy clung to power. It seemed wiser to keep myself out of his range.

"Sure. See you around, Mo."

She tucked some money under her plate, which I still hadn't cleared, and left without another word.

"We're already late," Billy said, glancing around the nearly empty Slice. "Best to clean up your friend's mess quickly."

CHAPTER 10

Here's something you should know about my school. St. Brigid's, while being one of the most expensive and prestigious girls' schools in the city, is also a regular neighborhood church. This has its benefits—after all, few schools with such a sterling reputation to uphold would accept the daughter of a convicted felon, unless the family was a member of the parish. A family who was happy to make sizeable donations every time the kitchen needed repairs or the air conditioning went out or the rectory was being remodeled.

There are also drawbacks. In my case, it meant an increased chance of my family running into my teachers, or at least the ones who wore white collars or black habits. A year ago, it wouldn't have been a problem—they would have sung my praises, all about how nice and hardworking and responsible I was. These days, it was a different tune.

After the service, we joined the crowd in the parish hall, everyone clutching cups of weak coffee and pumpkin loaf on paper plates. The kids my age—some who went to school with us, a lot who didn't—stood in a circle, talking and texting at the same time. Their language was as foreign to me as the Arcs'. I'd never be fluent in such carefree chatter.

Slumping against the wall, exhausted and suddenly, throat-tighteningly lonely, I watched as my uncle worked the room. He was in rare form, jovial and expansive. Maybe it had something to do with Elsa's visit. He shook hands, inquired about people's families, made sure everything in his little empire was running as it should. It was only recently that I'd started to notice what had been there all along—the thin coat of fear that overlaid the respect everyone treated him with.

Fresh anger surged through me. He'd cost me so much, and he didn't even care, because he still got what he wanted, and I got . . . nothing. A guy who wouldn't be with me, a school full of people who thought I was a freak and a criminal, an absentee father. My fingers curled into fists. I needed to escape before I created a scene that would only confirm everyone's belief I was losing my mind.

Ducking my head, I started for the exit, only to stop as someone grabbed my arm. I stumbled at the unexpected change of direction.

"Who's got you lookin' so fierce?" Luc asked.

"I'm not—" The words were automatic, and totally untrue. I shook off Luc's hold and glared at him. "What are you doing here? Did Orla change her mind?"

"We need to talk."

"I'm at church. It's kind of a bad time."

"Can't be helped." Even casually dressed, in a black sweater and dark jeans, he still managed to look more elegant and appealing than anyone else in the room. His eyes swept the clusters of people. "Where's Cujo?"

"His place, I guess." I didn't want to talk about Colin. It was too raw and Luc was too perceptive.

"Doesn't seem like him, letting you out of his sight. Sloppy."

I'd forgotten how quickly Luc could make me bristle. "We're here with my uncle."

"No need for your own personal guard dog, hmn?"

"Billy takes care of us." And better care of himself. I scanned the room. No one had noticed Luc, and when I concentrated, I could detect the faint hum of magic coming off him. He'd cloaked himself. Everyone probably thought I was talking to myself. Great.

Luc could talk if he wanted. I didn't have to say anything.

Instead, I watched the people, like I always did. They were so predictable—the same groups, week after week, taking up their same positions, having the same discussions. But something seemed off, like the camera didn't quite have the right angle. Something was different, more than Luc's presence at my shoulder, a centimeter too close, like always. I listened to the ebb and flow of conversations, the way voices rose up in excitement and dropped off to a hush, the lulls that sometimes overtook the whole room. When I heard the quiet burble of my mom's laughter, I zeroed in on it. That was the difference: my mom.

Usually, she drifted around the room, stopping to visit with acquaintances. It was the opposite of my uncle, who let everyone come to him. He moved, and the room moved with him, another reminder of who held the power. In contrast, my mom always approached each little group, like she was seeking admission. Tonight, people were flocking to her side. Clusters of women around the room murmured to each other, eyeing my mother discreetly. One of them would break away, oh-so casually, and sidle up to Mom, who glowed under their attention.

I thought back to Elsa's visit, Mom's hasty exit. If there was one thing my family excelled at, it was keeping secrets. "I'll be right back," I murmured to Luc, barely moving my lips.

He frowned, fingers brushing my sleeve. "Mouse, I'm serious. Let's go someplace we can talk."

I waved him off, starting across the room at the same time I spotted Sister Donna making her way toward my mom like a black-sailed ship. The crowd scattered once Sister's intentions were clear, but I edged closer.

A brisk greeting, and Sister launched right in. "I have concerns," she said. Forget the nurturing nun who passed out cups of Earl Grey in her office—that was an act reserved for college recruiters. The real Sister Donna was as ruthless as one of the traders at the Board of Trade. "Grave concerns."

"Is Mo acting up?" Mom asked, worry settling over her

like a damp wool blanket. It was her greatest fear—I might be causing trouble, bringing shame on the family. Because we didn't have enough already.

"She's distracted. The quality of her work is merely adequate, not at all what we're accustomed to. Her class participation has subsided. Several of her teachers are rethinking their decisions to write letters of recommendation."

My legs went numb. I hadn't known.

Sister continued, folding her hands at her waist. "We're sympathetic, of course, and I have tried to help, but she's making it quite difficult. She refuses to speak with her guidance counselor since the incident." Verity's murder. Which was apparently now referred to as "The Incident."

My mother frowned, twisting her fingers together. "She said everything was going well."

Sister Donna shook her head. "She lied, Mrs. Fitzgerald."

"She wouldn't do that. Not my Mo."

"She cut class today."

Damn. I ducked behind a group of young moms and squabbling preschoolers as my mom said, "There must be some mistake. Mo doesn't cut class. She's never cut class."

"Earlier this fall," Sister reminded her. "During her meeting with the representative from NYU."

"That was stress," Mom protested, head swiveling back and forth as she searched the room for me. "She's not serious about going to New York, you know. It's just a phase. It didn't hurt anything for her to leave."

Sister Donna's forehead crinkled slightly, incredulous. "Perhaps there's something else going on?" she said, dropping her voice to a near whisper. "Something at home that might trigger this sort of behavior?"

There it was: the real reason Sister Donna had sought out my mom. She wanted the gossip as much as anyone—she was simply more direct about it. I inched toward them, hoping to catch my mother's reply, when Luc's hand cupped my elbow.

"When you gonna learn, Mouse? You ain't invisible any-more."

"I'm in the middle of something," I said. "Can we do this later?"

He sighed dramatically, cutting his eyes to where his fingers pressed against the crook of my elbow. The faint hum of magic I had sensed before was now encircling me, too.

"C'mon," he said. "We're on a schedule."

"—about her father," Mom was saying as we approached. "But she hasn't even heard the good news yet."

I went still so abruptly, Luc almost let go.

"Oh?" Sister Donna asked.

"He's coming home soon. We'd thought it would be late spring or summer, but he's been a model . . . citizen. They're releasing him early. February."

A buzzing sounded in my ears, a hum that was more misery than magic, and my vision narrowed, the rest of the room falling away. All I could see was my mom, so delighted with her news, practically radiant. My father was coming home.

Early. *Months* early.

No matter where I went to school, we'd be under the same roof for almost six months before I could escape.

My entire body went hot, then cold, and I swayed, suddenly grateful for Luc's hand at my elbow. Even though I knew his spell hid us, it felt like everyone in the room was staring, the intensity of their interest in our little family drama suffocating me.

"Let's go," I said to Luc.

"What?"

"You wanted to talk? Let's talk. Just get me away from here."

His mouth curved upward, but it didn't quite reach his eyes. "Thought you'd never ask," he said, and ushered me out into the biting November night.

CHAPTER 11

Maybe it was because I was out of practice, or because I'd done it too many times in one day, but the brief journey to Luc's apartment left me retching and miserable. I wasn't meant to go Between. An Arc had to bring me through each time. Maybe it was the magic's way of telling me I didn't belong, a reminder that I was trespassing, a warning not to do it too much. Maybe the magic just didn't like me.

The feeling was mutual.

Like a gentleman, Luc waited in the living room while I put myself back together in the bathroom. I sank down, feeling the solidity of the floor beneath me, pressing my cheek against the cool tile wall, willing the room to stop spinning. Every heartbeat sent a fresh pulse of pain through my temples. The mere thought of my dad coming home sent a new wave of nausea running through me.

Living in the same house as my dad would be impossible. I'd given up being mad at him years ago. My anger had turned into something bleak and vast, a wasteland of indifference. He'd been stupid, laundering money through my uncle's many businesses. Greedy, too, because when that wasn't enough, he'd embezzled. After my dad left, Billy had stepped in, making sure that my mom could pay the bills, covering my tuition, selling my mom The Slice so she could be independent. Billy saved us. It was what my mom had always told me. My uncle had saved us when my dad had bailed.

The truth was a lot less noble. I didn't know the specifics. Colin wouldn't talk, and my mother refused to say a word against either my dad or my uncle, so I was left with nothing but the newspaper accounts of the trial. And while the official story was that my father had taken advantage of his brother-in-law's trust and generosity, I knew now that they'd both been mixed up with the Chicago Outfit the whole time.

New York was supposed to be my escape. After Verity's death, it had seemed more important than ever, a way of fulfilling our promise to each other, of living out the dream we'd shared. But it turned out, Verity wouldn't have gone to New York anyway. Her plans had changed when her powers came through and she'd discovered she was the Vessel, destined to save the Arcs and their magic. The last thing we ever did together was fight about her plan to move to New Orleans instead of New York. And now, here I was, in New Orleans, fulfilling a different promise to her.

"You okay?" Luc called through the closed door.

"Yeah." I stood, bracing myself against the wall. I made my way into the living room. I loved Luc's apartment. The crown molding, the old pictures, the careless clutter of beautiful art from around the world . . . everything here begged to be examined and touched and explored, because a quick glance wasn't enough.

The boy sitting on the couch was no different.

He stood as I entered the room, all long lines and lean muscle, concern softening the harsh angles of his face. He watched closely as I shuffled to the sleek black couch.

"You're looking a mess," he said, and even though his tone was light, the worry underneath was genuine.

"Thank you." I sank into the buttery leather, tucking my feet under me.

"Out of practice?"

"Maybe you are," I said. "Operator error. Isn't that what they call it?"

"I operate just fine," he said, amusement brightening his sharp, exotic features. "And you must be feelin' better already. You asked to come, remember?"

I shivered. The French doors to the balcony stood open, and even though it was warmer here than at home, I was chilled. Luc noticed—nothing escaped him—and with a single, shimmering word, the fire in the hearth caught.

"Here." He went to the kitchen and returned a moment later with a steaming teacup. "Want a little something extra?" He cocked his head toward the sideboard, with its cut crystal decanters.

"No thanks." Luc muddled my thoughts all on his own. I didn't need to hand him any unfair advantages. I sipped at the tea, aware of his eyes on me, a shifting green gaze that reminded me of trees in summer, warm and beautiful and secretive.

He sat down, stretching his arm along the back of the couch. He wasn't quite touching me, but warmth radiated from him. It made me want to curl up like a cat. "Church was . . . nice," he said.

"Church was a train wreck." I inhaled the sweet, flowery scent of the tea, shoving back the memory of my mom's announcement and Sister Donna's "grave concerns." "I'm screwed. You know that, right? I need those teacher recommendations to get into NYU."

"They'll be falling all over themselves trying to land a girl like you. But the news about your daddy rattled you pretty good. Thought you were going to keel right over."

"I didn't." It seemed important to remind him.

"I'd have caught you."

"What did the Quartoren say?"

"You sure you're up for it? Little worried 'bout you, Mouse."

"I'm fine." Sort of.

He stood abruptly. "Think you're steady enough for a walk?"

"You brought me nine hundred miles so we could take a

walk? We have sidewalks in Chicago, you know. Lots of them."

"It's a beautiful night. You could see my city. I've certainly been spending enough time in yours."

Reluctantly, I set my teacup down. "Where are we going?"

He watched my hands instead of meeting my eyes. "The Quartoren's willing to deal. But it has to be tonight."

"It's only been a few hours," I protested. "Why the hurry?"

"It's a bit of a pressing situation. Besides, what is there to think about?"

We walked side by side down the narrow staircase, Luc's hip bumping against mine. "They don't like me very much."

"It's not you, exactly." He looked faintly ashamed, a rarity. "You're not an Arc. And they're none too fond of Flats."

"Shocking." I'd witnessed that firsthand, when the Seraphim had tried to kill me in a bar full of Arcs and everyone had very deliberately looked away. "They're bigots."

"What would happen if Arcs were revealed in your world?" We crossed the familiar courtyard, gravel crunching under our feet. He opened the gate with a word and a touch. "Do you think Flats would accept us? Or would they think we were dangerous? Call us witches? Burn us at the stake, press us under stones? Human race is a lot of things, but tolerant ain't one of 'em."

We passed another couple on the street, arms wrapped around each other's waists, goofy, love-struck expressions on their faces. They smiled at us, so caught up in their romantic haze they assumed we must be, too. I stepped away from Luc and kept my voice low.

"I'm not just some Flat. I nearly died saving your stupid magic. And rather than return the favor—by helping one of your own—the Quartoren want to blackmail me? I'm having a hard time seeing them as the good guys."

"The Quartoren put the well-bein' of the Arcs above everything and everyone else. They have to look at what's best for all our people, not just a single girl. Whatever's wrong with the magic is putting us in danger. It's costing us *lives.* It ain't noble, but if the Quartoren need to use Vee's baby sister to convince you, they will. And they won't lose sleep over it."

"These are the people who are going to take care of Constance? Maybe she'd be better off without them."

We turned down a brick-paved street, so narrow it was more like an alley. Luc had slowed his pace for my benefit, despite the strain between us, and I appreciated it. In the darkness, the streetlamps turned the candy-colored houses into something shadowed and lovely, the fanciful wrought-iron casting lacy silhouettes on the clapboards and bricks. My fingers itched for my camera. Verity's pictures of the city hadn't done it justice. No matter where you looked, the past overlaid the present like the finest layer of dust. Every corner had plaques displaying the Spanish names of the streets, every third building bore a historical marker. Knowing the Arcs existed here added another layer of stories.

"You've seen what will happen to Constance if she's left on her own. Maybe you'd best reserve judgment until you see what we could do for her." He kept his hand on the small of my back as we walked, turning down streets seemingly at random, leaving behind the overbright neon and raucous noise of the Quarter.

"Where are we going?"

"The House of DeFoudre."

"There's an actual house?" I shook my head. It was just surreal enough to be funny.

" 'Course there is. Each element has one. You can come here with me, since we're bound. Bein' the Vessel, you're allowed into the other three."

"Then let's go visit the House Constance would be in."

"Because you and Orla are such good friends? Don't think so. Besides, I can't play tour guide half so well in another House."

We walked for a few minutes longer, alongside an elaborate fence, the wrought-iron posts tapering to wickedly sharp points. Our view was blocked by dense green bushes towering overhead. Luc paused in front of the main gate, and it swung open.

"You didn't even try to open it," I said. "What kind of spell was that?"

"Spell's in the lock. It recognized me as one of the House, so I don't need to cast anything."

"What if I came here without you and tried to get in?"

He winced. "Don't try that."

"Are the other Houses the same way?"

"Sure. Makes for a pretty safe environment. You wouldn't have to worry that Constance was bein' looked after."

I started to respond, but my breath was snatched from my chest as I marveled at the sprawling mansion. Three stories, white clapboard, a Georgian-style dream. Mansions on the North Shore had nothing on this place. "*This* is your House? Or is this just headquarters?"

"The Patriarch resides here. The rest of the Arcs have their own places. Spelled, usually, to conceal them from Flats."

"Like the Dauphine?" An Arcs-only jazz club, sumptuous and moody inside, an abandoned storefront on the outside.

"Yeah. They cluster together, most of the time. There's whole blocks of the city Flats don't see."

"You don't live here now, do you?" I'd always assumed Luc's apartment was his home.

"No. Once an Arc's powers come through, they usually leave home within a year or so. I'll be back eventually."

Because he was the Heir, I realized. When he took over as Patriarch from Dominic, this would be his home and his work. This place was Luc's future. Because we were bound, he assumed it was mine, too. I wrenched my attention back to the present.

"Constance couldn't move down here," I said. "We couldn't explain it to her parents."

"Wouldn't need to. She could come down for trainin' and be home again before anyone noticed she was gone."

"You trained here?"

He hesitated. "My upbringin' was a little different."

"Because of the prophecy?"

"Somethin' like that." He jogged lightly up the porch steps and opened the door to a massive, two-story foyer. A staircase spiraled upward, the dark wood floors contrasting sharply with the delicate brocade wallpaper and wide white trim. I tried not to gape, but it was like something out of a movie. I wouldn't have been surprised to see debutantes sashaying down the steps in heavy satin and lace gowns or a duel being fought on the lawn.

"I can't believe you grew up here." The air was so heavy with magic, it seemed to cling to my skin. I brushed at my arms, but the sensation remained.

"You get used to it," he said absently, guiding me through the foyer. "This is what I wanted you to see."

In the movies, it would have been the ballroom—glossy parquet floors, a soaring ceiling, Palladian windows and French doors lining one wall. The same debutantes who would make a grand entrance in the foyer would glide across this room on someone's arm, twirling until their dresses were a blur.

But here, now, it wasn't a ballroom. It was a school. Scattered across the room, groups of kids, from grade-schoolers to teenagers, practiced different spells. The room fell silent as we entered, everyone bowing their heads and extending a hand, palm up, to Luc—a gesture of respect. He cut a glance toward me and then returned the gesture, almost self-consciously. The kids went back to their activities, but many of them darted nervous glances at us as we passed by.

In one corner, I watched a girl a few years older than me work with a group of five or six little kids. She held out her hand and a ruby red flame appeared in the center. Nimbly, she passed it to the cupped hands of a gangly looking boy, whose thin face was screwed up in concentration. He passed it to the next child, whose shaking hands made the flame gutter and nearly go out, until she passed it to the next. Faster and faster, the flame traveled around the group, the teacher nodding encouragement and offering words of advice, until a pudgy redheaded girl dropped the flame. There was a faint pop as it went out, the scent of sulfur lingering.

"Beginners," Luc said, nodding at them. "Once they've gotten some control, they'll call it up themselves."

In a far corner, three kids Constance's age practiced pulling objects out of thin air. Oranges, a book, and a skateboard, of all things, would appear in their hands and then, just as suddenly, be shoved into space and disappear. "Always liked that lesson," Luc said fondly. "You find a little pocket of Between, stake your claim, and it's like a moving storage unit."

"Your sword," I said in sudden understanding. "That's where you keep it? Between?"

"Can't expect me to carry it everywhere, can you? But it's good to have at hand."

Since that sword had saved my life on more than one occasion, I had to agree.

In another group, kids practiced going Between. The older ones were playing tag, dodging in and out of the room trying to catch each other, while a little girl cut a flaming rectangle in the air, tongue caught between her teeth. Before she could close the shape, the flames dissolved and she stomped her foot in frustration.

The whispered language of the Arcs surrounded us, glimmering and diffuse. Everything was drenched in magic, overwhelming me. My knees buckled and I barely managed to stay upright.

"This is what we could give her," Luc said, surveying the room with obvious approval. He didn't seem to notice I was struggling. "A safe place to practice and learn. She'd meet other Arcs of her kind. Make friends."

"They seem so young," I murmured. The magic was filling my head with a strange pressure, and I tried to concentrate.

"Most of them shouldn't be here. They only come to a House for training once their powers come through. This room should be filled with kids sixteen, seventeen. With the surge in the magic, we have to take them in early."

"Because of me," I said. Across the room, one of the children holding a flame in her hands cried out as it flared up, burning her. With a word, the teacher healed the injury and resumed the lesson.

Luc watched the scene unfold and took my hand, running a finger over the scar on my palm. "You're the Vessel. You're meant to take care of the magic. I know you don't like hearing it, but if we don't fix this, more Arcs are going to suffer. Flats, too."

My head spun. "Can we go?"

His eyebrows drew together, but he led the way back through the house. "I'd give you more of a tour, but the Quartoren's waiting."

"I don't really have a choice, do I?"

He shrugged as we crossed the verdant lawn and headed toward the French Quarter. "There's always a choice. It's just a question of how much you're willing to pay. But at least you've seen what they can do for Vee's little sister. What you'd be getting if you agree."

My headache eased as we moved away from Luc's House, and I wondered why. I'd taken the magic inside me during the Torrent; now something was wrong with it. The idea that there was something wrong with me, too, seemed entirely possible. But I shoved the thought away and focused on the city around me, so different from Chicago in November.

The streets were surprisingly quiet, only a few clusters of people toting giant plastic cups and laughing. Luc steered us away from Bourbon Street, chuckling as I craned my neck for a glimpse. "Nothing you need to see down there. We'll play tourist another time."

We passed boutiques, candy shops, art galleries, all with darkened windows. The red brick buildings were soft with age, the corners crumbling, the door frames canting to one side or the other. The cafés were still open, the people in the lighted windows laughing and eating. Some of them even had outdoor seating, and I marveled at the sight of sundresses and capris when everyone at home was wearing scarves and heavy coats.

"It was forty degrees at home today," I said as we passed an oyster bar with lines out the door, accordion music spilling out.

"Winter has its benefits. Good reason to cuddle up."

I elbowed him lightly, too intent on taking in the lush elegance of the buildings in the deepening night, the vivid colors, the ornate balconies with riotously blooming flowers. There was a smell, like vanilla and apricots, as we passed a glossy green shrub. I stopped, trying to capture the scent of the starlike flowers, but it was gone.

"Won't work," Luc said. "It's sweet olive. Get too close and the scent disappears. Let it come to you instead of chasing after it."

I shot him a dirty look, and he held up his hands in mock defense. "Try it."

Skeptical, I stepped back a few feet and closed my eyes, breathing deeply. The scent enveloped me, so heavy it felt like a caress. "That's incredible. It's what heaven must smell like."

"Told you. Hard lesson to learn, isn't it?" He led us through a square, bounded by hedges and fencing on all four sides, past a statue of a man on a horse. Beyond was a cathedral, three spires soaring into the night sky.

"You're taking me to church?"

"Not exactly."

The sight reminded me of my mom. If I'd worried my absence from school would attract attention, it was nothing compared to what would happen when my mom discovered me missing from church, right underneath her nose. And Colin's reaction . . .

I pulled away from Luc, opened my phone.

"Mouse, you're about to do business with the Quartoren. This ain't really the time."

I ignored him and texted Colin: had 2 leave church. cover 4 me?

"You two an item now? All official-like?" Luc asked. His arm tensed underneath my hand.

"Leave him out of this."

"Be happy to. You're the one who lets him tag along. Always nicer when it's just us."

My phone rang, as expected. But I thought better of answering and tucked it into my pocket instead. "I'll call him when it's over."

"Won't be over for a long time," Luc said, not unkindly. "Tell yourself anything else, you're lyin'."

CHAPTER 12

Magic was good for a lot of things: transporting you instantly from one corner of the earth to another, healing a near-fatal injury with a touch, and fighting off creatures intent on eviscerating you, for example. But it was especially good at hiding stuff. The Arcs were masters of it, and the result was that nothing and no one were ever quite what they seemed.

We stood outside a massive cathedral with three soaring spires. As we crossed the threshold, the air quivered and the nave disappeared, revealing an echoing white room. There were no windows set into the high ceilings, but it was bright as day, illuminated by an enormous iron chandelier overhead, crammed with candles as thick around as my arm. The scent of beeswax permeated the air, cloyingly sweet.

"What is this place?"

"This? Just the waiting room. The Quartoren meet through there," he said, pointing to the second set of doors. "Ready?"

Probably not. He raised a fist and knocked, the sound deeper than I expected. His knuckles left a glowing reddish imprint on the metal, like superheated steel. On the fifth strike, the doors opened as smoothly and silently as if they'd been oiled. Luc stepped inside, and I followed.

It was a cavernous room, rows of seats stretching skyward like a theater. They were empty, except for the first row. Marguerite sat alone, her expression serene. She tracked the sound of our footsteps as we made our way down the black and white checkered aisle. Along the walls, torches flickered noiselessly. Shallow stairs led to a stage at the front of the room, where Dominic, Orla, and Pascal stood behind a massive wooden table.

"Be nice," Luc murmured as he drew me up the stairs to the stage. This close to the table, I could see symbols carved into the ebonized wood, similar to the ones I'd seen in the Binding Temple. It was the language of the magic, and the markings shifted as I studied them, rearranging themselves at will.

Very slowly, I backed up, goose bumps raising on my arms and legs. If there was one thing I'd learned about magic, it was that anything that powerful deserved a wide berth.

Luc stood behind me, fingertips brushing the back of my neck, a tangible, reassuring presence. I turned, about to question him, but he shushed me.

"Welcome, Maura. The Quartoren are honored by your presence here." Dominic winked before nodding solemnly, like he'd remembered his role.

Directly to his right, Orla pressed her lips together, as if she wanted to argue the point. She settled for wafting an old-fashioned silk fan in front of her face. To Dominic's left, at the far end of the ominously shifting table, stood Pascal. His hair was pulled back with a narrow strip of leather, and his fingers twitched, though he didn't seem to realize it. Between the two men, an empty chair stood, like a reproach. Evangeline's, I guessed, and quickly looked away.

Luc bent, touching his lips to mine. The gesture was so brief I didn't have time to pull away. "For luck."

"I need luck?"

But he was already nudging me forward, directly into the Quartoren's scrutiny. He sat next to Marguerite, who patted his arm. I wrenched my attention back to the scene before me. The weight of the magic, their solemn expressions . . . I wanted to turn around and run back out the door, into the sweetly scented New Orleans night, away from this world and what it wanted of me. What would happen to Constance if I did?

So instead of fleeing, I locked my knees and folded my hands in front of me. I'd come to them. The next move was theirs.

Orla's fan beat faster, and finally, Dominic cleared his throat. "We summoned you here, hoping we could come to a mutually beneficial agreement. We got off on the wrong foot today. My son has suggested that perhaps we rushed you, and if that's the case, I apologize."

There was the barest hint of irritation underneath the words. I didn't know if it was directed at Orla, for storming off, or Luc, for daring to correct him, or me, for not falling into line. I pasted on a neutral smile and let him continue.

"Fact is, we are in a dangerous situation. The longer we wait, the more destructive the magic becomes. Our children suffer more every day. Weaker Arcs can't risk casting spells, because they can't control what happens. The Darklings are seeking out the breaches, killing any living thing that happens nearby—including Flats."

I shuddered.

"It's what the Seraphim wants," Dominic added. "To destabilize the Quartoren and all we stand for. They want to use this crisis to bring about their Ascendency."

Orla rapped her fan on the table. "Rumors. There's no proof, Dominic. The Seraphim's back was broken when the girl defeated Evangeline and remade the lines. They're no threat to us any longer."

"You've heard the talk, same as I have. The Seraphim are coming back, and they are bent on ruination," Dominic said.

"It's nothing but people who feel wronged, talking to hear their heads roar," she replied.

Pascal held up a hand. "We've all heard the rumors, but there's no evidence. No conclusive proof. But the danger to the magic is real, and we need to devise a solution. Immediately."

Dominic squared his shoulders, trying to regain control over the conversation.

"We realize we're asking much of you, but we're prepared to offer something in return."

Orla's face seemed to twitch just a little, and her eyes were hard. "I can retract my decree. We can make a place for the Grey girl in my House."

"She needs more than a House. She needs a guide. Someone who will teach her to use the magic and how the Arcs work. I don't want her getting in trouble because she broke a rule she didn't know existed." I'd had that happen too many times in my dealings with the Arcs. I wouldn't let Constance run into the same problem.

"And in return, you would aid the Quartoren? Fix the magic?" Dominic said.

"I'd do whatever I could."

"That's a broad statement," said Pascal. "Do you know what you can do?"

I swallowed, searching for my connection to Luc. It was faint, like an AM radio station, and I wondered if the symbols carved into the table were interfering. "I can save Constance's life. That's all I care about."

Dominic smiled broadly. "Let's make it official then, shall we? We propose a Covenant. A formal agreement, sealed with magic. When the terms are met, the seal is broken and everyone goes about their lives again. But if either party doesn't fulfill their portion, their life is forfeit."

"They *die?*"

"It ensures neither party walks away," said Orla. "Or fails."

"She won't fail," Luc cut in. "Mouse tells you she'll do something, she'll follow through. I guarantee it."

"We'd need something a bit more reliable than your word, Luc. You're hardly unbiased," she said.

Pascal pushed at his glasses and then held out his hands, palms up. One cupped a darting green flame, the other a wisp of gold mist. "Your cooperation, Constance Grey's life." He made a show of balancing the two. "We will tend to her as carefully as you do our magic," he said, and the two strengthened. "If you fail . . ." He let the green light fade, but my attention was riveted on the gold mist. With a short, sharp movement, he threw the mist to the floor, where it disintegrated noiselessly. "We will cast her out. All of us."

I looked to Luc, silently begging him to tell me there was another way, but he only nodded, an odd tension radiating off him. I was on my own.

"Will you agree to the Covenant?" There was an unmistakable finality in Dominic's voice. If I said no, there would be no second chance—for me or Constance.

"Yes," I said, my voice swallowed by the cavernous room.

With a rustling noise, Dominic lifted a sheet of parchment from the table, displaying it to all of us. Then, setting the paper down again, he reached for a glass pen sitting nearby and dipped it into a pot of ink. With a bold, sure movement, he signed his name. Orla and Pascal both signed in turn, the room so silent you could hear the faint scratch of pen on paper.

When they were done, Dominic held the pen out to me with both hands. "Maura?"

I glanced at Luc again. He stood completely still, lips parted as if he wanted to speak but couldn't find the words. His eyes were shadowed and intent in the torchlight. It was hard to tell what he saw when he looked at me, and I was afraid, all over again, that whatever he saw wasn't truly there.

Pascal whistled absently, bringing my attention back to the choice before me.

My life, I thought. That's what was on the table. My life and Constance's, and Verity's, too, twined together like a braid. I'd seen how cruel and unforgiving a force the magic was, how easily it could destroy people. The only reason I was alive, able to make this deal, was because Verity had sacrificed herself for me in that alley months ago.

I crossed the stage and took the pen from Dominic.

It was made of clear, cool glass, sinuous and heavier than it looked. The ink gleamed, black as Luc's hair, along the finely etched tip. I bent and signed my name, Maura Kathleen Fitzgerald. Next to the ornate script of the other signatures, my writing seemed messy and childish. The ink soaked into the thick, creamy parchment, the edges blurring. Dominic whipped the contract away with a flourish, and I jerked upright at the movement.

"That's all?" I whooshed out a breath. That wasn't so bad. The Binding Ceremony with Luc had hurt a lot more.

Dominic patted my shoulder. "One last task."

There always was, with these people.

CHAPTER 13

"The Covenant requires we forge a symbol of our agreement," Dominic said.

Luc guided Marguerite onstage. In her hands, she carried a box of age-blackened wood. "For you," she said, lifting the lid and holding it out to me. Inside were five silver rings, each as big around as an orange.

I took one gingerly. "A bracelet?"

"A link. Do well, Mo," she murmured.

Dominic stepped forward and took a ring for himself. At his nod, Pascal and Orla did, too. Wordlessly, Marguerite shut the box, and Luc escorted her down the steps.

I would have thought signing a contract was enough, but it made a certain sense. Arcs didn't need tools to work a spell—Luc had destroyed the Chicago Water Tower with words alone—but objects seemed to give their magic a focal point. Verity had been given a ring to help her with the Torrent; when Luc and I had gone through the Binding Ceremony, we'd wrapped our wrists with a fine platinum chain. It was invisible now, joined to the magic, but still a constant reminder of our connection. And then there were the weapons. Channels, Luc had called them, a way to direct a large amount of magic. He'd carried a sword, the edge dancing with ruby flames, and every time he'd drawn it, there'd been big danger and bigger magic.

Now, I saw, the Quartoren had weapons of their own.

They'd formed a loose circle, leaving space for me. Each held a ring in one hand and a weapon in the other. Dominic held a scimitar, a curved sword, and Orla carried a delicately carved bow and arrow. Pascal rested a huge hammer, the metal head incredibly heavy looking, against his leg.

"Come," said Dominic, crooking an elbow at the gap next to him. "No one will harm you here."

I moved into the circle, apprehensive.

In a booming voice meant to carry through the room, he said, "We have forged an alliance, which shall remain fast until the terms of the Covenant are fulfilled. We seal our words with magic, the source of our strength. Hold out your link."

I did, and Dominic placed his circle over mine. The room grew warmer, and as he spoke, the air seemed to tremble, like the surface of a pot about to boil. With the flat of the scimitar's blade, he struck the links sharply, and ruby sparks flew into the air. I turned away, squeezing my eyes shut.

A few feet away, Luc said, "Won't hurt, and it'll be over in a minute."

I looked back at the ring. The two circles were now linked together, no seam visible, no cracks in the surface. On the other side of me, Orla touched her ring to mine and tapped it with the tip of the arrow, speaking a similar incantation. The golden sparks were so bright I was nearly blinded. The air around me seemed to charge, my scalp prickling as my headache returned with a vengeance.

"You said it wouldn't hurt," I muttered to Luc. The bones of his face seemed even more prominent, and his eyes were gold-rimmed green as he moved toward me. "It feels like before. With Constance."

Only Pascal and Luc reacted. Pascal's expression turned thoughtful, and Luc reached for me through our bond, trying to gauge exactly how much trouble we were in. The connection still felt muted by interference, and that made me worry more.

"Stop the ritual," Luc said. "It's too risky."

"We can't stop now," said Orla. "The Covenant hasn't been sealed. We'd be no better off than before."

"And your friend will be on her own again," Pascal said to me. "You'll be safe enough to continue, I think."

"Safe *enough?*" I asked.

"Are you sure?" Dominic asked. "We can't lose her here."

I felt a rush of affection for Dominic. Finally, someone on my side.

Pascal waved a hand. "Yes, yes. I can't predict other ramifications, but she'll live."

The hair on my arms stood up as the magic filled the air with a crackling tension. Orla made a noise of impatience.

"Maura?" said Dominic. "Are you well enough to proceed?"

I grabbed the increasingly heavy mass of rings with both hands, trying to hide my shakiness. "Okay."

At Dominic's nod, Pascal spoke, words of power that seemed to rebound off the magic looming over us. I tightened my grip on the rings as Pascal bobbled the massive hammer, his thin arms straining under its weight. When he finally struck the links, it was only a glancing blow. The hammer head slipped off to the side with a faint clink. I wondered for an instant if it had worked.

And then the room went blindingly white as the magic ripped through it, throwing me backward. Luc caught me, shielding my body with his. I could see his lips moving, casting wards around us as the magic burned, but everything had gone eerily silent.

As the magic ebbed away, noise began to filter back in, popping and hissing like an old-fashioned record. Gradually, my hearing returned to normal. Luc hauled me to my feet, checking for injuries.

"I'm okay," I said. "My head's . . . better . . . I think." Better was a relative term, but the throbbing pain I'd felt before had passed.

Luc shot an angry glance at the Quartoren, but they were too dazed to notice. "I'm taking you home."

I was still holding the rings, fused together like a complicated silver flower. "What about this?"

"Keep it as a reminder of our Covenant," Orla said.

Like I needed one, after tonight. "C'mon," said Luc, leading me away. From the other side of the room came a soft sound of distress. I turned and saw Luc's mom crouched on the ground, arms covering her head.

"Marguerite!" Dominic cried, rushing to her.

Luc dropped my hand and dashed across the stage. *"Maman?"*

Dominic helped her to her feet, murmuring reassurances, his broad frame dwarfing her tiny one. Effortlessly, she shook him off and looked directly at me.

I clapped a hand over my mouth. Her eyes had gone milky white, and her hands were cupped in front of her like she was receiving communion.

"What do you see?" Dominic asked. There was no trace of the concerned husband I'd seen a moment ago. Then again, this was an entirely new Marguerite.

Despite her clouded pupils, she held my gaze as she spoke, her voice high and hollow, nothing like the way she'd sounded at the bayou cabin.

"I see a new age rising, and we are brought low before it. Against the tide stands the Four-In-One, the Vessel bound forever, all the magic seeks." She paused, gasping in a breath, hands trembling. "Listen to it. Join the heart. Seal it with yourself, or we are, every one, lost."

Her words echoed in the silent room. The color seeped back into her eyes, and she sagged against Dominic. He scooped her up like a sleeping child, concern creasing his face. "See to her," he said to Luc, nodding in my direction. An instant later, they had gone Between.

"What the hell was that?" Luc asked.

Pascal's brow furrowed. "As with all seers, Marguerite's

talent is unpredictable. Likely the surge triggered her ability, permitting her to voice a new prophecy."

"Was she talking about me?" I asked. *I have other talents,* she'd said to me. No kidding. How much of my future did she see?

"It would appear that way. We'll study it," he said.

"I don't like all this magic floatin' around," Luc said, taking my hand. "Let's get you home."

I was about to answer when something struck the side of the building. The torches along the walls guttered.

Luc swore. Pascal and Orla exchanged a look of dread. As usual, I was the one playing catch-up. "What's going on?" I asked.

Orla's lip curled as something jolted the wall again. "Darklings. We told you, they're attracted to raw magic. From the sound of it, no more than a pair."

That was two more than I was comfortable with. "They're attacking the building?"

"The surge must have brought them," Pascal said. "Don't worry. Orla and I can easily dispatch two Darklings. It's unlikely they'll even breach the outer doors. This is not a comfortable place for their kind."

"Not odds I'm willing to play," said Luc. "We'll go Between instead."

Even though my heart was thudding in my chest as loud the creatures outside, I couldn't leave yet. Orla was already heading toward the stairs, ready to do battle, but I blocked her path. "You promised to help Constance. That starts now."

The walls shuddered from another assault. "Priorities," she said, gesturing to the bow in her hand.

"Constance *is* my priority." I crossed my arms.

"Fine. I'll select a guide and they'll begin tomorrow. You'll be kept . . ."—she smiled thinly—". . . in the loop? That's what Flats call it, correct?"

The loop was feeling more and more like a noose. "How do I fix the magic? I don't even know what's wrong with it."

"Enough," said Luc, as several of the torches went out. "Figurin' out the next step is their job. I'm taking you home." With broad, angry slashes, he cut a doorway into the air.

"You ready?"

I nodded, and he pulled me through.

CHAPTER 14

We came Between down the street from my house. The lights were blazing from the windows, my uncle's Cadillac parked at the curb, Colin's truck right behind it. "The gang's all here," I muttered, nearly toppling over.

From behind me, Luc grabbed my shoulders, keeping me upright. "Easy, Mouse."

I peered down the block. No bony talons, no rotting arms or tattered wings pierced the amber glow of the streetlights. "Do you think the Darklings will follow us?"

He concentrated for a moment, searching along the lines for some hint of trouble to come. "Doubt it. My guess is Pascal and Orla took care of them quick. And they're not after you—they want raw magic. None of that floatin' around here."

"I'm safe now?"

"Let's not get carried away. Seraphim could be a problem. Covenant definitely is. But Darklings shouldn't be an issue tonight." He didn't let go of me, though.

I couldn't think about the Seraphim or the Covenant right now. There was enough trouble facing me inside the front door. "You should check on your mom."

His body tensed against mine, and he rested his chin on the top of my head. "She meant us, you know. In the prophecy."

"The Four-In-One." Luc had one elemental power; I had three because of my link to Verity. But thanks to our binding, we shared all four talents.

"Bound forever," he added. "You heard it, too."

I knew what he was going to say—Marguerite's vision was proof we were supposed to be together. But I couldn't talk about it with him. I needed time to think and recover. I heard Marguerite's voice again, and a splintering pain stabbed at my chest, making it hard to breathe. It must have been another aftereffect of the trip Between. I was grateful that we'd come through in a shadowy spot so he couldn't see my face. "I can't deal with this right now."

He tried very hard not to look hurt. "Let me walk you to the door."

"I'll be fine." I eased away. "Go ahead."

I forced myself to cross the street without stumbling, clenching my teeth against the pain. I could feel Luc's presence clearly again, the slight tension in the chain between us. When I reached for the doorknob, he left, the sound echoing down the street.

I paused, not ready to go inside. The Quartoren's rings weighed down my bag, and I dropped it with a clank. I'd done the right thing. Constance needed help, and I was the only one who could make sure she got it. I had to believe that keeping my word, even without the life-or-death incentive of the Covenant, mattered. It was the opposite of what my family had taught me—tell the truth, keep your promises, take responsibility. I'd done something to the magic, and now I owed it to Verity's people to fix it.

Through the window I could see my uncle pacing the living room, phone to his ear, barking orders. No doubt my mother was in the kitchen freaking out. Colin was leaning against the doorframe between the two rooms, watching it all. He spoke to my mom, probably trying to calm her, but I knew exactly what his lowered brow and crossed arms meant: There'd be questions—and hell to pay—later.

I unlocked the door and stepped inside. Silence fell like the curtain at a play, and then an explosion of noise, the tumult nearly knocking me backward.

"Maura Kathleen Fitzgerald!" Billy roared, his face nearly purple. He snapped the phone shut. "What in the name of sweet Jesus were you thinking? Don't you ever run off like that again."

"You're not my mother." I walked past him to the staircase. Forget confrontations and explanations. All I wanted was a handful of aspirin and my bed. Across the room, Colin took a step toward me, eyes locking on to mine.

My mom skirted him and stopped next to my uncle, her mouth a narrow line. "I am. And I would like to know exactly where you've been, young lady."

I dropped my bag on the staircase with a thump. "Out."

"Out? That's the best you can do? I suppose you were out this morning, too, when you skipped school. I talked to Sister Donna this evening, and she told me all about it."

"I know. I heard you." I crossed my arms and braced for the inevitable fight.

Her triumphant look faded, replaced with uncertainty. "I didn't see you."

"I heard about Dad coming home, too." Six months ago, I would have left it at that. Not anymore. "You should have told me. Everyone at church knew, Mom. It'll be all over school by tomorrow." Out of the corner of my eye, I caught a glimpse of surprise on Colin's face, followed by understanding. He hadn't known either, it seemed.

"I wanted to find the right time. . . ." She blinked, then beamed at me. "Isn't it wonderful?"

I laughed despite my exhaustion. "Are you kidding me? It's the exact opposite of wonderful. You are so delusional."

"Watch your tongue," Billy snapped. "And don't change the subject. Where were you tonight?"

Colin gripped the back of the ivory wing chair, and my heart broke a little bit at the worry in his expression.

I didn't care if my mom and Billy were angry with me. It felt good to be the one with the answers for a change, to give them a taste of their own medicine. But Colin was different. Since Verity had died, he was the person I was most myself with. I didn't have to pretend, or hide, or be ashamed. When I was with Colin, being Mo was enough. He'd given me that, like a gift, and in return I'd caused him nothing but worry.

There was no way to say that to him right now, though. The best I could do was mouth "Sorry" as my family continued to rail at me.

My mother crossed her arms. "March yourself right into the kitchen. We're not done discussing this."

Oh, good. Because I was really up for a family meeting. I started across the room, deliberately brushing against Colin's arm.

He jerked away. "I should go."

"Stay," my uncle barked, and a hint of temper flashed across Colin's face, so handsome that even anger looked good. "We're going to be making some changes around here, and you'll need to be aware of them."

That didn't sound promising. I was not a fan of change, and I doubted tonight would prove the exception.

"Changes?" I echoed, dropping into my usual chair.

"It's nothing too terrible." Mom followed me into the kitchen and stood at the counter. "We think it would be better if you stayed close to home for the next little while."

"Define 'close to home.' "

She squared her shoulders. "You'll still go to school and church. You can work at The Slice. But until we see some improvement in your attitude, and hear that your school performance is back to where it should be, you're grounded."

"You're kidding, right?" But my mom didn't kid. It wasn't in her DNA. "You're grounding me. My senior year."

"You've been through so much, honey. I think you need a little downtime." She picked up an apple from the pile on the counter and began to peel it, the skin coming off in one shining, red curl. Despite the wobbly corners of her mouth, her hands were sure and steady on the knife as she worked, something I'd seen her do countless times.

"Now," Billy said, settling himself at the head of the Formica-topped table and glowering. "Where did you go?"

I glanced at Colin, peering out the window that overlooked the screen porch. Fatigue overwhelmed me, and I folded my arms on the table, making a pillow for my head. "I told you. Out."

"Where is out?" he demanded.

"Not. In." Even though my voice was muffled, the sound of Billy's hand striking the table proved he heard me.

"That's not an answer."

I lifted my head and studied him, the way his hair, pure white, fell limply across his head. There were new lines etched into the corners of his eyes and mouth, and he seemed . . . tired. Older than I'd realized. He was a lot older than my mom, more than fifteen years. There'd been other siblings, but Billy was the only one who'd come over from Ireland with my grandparents; my mom had been born here in the States. Once my grandparents had died, he was the only one left to watch over my mother. For a moment, I felt a faint stirring of sympathy. Then I remembered that he might have taken care of my mom, but it was because of him we'd needed help to begin with.

Wordlessly, I let my aching head drop to my arms again.

"Fine. You'll tell us who you were with, then."

"Nobody you know."

"The girl from the diner today?"

Jenny Kowalski? Oh, God. How bad would it be if he found out Jenny was looking into her dad's death and blaming it on me? I didn't think he'd harm a teenage girl, not really. Then again, he hadn't agonized when he'd thrown me to the wolves a month ago, asking me to falsely accuse someone of Verity's murder to further his own standing in the Mob. If he thought Jenny was really a threat—and I knew by the fervor in her voice it was a definite possibility—there was no telling what he'd do.

I heaved myself up in the seat, the effort monumental, and met his eyes. "No. I told you, it was no one you know."

"A boy?" my mom asked, setting the knife down, her voice pitched higher. "Were you with a boy?"

Colin turned slowly, his expression absolutely blank. I chose my words carefully, meaning them for him.

"I had something I needed to do." I hoped like hell that Colin caught the implication—need, not want—but his eyes were shuttered, unreadable. I dragged my focus back to Billy, rubbing at my forehead.

"And you think you can simply disappear from church, all by yourself? Without so much as a good-bye?"

It wasn't simple, and I couldn't do it by myself, but otherwise . . . yeah, pretty much. I didn't think saying so would help me at that moment. "Why should I stay? So people can get in more digs about Dad coming home? I can't believe you didn't warn me."

"Sweetheart, why would I warn you? I know you're angry that Daddy left, but he's coming back. It's a blessing!"

"He didn't *leave*. He was convicted of multiple felonies."

"You're dwelling on the negative."

Could she really be this clueless? "There's not really a positive. I don't want him coming back here. I don't want to live in the same house with him."

"That's not your decision." My mom's voice had taken on a sharp, thin edge, her eyes dangerous. "This is my house, and I have worked my fingers to the bone to keep it that way. He is your father, and my husband, and you will treat him with the respect he is due. Everyone makes mistakes, Mo. Even you. But we forgive each other, because that's what families do. That's what this family does." She pressed her hand to her mouth and rushed from the room.

My family did lots of things, but I'd never seen forgiveness rank high on the list. I shook my head, trying to catch Colin's eye. But he was still staring out the window, like he might catch sight of Luc.

"Are you satisfied?" Billy asked. "The happiest day she's had in years, and you ruined it for her."

I put my head back down, not wanting him to catch sight of the guilt starting to nibble at me.

"You have been through quite a lot, haven't you?" he said after a long minute. His voice was gentler, and when I looked up, his hands were resting, loosely folded, on the table. He looked good natured and utterly reasonable.

He was after something.

"Mo, you're old enough to know the truth. Some of it I'm sure you've guessed already, smart as you are. Some of it . . . well, you deserve an explanation."

I propped my chin in my hand and waited to hear this new version of the truth.

"The men I asked you to identify this fall work for a man named Yuri Ekomov. He's not a good man. He's greedy, and violent, and unstable. He is looking to use our neighborhood as a place to expand his criminal activities. I believe with my whole heart he is responsible for Verity's death. But for the grace of God, it might have been you."

I could have corrected him, but I didn't. Billy wasn't the only one who could play things close to the chest.

He continued, "All I want is to keep him out of our neighborhood. To protect all of us. Our family, our friends, our way of life. You may have believed you were doing the right thing when you refused to identify those men, but you've drawn attention to yourself. You're in danger, and the time for this sort of recklessness has long passed. You can't be running around the city unsupervised."

I pointed to Colin. "Supervised."

"And yet you slipped out tonight." He frowned at Colin.

"The guys at church were yours, remember? Don't blame him because your muscle isn't up to the job. I don't care about Yuri Ekomov's business or yours. I told you before, I'm out."

Billy's eyes narrowed. "You forget exactly how much influence I hold over your life, Mo. You're still a child, under your mother's care, and she listens to me. You need to be careful how you proceed."

What I needed was to get the hell out of the house. Or at the very least, the kitchen.

"I'm going to bed." As I got to my feet, I clutched the edge of the table for balance, the room spinning around me. I bit down on my tongue to keep from moaning and focused on getting upstairs without falling over. If Billy noticed something was off, he'd administer a Breathalyzer on the spot. If Colin noticed—which seemed a lot more likely—he'd add it to the list of topics covered during my interrogation tomorrow.

When I reached my room, I threw my bag on the bed and myself after it. Grounded? I was nearly eighteen. I was a straight-A student. I'd worked in the nursery at church since I was thirteen. I had saved the freaking world, and now I was going to spend my senior year under lock and key for cutting class one time? A drop on the faded quilt caught my attention, and I leaned closer. Quickly, it soaked into the carefully pieced cotton. And then another appeared, red as roses, seeping into the other one. I touched the stain, my fingers coming away scarlet.

Blood, I realized, my exhausted brain slowly putting it together. And it was coming from me.

CHAPTER 15

The next morning, a bloody nose was the least of my worries. Colin was waiting in the kitchen, his face like thunder.

"Hey," I said, going directly to the coffeepot. Too many trips Between and another round of nightmares had left me achy and disoriented. "Want some?"

"No." He paused while I stirred in cream and sugar and took my first sip. "So. Last night."

I looked at him over the top of the mug. He was tall, easily six feet, and he leaned against the counter as if he didn't have a care in the world. Only the stormy gray of his eyes indicated the anger brewing underneath.

"It's complicated."

"That's what I don't get. You did what they wanted. Why can't they find someone else to help this time?" He pushed off the counter. "You've seen Luc twice in the last twenty-four hours, and both times you've turned up looking like you've been put through the wringer. I don't like it."

"How did you know Luc was there?"

"You disappear from church while Billy's got a full detail of guys watching the building. I don't need magic to figure out who was involved."

"It wasn't his fault." I set down the mug harder than I meant to.

"It never is. What does he want this time?"

"I have to go to school."

I could almost hear him grit his teeth. "Grab your bag."

If I'd thought the drive would be a reprieve, I was wrong. As soon as we were settled in the truck, heading into the stop-and-go morning traffic, he started in again.

"Well? That guy always wants something. Like I don't already know what it is."

"It's not like that," I said, flushing at the memory of Luc's fingers on my jaw. "I was very clear."

Colin snorted. "And he's so good at respecting boundaries."

Screaming wouldn't help, despite my frustration. "Well, you're too good at it. A happy medium would be nice."

"Don't push me."

"It's the only way I'm ever going to get anywhere with you." Suddenly, the path before us seemed rockier than ever, so I steered the conversation back to marginally safer ground. "Remember how I told you there was something wrong with the magic?"

"Yes."

"The Quartoren need me to fix it. They wouldn't help Constance unless I agreed to try."

Colin's voice was like ice. "What kind of people use a fourteen-year-old girl as leverage?"

"I don't have to like them," I said. "Just help them."

"You made the deal." It wasn't a question. He struck the dash once. "God. I wish you'd put yourself first sometimes."

"You'd have done the same thing," I shot back. "She's a kid. She's alone. I didn't have a choice."

"And Luc was happy to force your hand."

"He wasn't, actually. It was the Quartoren." It was Luc's idea to approach them, but I didn't mention that part.

"This is a bad idea," he said. "Billy's worried. I know you don't trust him—"

"With good reason."

"Some of what he said last night was true. Ekomov is cutting into your uncle's business. Billy's scrambling for any way he can to chip away at their organization. His bosses are pressuring him to move more aggressively, and word is, they're interested in you."

"Me?"

"You didn't really think people were going to forget about the lineup, did you? Billy's bosses noticed you, and he thinks he can use that."

"And you think the Quartoren are the bad guys?"

"Billy wants to protect you, but you're a wild card. He figures if he can keep you on a tighter leash, you're less likely to get hurt."

"And I'm less likely to do something to hurt him, right?"

Colin checked the mirrors and didn't answer. As usual, when the truck pulled up, the girls lingering in the courtyard stopped and stared. He tended to draw attention whenever he showed up on campus.

"What does he have on you?" I demanded, ignoring their simpering smiles and hair flips. "You never say, but I know you owe him. What is it?"

"History," he said. "Nothing you need to worry about."

My fists clenched in my lap. "Don't tell me not to worry. Billy does that when he's doing something awful and he doesn't want me to know the truth."

"Sometimes it's better not to," he said, covering my hands with one callused palm. The tenderness of the gesture made the words cut deeper.

"You're wrong. And wrong not to tell me. I don't care what you've done. It doesn't matter."

"Then you don't need to know about it, do you?" I started to argue, but he cut me off. "Do not skip class today. Whatever is going down in Magicland, it's nothing compared to what Billy will do if you disappear again."

Stung, I pulled my hand away and climbed out of the truck.

"Stay out of trouble," he said. I turned to look at him, taking in the way the overcast skies darkened his hair to chestnut honey, his eyes the color of slate and just as unyielding.

He wasn't going to change his mind—about the Arcs or his past—and I didn't know how we'd survive either obstacle. So I turned away and headed up the wide front steps, forcing myself not to look back again. By the time Lena found me at my locker, I could almost manage a smile.

"Wow," she said, scrutinizing me. "Colin?"

"It's better like this."

She didn't look convinced but nodded anyway. "You know what will cheer you up?"

"Brownies?"

"You wish. Chocolate later, okay? For now . . ." She did a brief soft-shoe routine, complete with jazz hands. "Gossip!"

I couldn't help smiling at her enthusiasm. I knew Lena watched everything that happened around school. But she didn't often share her knowledge. "Juicy, of course."

"Like a peach."

She pointed down the hallway leading to the guidance office. "So, it turns out that Miss Turner used her school e-mail to send naughty pictures to the St. Sebastian's basketball coach."

"Seriously?" Miss Turner was the guidance counselor for the first quarter of the alphabet—if your last name began with the letters A-G, she was your advisor for your entire St. Brigid's career. She'd spent a lot of time this fall trying to convince me to open up and share my feelings. She wore sweater sets and a blond bob that made her look too young to be advising anyone over the age of nine. I wouldn't have thought she was the Girls Gone Wild type, but I wasn't sure I knew anyone these days.

"Seriously. Sister Donna got a copy, too." We headed toward first period.

"I assume Miss Turner will be leaving us to seek other opportunities?" I asked.

"Already done. The new counselor starts today."

"That seems fast."

"This is Sister we're talking about."

"Good point."

I had hoped Miss Turner's scandal would be the only story of the day, but by third period, it was obvious that wasn't going to happen. While Lena and I worked on our chem lab, the rest of the tables were dividing their time between concentrating on their experiments—hydrochloric acid was nothing to play with, we'd been reminded a million times already—and observing me, like I was another science project. Doctor Sanderson strolled around the room, checking calculations and monitoring safety procedures.

It was reflex to take refuge in the experiment in front of me. This was exactly why I liked science. Things were predictable. There were rules to be followed, patterns to be observed. Even when the results were unexpected, you could eventually puzzle it out.

As I was measuring acid into a Pyrex beaker, Jill McAllister sauntered toward the pencil sharpener, a few feet away. Lena nudged me, and I looked up to see Jill, twirling her pencil, standing next to our lab table.

"We missed you in class yesterday," Jill said. "Did you have . . . family stuff?" Her smile was all teeth and no sincerity.

I checked the level of solution in my beaker, ignoring her. Jill's dad, as she liked to remind people at every opportunity, played racquetball with the State's Attorney. Jill believed this made her an expert on my family's legal woes. I believed it made her an attention-hungry shrew.

"Or was it Constance Grey?" she wondered out loud, her voice carrying to the other tables. "Somebody said she OD'd in the girls' bathroom."

I jerked my head up. "She's here today, you moron. If she'd OD'd, she'd be in the hospital right now. It was food poisoning." I'd tried to find Constance between classes, but she always managed to slip away before I could get to her. Besides, the looks she'd been sending me hadn't exactly been conversational.

"Food poisoning," said Jill, flipping her shoulder-length blond hair over her shoulders. "Funny how nobody else got sick, isn't it?"

"Don't you have something to do? Somewhere else?" I asked, adding the neutralizing agent to the acid-filled beaker.

Jill's eyes narrowed, moving back and forth between me and Lena. "You don't have to be a bitch about it. St. Brigid's is a family, remember? Speaking of families . . ."

I tensed, waiting for the attack, but instead she homed in on Lena. "How's yours, Lena? I never see them around at games and stuff. Why is that?"

"They're pretty busy," she said, bending over her notebook. The pen in her hand shook slightly.

"That's too bad," Jill said, her voice poisonous. "I'm sure lots of people would like to meet them. Maybe when Mo's dad comes back, you could all hang out together. You must be really excited to have him home, Mo."

"Thrilled." But I was barely listening—my attention was riveted on the way Lena had paled at Jill's words. I'd never seen Lena back down before.

"Well, can you let me know when the big day arrives? I want to make sure I don't leave my purse lying around," Jill said. Around us, the other tables snickered.

Instinct and temper took over. I met her eyes and, with a flick of my fingers, knocked the beaker over the edge of the table, the solution inside splashing across the tile floor. A few drops landed on her shoes.

Jill leaped backward, shrieking, "You did that on purpose!"

Doctor Sanderson came hurrying over, shooing us away from the spill. "Mo? Is that true?"

"No! I would never . . ." For once, my reputation as a nice girl proved useful. "It was an accident."

Next to me, Lena agreed. "We were almost done with the experiment. Why would she ruin it? Now we have to start all over again."

The teacher scrutinized all of us. "You'd adjusted the pH already?"

I nodded. The solution I'd dumped was no more acidic than orange juice, but it smelled a lot worse.

"Well, I'm going to get the hazmat kit anyway. Jill, go finish your lab. Mo and Lena, there's not enough time in the period to start over. Clean up. You'll have to come in during lunch to rerun the experiment."

As she left, Jill swept her hair back, her expression vicious. "You really are psychotic, aren't you?"

"Everyone knows I'm a klutz." I shrugged, putting on my most innocent smile. "What can I say? Accidents happen a lot around my family."

She went white, then flushed, and stalked back to her seat. An angry buzz rose from her table. Lena stared at me.

"Since when are you the badass Mafia princess?"

I began rinsing out test tubes and eyedroppers. "Since never. I just snapped. It was the only thing I could think that might shut her up."

We both glanced back at Jill's table, where she stood with her cronies clustered around her, outraged and squawking. She didn't say anything, but when she noticed us, her expression turned vengeful and calculating.

"Somehow I don't think she's the type to shut up," Lena said.

CHAPTER 16

Lena and I went back to the chem lab during lunch.

"I'm sorry," I said. "I didn't mean to make more work for you."

She brushed a stray piece of fuzz from her sweater. "Jill McAllister's a bitch. She's got it in for you, but I'm not her favorite person, either."

"Does she know your family?"

"No." Lena's tone made it clear she wasn't going to elaborate. "But do me a favor, okay? Next time she comes after you? Don't miss."

"I'll do my best."

Doctor Sanderson glanced up from a stack of papers and waved us toward our table. Before we could even put on our safety glasses, the intercom crackled, and the tinny voice of the school secretary was requesting my presence in the office.

Dr. Sanderson sighed heavily. "Go. You two will need to finish this tomorrow at lunch, unless you'd like to work independently this time, Miss Santos?"

For a second, Lena hesitated, running a hand over her thick ponytail. I tried not to feel hurt—it was my fault we had to redo the experiment, and it wasn't like she owed me any favors. I wasn't looking to make a new BFF, not when I was leaving soon. Besides, my life was complicated. And dangerous. Lena would be one more person I had to hide things from, and what kind of friendship was that? But it *did* hurt. Just a little.

"It's fine," I said. "You stay."

"Nah. Lunch tomorrow is fine with me."

To someone like Jill, it would have been a small thing. To me, it was a bright moment in a dismal day.

I was used to being called down to the office. I ran errands for teachers all the time, or went out on assignments for the school paper, but the echoing stairwell felt oppressive this time, and my feet dragged. As people passed me, their faces would light with recognition and then quickly turn away, like they were afraid to be caught staring. No doubt Jill had been spreading the word about Chem, giving the story her own spin.

I halted outside the office to straighten my sweater and smooth back my hair. I'd been wearing it down more often, leaving it a little curlier than usual, but at times like this it seemed sloppy instead of carefree. Taking a breath, I hauled open the door and stepped in.

The office smelled like tropical air freshener, the kind you plugged into an outlet, and the secretary peered at me from behind the main counter. "Go ahead. They're waiting for you in Father's office."

The hallway was lined with pictures of each senior class, more than seventy years' worth. Despite the dated outfits—wrist-length gloves, flowing hippie cotton shifts, shoulder pads like football players—each group looked happy and fresh, eager for whatever the world would bring them, confident they could handle it. I couldn't imagine feeling like that when I left St. Brigid's. The only expression the camera would capture on my graduation day was utter relief.

If I didn't get kicked out first, that is.

I knocked on the open door. "Come in," said Father Armando. He rose up behind the massive walnut desk to greet me. Sister Donna stood next to one of the burgundy armchairs, and she motioned me toward its twin.

"I expect you know why we've called you down here, Mo," Father continued after we were all settled.

Not to award me student of the month, I was pretty sure. Those days were gone. Had Jill filed a formal complaint about today's lab? I didn't think so. She'd be looking to make her revenge a little more personal.

"We're very concerned." Sister Donna leaned forward, radiating tough love. "You've had a terribly difficult time, and everyone here has tried to be accommodating."

"I know." I twisted my fingers together and kept my eyes down. I'd had enough experience at home with lectures to know the tricks to make them go quickly. "You've been great."

Father scanned the folder lying in front of him. "You seem to be struggling. Your teachers feel your performance has slipped. You're isolating yourself from the other girls. And I still don't understand what occurred during your college interview. That sort of impulsivity doesn't suit you. Who knows what the consequences will be?"

I thought I'd been covering well enough, but they'd seen through it. My cheeks felt hot, my hands cold, both of them burning with shame.

"Our other concern is your attendance," he continued. "You've cut class on multiple occasions. Including yesterday."

"Constance was sick," I said. "I took her home."

Sister set her teacup down. "Leaving campus without permission is a serious offense. You should have alerted the nurse."

The school nurse doled out Band-Aids, ice packs, and saltines. Not exactly what was needed.

"I guess I panicked. All she wanted was to go home."

"Constance's wishes are not the issue here. This isn't your first unexcused absence. We're trying to understand what's happening with you so we can help, but you're making it difficult." She shook her head ponderously.

"Nothing's happening with me."

Father's forehead creased, his voice full of gentle reproach. "That's not quite true. Your mother is very excited about your father's return. Is it safe to say you're not similarly enthused?"

"This doesn't have anything to do with my dad. My mom didn't even tell me until last night."

"Was that before or after you left church without notifying your family?" Sister Donna asked. "I know what you do on your time is not our concern, but it's a pattern, you see? And we find it troubling."

"I'm sorry I took Constance home without permission. It won't happen again."

Usually, an apology and a promise to do better will get you off the hook, especially if you're rarely in trouble to begin with. But judging by the solemn looks Sister Donna and Father Armando were giving each other, it wasn't going to be enough this time.

"You've had two unauthorized absences already this semester. According to school policy, disciplinary action should be taken."

Tiny beads of sweat sprang up along my hairline. They were going to suspend me? There was no way NYU would take me if I'd been suspended. Panic began to claw at my throat. "But . . ."

Father Armando held both hands up, fending off my protest. "As I said, we're aware you've had a difficult time lately, and we're prepared to offer you some flexibility. Rather than suspension, we're putting you on probation for the remainder of the semester. No more unexcused absences. Your classroom participation needs to increase. Your extracurricular participation, too."

"My extracurricular . . ." I played soccer, and I was co-editor of the paper and a member of National Honor Society. I'd worked on the stage crew for the spring musical three years in a row. They wanted me to join more activities?

Sister Donna chimed in, like she was reading my mind. "Ms. Corelli assures us your work on the newspaper, if not enthusiastic, has been adequate. And of course, soccer won't start until the spring. But your membership in NHS is a privilege, not a right. It can be revoked."

"My grades are fine."

"Honor Society is about more than a GPA and Advanced Placement classes. It's about character, and service, and contributing to the school and community. You were so active last year, helping out with food drives and service projects, and this year . . . nothing. According to Doctor Sanderson, you've skipped half the meetings."

"I . . . I've had a lot going on." Like saving the world. Which should absolutely count as a service project, in my opinion.

"Which is why we're giving you the chance to fix things. Doctor Sanderson pointed out that NHS is sponsoring the Sadie Hawkins formal. The proceeds, I believe, are going to Children's Memorial Hospital."

My stomach did a slow, unpleasant flop.

"Apparently, they're still in need of help. Decorating, taking tickets, cleanup, that sort of thing. You haven't volunteered yet."

"I wasn't planning to go," I said. It would have been one thing if I could have convinced Colin, but I'd known it was a lost cause before I'd asked. He hadn't proved me wrong, either.

"You don't need to attend. In fact, since you're on probation, you aren't allowed to. But you can donate your time to serve the greater good. It might help you to focus on something other than your grief."

I'd done a hell of a lot to help the greater good, actually, even if Flats like Sister Donna didn't realize it. It wasn't fair— I'd risked my life to help the Arcs, and all it had gotten me was trouble in my real life. Now it was starting again.

"What do you say?" Father Armando asked heartily, rubbing his hands together in satisfaction. "A little effort on your part and we can get you back on the right track."

"I'm grounded," I said, trying to look regretful. "I don't think my mom will let me out of the house."

"We've already spoken with your mother," said Sister Donna, settling back into her seat with a satisfied air. "Last night. It must have been after you left. She thought this was worth making an exception."

Of course she did. If I was suspended and kicked out of NHS, people might talk. And we couldn't have that, could we?

"So," said Father Armando, "are we in agreement? Is the old Mo back?"

I didn't even have to think about it. Lying was a sin, and lying to a priest had to be worse, though we'd never covered that specific topic in Theology. But I'd do whatever penance they asked to salvage my chance at NYU. If it meant bringing back the timid, obedient girl I used to be, I'd fake it for as long as I had to.

"She's back," I said, forcing my lips into a smile.

I had absolutely no appetite after my trip to the office, but there was still plenty of time left for lunch. As I made my way to the cafeteria, Constance fell into step beside me, and I stopped.

"Did they kick you out?" she asked. She'd lost the blood-less pallor of yesterday, and her eyes were back to normal, china blue and filled with malice.

"I'm on probation."

She seemed disappointed.

"How are you feeling?" I moved to touch her shoulder, but then thought better of it. The way she was looking at me, she'd probably rip my arm off.

"What did you do to me? I did not have food poisoning, and I wasn't on anything, even if that's what people are saying."

"People say all sorts of things, but that doesn't make them true."

"You would know."

Verity's sister, I reminded myself. Alone and confused and she didn't know about the magic. Like everyone else at St. Brigid's, she'd heard the rumors that Verity's death was meant for me. Obviously, she believed them. "I can explain what happened yesterday. Kind of."

I'd been on the receiving end of this talk once, with Luc. But I hadn't believed him, even though I'd watched him fight off monsters and transport me from Chicago to New Orleans in the space of a heartbeat. How was I going to convince Constance—not only that magic existed but that she could use it? It wasn't like I could demonstrate.

I peeked into a nearby classroom. French verbs were neatly conjugated on the board and various posters of the Eiffel Tower and the Arc de Triomphe were plastered across the walls, but there was no one inside. I opened the door and gestured for her to follow.

Once we were inside, I locked the door and moved away from the window, to the back of the classroom. The last thing we needed was someone interrupting us. "Tell me what you remember."

She scuffed her shoe across the linoleum. "I didn't feel good. My Bio teacher sent me to the nurse, but I didn't think I'd make it. And then, everything went . . . crazy . . . all these lights and sounds. It was like standing inside a tornado, you know, the way everything was happening around me, and I thought I was going to explode right out of my skin." Her eyes grew unfocused as she tried to remember. "I passed out. You were there, and that Lena girl . . . and a guy. The janitor, maybe?"

I nearly laughed, imagining the look on Luc's face if he heard someone mistake him for a janitor. She frowned at me.

"He's a friend," I said.

She looked skeptical but went on. "I dreamed we went somewhere, and he made the tornado stop, and it didn't hurt anymore. When I woke up, I was at home."

"It wasn't a dream. None of it."

She paused, her voice dripping with contempt. "Right."

I took a breath, feeling time slow, the way it did at the top of a roller coaster, that infinite moment before you hurtled toward the ground. There was no coming back from what I was about to say, for either of us. "Magic."

Her face went blank for a moment, then contorted into a sneer. "You really are crazy. Everyone said you lost it when Verity . . . they were right."

"I'm not crazy," I said. "What happened yesterday, that was magic. Your magic."

She took another step away from me, but I followed her, the words tumbling out. "Verity had it, too. They haven't caught her killers because the things that killed her weren't human, they were monsters. Actual monsters."

"You're insane." But she hesitated for a second before she said it, a chink in the wall of her disbelief. "You're making up delusions, or something, because you feel guilty!"

I closed my fingers over the scar crossing my palm. "I wish I was. But the magic is real. I've seen it. I've felt it."

She scoffed. "Oh, you're magical, too? Are we fairies? Do you have a wand?"

"I don't have any powers. It runs in families."

"There's no such thing as magic, you freak! And believe me, my parents do *not* have magic."

Her mom and dad weren't magical. They were completely, beautifully ordinary. "Not your parents. Verity, though." I paused. "Evangeline was teaching her."

She shook her head, so rapidly I knew fear was overtaking denial, even as she tried to keep it at bay. "Great-Aunt Evangeline? You're really losing it. She's not a witch. She went back to her stupid antique store, that's all. She doesn't have magic, and she doesn't care about us."

The last part was true, but this didn't seem like the time to mention it. "They're called Arcs, not witches. You're an Arc, too."

"And you're not."

I tried to smile. "Figures, huh? Yesterday, in the bathroom, your powers manifested. Luc says it's not so strong, most of the time."

"Luc. The guy?"

"Yeah. He's an Arc, too. He and Verity . . . were friends." I didn't try to define what Luc and I were.

"And he's"—she made air quotes with her fingers—"magical?"

"He's an Arc," I said carefully. "He wants to help you."

"I don't need help. *There is no magic.*" She rolled her eyes, trying to look nonchalant, but her hands shook. "And if I'm so magical, why wouldn't Aunt Evangeline help me the way she did Verity? Or am I not magical *enough?*"

"Your aunt . . . wasn't an option." I swallowed hard.

"Why not?"

"She's dead." There was probably a better way to say it. Something more sensitive, a gentler way to break the news. But though Evangeline was dead, my hatred for her blotted out everything else—rational thought and politeness included. Not even my concern about Constance was enough to make me sugarcoat it.

Constance froze, her eyes filling with tears. When she spoke, her voice was a cracked whisper. "She's . . . dead? What happened?"

Okay, maybe I could sugarcoat it a little. I needed Constance to trust me. Admitting I'd killed her aunt wasn't going to help.

"Verity and Luc were trying to fix a problem with the magic. When she died, I agreed to help. But at the last minute, things went bad." *As in, I found out your traitor of an aunt arranged for your sister's murder, so I killed her.* I bit my lip.

"Bad how? What did you *do?*"

"We went to a sort of temple. The magic was falling apart. We were able to fix it, but the temple was destroyed. Evangeline was inside when it happened."

"And you left her there?" Her face was blotchy, her breath coming shorter and shorter.

I swallowed the venomous words I wanted to say. Evangeline didn't deserve to be mourned, but telling Constance the truth would be taking revenge on the wrong person. "I couldn't help her. Luc and I barely made it out alive."

"How hard did you try? As hard as you tried to save Verity?"

Before I could respond, she raised a hand, screwing up her face in concentration. Nothing happened. "If I was magical, I would have knocked you on your ass right now. I *knew* you were crazy."

"You need someone to teach you." I ached to hug her, but it was too soon. "We're going to help, I promise."

"I don't want your help. And I don't believe you!" Her shoulders shook, tears pooling in her eyes. One escaped, trickling down her cheek. "I want Verity back. And Evangeline. Can it bring them back?"

I can heal people, not raise the dead, Luc had told me, and I closed my eyes, Constance's loss making my own fresh again. My skin prickled, alarmingly familiar, and my eyes flew open. "You need to calm down. *Now.*"

"Don't tell me what to do!" Her voice rose to a shriek. The temperature in the classroom dropped suddenly, and she paled. "What's happening?"

Pain lanced through my temples. "It's the magic. Breathe, okay?"

"Make it stop!"

"I can't!" I grabbed a desk as the air began to hum. Whatever line she'd tapped into was starting to surge. "Try to pull back, like . . . I don't know, you're turning down the volume."

She nodded, her breath too fast and shallow. "It's not working!"

My skin crackled as the energy coalesced around Constance, enveloping her and reaching for me, and I squeezed my eyes shut, trying to find the place inside me capable of tapping into the magic. I envisioned myself unfurling, welcoming it in, as I'd done at the Binding Temple. I'd done this before; I could do it again. Especially when it was Constance at stake.

And yet, when I was finally able to make the connection, the sheer force of the magic pouring out of the line knocked me across the room. I heard the crack of the blackboard as I slammed into the wall and slid to the floor, the dusty slate raining down around me.

CHAPTER 17

I heard Constance's scream as the magic crested, and then, blessedly, Luc's voice.

"Take care of it," he snapped. Another voice began to chant, the sounds soothing, like wind through leaves.

"Mouse?" I felt him crouch next to me, taking my hand. "You okay?"

"Constance got mad," I managed. "Is she . . ."

"She's fine."

"Darklings?"

"We got here early enough to shut it down. But you keep makin' a habit of running raw magic through the school, they're bound to take notice." He brushed my hair back, his fingers light and nimble as they searched for injuries. The energy was ebbing, drawing back into the lines as the chanting continued. He probed at a painful spot on the back of my head. "Let me fix this."

I nodded, too miserable to speak. He closed one hand over my wrist and trailed the other down my back, tingling warmth chasing away the pain. The room faded, and all I knew was his touch and his voice, foreign and silky as he cast the spell. Before his hand could travel too low, I opened my eyes and pulled back. "I'm better. Thanks."

Across the room, a familiar face was tending to Constance, who looked bewildered.

"Niobe's here?" I clutched Luc's arm. The last time I'd

seen her, in a bar that catered to Arcs, Luc and I were narrowly escaping an attempt on my life—one Niobe had made no move to stop.

"You requested a guide for the girl, didn't you? Orla sent me." Niobe regarded us curiously. "Playing white knight, Luc? Is that really wise, considering?"

He leaned against the cinder block wall and fixed her with a warning look. "What kind of companion would I be if I let her stay hurt?"

"A sensible one," Niobe said. She wasn't much older than us, probably in her midtwenties, with cinnamon-colored skin and hair cropped close, which emphasized her dramatic, elegant cheekbones. Her dark, almond-shaped eyes were constantly shifting between disdain and amusement. She made me feel drab and childish, especially as I sat on the floor in my uniform.

I struggled to my feet as Luc surveyed the classroom. Chairs were knocked over, the blackboard destroyed, papers blown off the bulletin boards. A toothpick model of the Eiffel Tower was smashed beyond repair. He rubbed a hand over his head. "What happened?"

"Remember how you said you wouldn't want to be around if Constance tapped into a line without having any control? You were right."

He smirked, but it was a faint imitation of his usual cocky smile. "I'm always right. You must've pissed her off somethin' good."

Judging from the look on her face, that hadn't changed in the last few minutes. I moved closer to Luc, only a few inches between us, and kept my voice low. "She wanted to know about Evangeline."

He swore under his breath.

"I didn't tell her."

Humor softened his features. "You? Lying to someone? This before or after you got walloped?"

"Don't be a jerk."

"I ain't the one with anger management issues," he said, giving Constance an unfriendly look. I made my way across the room, skirting upside-down desks, stepping over broken light fixtures and piles of books.

I stopped a few feet away from Constance. The magic in the room had dissipated, but I wasn't ready for another round if she lost control again. "Are you okay?"

"What do you think?" she snapped.

"She's not injured," Niobe said. "I wish I could say much has changed since the last time I saw you, but . . . it wouldn't appear so."

"Everything's changed."

She tilted her head toward Luc. "Not in essentials."

"You guys *know* each other?" Constance asked, accusation plain in her voice. "I thought you said you weren't magical, Mo."

"Mo has carved out a unique place among us," said Niobe. "Not an Arc, but bound and beholden to us, as we are to her."

"Whatever." Constance rolled her eyes. Behind me, Luc returned the books to the shelves with a few words. They slammed into place harder than necessary, and the noise made Constance jump, then glare.

"Orla sent you?" I asked Niobe, wanting to forestall another confrontation.

"Yes. I've already explained to your friend—"

"She's not my friend," Constance put in.

Niobe gave her a withering glance. "I've already explained to the girl my role in the Covenant."

"She says you made some deal with her boss, so she has to help me. You didn't even *ask* me."

"I'm trying to help," I said.

Behind us, Luc was reassembling the chalkboard with minute flicks of his fingers, the individual pieces flying up one at a time and fusing together, like a jigsaw puzzle. At Constance's words, he wheeled around, his voice like a lash. "She

struck a deal to save your life, little girl. You are small potatoes to most people in my world, and not one of them is
losin' sleep over how you handle this. She is the closest thing
to a friend you've got. Polite thing to do now is tell her thank
you."

She watched the chalkboard fragments spin slowly in
midair, and clamped her lips shut.

I pressed my fingers against my eyelids, trying to relieve
the pressure. I wasn't interested in playing referee, but protecting Verity's sister wasn't optional—and neither was my
bond with Luc.

Luc tugged on my arm. "Best we go. I concealed everything when we got here, but I don't know how well it
worked. Niobe, can you take Little Miss Temper Tantrum?
Figure you two have a lot to talk about."

You could see Constance calculating the distance to the
door and the odds of escaping. I knew the feeling; I'd done
the same thing when Luc had told me about the magic. I also
knew how useless it was to try to outrun this. She caught me
staring and crossed her arms defiantly. "Take me where? I'm
not leaving with you people!"

Niobe smiled at her, teeth brilliantly white against her
dark skin. "My office, of course." For the first time, I noticed
the St. Brigid's ID, clearly labeled STAFF, on a lanyard around
her elegant neck.

"Wait." I stared at her, remembering Lena's announcement
this morning. "You sent those pictures of Miss Turner?"

"Not personally."

"That was a crappy thing to do. She won't be able to find
another job." I shouldn't have been surprised. They turned
people's lives inside out all the time and never gave it a second thought.

"Let it go," Luc said, taking my elbow. "It's what you
asked for."

Niobe shrugged. "Would you prefer we leave Constance
unsupervised? Think of it as collateral damage."

"We aren't at war," I retorted.

"Not everyone believes the Seraphim are regrouping. But if the rumors are true, rest assured they will do what they can to overthrow the Quartoren. What else would you call that?"

I didn't answer.

"Hey!" Constance stamped her foot, eyes flashing. "I don't care about Miss Turner or your stupid Quarters, or anything except what just happened. The room is still trashed. How are you going to explain it to Sister Donna and Father Armando?"

Niobe turned, appalled. "It's hard to believe you could come from the people you do, yet know so little."

Luc stepped forward and, with a few words, righted the desk. Niobe's spell rebuilt the toothpick Eiffel Tower and reattached the light fixtures, filling my head with the sound of rushing magic. They worked perfectly together, wordlessly coordinating their movements, and something inside me twinged unpleasantly at the sight. I studied Constance instead. Had I looked like her the first time I'd witnessed magic? Had my eyes gone so wide and startled? Maybe, but the hunger on her face seemed more avid than anything I'd experienced. As the scattered papers reassembled into neat piles, the sheets swooping through the air like gulls, Constance reached for one, finally convinced. Luc and Niobe's actions were better proof than my words.

"Come," Niobe said to her when they'd finished, and Luc made a shooing motion. Constance trailed after her, pausing only to shoot us an expression of utter dislike.

I sank into a desk. I hadn't wanted to look weak in front of the others, but my headache had returned in a rush, black spots obscuring my vision. I blinked them away.

"You all right?" Luc asked again, coming to stand next to me.

"Fine. Just a little wiped out." I wasn't so sure, though. Each time I interacted with the magic, the pain was worse. It hadn't been like this before the Torrent; I'd hated going Between, but it hadn't been harmful. I was starting to worry that whatever had gone wrong with the magic had hurt me, too.

"I could heal you again."

"Niobe said it was risky. What did she mean?"

He sat on the edge of the desk, one long leg swinging, and said, "Niobe's a prickly sort. She's happiest when she can set other people on edge."

"Luc, she was definitely implying something."

He shifted. "It's just a little dig. Suggestin' I'm too caught up in worrying about you. Frowns on that, you bein' Flat."

I squinted at him. "That's it? You're sure?"

He reached out and drew an X over the school crest embroidered on my sweater. "Cross my heart, Mouse."

The moment seemed to catch and stutter in time with my breath. "This is bad," I said finally.

He raised one eyebrow, his finger hooked in my V-neck. "Respectfully going to disagree."

"I'm serious. What if someone had seen us? What if the Darklings had come? The magic is dangerous, Luc. I can't let it cross over to my real life."

"We're just as real as anything here. Anyone, for that matter. And if you don't like us coming into your world, take your place in ours." I started to disagree, but he cut me off. "Quartoren have kept their end of the bargain. They'll expect you to do the same."

I looked around the room he'd repaired so easily, knowing he was right. The longer I fought against it, the worse the damage would be.

"I'm ready," I said. But I knew there was no preparing for what was coming at me.

CHAPTER 18

A nasty, ice-cold rain pelted me as I left school, and I ran for the truck. The sky was gunmetal gray, a perfect match for Colin's eyes.

"Good day?" he asked, helping me inside.

"Not really." I held my hands toward the ancient heating vents, breathing in the scent of toasting dust.

He looked me over. "Magic, huh?"

"How'd you know?"

"You walk differently after a run-in with the magic. Like you're carrying a glass of water, and if you trip, it'll spill."

This was not comforting. "I trip a lot."

He scowled, pulling into traffic. "I know. Are you going to tell me?"

"It's Constance. We had to tell her about the magic. It got a little crazy."

"And by 'we,' you mean you and Luc?"

"And the woman assigned to help Constance. Niobe. She's got a job at the school now."

"How did Constance take it?"

I lifted a shoulder. "About as well as you'd expect. She thinks Evangeline died stopping the Torrent."

"And you didn't correct her thinking." He shook his head. "This won't end well. She'll find out eventually."

"Maybe not."

"The truth's a hard thing to keep buried."

"You manage," I said, narrowing my eyes. "Maybe you could give me some tips."

"Jesus, Mo. Don't start."

"What? You can't have it both ways. Either it's important to tell people the truth, in which case I'd like to know what Billy has on you, or it's okay to lie, in which case I didn't do anything wrong."

He didn't answer, not that I expected him to. "What's the rest? There was school stuff, too?"

"They're threatening to kick me out of NHS. If that shows up on my application . . ." My voice hitched. "I won't get in to NYU."

He rubbed a thumb over my knuckles. "We can fix it. Did they tell you what they want you to do?"

"You won't believe me."

"You've already told me the unbelievable stuff," he said, a smile tugging at the corner of his mouth.

"I have to work the dance." At his blank expression, I added, "The Sadie Hawkins dance."

"That's not so bad. You wanted to go, right?"

"I wanted to go with you. And you're not interested."

He released my hand. "It's complicated."

"No, it's very simple. Keeping your secret is more important than being with me. It's hurtful, Colin, not complicated." I balled my fists in my lap. He kept his eyes on the road.

"You don't understand."

"Because you won't explain."

"And I'm not going to," he said, utterly final and unyielding as stone. "I shouldn't have kissed you yesterday. I shouldn't be kissing you at all."

For a second, I didn't even feel the cut of his words, like when you're slicing a loaf of bread and the knife slips. You know something's wrong, you know you should be in pain, but shock keeps you numb, even as you start to bleed. And then the shock wears off.

It had been so long since Colin had spoken to me in that insufferable, world-weary tone, but hearing it took me back to the first day we'd met, when he'd called me "kid" instead of Mo, when he'd written me off as a spoiled brat and I'd assumed he was a brainless, heartless thug. If he really thought kissing me had been such a mistake, we'd changed less than I thought.

"Then don't."

"Mo—" He parked the truck in the alley behind The Slice, killing the engine, and the warmth of the cab evaporated.

"You said you knew me." I was furious with him for not trusting me, furious with myself for pushing it this far. "You should know how much this hurts."

"I do." He reached for me, and I shoved his hand away.

"Then stop. Go back to being my bodyguard. Better yet, get me a new one. I'm done with you." I hopped out, slamming the door so hard the impact jolted my shoulder. Without looking back, I stomped into the kitchen. Never before had I looked forward to the monotony of coffee refills and pumpkin pie à la mode.

He didn't follow me inside, and I told myself I was glad.

As I tied on my apron and kerchief, I studied the day's customers over the kitchen counter. My mom stopped to chat with one of the regulars, Brent, who ran an insurance company a few blocks away.

"Great pie today, Annie," he said. "Men have proposed for less than this."

She gave him a quick, absent smile as she refilled his cup. "Oh, I don't know about that."

"I do. Can't figure out how you keep it all running so smoothly. You must get tired of cooking. When's the last time someone took you to dinner?"

He was hitting on my mom. A normal, decent, noncriminal guy, hitting on my mom. I didn't know if I should laugh or be offended or cheer. What would our lives have been like if she'd left my dad and found someone else all those years ago? She'd never considered it, I was certain. Too loyal to my father, too mindful of her wedding vows. She probably wouldn't even recognize that he was asking her out.

"I spend all day at a restaurant. I'm not really one for going out." She twisted her wedding band and breezed away to take care of another customer. Brent's face fell, but I was the only one who saw it.

I was surprised at how deftly she'd turned him away, like she'd had practice. How often had it happened over the years? How many times had I failed to see it? It was like looking through the viewfinder of my camera and discovering the focus was all wrong. I didn't like the feeling.

"Sweetheart!" My mom smiled as I pushed through the swinging doors into the restaurant. I grabbed an order pad from the counter. Brent was gone. "How was your day?"

"Fine," I said, trying to stuff an escaped lock of hair back into my kerchief unsuccessfully. We'd never had the kind of relationship where I talked to her about guys. Considering the guy in question, I planned on sticking to that policy.

She peered at me. "You're unhappy."

"Just tired," I said, remembering Billy's words from the night before about how I'd ruined her day.

"Sit for a few minutes." She gestured toward an empty stool at the counter and I obeyed, watching as she fixed me a cup of tea. While I warmed my hands on the white stoneware, she plated a brownie from one of the dessert stands and slid it across the counter. "You can't be waiting on customers with that face."

I blinked at her. Either she was feeling badly about last night or I looked even more miserable than I felt.

"I'm on my way out to do the deliveries, unless . . . you need me here?" There was a hopeful note to her voice, and I smiled weakly.

"I'm okay," I said. "The tea helped."

"Maybe you need a break." She leaned over and adjusted my kerchief. "I've been thinking we should take a trip."

"A trip," I echoed, some inner alarm triggering at her determinedly bright tone.

"You and me. The Fitzgerald Girls, getting away for a bit. Not long, just a weekend, so you don't miss school."

We didn't have money for a spur-of-the-moment vacation. And where would we go? I was a little old for Disney, and my mom wasn't exactly the spa type. Either she was trying to get me out of town on Billy's orders, or . . .

"We could go see Daddy."

"No." My response was instant, a reflex I'd honed over the last four years.

Her brow furrowed. "But he wants to see us, so we can celebrate the good news."

I managed to stop myself from pointing out that not everyone considered his early release good news. "I'm not going to Terre Haute, Mom." Before she could ask why, I answered with the only reason she would accept. "You know they always pile on a ton of work before Thanksgiving."

She smoothed her hair back into its bun, disappointment tightening her mouth. "But it doesn't seem fair to make him wait until the break."

"Sorry." I could not have been less sincere if I was trying to sell her a used car, but she cheered up when I said it.

"We could go this weekend," she suggested "A quick trip."

"I can't. I have to work the dance, remember?" How many other excuses could I drum up?

She paused, then rallied. "Surely Sister Donna would understand if we found some other way for you to volunteer. This is family!"

Maybe so, but I wasn't about to take the chance. "Do you have any idea how ungrateful I'll seem? They gave me a second chance—I can't blow it off."

"But I promised your father."

"Go and see him, then."

She frowned. "I don't like leaving you alone."

"I'm never alone. I have a bodyguard. And a very expensive alarm system." Not that I had any intention of speaking to my bodyguard for the next, oh, fifty years or so. "You can go if you want. But I'm staying here."

"We'll see," she said. "Sister Donna probably wouldn't appreciate you backing out of your commitment. It's important that she knows you're the same reliable, level-headed girl you've always been. We could always go another weekend. Maybe after Christmas. That might work out better, to go between semesters."

I watched as she convinced herself she hadn't really lost—she'd found a way to want the alternative. She'd gotten really good at it over the years.

Finally, she nodded. "I'll think about it."

"Great." As I took my place behind the counter, I pasted a smile on my face. Bigger smiles meant bigger tips, and bigger tips meant more money for the New York fund. Plus, I knew Colin was watching me through the window, and I wanted him to see exactly how happy I was without him.

CHAPTER 19

An hour later, my smile slipped as Jenny Kowalski came in, huddled into her North Face jacket. I was behind the counter, rolling place settings into napkins. I was definitely not looking out the window toward Colin.

"Fancy meeting you here," she said, turning over her coffee cup. I filled it with decaf, not bothering to ask which kind she wanted. If there was anyone in the world who needed to lay off the caffeine, it was Jenny.

"What do you want?"

"I heard the good news. Congratulations."

"The good news?"

"About your dad." She dumped three packets of sugar into her coffee. "It must be nice, to have a dad coming home."

I exhaled slowly and rolled my shoulders. "Can you do me a favor? Either tell me what you're doing here or don't be here at all."

She toyed with the menu. "I told you to look into your family. Did you?"

"I've been a little busy," I said through clenched teeth. "And I have other tables. Besides, whatever you're hoping I'll dig up won't have anything to do with me."

Jenny laughed. "Aren't you supposed to be smart? It's got everything to do with you. Your uncle's done all sorts of things to keep control of his territory. Asking you to fake that ID was nothing."

Booth four signaled for their check. "Where are you getting all this?" It wasn't the sort of thing she would have figured out by herself, even if she'd been listening to her dad. Someone had to be feeding her information. Someone in Billy's organization? Ekomov's people? One of her dad's poker buddies? Jenny was trouble, but whoever was helping her was *dangerous*. The person behind the scenes always wielded the most power.

"Does it matter who told me? I'm trying to do you a favor."

"Really? How's that?"

"I thought you'd appreciate a warning. Yuri Ekomov's been asking about you. So have your uncle's bosses. You should be careful."

"I have a bodyguard."

"Colin Donnelly? Do you know his story?"

Somehow, I managed to keep my voice even. "He doesn't have one."

"Or you don't know it."

"And you do?"

"More than you." She smirked and pulled two file folders from her backpack. "Donnelly," she said, pointing to the thinner of the two. "Your family." The second folder was overflowing, held closed with rubber bands that looked as if they might snap at any moment.

I waved at booth four. People were starting to notice our conversation. "What do you want?"

"Proof that your uncle killed my dad."

"I can't prove something that's not true."

She tapped the folders with her nail, bitten to the quick. "There's a lot of information in here. I'd be willing to trade."

"I don't know anything." The folders looked so harmless, even a little dull. But inside were answers to questions that burned in my veins like magic.

"Only because you won't look. We know what he's involved in. All we need is the proof, but he's really careful."

"Maybe he's innocent."

She scoffed. "You don't believe that."

No, but refusing to help my uncle was one thing; sending him to prison was another. Besides, I didn't care about taking down Billy. All I wanted was to get Colin free. Jenny—and the people feeding her information—dangled those folders in front of me like bait. But the whole point of bait was to conceal a trap, and until I knew how this trap worked, I couldn't risk it.

"Not interested," I said. It might have been my biggest lie yet.

CHAPTER 20

There's nothing like a dead restaurant to make you think. The next afternoon, The Slice was practically deserted. I passed the time by refilling the ketchup and mustard bottles, restocking the napkins, and organizing the sugar packets by color—white, yellow, pink. Anything to keep my mind busy. But eventually I'd taken care of any possible chores, and there was nothing left to do but think about yesterday's fight with Colin, the strained silence between us today and Jenny's offer. She'd scrawled her phone number on a napkin, in case I changed my mind. I'd pulled the crumpled paper out a dozen times today, but couldn't bring myself to pick up the phone.

"Slow, huh?" Tim, our cook, remarked as I carried a barely filled tub of dirty dishes in back.

"Yeah. The weather's keeping people in." I loaded the industrial dishwasher slowly, my eyes on the door to the storeroom connecting The Slice and Morgan's, my uncle's bar. Maybe I didn't need to call Jenny after all. Maybe my answers were on the other side of that door.

It was a completely stupid and impulsive plan, and if I wasn't so desperate, I would never have considered doing it. But an afternoon alone with your increasingly depressing thoughts can warp even the most reasonable mind.

So I did it.

You could tell the second you passed from The Slice into Morgan's. The warm, sugary aroma of perfectly browned pie crust was replaced by the yeasty tang of beer and sharp scent of whiskey poured out liberally. No one ever complained that Morgan's watered down their drinks, mostly because they didn't serve many drinks that required mixing.

I paused. Below the regular noises of the bar—ESPN, clinking glasses, good-natured arguments over Fords versus Chevys—was the sound of Billy's voice, rising and falling. I could picture his hands waving to punctuate whatever point he was making or story he was selling. Every so often, a second voice would say a few words, slow and rumbling, and Billy would jump in again. I cracked the door a little, but the hinges squeaked and the voices fell silent.

So much for stealth. I pushed the door wide open and strode in, trying to look nonchalant.

"Now, this is a surprise," my uncle said. He smiled heartily, but his eyes were slits. "My niece," he said to the man sitting opposite him.

He'd switched places. Billy always sat in the last booth, facing the front door. Everyone who wanted an audience had to be escorted to him. They sat with their backs to the bar while my uncle surveyed his domain.

But now, Billy was in the visitor's seat.

"Wait up front," he instructed. "Have Charlie get you a Coke and I'll be done shortly."

"Mo, right?" The other man stood and shook my hand. He peered at the room I'd just emerged from. "Where's Donnelly?"

Billy shrugged. "He doesn't always come in. No need to, here."

"Marco Forelli," the man said, returning his attention to me, still gripping my hand. "You're even prettier than your pictures."

"Thanks," I said uncertainly, and watched as Billy's face clouded over and cleared in the space of a breath.

Marco Forelli wasn't talking about my senior portrait. He meant the pictures someone had taken earlier in the fall and sent me as a warning—*we can get to you*. My skin felt like a hundred beetles were scuttling across it, and I pulled my hand away.

He glanced at my uncle. "She looks like Jack. The eyes, I think. And the mouth, too. Billy says you and your old man got a lot in common."

I folded my arms across my chest. "I wouldn't know."

"No, it's been a while, huh? You must be excited, having him home so soon."

"Thrilled."

"Well, we're all looking forward to seeing him again." He reached out and ruffled my hair. I barely kept myself from hissing. "I'd better get going. It was nice to meet you, Mo. I'm sure we'll run into each other soon."

I didn't trust myself to speak.

Billy walked Forelli out. When he returned, his darting, nervous energy was replaced with something infinitely more destructive—anger, focused squarely on me.

"Do you know who that was?"

"Marco Forelli?" The name didn't mean anything to me, but I was pretty sure it should.

"Yes, Marco Forelli! He's not to be trifled with."

"I didn't trifle," I protested. But Billy's fury was tinged with genuine fear, and it was contagious.

"The man deserves your respect, and you treated him like a substitute teacher, with your attitude and your snide comments."

I shoved back at the fear. "That man took pictures of me. To scare me. You think I should respect him? Don't you mean suck up?"

Billy's mouth worked in noiseless outrage for a moment. He pointed to the booth. "Sit. Down."

I did, not because he told me to but because I still had questions to ask.

He sat, leaning forward, shaking his finger like he was scolding me. "All we asked was that you do your part. Make our neighborhood safer. Preserve a way of life that has benefited you and everyone you know for years. We asked you to do one small thing, and you failed."

"You asked me to lie to the police. I could have gone to jail."

"Nonsense. That would never have happened."

"Is that what you told my dad?"

"Your father knew exactly what he was doing." He settled back in the booth, crossing his arms across his chest. "And considering the lack of concern you've shown for the man over the years, you've little grounds to play the outraged daughter now."

"I'm not."

"That's something, anyway. Marco Forelli's taken an interest in you. It's a very dangerous position to be in."

"He doesn't scare me," I said, trying not to remember the picture of Luc and me kissing on my front porch. The look on Colin's face when he'd seen it.

"He should. Now, what brought you over here today? I doubt it was to say hello."

"I want to know what you have on Colin." I gripped the edge of my seat. "It must be something big. Some information about his past, and you're lording it over him so he'll do what you want."

Billy shrugged. "Donnelly's free to leave my employment any time he likes. He chooses to stay."

"Why?"

"He's loyal." He gave me a sour look. "A scarce commodity these days. The better question is, what business is it of yours?"

I stayed absolutely still as he scrutinized me. His eyes lit with amusement. "You've got a crush on Donnelly?"

Heat flooded my cheeks, and he chuckled. "You're a darling girl, but he's unsuitable. You'll only embarrass yourself."

I'd done that anyway. "I don't have a crush on him. I'm just . . . curious."

"Ah. You know what they say about curiosity and cats, don't you?"

The ground beneath me suddenly felt boggy and treacherous. "He's a nice guy."

"That he is. But the place he comes from is blacker than pitch. Leave him alone."

"Why? What could be so terrible?"

Billy's face went hard. "More than you can imagine. More than anyone should. Find someone else to dream of, Maura Kathleen. Donnelly will never look at you that way."

"What way?"

He scored an oval in the air, like he was outlining my face. "That way. And don't look so disappointed, either. The man would be dead before the next sunrise if he touched you, and he knows it. He'll risk his life to protect you, but it's not only his life he's concerned with." He stood. "You're supposed to be at home, if I'm not mistaken. You've caused enough trouble for your mother lately. The least you could do is show up to dinner on time."

I slid out of the booth, the sting of his dismissal barely noticeable compared to everything else he'd said. Billy had never threatened anyone in front of me before, but he'd been so nonchalant when he'd mentioned killing Colin, like it was no bigger an item on his to-do list than picking up the dry cleaning. My stomach twisted at the idea of putting Colin in danger, all because I wanted to go to a dance. God, how shallow could I be?

And then the second part of his declaration hit me: *It's not only his life he's concerned with.* Whose life, then? Mine? My uncle was manipulative and power hungry, but he'd never hurt me. It was one of the only things I was certain of when it came to Billy—my mom's safety and mine were absolute. Who was Colin protecting?

I touched the mark on my palm. Only a couple of months

old, and it was changing from a mottled red line to a pale pink, lighter and thinner every day. It would never disappear completely, the doctors had said, but it would fade. The scars across Colin's back were pure white, long healed but sorrowful and secretive.

Scars didn't go away, I reminded myself. Why had I expected them to?

CHAPTER 21

If I'd thought I could get away with walking home, I would have tried it. Instead, I did the next best thing—I pulled my iPod from my bag, fitted the earbuds in, and cranked up the volume. The music made a sort of sulky cocoon as I threw open the door to the truck and boosted myself in.

The press of Colin's hand on my arm, even through my wool peacoat, seemed impossibly heavy. Instead of looking at him, I slumped into the corner of the seat and stared out the window. Outside Morgan's, the neon Harp and Guinness signs were reflected in quivering puddles, the words broken apart into random chunks of color by the rain. We drove home without another word.

I didn't tell him about the mysterious flowers, or Jenny's offer, or meeting Marco Forelli. He didn't tell me what Billy had on him. All the things we weren't saying stacked up like a wall between us, and I forced myself not to be the one to break through. I'd pushed as far as I could, left myself vulnerable, and Colin still didn't trust me. There was nothing left to say.

When we pulled up to the house, I took out my earbuds and groaned. Sitting on the front porch in the pale light, huddled against the chill in a black leather jacket, was Luc. Colin sucked in air, a harsh sound. "Let me guess. The world needs saving?"

"I don't think he'd hang out on my porch for that."

"Right. Go deal with whatever today's crisis is. And don't leave without telling me."

"So you don't worry?"

His eyes were unreadable. "So I can cover for you."

I didn't know what to say.

"Cujo didn't feel like chattin'?" Luc called, waving to the truck as I crossed the lawn. Even in the chilly night, his drawl sounded languorous and warm.

"Imagine that. What are you doing here?" Before I could pull out my keys, he touched the lock, the metal sending off red sparks. The dead bolt snicked open, and he grinned at me.

"I need a reason to stop by?"

I had never invited Luc into my house before. He'd come Between in my bedroom but never stayed more than a minute. This felt normal, and with Luc, normal felt strange.

"You want something," I said, dropping my bag on the stairs and hanging up my coat.

He toyed with a loose strand of my hair. "I always want somethin'. Sit with me."

I sank onto the couch and he flopped down next to me, propping his feet on my lap.

"Is something wrong?" I asked. "Is Constance okay?"

"Bratty as ever," he said, glancing around. I wondered what he thought of my house. Compared to his elegant, exotic apartment, it seemed cramped and dull. I poked a finger through the afghan and tried not to feel defensive. "Niobe's got her at the House right now. She's making friends already."

"That's good. They don't mind that she's got Flat parents?"

"Apparently not. Can't imagine what they see in her," he said.

"Cut her a break. She's had a lot to deal with."

"Same as you, but I don't catch you throwin' a tantrum every five minutes. Nice flowers, by the way. Cujo?"

"Flowers?" I asked, and he tilted his head toward the kitchen.

Sitting on the table was another vase of sunflowers.

I shoved his feet off my lap. "Those aren't from Colin."

"You got somebody else on a string now? Ain't it hard to keep track?"

Same vase. Same bright, happy blooms. But The Slice was a public place. My kitchen had a silent alarm system, installed by Colin the day after we'd met. "Can you tell if someone's done magic in here?"

He stretched out a hand, his expression going distant as he concentrated. After a moment, he came back to himself. "An Arc's magic carries a signature, like a fingerprint, or DNA. This place is clean, 'cept for me." He touched my shoulder. "What's goin' on?"

"I wish I knew."

By the time I'd reached the sidewalk, Colin was climbing out of the truck. The cold rain soaked into my thin sweater and I shivered.

"What's wrong?"

"There's something you should see. In the kitchen."

Before I could say more, he was sprinting for the house, dragging me behind him by the wrist.

"Down, boy," said Luc as we burst inside. Colin ignored him and went straight to the kitchen, while I dug in my bag for the sunflower drawing.

He grabbed the vase, tilting it from side to side until he found what he was looking for. "Here," he said, pulling out a card.

I held out the drawing. "Trade you." His head snapped up, expression turning to disbelief as he took it.

The small white envelope fluttered like a moth in my hand. Gently, Luc steered me toward the couch. "Sit down."

The paper tore under my fingers and my heart sank at the unfamiliar alphabet. "I can't read this."

Colin reached for it, but Luc was faster.

"It's Russian. First line says 'Thank you.' " He glanced up, a quizzical crease above the bridge of his nose. "Who you helpin' out in Moscow?"

"Keep reading," Colin said.

"Second part's an idiom. Means, 'The enemy of my enemy . . .' "

". . . is my friend," Colin finished. "Great."

He paced the room while Luc laid one arm across the back of the couch. "Care to fill me in?"

"The Russian Mob sent me flowers," I said. "Wait. How do you know Russian?"

"Languages come easy for me."

"Everything does," I muttered.

He raised an eyebrow. "Not everything, Mouse. Question is, why are they sending a thank-you note? Thought you were limitin' your favors to the criminals you were related to."

I slumped back on the couch. "I wasn't trying to help them. All I did was tell the truth."

Colin spoke from his position by the window, his voice brusque. "The end result was the same. It helped them get a toehold here. Left their guys on the street."

"But the guys from the lineup are dead now."

There was a beat of silence, and then he turned to face me. "Where did you hear that?"

Too late, I remembered Jenny was a secret. "Aren't they?"

"Yeah." He pressed the corner of the note into the pad of his thumb, his eyes never leaving mine.

Luc whistled. "For someone who says she likes quiet, things do seem to pick right up when you walk into the room, don't they?"

"When did you get the drawing?" Colin asked.

"Monday. I bumped into an old guy at school. He must have put the drawing in my bag then. They sent flowers to The Slice, too, but there was no note." Before he could ask, I added, "I didn't want to worry you."

"It is my *job* to worry about you."

"I'm tired of being your job," I shot back, scrambling up.

Luc stood. "Anybody else want somethin' to drink?"

Colin sat on the arm of the couch, his hand closing over my wrist. "You should have told me."

"I thought it had something to do with the Arcs," I said. Not that I'd mentioned it to Luc, either. "Who killed the guys from the lineup?"

"Who told you about that?"

"Not you, that's for sure."

"Now is not the time to prove a point. Ekomov is dangerous. If he's feeding you information, it can only end badly."

"It's not Ekomov. I promise." I pulled my hand free as Luc returned. "Colin, you have to trust me."

"This is touchin', but I ain't here to watch you two hug it out." Luc shifted, and I could feel his nervousness crackling along our bond like a lit fuse. "We have work to do. Can't be putting it off because Cujo's falling down on the job."

Colin bristled, and I glared at Luc. "Stop it."

"I have to tell Billy," Colin said, sounding less than enthusiastic. "You stay home."

Luc coughed. "Pascal wants to see you."

"Who the hell is Pascal?" Colin asked.

"Arc. Big fish. It ain't like we got all the time in the world, Mouse."

"I can't leave now. My mom is going to be home soon."

"After she's asleep, then."

I sagged at the thought of going Between again. He touched my shoulder and smiled encouragingly.

"Meeting's here in the city," he said. "No going Between if you're not up to it."

Colin shook his head. "You're not running off with this guy in the middle of the night."

"You're worried 'bout her breaking curfew?"

"You can't keep her safe."

Luc extended a hand, palm up, and a flame danced harmlessly along his skin. "Shouldn't be a problem."

Colin's jaw flexed, but he didn't say anything.

Luc extinguished the flame. "Ticktock," he said. "I can

put Pascal off for a few hours, but I need to tell him what the plan is."

"You have to take care of the Russian thing tonight?" I asked Colin.

"Billy needs to know." There was no apology in his voice—he was all bodyguard now, remote and focused, as I'd predicted. "The sooner the better."

"Fine." There was no point in arguing. Turning to Luc, I said, "Come back at eleven. I'll meet you by the garage."

"Lookin' forward to it." He touched my cheek and strode out the front door. Red lights crackled across the front lawn, and then he was gone.

"I really hate that guy," said Colin.

"The feeling's probably mutual."

While Colin called my uncle, I took my bag upstairs and started on homework, trying to lose myself in differential equations and imaginary numbers. I wondered what Constance was doing, if she was at the training house with Niobe or sitting in her room, afraid of her powers, hating me, missing Verity. My eyes fell on the strange jumble of links the Quartoren had given me. Fused together, they looked like some sort of atomic model, the links tracing the patterns of electrons orbiting a nucleus. I poked my finger through the center, half-expecting to find resistance, like a force field, but there was nothing except a hum that raised goose bumps along my arms.

Exhausted, I dropped the links on my nightstand and lay down on top of the covers with my AP Chem book. The tiny print squiggled and swam across the page, and my eyes drifted shut. I heard my mom come home, chatting with Colin, urging him to stay for dinner. Nothing in the tone of her voice or the muffled conversation sounded urgent—Colin must have gotten rid of the flowers.

Her footsteps squeaked on the stair treads, and then she appeared in the doorway, her face drawn with concern. "Hi, sweetheart. Colin said you've been studying all evening."

Trying to, anyway. "Pretty much."

"I made a brisket for dinner. Biscuits, too. Do you want to come visit while I finish up?"

"I'm not hungry."

She moved closer, laid a cool hand on my forehead. "You feel a little warm. I hope you're not coming down with something."

"Tired," I said, fighting back an enormous yawn. "Can I skip dinner? I'll be better if I nap."

"It might help for you to eat," she chided. "We never got to have our talk."

"Mom, please. I just need to rest."

Worry etched little lines at the corners of her mouth and nose. "If you say so. Colin said he'd see you tomorrow, the usual." She bent and kissed my forehead lightly. "Get some sleep."

I understood his message. "The usual" meant Billy wasn't putting more guards on me yet. I knew how to decode Colin's words. I knew his moods and gestures, I knew the meaning behind his looks—even the ones he didn't realize he was giving me—and I'd thought, naively, that was enough. He'd said it was enough for us to know each other, that his past didn't matter. But whomever he was protecting was very much a part of his present. A present he was deliberately excluding me from, despite having an all-access pass to my entire life. Until I figured out what he was hiding, we didn't stand a chance.

After reaching for my phone, I dug out the crumpled napkin with Jenny Kowalski's number and keyed in a text, trying to ignore the feeling I might be betraying Colin's trust. It was precisely because he didn't trust me that I had to do this.

CHAPTER 22

Jenny's response never came. As I waited, sleep dragged me under like a riptide, sinister and suffocating. In my dreams, I breathed in tar and it filled my body, squeezing the blood from my veins and the air from my lungs. The more I fought, the faster it overtook me. There was a splintering sound, and I lurched awake to see Luc standing at the foot of my bed.

"You're supposed to be outside," I whispered after I caught my breath.

His voice was so low I felt it in the base of my spine. "You're supposed t'be awake."

"I am. Kind of. What are you doing in here?" I glanced at the clock on my nightstand. 10:42. "I'm not late."

"Figured it would be easier to sneak out if you had a little help."

I scrambled out of bed, still dressed in my school clothes. Hastily, I tugged my skirt down. He raised an eyebrow. "Gotta say, I was hopin' to see you in pajamas. Or do you not wear them?"

"Pervert."

"This look is fine, too. Better with some kneesocks, maybe." He came closer, touched my elbow lightly. The faintest shimmer of magic rose up around us.

"What are you doing?"

"You're making a lot of noise. Rather not explain to your mom why I'm here."

I had a sudden, vivid memory of another time he'd cloaked himself. We'd been on the front porch, kissing, and he'd simply . . . disappeared. And kissed me anyway, like a ghost, invisible hands on my skin, a mouth I couldn't see trailing kisses along my throat. I shivered at the memory.

A concealment would work only if he was touching me, though, and I needed to change clothes. No way was I going off to do magic in my school uniform. I'd already ruined one this week; I wasn't going to chance a second. I snagged a pair of yoga pants out of my dresser and gave him a gentle shove.

"Turn around."

"It's nothin' I ain't seen before."

"Not on me, you haven't. Turn around."

He let go, and the magic dropped away, leaving the room colder. I pulled the pants on before shimmying out of my skirt, then quickly traded my wrinkled button-down for a long-sleeve tee and heavy fleece. For a moment, I studied the line of his shoulders, confident to the point of arrogance. He was lean and angular, even under the black leather coat, and you would think you'd cut yourself on the sharp lines of his body if you got too close. But I knew from experience how effortlessly you could fold yourself up in him. It didn't make him any less dangerous, though. His hair, black like a raven's wing, begged to be touched. I curled my fingers to stop myself from trying.

"I'm ready."

He took my hand again. The magic came back like a caress, and I swayed into it. "Hope you're warm enough. Bit of a walk."

"We're not going Between? Really?"

"I like these shoes. Don't want you castin' up your accounts on them." Keeping my hand firmly in his, we tiptoed down the stairs. There wasn't any need for stealth—my mom was fast asleep, Colin knew we were going, the cloaking spell made us invisible—and yet, when you're strolling out of your house in the middle of the night with a boy who looked like Luc, sneaking is the only way to go.

"Where are we going?" I asked when we'd reached the street. It was cold now, just above freezing, and I took a hat from the pocket of my fleece.

"Open space."

"We're in the middle of the city, Luc. The nearest open space is a golf course."

"Got it in one," he said. "It's better for this sort of thing. Things go wrong, we don't have to worry about taking out passersby or property damage."

"You think things will go wrong?"

He stopped. Under the streetlight, his hair gleamed and his eyes were lost in shadows, but he brushed the back of my hands with his lips. His voice held the slightest hint of strain. "Won't let anything hurt you," he said. "No matter what else you think 'bout me, you should know that."

"I do." For one brief instant, I let myself believe he was talking about me, Mo. Not just the Vessel. I wasn't even sure he could separate the two. We started walking again.

"What does Pascal want?"

"To test some ideas."

"I'm a lab rat?"

"Nicer to think of you as one of a kind," he returned. "Things were different, you might like Pascal. He was a scientist before he was elevated to Patriarch. He's still who we go to when we have questions about how the magic works."

I could envision him as a scientist, but it didn't make me feel any better about being his experiment. "How do you choose someone for the Quartoren? You're Heir to your House, right? Is it hereditary?"

"Tricky business," Luc said as we waited for a light to change. "It's passed down through bloodlines for the most part. Sometimes there's a prophecy, but that's rare. In Evangeline's case, there's no clear successor, so people can throw their hat into the ring and the House will hold a ceremony, let the magic guide them to the right choice."

"So Pascal didn't want to be on the Quartoren?"

"Happened before my time," Luc said. "But from what my father said, I don't believe he was necessarily thrilled."

I felt a sudden kinship with Pascal.

We walked in silence for a few minutes. Every so often, I'd check my phone for a message from Colin, but the screen stayed blank.

"Problems with Cujo?"

I bit my lip. "Why do you say that?"

"Why you denyin' it? I've got eyes. You're walking around like someone told you there's no Santa. And he's looking at you like . . ."

"Like what?"

He seemed to struggle with the words. "Somethin' precious. Somethin' fine and delicate, like china. And he's scared to death he might break you."

He paused, and I stared at the ground, unwilling to meet his eyes.

"He ain't the only one who sees it. He got there first, is all."

There was nothing I could say to that.

His voice was gentle. "Maybe it's for the best, you two ending things now. You're not meant for him."

I stuffed my hands in my pockets, walking faster. "Do not start with the fate thing. I'm not you, Luc. I'm not going to base everything in my life around a stupid prophecy."

"Even if it's true?"

"The prophecy was about Verity."

"It was about the Vessel. That's you, like it or not. You don't see me complaining."

"Because you don't argue with fate."

"Bad things happen in the world. Terrible things. You can rail against it, but there's no point. Fate gives us those things for a reason. And sometimes they bring you something good along with it."

He spoke with a fierceness, a sort of desperate conviction, that reminded me of what Marguerite had said the first time

I met her. *He holds his grief so close I'm not sure he even realizes what it does to him.*

I wanted to ask more, but some instinct held me back. Instead, I stopped, sliding my fingers along the chiseled line of his cheekbone. He swallowed, like he was trying to shove the grief down, and pressed his lips to the scar crossing my palm. The warmth of his breath drew me in.

"You laugh at fate," he said hoarsely. "You don't believe in it, but it's still there. You believe in gravity. You believe in quarks and God, dark matter and planets you've never seen. You believe in magic. Why not believe in me?"

"I do." The words hung between us, smoky puffs in the night air.

"Then why are you fighting so damn hard?"

I was tired, suddenly, like I'd never taken that nap, like I'd been running forever, since the first time I saw him. Maybe it was time to take a stand. "Because it's not your decision. You never even question the prophecy. You don't wonder what your life would be like without it. So when they tell you that I'm the one you're supposed to be with . . . you don't think to yourself, 'Hey, I might not want to spend the rest of my life with a girl I barely know.' You just fall in line with what's expected."

I pulled back, rubbing my thumb over the spot he'd kissed.

"It's not you choosing to love me, Luc. It's fulfilling a duty. I don't want to be your obligation."

He raked his fingers through his hair. "Tell me how to convince you it's more than that."

"I can't tell you what I don't know."

He caught my hands before I could walk away, his eyes blazing green under the streetlights. "You think I don't care, but I do. If you're lookin' for me to prove it, best be ready."

My heartbeat picked up, so loud I was sure he could hear it. For an instant, his words were thrilling instead of terrifying. "Ready for what?"

"Me."

CHAPTER 23

If you're going to mess around with a force capable of flattening a city block, the Beverly Country Club was one of the prettiest places in Chicago to do it. A world-class golf course dropped into the middle of the city, it was bounded on one side by train tracks and on the other a forest preserve my mom forbade me to visit. I was never sure if it was the rumors of the wild dogs or the wild parties she was more worried about.

The BCC itself was a lush green rectangle lined with trees, plenty of wide open space, and an easily circumvented security system. Perfect, Pascal assured me, for the experiment he had in mind.

To look at Pascal, you wouldn't guess he was an Arc, let alone one of their leaders. Slightly built and a little unkempt, he seemed like the kind of guy who'd be more comfortable in a chem lab than governing a secret society. Dominic clearly ran the show, and Orla seemed most concerned with propriety. I wondered what Evangeline's role had been, and who was going to take her place.

Pascal was in full-on absentminded professor mode, muttering over notes scrawled in a thick, leather-bound book, stopping every so often to close his eyes and concentrate on something I couldn't see.

When we were bound, Luc had given me a ring to help

stop the Torrent. It had allowed me to see the ley lines threaded through the world. Evangeline had taken the ring from me. Now I could sense the lines, like a current of warm water in a cold lake, but I couldn't see them on my own.

"I've been meaning to ask," Pascal said, looking up. "How are you feeling?"

I doubted he was digging for answers about my love life. "Okay, I guess."

"No lingering effects from the other day? Headaches, dizziness?"

I tugged off my hat, twisting it with both hands. "How did you know?"

"Another theory," Pascal said. "Nosebleeds?"

"A couple. Why?"

"I healed that up," Luc said, eyes roving over me like he was trying to see past my skin. "I fixed it."

"What's your theory?" I asked Pascal.

"Well, it's only an idea, you understand. You're quite the anomaly."

I'd known something was wrong. And clearly Pascal had, too. Even Marguerite had suspected, but she hadn't mentioned it to Luc. Why not?

"What's wrong with her?" he demanded. "You know what it is, you always do. Quit dancin'."

"When the raw magic passed through you during the Torrent, you became joined to it, somehow. Now the magic is treating your body like another line, attempting to flow through you." He shook his head, in wonderment or pity, I couldn't tell. "But you were never meant to do magic. Your body can't handle the buildup of energy, and so it rebels. The nosebleeds, the headaches . . . they're symptoms of the pressure building inside you. When an Arc calls on a line near you, that magic inside you responds, bursting free. It intensifies the effects of the spell as well as your symptoms."

"At the Covenant," Luc said. "That's why it got so wild; you made the magic amp up."

"Yes. I don't have diagnostic equipment, but I think one of your flat scanning exams would show a substantial amount of internal damage after each encounter."

The image of Kowalski, caught in a blast of raw magic, came back to me in a rush, and my knees started to give.

Luc pulled me close, tucking my head under his chin. "Fix it," he ordered. "Fix her."

"That's what we're trying to do." Pascal pushed his glasses up. "Tonight I'd like you to interact with a line. A minor one, nothing too powerful. I'll open it, and you can get your toes wet, so to speak. Once you're comfortable, try channeling the magic as you did during the Torrent."

I was not looking forward to repeating the Torrent, but Constance's face, so much like Verity's, lingered in my mind's eye. "I'm not sure that's a good idea, considering what happened at the Covenant ceremony."

"It's a very small line. One of the weakest in the vicinity. I'll be monitoring the whole time. If a problem arises, I'll close the line down."

"What's my part?" Luc asked, his arms still encircling me.

"Lend her support. Your mother's prophecy speaks of the Four-In-One. That's both of you. She can't do it alone. Even if she could, without your contribution, the magic would end up horribly unbalanced."

I was not thrilled at the idea of needing Luc for anything, especially after our exchange on the way here. Thinking about Pascal's experiment was more comfortable.

"This sounds dangerous."

"It is," Pascal said, closing the book with a thump. He suddenly looked a lot more like a Patriarch than a mad scientist. "You agreed to the Covenant. Under those terms, you'll do whatever's necessary to fix the magic. This is a necessary step."

"Risking my life is a necessary step?" I said, as Luc's fingers tightened on my arms.

"I need to see what occurs when you interact directly with the magic, so I can determine a plan for how to fix it. The alternative is to send you into the source of the magic and let you fumble your way through."

Luc murmured into my hair. "Might be best to start small, hmn?"

"Best" didn't apply here. All of my options sucked. I'd known it when I agreed to the Covenant, but standing on the eighth hole on a frigid November night made that knowledge much more real, much more terrifying.

I squeezed Luc's hand, drawing strength from the fact that he wouldn't let anything bad happen to me. He squeezed back, and I nodded at Pascal.

"Let's proceed," Pascal said.

Around us, the trees stood like dark, silent sentries. The grass underfoot was dense and springy, nearly black in the moonlight. Pascal waited until a passing freight train had rumbled a safe distance away. As the sound faded, he began to chant, making the line visible. Its surface swirled like mercury, a slender thread that seemed to pulse in time with my heartbeat. The lines I'd dealt with in the Torrent were massive ropes that rippled beneath my touch, much more difficult to control. Shoving aside my nervousness, I closed a hand around the line, allowing its energy to flow into me.

The initial contact was a rush, jarring but almost exhilarating. It was an earth line, the texture sturdy and cool against my fingers. I opened myself a bit more, tentatively, and the power glided smoothly through my veins.

"The line is healthy. There's nothing wrong with it," I said. I'd expected to feel some sort of brokenness. During the Torrent, the lines had corroded under my fingers, unleashing raw magic as they crumbled away. But this was full and rich, firmly grounded in its element.

"Good," Pascal said. "Try increasing the capacity."

I didn't need his instruction—already the magic was tumbling, straining against the filament-like line. I drew on Luc's power to bolster it. The surface was like clay, malleable to the touch, and I tried to reshape it, working as fast as I could. Not fast enough.

The magic destabilized the line gradually, like the tide lapping at the base of a sandcastle, sagging and crumbling before it washed away completely. It slipped out of my control in slight, ominous increments. Next to me, Luc's muscles trembled as he fed his strength into our connection.

This wasn't right. They'd warned me the magic was stronger now, but this was more than powerful—it was all-consuming, almost hungry. I could feel the force of it in my bones, racing toward us, and tried to deflect it.

"Shut it off!" Luc shouted to Pascal, who was scrutinizing me and muttering to himself. He nodded and made a few sharp gestures. For a moment, there was only silence, and relief. My breath came more easily, and my shoulders relaxed as Luc's hand found mine.

And then the magic surged, retaliating against Pascal's attempt to stop it. It was like an avalanche, the power roiling around us, grasping and ravenous. I felt myself being lifted into the air. All I could think was that I must look like Kowalski had when he died.

Then the magic left as abruptly as it had come, throwing me to the ground like a rag doll. Something in my leg snapped.

"Mouse!" Luc dropped to his knees next to me. "Don't look."

"Okay." I covered my face with my hands, whimpering at how badly it hurt.

"Stop, Luc." Pascal's voice was hoarse.

"She's losing blood. I need to—"

"You need to protect her."

Luc fell silent. With my eyes closed, I could hear the trees creaking in the wind, the shuffling sound of the leaves, the rumble of an approaching train. I felt Luc's breath against my cheek, his words low and urgent. "I need to take you Between. Right now."

I dropped my hands. "No!"

"Darklings are coming. Three, at least. Maybe more."

"Luc, I don't think I can go Between." It wasn't that I

wanted to stay here, a target for Darklings. Black spots swarmed over my vision, and the shallow panting I heard was coming from me. Internal damage, Pascal had said. Judging from the stabbing pains radiating from my stomach, a broken leg was the least of my injuries.

Pascal stood on the other side of me. "You can't take her in this condition. It would kill her."

Three forms seemed to ooze from the grove of trees bordering the golf course. Even from this distance, they were tall, wearing tattered black remnants that flapped in the cold wind. The air carried the stench of decay, and bile flooded my mouth.

"Heal me," I said. "We'll go Between and they won't follow."

Luc and Pascal exchanged glances, and Luc turned, wrenching his sword from thin air, the blade shining from within. He shrugged off his coat and pressed the leather hard against my leg wound. I screamed through clenched teeth, and he flinched. "Keep pressure on it. I'll be back as soon as I can."

"Luc!" I cried. An instant later, a glowing red lattice sprang up around me. Wards, designed to prevent the Darklings from reaching anyone inside.

Luc was outside the wards.

He and Pascal stood crouched as the Darklings loped toward them. The noise I'd thought was a freight train was them, snarling and roaring. Bloodlust, I thought dimly. I was losing blood, and they could smell it. I wondered if it was the cold ground or shock causing me to shake so violently.

On the other side of the wards, Luc and Pascal battled the Darklings. I would have thought Pascal would be a lousy fighter, but he seemed to be holding his own against one of the creatures. He wasn't graceful, but combined with whatever spells he chanted, he was able to keep it at bay. Once in a while, he even managed to land a blow with the massive hammer.

Luc moved so beautifully, I could almost forget how lethal he was—slashing and parrying, leaping away from their curving talons at the last possible moment. One struck him in the leg and he dropped to the ground. The wards dimmed, and two Darklings lunged toward me.

I screamed again, and Luc sprang up, shouting something. Instantly, the red lines brightened like a road flare the same moment the monsters reached through. Sparks scattered, the air turning acrid and smoky. The first Darkling howled and stumbled away, leaving behind part of its arm.

Still calling out spells, Luc pressed the advantage, beheading the creature, plunging his blade deeply into its chest, setting the body aflame with a word. I gagged at the smell.

I should have been able to see the wards above me, but the black dots spotting my vision were expanding. On the far side of the golf course, something moved. I squinted at it. More Darklings? A passerby? Grunting, I leaned forward. Too small for a Darkling, feet that looked like a human. The black spots were winning.

I had the impression of hands on knees, as if someone was bending over to peer at me, and then a flash of light. My eyelids were too heavy to open again, my hands too weak to hold Luc's jacket, and the outraged howl of another Darkling, abruptly silenced, came from such a long, long distance. . . .

And then Luc's palm was hot against my stomach, his other hand hovering over my leg. His words seemed to pierce my skin, the numbness that had overtaken my leg becoming painful tingling as blood started to flow normally again and the bone reknit itself. There was a stretching, pulling sensation along my skin, and Luc's hands slid away.

"The Darklings?" I whispered.

"Gone. We're safe." He flopped on the ground next to me.

"What about the guy? Did they get him?"

"What guy?"

"Someone else was here. I saw him." Maybe Colin had followed me after all.

"Shhh." He reached over, brushed my hair away from my

face. "Nobody else is around. You were in shock. Probably hallucinatin'."

I sat up and checked my leg. I hadn't imagined my injuries. The gray jersey pants were ripped at the thigh, drenched in blood. But underneath my skin was unbroken. I sank back onto the cold, damp ground, too weak to stand.

"See? All better."

"Thanks," I said.

"Are you sure that was wise?" Pascal asked, addressing Luc.

"You had a better plan?" he asked through clenched teeth. I shifted to see Luc's face, stunned to find an ashen cast to his skin, usually the color of melted caramel.

"You're hurt." I sat up, fear worming its way through me. "Was it the Darklings?"

"They barely touched me. I just need to rest," he said.

His forehead was clammy to the touch, and I looked balefully at Pascal. "The lines? You didn't say the magic would hurt him, too. You should have told me."

"It wasn't the line," Pascal said. "It was—"

"That's enough," Luc said. Even though his voice was weak, there was an unmistakable note of command in it.

Pascal peered over the tops of his glasses, face forbidding. "Don't forget who you're speaking to, boy. You haven't succeeded Dominic yet."

"Mouse, leave it." He struggled to sit up. I threw an arm over his chest, pressing him toward me.

"The hell I will." I knew that voice. That was Luc's "I am keeping something important from you" voice. "One of you start talking."

"It's nothing," Luc said. "Hardly a trifle."

"Good. Then it won't take long to explain."

"You were easier to manage before," he said. "Little alarmin', the new you."

I folded my arms and stared him down.

"Fine." He looked sulky, a little boy forced to divulge a secret. "It's transference. From healing you."

"Transference?"

"Arcs can't use the magic to create things, only change 'em. So when you get hurt, I convert the physical injury into a magical one, then move it into me."

I ran a trembling hand down my thigh, feeling the lengths of muscle over bone. Without thinking, I reached for Luc's leg, and his face tightened. He was still recovering. "Your leg is broken now?"

"No. Hurts like it, but the damage is magical, not physical. It'll pass soon enough. It's just hard to work any spells in the meantime."

"All this time, you've been hurting yourself when you healed me?"

"Only since your binding," said Pascal, finally wandering back over a sand trap and rejoining the conversation. "When an Arc heals someone, much of the transferred energy is lost as it moves between healer and patient. But with bound couples, their link makes the process more efficient, converting more of the damage to the healer."

How many times had he healed me? Too many to count, and every time, he'd taken on my pain. But he'd never used it as leverage or made me feel guilty. Guilt soured my stomach now, and with it came a flash of anger. "You lied to me. I asked what Niobe meant, and you lied straight to my face."

"You lied to me," he shot back, completely unrepentant. "Told me you were healed."

"Now you know how it feels. And you wonder why I can't trust you? No more healing." The cost was too high. It was too much responsibility. The anger trickled away, leaving behind something . . . warmer. Carefully, I pressed my palm against his chest, meeting his eyes. "Promise me."

"I can't. What if you're hurt? Should I let you sit around with your brain scrambled like an egg? Without me running interference, you won't last long enough to do the job."

Irritating, but true. "Not unless it's necessary," I said finally. "Not unless you ask."

He scowled. "I always do."

"Now that we've settled your quarrel," said Pascal, "may we discuss strategies? Based on what we've seen tonight, I believe that if you try to access the joined lines—all four at once, as the prophecy requires—there are two possible outcomes. The first is that you could increase the capacity of the current lines and create new ones, diffusing the pressure. It's similar to what happened when you entered the magic during the Torrent."

"Isn't that dangerous?" I asked.

"Of course. Last time, you survived because you didn't use the magic. Not much, anyway," he said with a sly smile. "You managed to hold a bit back."

"Evangeline," Luc swore.

A blue-white line of magic flying from my fingertips directly into her heart. "That's what caused all of this? I used a little bit of magic? It's not like I cast a spell, I only directed it."

"You created a link between the magic and yourself. Now you need to use that link—create new lines, direct the magic through them."

"What if I can't?" I'd failed tonight, with only one line. It didn't bode well for working with all four at once, no matter what the prophecy dictated.

"You saw what happened to Constance. That sort of overload would happen to every Arc on the planet, and only the very strongest could withstand it." Any Flats nearby would be killed as well. But that wouldn't occur to Pascal or the Arcs.

"What's the other choice?"

He studied me for a long time before answering. "You could enter into the source of the raw magic again. But this time, you would remain there."

"Like before," I murmured, flashing back to the Torrent,

the sense of omniscience and peace I'd experienced while caught in the swirling nebula of raw magic. At the time, I'd been tempted by all the knowledge and power. I'd considered staying, but Luc had pulled me back. Pascal's words had the same effect now. "Permanently?"

"Yes. You'd be trapped there. Once you were, however, you'd be able to direct the flow and velocity of the magic, ensuring the integrity of the lines and returning our world to normal."

Luc turned away, looking miserable.

I tried to picture abandoning everything in my life—my mom, Lena, Constance. I wouldn't go to New York. I'd never see Colin or Luc again. I'd be alive, but not in any way that counted. My mouth felt filled with sand. "That's not an option."

After that, there wasn't much to say. Luc and I walked slowly home, neither one of us fully recovered. Luc kept my hand firmly in his.

"I don't suppose I could just walk away, huh?" I asked after a few blocks.

"Wish you could," he said in a voice as raw as the wind whipping past us. "But you swore a Covenant. Break it, and you're dead."

I should have been terrified to hear him put it so plainly. I'd known it all along, but it had been so much easier to push the knowledge away, busy myself looking for answers instead of considering consequences. But I couldn't ignore it any longer. "I'll have to go back in. Make more lines. It's the only chance I've got."

"Pascal's not often wrong," Luc said, sounding like he was fighting to keep his voice even. "He was right about the magic makin' you sick. Does it happen every time I use magic around you?"

I shook my head. "Going Between is the hardest. The other spells, like fixing the French classroom or cloaking us, I barely notice. Other people's magic seems to be worse."

"Probably somethin' to do with the binding," he mused.

"Makes me feel a bit better. Don't much like the thought I'm hurting you."

It wasn't only the magic that hurt with Luc.

When we reached the house, he opened the door and led me inside, up the darkened stairs to my room.

"I could have gotten in by myself."

"You don't sneak around so well," he said. "And I will admit to harborin' some hopes on the pajama front."

I paused in the middle of taking off my fleece. "Dream on, sword-boy."

"I will." He sidled closer, touching my collar.

Heat crept up my cheeks, but I kept my voice light as I wriggled away. "Don't let me keep you, then."

Grinning, he stepped back. "Always a pleasure."

He vanished Between, but the afterimage of him slipping through the flames stayed with me until I fell asleep.

CHAPTER 24

I'd gotten Colin's message right for once, because he appeared outside the house, just like normal, the next morning.

"You talked to Billy?"

He made a noise halfway between agreement and irritation. "A little. I'm going to meet with him while you're at school today."

"Isn't that something I should be involved in? Ekomov sent the flowers to *me*."

"I'm trying to keep you *not* involved. Bringing you to the meeting defeats the purpose." He paused. "Why didn't you tell me about the first batch of flowers?"

"I didn't know it had anything to do with Billy. It was just weird, and when weird stuff happens these days, I assume it's magic related." Partly, that was true. Partly, I'd kept quiet because the more Colin worried about me, the more he retreated into bodyguard mode. My strategy hadn't worked, but he seemed to accept my explanation.

"Speaking of magic, what happened last night?" he asked as we pulled up to the school.

"Arc stuff. It's not really anything you can help with." I gathered my bag and opened the door.

His hand caught my sleeve. "I'd still like to know."

The irony wasn't lost on me—four years of honors English

will do that for a girl—but I tugged away. "Important stuff in my life and I'm not telling you about it. That must totally suck."

School was uneventful. There was the usual—avoiding Jill McAllister and her snide comments, surreptitiously checking in on Constance, making sure I adequately participated in class, fending off Lena's probing about Colin and Luc—but no one suspicious tried to approach me. Nothing out of the ordinary, unless getting the last salad in the cafeteria counted. By the time I walked outside, I'd forgotten all about Colin's meeting with my uncle.

The look on Colin's face as I crossed the courtyard quickly brought it back.

He scowled through the truck window as I waved to Lena. While I buckled in, he drummed the steering wheel in frustration. Even the sound of the engine turning over seemed angry.

When I couldn't take his glowering for another second, I threw up my hands. "What?"

"Tell me you did not go toe-to-toe with Marco Forelli."

I blinked. "Wow. So not the response I was expecting."

"What response were you expecting when you waltzed into Morgan's and mouthed off to your uncle and his boss? And dug around for information on me? Please tell me you didn't really believe Billy would talk. Tell me you are not that naive."

"Of course not. But no one ever says what they mean. I figured if I surprised Billy . . ."

"He would what? Tell you all my deep, dark secrets? My secrets, Mo. *Mine*. Jesus."

"I'm sorry."

"Stop pushing. If I wanted to tell you, I would." He blew out a breath and tightened his grip on the wheel. "You should be more worried about Marco Forelli. If he noticed you, it's because he thinks you're useful."

"Useful how?"

"I'm looking into it," he said. "Quit talking to Billy about me."

"Done." The rest of the ride was fraught with silence, but as he parked in front of The Slice, I asked, "What about Ekomov?"

"If he wanted to hurt you, he would have by now. We let it play out, see what he's after."

"Are there any theories?"

"None I want to share."

"Shocking," I said, and went inside.

"Mo," my mom called with relief when she spotted me. "Finally!"

"Mom, I'm three minutes late." The Slice didn't seem any busier than usual, but she was clearly starting to freak out. I scanned the room for a clue as to why.

She tucked the cordless phone between her shoulder and ear. "I need you to take the delivery over to Shady Acres. The computer isn't working right, and I've been on the phone with someone from technical support for over an hour. And now they've put me on hold."

"Maybe I can fix it."

"It's something to do with the hard drive, and a fan, and . . ." She waved her hands around, flummoxed. If she could have, Mom would have kept the books in a paper ledger, but at some point Billy had managed to drag her into the twenty-first century. "I don't understand it, but if I'm not here when they come back on the line, I'll have to start all over again. Please don't argue, just run the delivery over. You've done it before."

"Not happily." They could call Shady Acres assisted living if they wanted to, but really, it was the last stop before the nursing home. It wasn't shady. It didn't sit on an acre. And I didn't have it in me, today of all days, to chat pleasantly with the residents the way I usually did.

"They're old. You'll brighten their day."

"They'll make me play bridge."

"That's not so bad. Go on," she said, pointing to a stack of pies already loaded into the little grocery cart we used for deliveries.

"Fine," I muttered, pulling my coat on.

Towing the cart behind me, I stopped by the truck. "I have to drop off pies. Do you need to come with?"

He grimaced and reached for the door. "I'll walk you there, but I'm not going in."

He was still mad. I could tell because he didn't offer to take the cart from me, and we barely spoke on the three-block walk. Shady Acres was a renovated apartment building, so I pressed the buzzer and waited to be let in while he sat on the bench outside.

"So nice to see you, Mo!" said Edie, the front desk manager from behind her perpetually cluttered desk.

"You too," I said. "The kitchen, right?"

"Yep. You can leave everything on the counter."

I crossed the lobby, past the library—a small room with three mismatched wing chairs, a gas fireplace, and a truly impressive collection of large-print *Reader's Digest*s—and the game room. Two residents were engaged in a vicious ping-pong game, and another group played bridge. I walked a little faster. The corridor smelled like pot roast and disinfectant, and I rounded the corner into the big industrial kitchen.

Alone in the room, I began unloading the pies onto the counter: three apple, three cherry, two mince, and two of the day's special.

"I'm always so glad when chocolate pecan is on the menu," said a faintly accented voice behind me. "Hello, Mo."

The white cardboard box nearly slipped out of my hand as I wheeled around.

"You're . . . the guy."

"Yuri Ekomov. It is nice to see you again."

"What are you *doing* here?" It seemed impossible that the Russian gangster my uncle was so worried about would be living in the local retirement home. But there was no mistaking the old guy from school. He was wearing another slightly unfashionable suit and favoring the ivory-handled cane he'd carried that day at St. Brigid's.

He seemed to read my mind, because he smiled, like we were sharing an inside joke. "I'm getting acquainted with your neighborhood," he said. "I've only been here a short time, but it's a fascinating place."

He stood between me and the door, but I wondered if I could make it past him. He wasn't a small man, and the cane could be a problem. "You live here?"

"Not all the time. The apartment is rented under another name—Mr. Eckert. Better, don't you think, not to advertise my presence to your uncle? It's so convenient for business, though. And I enjoy your mother's baking."

I shrank away as he stepped closer, but he simply took the pie box out of my hands and set it on the counter.

"It would be a crime to drop that," he said. "Did you like the flowers?"

I trembled. "You've been watching us. Watching me."

He inclined his head. "You are a girl who bears watching. I'd heard Billy Grady had a niece, but up until this fall, your uncle worked hard to keep you and your mother away from his business affairs. He should have stuck to his decision."

"I didn't identify your men."

"Yes. I'm aware."

"And I didn't know anything would happen to them afterward. You have to believe me." I backed up until the edge of the counter was digging into my back.

"I do. Do you believe we had nothing to do with your friend's death?"

"I do." It was true.

He studied me the same way he had at school. "You have no reason to be afraid. I arranged this meeting so I could introduce myself properly, that's all."

When people tell you not to be afraid of them, it's usually because they've done something really scary. I turned my head slightly, looking for the knife block a few feet down the counter.

He reached over and patted my hand, his fingers gnarled to a claw, and I managed not to flinch. He was a lot older than my uncle. I didn't know if that made him weaker or cagier. Either way, I stayed frozen as he said, "We could be helpful to each other. As I told you, one good turn deserves another."

"How's that?"

"We'll see. Today, I only wanted to meet you without interference. But things in your uncle's world are going to change soon. When they do, you should know that siding with him is not your only option."

I swallowed. "I'll keep it in mind."

He tapped the cane once, with a satisfied air. "Do."

"Can I go?" I reached blindly for the empty grocery cart.

"Certainly. If I were you, Mo, I wouldn't mention this conversation to anyone," he added as I made my way to the door. "I'm afraid our friendship would be over before it started if your uncle found out I was a guest here."

I fled, the cart bumping along behind me, and didn't slow down until I spotted Colin. I should tell him, but something in me resisted. Maybe it was Ekomov's warning not to talk, or Billy's willingness to use me as bait, or Colin's own insistence that I shouldn't be involved. Maybe my family had rubbed off on me a little too much and keeping secrets was becoming second nature.

"How was it?" he asked when I'd rejoined him.

I was careful not to look back at the door. "The usual."

He nodded, and I returned to The Slice without a word to anyone about Yuri Ekomov's new address.

My mom was still on the phone. "You'll send a new one? Will I be able to save my files?"

That didn't sound promising, and sure enough, her face fell. "Yes, I back it up regularly. It's really that simple?"

I ducked into the back, hanging up my coat and pulling on an apron, trying to calm down before I faced my mom again. By the time I returned to the register, she'd hung up and was straightening menus with a frazzled expression.

"Bad news?"

"They said the hard drive is ruined. They're overnighting a new one, but I have to install it myself."

"At least you don't need a whole new computer."

"I might as well. I'd as soon do open-heart surgery as look inside that machine."

I smiled despite myself and started a fresh pot of coffee. "I can do it. It's not that hard."

"Really? Oh, Mo, you are a godsend!" Problem fixed, she rang up a customer. "How was Shady Acres?"

My hand slipped, sending coffee grounds across the counter. Sighing, I grabbed a sponge and began cleaning up. "The usual."

"See? I told you it wouldn't be terrible."

I didn't answer.

CHAPTER 25

The next day, midway through second period, one of the office aides dropped off a note for me. It was written on such thick, beautifully textured paper I knew it had to be from Niobe. Someone needed to explain to her that guidance counselors did not make enough money to waste high-end stationery on their students. A notepad with "From the Desk of Niobe" printed across the top would blend better.

Then again, what did she care about blending in?

In bold, navy script, the note read, *Pascal will meet with you and Luc this evening. Seven o'clock.*

Nice, the way she informed me instead of asking.

Lena nudged me. "So, are you excited?"

"Not particularly." Pascal would either want to run more tests or deliver more bad news. Neither one appealed very much.

She grimaced in sympathy. "Are you sure they won't let you in? It seems stupid to make you come and sit in the lobby the entire time."

"The lobby?" Lena meant the Sadie Hawkins dance, which had slipped completely off my radar. I frowned. How was I supposed to work the dance and meet with Pascal? Even if I went Between, I couldn't be in two places at once. "What do you think Sister would do if I left once the dance started?"

Lena stared at me, mouth agape. "You really are crazy," she said finally. "Look, I know your year has sucked beyond belief. But not showing at that dance? That's academic suicide."

I sighed. "I know. There's someplace I need to be, though."

"I thought we had plans," she said quietly.

"We do. We totally do. This meeting is during the dance, not after." I'd explain to Luc that I only had an hour or two.

"I don't care how hot the guy from this summer is or how hard you're crushing on Colin. Sister will boot you out of NHS and suspend you. Life as you know it will be over."

She didn't need to know it already was.

"And since when did you get so guy crazy, anyway? I didn't think you were one of those girls." She flipped her ponytail over her shoulder, disdainful. "Maybe we should just forget it."

I shook my head rapidly, not wanting to offend her any more than I had. "No way. I would much rather hang out with you than do the other thing. I can reschedule." I hoped.

Lena sat back, eyes still flashing. "Don't let me interfere if you've got something better to do."

Other than Verity, I didn't remember how long it had been since I'd had a true friend. I missed having someone to talk to. Even with Colin, there was always something left unsaid, our feelings running just under the surface of our conversations. "Nothing's better than hanging out with you."

The bell rang, and I hoisted my books. "I have to run down to the office. We can talk later, figure out times and stuff?"

"Sure." She didn't look like she believed me, and I couldn't blame her.

I made my way to the guidance office, and the secretary waved me through to Niobe's tiny room. She'd redecorated, scrubbing away all traces of poor Miss Turner. The motivational posters of baby animals were gone, replaced with a series of moody black-and-white landscapes. Instead of the electric teakettle and overcrowded bookshelf I'd stared at all semester, a Japanese tea set sat atop a low table, two chairs pulled up next to it as if inviting conversation.

"No students? Shouldn't you be helping people figure out their lives?"

"Regardless of the sign on the door, I'm not a guidance counselor. I try not to encourage repeat visits." She dropped into one of the chairs and crossed her legs at the ankles.

"Nice. Listen, I need you to take a message to Pascal."

"I'm also not an errand girl."

"This is important. I can't meet him tonight."

"Excuse me?" she said, as if she hadn't heard me correctly. "You're going to cancel a meeting with a member of the Quartoren? What could possibly be more important?"

I gritted my teeth. "The dance."

She laughed, the sound mingling horror and mirth. "A high school dance?"

"I know it sounds stupid."

"It *is* stupid. Mind-bogglingly so." She leaned forward and poured a cup of tea for herself.

"Maybe to you. But there's exactly one person in this school who's willing to hang out with me. If I bail on her tonight, that number drops to zero. Not to mention, if I don't work this dance, Sister Donna will revoke my probation. I'll never get into NYU."

"And you truly believe your simple Flat problems matter when placed next to the dangers facing my world?"

"They matter to me. And since you're relying on me to fix your world, it might be a good idea to help keep mine from imploding."

She waved a hand. "Fine. At the very least, I'm sure his reaction to the news will provide some entertainment. Is that all?"

"How's Constance doing?" I asked, sitting down. This seemed like as good a time as any to make sure the Quartoren were holding up their end of the bargain. "Is she making progress?"

"Some. She'll end up wielding considerable power, I think."

She sipped at the tea before continuing. "She's highly emotional. It makes her control of the lines unpredictable."

"You can teach her control."

"To a degree. I can give her techniques for mastering her emotions, but she's alone, and frightened, and very confused."

"She's not alone. She has me."

"That's less of a consolation than you seem to think."

"Luc said she's making friends."

"I believe so, yes. Others in her training sessions. They're from established, respected families. It should smooth her way." She shook her head. "There is something else. My sources tell me that the Seraphim are planning to move against the Quartoren soon, and publicly. And they'll use you in order to do it."

Unease made my scalp prickle. I didn't ask where she'd heard it. Niobe knew things. She had connections to parts of Arc society even Luc couldn't penetrate, and he'd relied on her information in the past. "How?"

"I don't know. Keep in mind that, while the Arcs are indebted to you for stopping the Torrent, they're also leery of how much influence you wield—a Flat who knows their ways, bound to someone of Luc's standing. It wouldn't take much to tip feelings from gratitude to resentment, and the Seraphim are counting on that."

"Why are you telling me this? You don't even like me."

She seemed to consider the question, and the wind chimes stirred for a moment before falling silent. "Not particularly. But Luc does, and I have a . . . fondness for him. It's sentimental, but there you have it." She handed me a hall pass. "I'll send your message to Pascal. You should go back to class."

CHAPTER 26

Jenny Kowalski's e-mail came through during Journalism. I sat at my work station and let the pointer hover over the subject line, thinking about rumors and how the story you heard was almost never the one that really happened, even in the papers. I thought about how long ago my dad's trial was, and how over the years, the truth had rippled and faded like an echo, only certain parts coming through. I'd done research, but even the newspaper accounts at the time seemed biased and incomplete, like the authors knew more than they could say. Jenny knew things, and she wasn't afraid to say them.

She knew Colin, too.

I opened the e-mail, my limbs tingling.

> Mo—
> *Let me know when you want to talk.*
> J.

I skimmed the first attachment, the unofficial court transcript of my dad's trial. I'd tried over the years to get a copy of the official version, but it was sealed. This file was the truth, unfiltered by people's agendas. Without hesitation, I printed it out, hearing the ancient laser printer wheeze to life across the room.

Colin's file was much smaller, and somehow more complicated. If I looked at it, I was pretty much confirming he couldn't trust me. But I didn't see another choice. My uncle had said Colin was free to leave, but he said it with the confidence of a man who knew it was never going to happen. If I was going to help Colin get free, I needed to know what Billy had on him.

I clicked print and headed across the room to pick it up.

"Research?" Lena asked as I scooped up an armload of paper.

"Sort of." I hugged the stack to my chest so she couldn't see what it was.

"What time should I pick you up tonight? Seven sound good?"

"Sure." It wasn't like I had to worry about my hair and makeup. Usually, the job of running the check-in desk went to some sophomore desperately hoping to get into NHS. This year it would be me, desperately trying not to get kicked out. When I'd hoped for a memorable senior year, this wasn't quite what I'd had in mind.

"Maybe you could slip in, once everyone's arrived," Lena said with obvious pity.

I shrugged. Without Colin, the dance had zero appeal. "What's the point?"

She shook her head, baffled. "To see and be seen? To witness firsthand the stuff everyone's talking about on Monday? You are starting to worry me."

I waved away her concern. "Seven o'clock, right?"

She flashed a grin, twin dimples appearing. "Can't wait!"

The bell rang and I loaded up my messenger bag, carefully tucking the files inside. Colin's was such an innocuous-looking sheaf of paper. It didn't seem possible that his past—the one he hid from me at every opportunity—could be summed up in so few pages. Surely if things were as bad as he implied, the file would have been as thick as a phone book.

When I stepped outside, the wind slapped at me, stealing my breath. Colin lounged against the truck, his only concession to the cold a dark gray knit cap that matched his eyes. I tried not to look guilty as I crossed the sidewalk.

"Your bag looks heavy." He held out his hand to take it, but I clutched the webbed strap and ducked away.

"No! It's not too bad, just bulky. I've got it." I was babbling, protesting too much, and he squinted at me for a second before pulling open my door. "Lot of work this weekend?"

"Yeah." I waited until he'd climbed in and started the engine to continue, holding my fingers up to the heating vent. "It's like the teachers know we have something fun scheduled and they want to balance it out."

"Something fun, huh?" There was more than curiosity in his voice. Approval, I thought, as if he was pleased that I was taking his suggestion to act like a normal teenager. "What's that?"

"The dance. I'm not actually dancing, just taking tickets. Lena's driving me."

Abruptly, the mood in the cab shifted, Colin's expression turning suspicious. He wasn't storing the gun in the glove compartment anymore, I noticed. He kept it on him all the time, tucked into the holster at his back. "You're not supposed to go anywhere without me."

My temper started to crackle like tinder. "You didn't want to go, and Lena's staying over tonight."

"While your mom's out of town? Is she okay with that?"

"Yes. She thought it might be nice for me to have company."

The muscles in his jaw jumped. "You can meet her there. I'll drive."

"No. If you're that worried, follow us. You'll have to sit outside, though. Only ticketed guests are allowed in."

He ignored the dig. "I can't believe your mom is letting you stay home while she goes to Terre Haute."

"I can't believe you'd think I would go."

"I'm not crazy about you staying by yourself. Too many people are interested in you."

"I won't be by myself. Lena will be there. You said yourself that if Ekomov wanted to hurt me, he would have done it by now."

We pulled up in back of the house and I felt the tight knot of fear in my chest loosen slightly, the concern he might discover the files in my bag dissipating.

"Are you coming in?" It was our usual routine when I wasn't working. He'd have a snack and watch sports while I did homework. Sometimes he'd tinker under the hood of the truck or do some little household repair that had been bothering my mom. We'd flirt and joke around, and it was the closest thing to normal since Verity's death. Sometimes, when the snide comments and sideways glances during school were especially cutting, those moments were all I had to look forward to.

But nothing between us was normal anymore. Nothing was easy. And today, with a bag full of Colin's secrets resting at my feet, his company was the last thing I wanted.

"Your mom's home," he said. "You two should visit before she leaves for Terre Haute. I'll sit this one out."

In the kitchen, Mom was wiping down counters and rearranging the pantry, determined to put everything in perfect order before she left. I watched her from the screened porch. She was wiry—small but strong, her hands red from all her work at The Slice. Growing up, I'd watched her roll out countless pie crusts, handling the delicate pastry with confidence. Outside the restaurant or our house, that confidence seemed to evaporate, and the transformation always made me sad. Now, as she darted around the room, I felt a twin rush of affection and irritation. She wore herself out to make things as perfect as they could be, but she refused to see that it was my dad's fault she had to work so hard.

"You're home early," she said, rinsing out the sink. The scent of bleach and artificial lemon filled the air, and my nose wrinkled involuntarily. "Where's Colin?"

"Outside."

She looked crestfallen. Something in Colin's unflappable

manner diffused the tension between us. I kept a better hold
on my temper when he was around; Mom hovered less. Plus,
he loved her cooking. She was always happiest when feeding
someone who went back for thirds. Most important, he was
dedicated to keeping me safe. For that alone, my mother was
ready to have him canonized.

"Daddy's going to be so disappointed when he sees you
stayed home," she said. "You could still come with."

I dropped my bag on the recently washed floor and slipped
off my Birkenstocks. "It's been four years. He's probably not
expecting me."

She shook her head. "He misses you."

I stifled the urge to tell her that if he really missed us, he
should have stuck to accounting instead of branching out
into money laundering and embezzlement. Good dads
coached soccer. They taught you how to ride a bike. They
videotaped your performance in the annual Christmas
pageant. They didn't commit felonies and get arrested at the
Fall Festival when they were supposed to be working the
beanbag toss.

"He's coming home soon. You owe it to him to bend a
little."

"What could I possibly owe him?"

She set the sponge down and turned to face me. "Your father sacrificed a great deal for us. You act as though he
wanted to leave, but nothing could be further from the truth.
It nearly killed him, but he did what he thought was best. For
us."

"You sacrificed, too. Didn't you ever want . . . more?"
More kids, a bigger restaurant? A car with a muffler that
wasn't constantly in danger of falling off? A husband to sit
next to on Sundays at church? "Nobody should have to
work as hard as you do."

She smiled, a little sadly. "I have a beautiful daughter and
a business that brings people happiness. Hard work seems
like a small price to pay."

I picked at a snagged thread on my sweater, feeling petty

and ashamed, like my question had diminished all that she'd worked for over the years. "All I meant was, you deserve to be happy, too."

Turning away, she dumped more Comet into the already-spotless sink and scrubbed feverishly. "I'm content. And when your father comes home, I'll be happy."

"You gave up so much."

"Sometimes you do," she said over her shoulder. "Sometimes you have to choose between the dreams you've carried and the person you love, because without them, the dreams turn to ash. The people you love matter more than ideals. Always."

I scoffed. "If that were true, Dad would be here, not in prison."

"Oh, Mo. The truth is always more complicated than you'd like."

"I'm going upstairs. Schoolwork." I lifted my bag for emphasis.

Mom swallowed, as if there was something in her throat that wouldn't quite go down. "I'll come up in a little bit to say good-bye."

My room was spotless. Mom had already cleaned in here, no doubt looking for something—anything—to explain my recent behavior. But the only things I'd kept from my time with the Arcs were the strangely fused Covenant rings.

I tossed Jenny's files onto the bed and leaned against my dresser, staring at the two stacks of pages.

Maybe this was a mistake.

The front door banged. Through my window, I watched my mother approach Colin's truck with a thermos and a foil-covered plate. She was probably giving him last-minute instructions before she left, like he was a babysitter. It made sense, because deep down, he still saw me as a kid.

He was deliberately keeping me in the dark, trying to protect me, but the dark was where the scariest things lived. I wasn't going to stay there anymore. I climbed onto my bed and picked up his file.

The first several pages were scans of handwritten reports from Denver Child Services, detailing a visit to the Donnelly-Gaskill home, eleven years ago. The words looked like bruises on the page.

Compound fractures, multiple lacerations, cigarette burns.
Ages eleven, eight, and six.
Mother refused to press charges.
Girl, six, demonstrates play patterns consistent with re-
*   peated sexual abuse.*
Recommend removal from home.

I pressed my fist to my mouth. The scars across his back made sense now, in the cruelest possible way. My eyes filled, grieving for those kids as I flipped through the other pages. There was no follow-up, no formal report. Nothing to show that the children—Colin and his siblings—had been saved.

The next few pages were a rap sheet for a man named Raymond Gaskill, Colin's stepdad. A string of thefts, from breaking and entering to auto theft and armed robbery, interspersed with assault charges—domestic and otherwise. In nearly every case, the charges were dropped or the cases dismissed. A few stints in jail, none lasting longer than ninety days. And then, suddenly, nothing.

I turned the page. An EMT logbook—a response to a 911 call in an apartment in Denver, shots fired. A man and a woman, both dead at the scene, and a boy, eight, who'd died en route to the hospital. A girl, six, unconscious with massive head trauma. And another boy, eleven, in shock and badly beaten, with multiple fractures but expected to survive.

Greasy nausea swamped me, and I curled in a ball, trying to stave it off. The image of an eleven-year-old, alone in the ambulance, alone in his pain, wouldn't go away. And Billy had told me. *A nightmare.* Billy had told me the truth, and I hadn't believed, because I thought nothing could be as bad as Verity's murder.

So *stupid* to think I'd cornered the market on misery.

My fingers shook so badly as I turned the page that the paper ripped. I was desperate not to see the catalog of injuries Colin and his siblings had sustained, but it was pointless. I'd see it anyway, for a long, long time.

A newspaper story—a small one, only a few paragraphs, buried on page twelve, about a home invasion that had left a mother and son beaten to death. The survivors, a boy and girl, were handed over to the custody of distant family members. No mention of a stepfather or anyone else at the scene.

I pressed my back into the wall, trying to piece together the information in front of me. Colin's stepdad had abused the whole family. I remembered the lattice of scars down Colin's back, and my stomach twisted, picturing how big Raymond Gaskill looked in his mug shot, a hulking brute of a man, and how small an eleven-year-old boy was. How impossibly, terrifyingly unstoppable he would have seemed to a six-year-old girl.

Why hadn't Colin and the other kids been put in foster care? Why wasn't Gaskill in jail? The caseworker's notes were dated only a few days before the EMT report. Either the kids hadn't been removed or they'd been sent back, and Gaskill had picked up where he'd left off. When he did, something had snapped, and Colin was the only one left standing.

It didn't fit. I had this feeling of looking at a jigsaw puzzle, all the pieces laid out before me, but I wasn't turning them correctly, couldn't nudge them into place. Jenny had wanted me to see the whole picture, but my vision kept blurring. Neither the newspaper nor the police had mentioned Gaskill at all. Was it possible the EMT report was wrong? Was he still alive?

The last page was simply an address on the west side of the city. I put it aside. Nothing in Chicago interested me right now. It was what had unfolded in Denver, eleven years ago, that I needed to understand. I studied the papers again, scattered across my bed like leaves, a cold dread creeping over me. There were five people in that apartment. Four of them were badly beaten. One of them was shot. Either Raymond

Gaskill had committed suicide—and he didn't seem like the kind of guy who felt a lot of remorse—or someone else had pulled the trigger.

I knew, with a sudden, hideous clarity, who that someone was.

So much blood. So much loss, and Colin carried it with him every day. I wept for him, for the scared little boy he must have been, and the solid, fearless man he'd grown into. He'd survived and carved out a life for himself, and all I did was batter against it, demanding answers to something I had no business asking after. He'd been right. Billy had been right.

My mom knocked on the door. Hastily, I gathered the papers and shoved them under my pillow.

"I'm about to get on the road," she said, sticking her head in. Even though she'd arrive in town after the prison's visiting hours were over, she wore a nice skirt and pearls with her mock turtleneck sweater, the kind of clothes she wore for company and special occasions. "Are you sure you won't come along?"

"Positive." I kept my face turned away and my voice nonchalant, hoping she wouldn't notice anything amiss. My ability to lie convincingly had improved in the last few months, but I was too fragile to pull it off now. "Have a good trip."

The cheery tone must have been too much, because she crossed the room and sat down next to me. "You're upset. Is it about this trip? It's not too late to change your mind."

"It's not the trip," I said, tracing the hand-stitching on my quilt. My dad's return seemed simple compared to what I'd just read. "It's . . . complicated."

She pressed her lips together. You could practically see her fighting off the urge to pry, but she smoothed my hair back from my face and smiled weakly. "I made a lasagna," she said. "And there's waffle batter in the fridge, so you and Lena can have them fresh tomorrow morning."

"Sounds great. Thank you," I whispered.

She squeezed my hand. "Could you do me a favor while

I'm gone? The parts to fix the computer came, and I'll need to do payroll when I get back. Can you see what you can do?"

"Sure." It would be nice to try fixing something where I might actually succeed.

"Thank you, sweetheart. I'll tell Daddy you said hello."

"I . . . sure." She was trying. I could too, a little. "See you Sunday night."

As soon as I heard our Ford Taurus shimmy to life, I turned on my computer and Googled "Raymond Gaskill," but there was nothing. I'd already looked for information about Colin, but even when I added Denver and the year on the reports, I found nothing. They were all ghosts. I fumbled for my cell and dialed Jenny's number, fingers slipping on the keys.

"Why did you send me this?"

"Mo." Her voice was cautious. "You read both files?"

"I read Colin's. You don't know him," I said, my voice cracking.

"Do you?"

The question caught me off guard. Did I know Colin? Or had I only known *about* him, the way people thought they knew about me?

"Colin didn't kill your dad."

"Maybe not. But he's still connected."

"And this is what I needed to unconnect him. Thanks."

I threw the phone onto my bed and sat down on the floor, clutching the sheaf of papers. I didn't need to read them again—every word was seared into my brain, and nothing would soothe them away. All I'd done was read a few reports. I could only imagine the kind of damage living it had done to Colin. My eyes filled again, and I swiped at them with the heel of my hand.

Why hadn't Colin trusted me with this?

He knew all my secrets, all the dark and terrible things I'd done or lived through in the past few months. He'd watched me grieve for my best friend. He'd seen me plunge into magic and fight my way back. He'd seen me kill. And he'd stayed silent.

His silence *hurt*. Maybe it was selfish, to be thinking of my own pain instead of Colin's, but I didn't understand. He'd kept the most important thing that ever happened to him a secret from me. Worse, he'd told Billy. Even though my uncle was using Colin's past to blackmail him, he trusted Billy to keep his secret, but not me.

He didn't trust me. He'd never trusted me, and he never planned to. I couldn't possibly have made a bigger fool of myself.

I heard the door slam again, the creak of Colin's foot on the bottom stair, his voice rising up from the living room. "Your friend's here. You coming down, or should I send her up?"

"I'll be down in a minute." I scooped up the papers and dropped them on my desk, then threw on the first clean dress that looked like it might work—dark green jersey, edged with lace at the neckline and hems, a swingy skirt. Half as dressy as what everyone else would wear, but no one would care since I'd be sitting behind a table the whole time. I put on a very sensible pair of low black heels and pulled my hair back into a knot, jamming a clip in to hold it.

"Mo, come on!" Lena called. Her conversation with Colin sounded light and inquisitive. I took a grim satisfaction envisioning him trying to evade Lena's questions. The smile dropped away as I peered at my blotchy reflection. No amount of makeup could hide my swollen, red-rimmed eyes.

Colin would guess that something was wrong the minute he saw me. I didn't know how to keep this secret, so huge it eclipsed everything between us. I didn't know how to look at him without pity for everything he'd gone through, and anger at not telling me about it. It was his past, but our future. At least, that's what I had thought. Now I knew the truth—we'd never had a future at all.

I grabbed my purse, tossing in the essentials, and clattered down the stairs to meet Lena.

Colin was waiting in the living room, one hand on the banister, looking like he wanted to flee from Lena's brightly persistent questions. He looked up, obviously relieved I was taking Lena off his hands.

"You okay?" he asked, relief turning to concern as I fumbled for my coat. "You look . . ."

"She looks great," Lena said, catching my eye. I thought she'd say something—she wasn't the type to censor herself—but she grabbed my hand and reached for the door. "We should have left ten minutes ago."

I struggled into my coat, shaking off Colin when he tried to help. "Ready."

He caught my arm at the door. "Something's wrong."

"You wouldn't understand," I said, yanking away. Not a lie—if he didn't understand why he should have told me, he wouldn't get why I was so upset. And he definitely wouldn't understand why I'd read his file in the first place.

CHAPTER 27

L ena's little Chevy had barely made the turn onto Western before she broke the heavy, miserable silence. "You are clearly not okay. Did you guys have another fight?"

"No."

She waited for me to say more, but I pressed my icy fingers to my eyes, trying to erase the damage. After a few minutes, she glanced in the mirror. "He's back there, you know."

"Yep." This was why it was pointless for me to try to make friends. I couldn't tell Lena any of what I'd learned—not about Colin, or my uncle, or even why Jenny Kowalski was hounding me.

"He seems like a nice guy," she said cautiously. "Like he cares about you."

"He's a great guy."

"Who is making you miserable."

"It's not his fault," I said.

She frowned. "Are you sure? Because if he's hurting you, I can help. I know people who can help."

I laughed once, the sound too close to tears. "You think he's . . . Colin isn't beating up on me, Lena, I swear. If anything, he's too careful."

"Better than the alternative."

I whooshed out a breath. "Can we talk about something else? Please?"

"Sure." Lena prattled on, deliberately keeping the conversation light. I used the rest of the car ride to pull myself together.

We entered the school, and Sister Donna was waiting for us. "Right here," she said, gesturing toward the table. "Mo, you'll check people in. Take their tickets, check the IDs of the guests to make sure they match the names we've been given, and mark them off the list. I'll come by once the dance has started, to make sure everyone's accounted for."

"Got it."

"Lena, you can help test the sound system. People should be arriving shortly."

"Later," Lena said, waving a hand.

I sat down in the empty lobby, toying with a pencil. A book would have been nice. Or a video game. A manicure kit. A large stack of homework. Anything to help me pass the time and not think of Colin. It was only slightly easier when couples began to filter in, the girls in clouds of sequins and satin, accompanied by guys in dress pants and ties, looking uncomfortable. I worked as quickly as I could. I wasn't in the mood for conversation, especially not when the topic was going to be why I was sitting out here doing an underclassman's job when the rest of the seniors were inside dancing to Top 40 hits deemed appropriate by the administration.

And then, because my day couldn't get any worse, Jill McAllister strutted in. She was surrounded by her entourage and their dates. Jill was always at the center of a carefully selected group of girls—pretty, wealthy, popular girls who would enhance her reputation but not overshadow her. Even tonight, in a shimmery gold dress that highlighted her spray-on tan, spiky heels, blond hair artfully messed—she was the sun, and everyone else orbited around her. When she caught sight of me behind the table, she brightened even more.

"Mo! Ready to celebrate? We've already started!" She twirled, giggling as her date steadied her. I sniffed discreetly, but I couldn't smell anything on her breath. She threw the tickets on the table and made a show of examining me. "Nice dress. Did your mom pick it out?"

Did your pimp choose yours? I wanted to ask. But I didn't have the energy for Jill tonight, so I double-checked the guys' IDs and waved toward the cafeteria. "Have a great night," I mumbled.

"Wait." Jill held up a hand and the crowd rippled to a halt. "Aren't you going to congratulate me?" She smiled, showing too many teeth like a horse. Then again, her dress was so low cut, no one was looking at her face.

I sighed. "What are we celebrating?"

"NYU! I got my letter today! Didn't you?" Her eyes widened in mock apology, but her eyes glittered brighter than the sequins on her dress. "I forgot. You didn't even apply, did you? It might be nice for you to go somewhere local. Stay here, spend time with your family. I'm sure your dad would love that. Maybe NYU isn't the school for you."

"Yeah, their standards have really slipped lately," I said, curling my lip as I looked her up and down. "They'll let any piece of trash in, if it's dressed up shiny."

Her face flushed as she leaned in, earrings swinging. "It's not St. Brigid's," she said. "Your uncle's money isn't going to buy you a spot. And in New York, his connections aren't going to matter. No one's going to care if he's Mob."

That's what I was counting on.

"Ladies," said Sister Donna from behind me. "Everything going smoothly?"

"Perfectly, Sister," Jill simpered, backing up quickly. "We were just going in. I don't want to miss anything."

"Indeed. Mo? Are we nearly done?"

I checked the paper in front of me. "Only a few left."

"I'll take the list and start calling. They're probably still taking pictures, but better safe than sorry. Stop by the office if our stragglers show up, please."

I settled in to wait, alone with my thoughts in the dim hallway. Behind me, music drifted in from the dance. The massive front doors blocked my view of the courtyard, but I knew Colin was there. He was always there, the surest, steadiest thing in my life. And it turned out I didn't know him at all.

"Doesn't seem right," came Luc's voice from the darkness. I jerked, looking around, and saw him on the other side of the security gate blocking the stairwell. He tapped the padlock lightly, and it fell open with a sizzle and pop. I watched, openmouthed, as he pushed the gate aside, the creak echoing in the high-ceilinged lobby. "Pretty girl, all by her lonesome on a Friday night. Shameful, really."

"What are you doing here?"

"You stood me up to sit in the dark by yourself? You ain't exactly doing wonders for my ego, Mouse."

"I told Niobe I couldn't make it. You didn't get the message?"

He chuckled, perching on the table in front of me. "Easy, now. She delivered."

"Oh." If he'd known I couldn't meet him, why come here? "Is something wrong? Is it Constance?"

"She's off trainin'. Niobe told her mama it's a grief support group. I figured it might be nice to pay you a visit." He tilted his head, studying me. "What's eatin' you?"

"Nothing."

"Mmn-hmn. Does nothing stand about six feet, wear a lot of canvas, and think waving a gun will make all the bad things go away?"

"Please don't. Not tonight."

He held up his hands. "All done. How are you feeling? Magic-wise, I mean. Any more symptoms?"

"Not really."

He gave a satisfied nod and prowled around the lobby, examining the trophy cases, pictures of distinguished alumni, and the portrait of the current Pope. Despite my wretched mood, I had to smile. Watching Luc in my world was like seeing a movie in 3D for the first time. Everything around him was two-dimensional, while he stood out, vivid even in the dim light.

"Music's nice," he said over his shoulder, peering down the corridor to the cafeteria. "You been to a lot of these?"

"Dances? A few. My mom's not really a fan," I said with a grimace. "What about you? Do Arcs have school dances? Do they even have schools?"

"Sure. Little different from yours, 'course. You can sit next to someone from Sri Lanka, and they go halfway around the world for lunch and back again before you've finished your sandwich." His voice sounded strangely wistful.

"Do they have dances?"

He turned back to me, ambling down the hallway like he wasn't the slightest bit worried Sister Donna might come around the corner. "No idea. I'd imagine so, but I couldn't tell you for sure. I didn't go."

"You were homeschooled?"

"In a manner of speakin'," he said. There was a lot about Luc that was a mystery to me, but in that moment, I saw him perfectly, how resolutely he tucked the pain away, cocking his head toward the music. "Sounds like fun. You sure you don't want to pop in?"

"I show my face in there, my probation is officially over. And not in a good way."

"Then we'll have to dance out here," he said, holding out one hand. His eyes traveled over me as he gave the slightest of bows.

"Luc, I'm not dancing."

"It's easy," he said. "And you could use a bit of fun." Before I could protest, he tugged me out of the chair. With a quick curl of his fingers, the music increased, swelling through the lobby, slipping irresistibly beneath my skin. Around us, tiny flames like fairy lights appeared, brightening the gold flecks of his eyes. As I peered at the nearest flame, trying to figure out how it worked, he slipped one arm around my waist and took my hand in the other. With practiced movements, he guided me through a simple box step, and I stepped on his feet.

"Sorry!"

"No worries." He spun me out and back, and I stumbled, knocking into him. "Relax."

"I am not really in a relaxing mood." The press of his fingers through my dress wasn't helping, either.

"One dance. You been carryin' the weight of the world for as long as I've known you. You can set it down for one dance, right?"

I exhaled slowly, feeling a bit of the tension flow out of me, as if he was drawing it away.

"Better already. See? You just have to trust your partner." He kept the steps simple and his hold firm, and for a few minutes, there was nothing but the music and the rhythm of our breathing. He eased closer, narrowing the space between our bodies, and I resisted the urge to pull away.

"Why were you homeschooled?"

He sighed, the exhalation stirring my hair. "Long story. Let's just say the Quartoren decided it would be better."

Maybe. But something had made him look so unhappy earlier. It made me reluctant to push, but I needed some part of him, something to hold on to. "Tell me something about you. From before we met. Tell me something true."

"Something true," he mused. He drew me closer, until my cheek was resting on his shoulder and I could smell him, cinnamon and saltwater. After a moment, he said, "You'll like this. One of my favorite things when I was little, five or six years old, was learnin' my letters. Arc kids grow up learning both kinds—yours and ours—because it's good to get the language of spells down before you actually cast 'em. Less of a mess later on."

"I can imagine." I relaxed into the cadence of his words.

"You practice by tracing on glass slates with the characters carved in. You follow the paths of the letters with a brush. One of the most beautiful sights in the world," he said, lost in memory. "The ink glows like jewels, and the light shinin' through the tablets makes patterns of the spells. On a sunny day, there's words of power on every surface—the walls, the floor, your skin, the dust in the air. Like you're inside the spell."

He looked sad again, and I squeezed his hand gently. He blinked, seemingly dazed.

"It sounds amazing."

"I'll show you someday."

"I'd like that. Why did the Quartoren pull you out?"

The slightest tension rippled through his body. "Once fate lays out a path for you, best to start walking it, even if it's not what you planned for." His eyes, a dark, bottomless green, met mine as he twirled me out and back in again. He stopped moving completely, catching me off balance amid the golden lights and lush music.

"Sometimes, the two overlap. The life you're supposed to have, the life you're dreamin' of . . . they come together. It's a rare thing." The corner of his mouth turned up. " 'Bout as rare as you, I'd bet."

"Luc . . ."

"I could dazzle you with magic," he said softly. "I could wrap you up in our binding, shower you with diamonds, set a spell to make you forget everything in the world but me. There's a hundred different tricks I could use to convince you about us."

He brushed his mouth over mine, a whisper of a kiss, and stepped back, breaking all contact between us. With a short, sharp gesture, the fairy lights vanished. The music he'd brought into the room went silent, only faint snatches audible from the other end of the hallway. The hint of magic that had skimmed over me ceased, and the room felt vast and intimate at the same time, as big as the world and small enough that it contained nothing but us.

"No tricks this time. No magic. Just me, and you, and the truth, for once. Truth is, we're right."

I couldn't take my eyes from him—hair falling into his face, shining like water in moonlight. His lips parted as if he were about to speak, and he reached across the space between us, beckoning. I looked at his hand for a moment, those long, clever fingers that could wield magic like a weapon or a caress, knowing exactly how they would feel. He wasn't trying to persuade me, he was stating a fact. This moment was about us—no one else, no magic or fate or excuses. Just us. It was a challenge, and an invitation, and it was as vulnerable as Luc had ever let himself be in front of me.

I slipped my hand inside his.

His smile blazed as he yanked me toward him, as if he couldn't wait any longer to close the gap. I stumbled into the kiss, his mouth searching, shockingly hot. The world fell away in a rush, like we were flying, and I kissed him back. His fingers tangled in my hair, traced down my neck, and it seemed stupid that there was any space between us at all. I pressed closer, biting his lip, and he made a noise deep in his throat, contentment and hunger at the same time.

I opened my eyes, startled to find him staring at me. This close, I could see the gold flecks in his irises, luminous and intent. I stared back, unafraid for once in my life. The rightness of it all—our feelings, the way we fit together, made me dizzy. It wasn't just Luc's truth anymore. It was mine, even if it made everything else more complicated.

"Stop thinking," he said against my mouth. So I did, learning him through touch alone, feeling the pulse at his throat quicken, breathing in the scent of him, smoke and secrets.

Behind us, someone coughed.

I scrambled back as the real world crashed in, my face flushing scarlet.

"Sorry to interrupt," Lena said, sounding more entertained than apologetic. "Nice to see you, Secret Guy. Again."

Luc dropped into my chair and waved at her, maddeningly collected.

"I came to see if you were bored," she said, turning to me. "Since you're not . . . I'll catch you later."

"Do," Luc said, twining his fingers with mine, tugging me onto his lap.

She dimpled and left.

"Nice girl," he said. "But she's got a nasty habit of inter-ruptin' at the worst possible moment."

"I'm not sure if that's your timing or hers. You should probably go," I said, squirming as his fingers trailed along the lace-edged neckline of my dress.

"We were just getting started."

I batted his hand away. "Lena's not the only person who's going to be wandering around. Do Arcs have nuns? Trust me, you don't want to meet Sister Donna."

He sighed heavily and kissed me again. "Do you believe me now? It's not just magic."

"I believe you." It had seemed simpler before Lena had come in and brought the rest of the world with her. "I don't know what to do with it, though."

"Plenty of things we could do," he said, eyes gleaming with suggestion. "Want me to tell you about 'em?"

"You are such a guy."

"Glad you noticed."

I'd always noticed Luc; from the day I met him, it had been nearly impossible to look away. Something about him compelled me. He made me question things, want things, want *more*—from myself and from the world—and he made me believe I deserved it.

"Come with me." He was asking, not ordering. "Not home. Don't want to take you Between if we can avoid it. Somewhere, though. Your place?"

The thought of being alone together, with no chance my mom would come home, sent a charge running across my skin. Every nerve in my body strained toward him. "I want to . . ."

"Good." He kissed the spot where my jawline met my ear.

". . . but I can't leave." I hadn't expected the disappoint-ment to be such a sharp tug.

His thumb brushed the back of my knee, and my eyes drifted shut. "Why not? There's nothing here worth staying for."

I slipped out of his reach, afraid of how little it would take for him to change my mind. "I made plans with Lena, for after the dance. I promised."

"You and your promises," he grumbled. "Awful convenient."

"What's that supposed to mean?"

"Never met anyone who makes excuses the way you do. There's always some reason you can't go all in. Always logical sounding and proper, but underneath it's because you're scared. Couldn't meet with Pascal because you have this dance, can't come with me because you've got a sleepover. You're not lyin', exactly, but it ain't the whole truth, either."

"Maybe you're just jealous because you didn't get an invitation," I said, trying to ease the tension. Something inside me resonated at his words, and I touched his arm in apology. "I didn't know you'd be here, Luc. Don't make me choose."

"Not tonight." He frowned. "But eventually you're going to run out of excuses. You'll have to choose, or you'll end up with nothing. I wish I could make you understand."

"I do," I said, resting my head against his shoulder. He was talking about more than our relationship, and I wanted to give him the truth he deserved. "I'm figuring it out, okay? That's the best I can do."

"I know." He leaned down and kissed me, his mouth lingering on mine like an echo. "Missing that already," he said, and vanished.

CHAPTER 28

"I cannot figure you out," Lena said as we walked to the car.

"Welcome to the club."

"Seriously. You're crazy about Colin. Anyone can see that. He walks into the room and you light up. One fight later, and you're sticking your tongue down Secret Guy's throat. Which I get, because he's, like, nuclear-reactor hot, but really? What is the deal?"

I didn't say anything as we pulled out of the parking lot. "I wish I knew."

"You said he was Verity's boyfriend."

"I might have jumped to conclusions."

"You jumped *something*," she said. "What about you and Colin?"

I glanced back at the truck following us. "There is no me and Colin. He has made that abundantly clear."

"Oh. That was the fight. Earlier."

"Yeah."

She fiddled with the radio, regrouping. "Does Secret Guy have a name?"

I paused. "Luc."

"Are you guys serious?"

I touched my wrist. "Hard to say. We're figuring it out."

Lena pursed her lips. "He looked pretty serious to me."

"Yeah. It's . . ."

"Complicated," she finished. "Everything is with you, lately."

The rest of the night passed in a blur of popcorn and chocolate chip cookies, cheesy romantic comedies, and school gossip. It was exactly what I needed, and I forced myself not to think about Colin's file or Luc's ridiculous accusation that I was scared of us. I wasn't making excuses, I was trying to find a balance between his world and mine.

Lena finally crashed sometime around two AM, snoring daintily on the couch. I burrowed into my nest of pillows and blankets on the rug, feeling nostalgic. Verity and I had slept over at each other's houses at least once a week, just like this. A friendship with Lena wouldn't be the same. I knew that. But it was a start, one small aspect of my life that was a little bit normal again. The thought cheered me as I drifted off.

An hour later, I jolted upright as the sound of shattering glass filled my ears. I struggled against the tangle of blankets wrapped around my legs. Lena jerked awake just as another brick came sailing through the front window, landing at her feet.

"Out the back!" I shouted, pulling her off the couch and shoving her toward the kitchen. "Go!"

I was about to follow when someone kicked open the front door. A man in a ski mask filled the doorway, and I screamed.

"Mo!" Colin burst through the kitchen door, gun drawn. "Upstairs. Now!"

But I stood, frozen in place. Lena hauled on my arm. I barely registered the movement.

"Come on!" she cried, pulling me up the steps. I shook her off, unable to take my eyes from the scene in front of me. The stranger pulled a gun—the biggest I'd ever seen—and aimed it at Colin, shaking his head in warning.

"Snap out of it!" Lena hissed, dragging at me.

A second man appeared behind the first, gun in hand.

Aimed directly at me.

My legs gave out, and I sank down on the step, clutching the banister.

Colin glanced up at me, and retrained the gun on the second man, eyes hard. "You've got no beef with her," he said. "It's smarter to walk away."

The door creaked, swinging drunkenly on its broken hinges.

"Walk away," Colin repeated. His finger moved the tiniest bit on the trigger. "Walk away now, or I will end you, and everyone you've ever loved, and it will. Not. Be. Quick."

On the landing above, Lena was begging me to move. The curtains twisted in the night air, and the temperature plummeted so rapidly my teeth chattered. I gripped the banister, feeling the wood splinter underneath my nails, anchoring myself with the pain.

Colin never wavered, his grip perfectly steady, his gaze never shifting from the man still pointing the gun at me. The barrel seemed impossibly long, the hole in the center infinitely deep. I wondered if it would be the last thing I ever saw.

And then he lowered the gun and tapped his partner on the shoulder. Silently, they backed out the door. Colin kept his gun on them the whole time, glass crunching under his feet, edging toward the door to get a better view as they escaped. Across the street, an engine revved, tires squealed, and they were gone.

I squeezed my eyes shut, curling myself tighter and tighter against the shivers racking me, and then Colin was kneeling on the step below, wrapping me in his arms. "Mo? They left. They're gone. They didn't hurt you." The stubble covering his jaw was the color of wheat, but the skin underneath was pale.

"They had guns," I said.

"I know. It's okay. You're okay. Jesus," he said, blowing out a breath. "You're okay."

Lena appeared at the top of the stairs, phone in hand. "I'm calling 911."

"Don't," Colin said. "Leave the police out of this."

"Dude? Those people just tried to kill us. Of course I'm calling the police."

He let go of me and bounded toward her. "No. You'll make it worse." Neatly, he plucked the phone from her hand.

"Hey!" She shoved at him. "Did you miss the part with the guns? It can't get worse!"

"It can. If we report this and make her a target, it will."

Lena shook her head. "The alarm company will call them anyway."

"The alarm only notifies me," he replied. "No police. There are times they can't help, and this is one of them."

She looked at me. "Are you sure?"

"No police," I agreed, pulling myself up. "I'm so sorry, Lena. Are you okay?"

Her hands shook as she pushed her hair out of her face, but she said, "I'm fine. You?"

"Yeah."

"We should take you home," Colin said.

"Right. Because that won't raise any red flags, showing up at my house at"—she checked her watch—"four AM. I'll go home in the morning. Can I have my phone back?"

He studied her for a moment. "Here."

"Thank you," she said stiffly. "It's freezing in here."

"I'll get something on the windows," Colin said, pulling out his phone, no doubt calling my uncle.

"I'll make tea," I said, needing something to do. "Meet you upstairs?"

She hesitated, cutting her eyes toward Colin, then nodded. Picking my way around the glass-strewn living room, I made my way into the kitchen. The rear of the house wasn't damaged, but the alarm panel was flashing wildly. As I punched in the code, I caught sight of Colin's truck in the driveway. He must have sent the other guard home and instead stayed to watch over us himself. I refused to wonder what would have happened without him.

Mechanically, I filled the blue enameled kettle and waited for it to boil. Chamomile, I decided, getting down mugs. I stretched to get the box down from the top shelf, going up on tiptoe, not quite able to reach.

"Got it." Colin set it down, then leaned against the counter, arms folded.

"Thanks." I placed a tea bag in each cup, arranging the tags just so, keeping my back to him the whole time.

"You were supposed to go upstairs."

"I forgot." Funny how having a gun aimed at you will do that.

"Remember, next time."

"There's going to be a next time?" The kettle shrieked and I poured water into the mugs.

"We need to get you out of town for a little while."

"No." I turned around. "There's too much going on. School. Magic stuff. I can't leave."

"Screw the magic," he said. "Your life's more important."

"I'm staying." This wasn't the time to explain the two were interconnected. "It's not your call."

His eyes were weary, and the square line of his jaw clenched at my words.

"When you left for the dance, something was off. I could see it in your face. What am I missing?"

I steeled myself. "Nothing. You were right, that's all. We don't work—not while you're working for Billy. I don't see that changing, do you?"

"Mo—"

"Billy wins. I've had enough, Colin. You trust him, not me, and I can't fight that." I picked up the tea. "That's what I decided today, before the dance. That's why I was upset. Billy gets you, and I don't."

He covered my hands with his own, chamomile-scented steam curling up between us.

"Do you know how many times I've watched you almost die?" he asked, staring into the mug.

"Counting tonight? Three."

"Too many. I can't let that happen."

"You wouldn't." I thought about his family, about the little girl that was his sister, out in the world somewhere, and pulled away. "But you can't stop all the bad things. You can't save everyone. Not all the time."

"I don't care about everyone. Only you."

I thought about how he was keeping entire parts of his life secret, just to spare me. Keeping me from knowing him, shutting me out with the very noblest of intentions. He was so devoted to protecting me that he would never trust me. We'd never stood a chance.

I picked up Lena's tea and left.

Lena sat on my bed, huddled into an tattered Northwestern sweatshirt. One hand twirled her ponytail, and the other was holding the transcript of my dad's court case.

"What are you doing?" I asked, coming to a halt. Hot tea sloshed over the side of the mug and burned my hand, but I ignored it.

Lena looked up, mouth agape. "Your family is seriously messed up."

I shoved the mugs onto the dresser and snatched the file away. "That's private! What gives you the right to go through my stuff?"

"You left it on your desk," she said. "Not very private."

I paged through the papers I'd taken from her. "This is the just the trial transcript," I mumbled, shoulders dropping in relief. Colin's file was still safely tucked away in my messenger bag. My family's secrets were bad enough. I couldn't bear the thought of anyone else knowing Colin's past, especially when I'd only started uncovering it myself.

"*Just* the transcript? There's more? Have you read this?"

"Not yet." I set the stack of papers in my top drawer, shoving it closed with both hands. There weren't enough drawers to hold all my secrets these days, and I was struck with the sickening certainty that nothing I did could keep them all back. Lena's expression was pitying. "You knew what it was," I said. "Why did you keep reading?"

She threw up her hands. "Because people in masks broke in here tonight, threatened us with guns, and your reaction was to *avoid the police*. Because your bodyguard threatened to go scorched earth on the bad guys and you didn't flinch. Because I think you are in really, really big trouble, and I'm trying to be a friend."

"By snooping?"

"I'm trying to figure out what's going on with you. So I can help. That's what friends do, unless you've forgotten." She exhaled slowly, staring at the ceiling for a long moment before meeting my eyes. "Are we friends?"

I hadn't forgotten the way Lena had covered for me, more than once, without batting an eye. When everyone else had decided I was responsible for Verity's death, she'd ignored the talk and sat with me during lunch, and without making it seem like she was doing me a favor. Until tonight, she'd let me keep my secrets without a fuss. Not for the first time, I wondered what secrets she held that made her so accepting of mine.

What kind of friend would I be if she got caught in the crossfire between my uncle and Ekomov? Or attacked by Darklings? There was so much I couldn't tell her, so many things I couldn't warn her about. Then again, she could have left tonight, when Colin offered to take her home. Most people would have run screaming out the door. Lena had stayed. Maybe she could handle it. Maybe I could trust her.

"We are friends. I mean, I hope so. But my family . . ."

"You are not your family. You need to read the file."

I toyed with the drawer pull. "I'm familiar with how the story ends."

"It's not the ending," she said. "Everyone knows the ending. You need to see the beginning."

"But . . ." *I'm scared,* I wanted to say, but couldn't.

"Those guys tonight could have killed us." She shuddered

and took a sip of tea. "Someone's after you, and I am way grateful that Colin was here, but you can't keep living like this. If we find out the truth, we can find a way to fix it."

She took the second mug of tea from the dresser, carried them to my bed, and sank down onto the floor.

"Read the file, Mo. I'll keep you company."

I opened the drawer and took out the stack of papers. If my world was going to explode, better that it happen with a friend at my side.

Chapter 29

I paged through the stack of documents. Languages weren't my strong suit, and legalese was no different. "I don't even know what I'm looking for."

"A little farther back," she said, pointing. "There."

"A plea agreement? He didn't sign it. Why does this matter?"

"Read," Lena instructed.

I scanned the tiny print three times. "Still lost."

"The DA offered your dad a reduced sentence. Five years with the possibility of parole. He would have been out by the time you turned ten. All he had to do was talk."

"Talk about Billy," I mused. "And all the things they did, like launder money through Morgan's and The Slice."

"It makes sense," Lena said, pursing her lips. "You can't make a ton of money illegally and deposit it at your bank, because it gets reported to the government, and they investigate. Money launderers find a business that will report the cash as income, pay taxes, and give it back clean."

"How do you know this stuff?" I asked.

"Econ class," she said blandly. "The Slice doesn't take credit cards, right? It would be easy for your dad to make the books look like you'd taken in more money than you actually made. But they'd have to be careful. The Slice does okay, but they couldn't funnel tons of money through. They couldn't get greedy."

Colin's words floated back to me. *Billy's survived as long as he has because he's smart—he doesn't get greedy, he doesn't overreach.*

"Billy owns a lot of businesses. It's not just Morgan's and the construction company. There are others, too. He owned The Slice, before my mom took it over." He'd had a dozen opportunities to make Mob money look squeaky clean. When my dad was the accountant, it would have been even easier to hide the trail. "But my mom would never agree to it. They must have done it without her knowing."

Lena stared at the paper in front of us. "Why didn't your dad take the deal? He must have had a reason. Five years with parole is a lot less than twelve."

"I don't know." I scanned through the prosecution's cross-examination of my dad. No matter how they'd put the question, Dad was adamant—no, he didn't have help. No, he didn't work for someone else. No, there had never been any suggestion of favors for his family. No, he'd never had any dealings with Marco Forelli or anyone else in the Forelli family. Jack Fitzgerald had acted alone, and no amount of hounding, threatening, or leading by the prosecution was going to change his story.

"He was the fall guy," I said.

"The Outfit must have had leverage," Lena said, eyes troubled. "Something to keep your dad in line."

I felt a chill that had nothing to do with the window downstairs. "Us. My mom and me. And if my uncle went free . . ."

"He was in on it."

I nodded mutely, thumbing through the rest of the pages. And then I stopped, because at the end, after the transcripts of the closing arguments and the sentencing hearing, was a single piece of paper, separate from the legal documents. It was the deed to The Slice, transferring ownership from Billy to my mom. It was dated the day after my father's sentencing.

"Lena," I said, unwilling to actually touch it. "Not just leverage. A bribe."

She took the deed and read through it, hand covering her mouth. My dad wasn't the only person cutting deals before he went to prison. Mom had made one of her own. Her neat, rounded signature was right there. I'd never noticed before how similar our handwriting was. "Holy hell," she said softly.

Something moved inside me, a slow and painful grinding. I leaned my head back against the bed and let the ground shift beneath me, wondering when it would stop, wondering if there'd be anything recognizable left in the end.

CHAPTER 30

Lena cleared out early the next morning, irritated by Colin's insistence that one of Billy's guys follow her home. "Sorry," I mouthed as she left, staring daggers at Colin.

"Was that really necessary?" I asked him.

"Yes." He met my frown with cool indifference and went back to chiseling old putty out of the window frame. A few feet away, replacement panes of glass leaned against the bookshelf. "What's the plan for today?"

I thought about the file sitting in my dresser. Then I looked around my ruined living room, at the guy who would take a bullet for me.

"I'll think of something."

"Billy's pretty upset," he said over his shoulder, intent on his work. "He wants you out of town, at least for a while."

"Right. You know how much he hates it when people threaten me."

Slowly, he set the chisel down and turned to face me. "Something you want to get off your chest?"

"No." It was the truth. "How about you?"

"You're angry," he said.

I pulled the sleeves of my sweater over my hands. "I was scared."

Colin tugged at his work gloves and watched me closely. "Now you're angry. There's a difference."

I lifted a shoulder. "I have a right to be, don't you think?"

"Yeah. Promise you won't do something stupid and reckless," he said.

"Never. You know me."

He snorted and went back to work. I went upstairs and scrutinized my dad's files again, but everything read the same as it did last night. My anger mounted, but with no clear target, I felt jittery and useless. I needed to do something, and so I fished out the lone address from Colin's file and Googled it.

I don't know what I'd expected to find, but a nursing home definitely wasn't it. I zoomed in on the map, trying to figure out what combination of buses and trains would get me there fastest. There wasn't time to finish, though, because a minute later, my mom came home. My temper had found its target.

"Mo?" Her footsteps were quick taps on the stairs, and then she was in my room, all fluttering hands and ineffective bustle. She gathered me up in a hug, but I didn't let myself relax against her. "I should never have left you here alone! Billy should have called me the minute it happened. You must have been so scared. And your friend was here! I can only imagine what she's going to tell people. Thank God for Colin." She paused for breath, finally noticed my silence. "Are you hurt, honey? Colin said no one was hurt. Are you okay?"

"How's Dad?" I asked, barely recognizing my own voice.

"He's fine, sweetie. Excited to come home. He can't wait to see you." She toyed with the buttons at her sleeve. "Billy's going to fix this. Just watch."

"I've watched enough." I straightened the stack of papers in front of me. "Tell me about Dad's trial."

Her mouth thinned, lines radiating outward in disapproval. "Daddy's coming home soon. Why focus on the past?"

"Uncle Billy was charged, too."

"It was a witch hunt." She began straightening the books

on my bookshelf, making sure the spines lined up perfectly. "The district attorney was out to get him. Daddy, too. They dismissed the charges."

"Billy's. But not Dad's."

"No. Daddy wanted to give us a better life. He went about it the wrong way, and he's so, so sorry, honey. But he's repented, served his time. It's over now."

"You can't believe that. People broke into our house last night. With guns. Does that seem over to you?"

"I don't like your tone. I told you, your uncle will take care of it."

"Right. And he takes care of everything because why, exactly?"

"We're family," she said tightly, twisting her wedding band around her finger. "That's what we do. Take care of each other."

"The DA offered Dad a deal. He could have been out years ago. Why didn't he take it?"

"Where is this coming from?" She shook her head. "It doesn't matter. We got through it. You and me, the Fitzgerald Girls. It wasn't so bad, was it?"

"Billy leaned on Dad, right? Did they threaten you? Me?"

"Billy would never threaten us. How do you think we've managed all this time? Your father was going to jail. There was no escaping that. There were records, tax returns. They had proof. If Billy had gone to jail, we would have been on our own. The restaurant wouldn't have been enough to support the two of us, to give you the life we wanted for you. And there was no one else, no other family to help. Should I have sent my husband *and* my brother to prison? We would have been alone."

"So Dad took the fall." And Billy signed over The Slice to my mom, like hush money.

She whirled, color high. "We had you to think of! I tried to tell you before, sweetheart. Sometimes you have to give up the life you want in order to protect the people you love."

"I lost him for twelve years. *Twelve.* So you could keep a

restaurant. And Billy kept everything." I grabbed my messenger bag and shoved the assorted files inside. "I'm going out."

"Honey, wait!"

I ignored her, nearly tripping down the stairs in my hurry to be gone, shoving my feet into my shoes, grabbing a coat and scarf from the closet.

Colin had just finished the second window, cleaning his tools and carefully replacing them in the box.

"Going somewhere?" He set down the rag he was using. "I don't think—"

"I don't care," I snapped, and headed out the back door, not waiting to hear the rest of the sentence. He was just another thing Billy had taken from me.

It's a lot easier to storm off when you're actually allowed to be alone for longer than five minutes. I hadn't gotten much farther than the alley before Colin caught up with me.

"What the hell is your problem?" He put his hand on my shoulder, and I knocked it away.

"You *knew*."

"Knew what?"

"About my dad's trial. You knew, this entire time. And you never said a word."

I shoved my fists into the pockets of my coat and continued walking. Colin kept pace with me, and out of the corner of my eye I could see his scuffed leather work boots and jean-clad legs flashing in a steady rhythm.

The air was sharp, spicy with the scent of burning leaves, and I resisted the urge to scuff my feet through the piles of russet and gold lining the sidewalk. This was the street I'd lived on my whole life. I'd trick-or-treated at these houses. I'd learned to ride my bike here, my mom running beside me with one hand on the seat until I'd begged her to let go. My life here was what had sent my dad to prison. My feet carried me automatically toward The Slice, and I braced for Colin's explanation, knowing it wouldn't be enough.

"Billy asked me not to tell you," he finally said.

"Screw what Billy wants!" I might not have a right to Colin's past, but I had every right to my own.

"What could you have done? They wanted to keep you out of it."

"To protect me."

"Yes."

"Because I'm too stupid and weak to protect myself?"

"Hey." He grabbed my arm and forced me around. "I know exactly how smart you are. And I've seen you in action—there's nothing weak about you. But you can't fault the people who love you for trying to keep you safe."

My stomach did a strange, tumbling dance. "The people who love me?"

He curled a finger around the lapel of my coat. "Yeah."

I twisted free. "The people who love me have a really crappy way of showing it." No matter what he said, his past stood between us, a hulking, shadowy thing.

"Here's what you need to understand." He sounded exhausted. He must have stayed up all night, guarding the house. "People think you have power. They will tell you what you want to hear, show you what you want to see, in order to get it. Everyone wants something from you, but they're not always going to be up-front about it."

"Even you?"

"What do you think?" he asked as we stopped in front of Morgan's carved oak doors.

"I think it's time Billy and I had a chat."

Colin blocked my path inside. "How'd that work out last time?"

"This is different."

"It's the same. You think you're going to outmaneuver Billy. It won't happen. He might let you think you've won, but trust me—he's playing on a much bigger board than you. Besides," he added, "You've got a visitor."

He jerked his chin toward the window of The Slice. From our position on the sidewalk, I could just see Luc in the corner booth, building a miniature castle out of sugar packets.

When he noticed me staring, he knocked it over with a flick of his finger and raised his mug in a mock toast.

"Are you coming in?" I asked.

"Lost my appetite," Colin said.

Luc rose as I stepped inside. I waved to the waitress on duty, my mouth suddenly too dry to speak. My coat seemed stifling, and I tried to unbutton it as I made my way toward him. My hands were clumsy, and then Luc's long, elegant fingers were on the buttons, maneuvering them with practiced ease. Jealousy flared—how exactly had he gotten so good at helping girls out of their clothes?

"Cold," he said, eyebrows raised. "You're all pink."

"I walked." He nodded. I expected him to kiss me, but he only touched his thumb to the center of my lower lip, forehead creased with concern.

"Brought you some company." He gestured toward the booth.

"Company?" I leaned to look around him.

Jenny Kowalski smiled up at me, not at all friendly. "You probably don't need a menu, do you?"

CHAPTER 31

Luc slipped my coat from my shoulders and placed it in the far corner, then waited for me to sit, sliding close to press his leg along mine. He draped an arm around my shoulders and smiled approvingly at both of us. He'd left sugar packets all over the table, and I busied myself, putting them back neatly in the black plastic box, sorting out pink and yellow and white as I went.

"Stopped by your house this mornin', saw Jenny on the porch talking with your mom."

I crumpled a packet of artificial sweetener. "You came by my house?" I asked her. "My uncle will freak if he finds out."

"Why? According to you, he's totally innocent."

I reached for Luc's water and drank deeply.

"Your uncle's guys were all over the place, putting a new front door in," Jenny added. "Your mom didn't say what happened."

No, she wouldn't. If there was one skill my family had mastered, it was not answering potentially awkward questions. And Luc wasn't too bad at it, either, because he cut in. "Figured any friend of yours was a friend of mine. Offered to buy her a cup of coffee while we waited for you."

"Fabulous. Have we done the formal introductions yet? Jenny, this is Luc. Luc, meet Jenny. *Kowalski*."

"The cop's daughter?" His expression turned kind. "I'm sorry."

Jenny nodded, blinking rapidly. One of the weekend wait-
resses, her blond pixie cut streaked crimson, set down two
pieces of pie and a cup of coffee. She looked pointedly from
me to Luc and flashed a quick smile.

After she'd left, I focused on Jenny again. "Who are you
working with?"

"I can't tell you that."

"Then I can't help you. What if you're working for someone just as corrupt as my uncle?"

She leaned across the table, knocking over the saltshaker.
"I am *not*. They're good people. They want to make this city
better, and that includes putting your murderer of an uncle in
jail."

"Nothing in those files even hints Billy had something to
do with your dad's death."

Luc frowned. "You think Mo's uncle killed your daddy?"

"It makes sense," she insisted. "There's no other explanation."

"It's neat," he agreed. "Wrong, but neat."

She glanced at him. "What do you know about it?"

The last thing I needed was Jenny deciding Luc deserved
his own file. "What are you after?" I asked. "I can't help you
prove something that's not true."

"My dad . . ." She began to shred her napkin. "My dad
wanted to take your uncle down. It didn't start out personal.
Billy Grady's a cog in the Chicago Machine. Take out enough
cogs and the whole machine breaks down. But he spent his
entire career watching your uncle in action. He saw enough
people hurt, and he made it his life's work, putting Billy
Grady behind bars."

"And you're going to finish it," Luc said. It wasn't a question, and a bit of the fight went out of her shoulders as she
nodded. "To honor him. You can respect that, can't you,
Mouse?"

I knew he was talking about Verity, and I elbowed him.
"This is not the same."

"Sure it is." He rubbed the back of my neck, working out

the knots that had taken up permanent residence there. "Perhaps you're gainin' a bit of sympathy for my position."

"Don't be smug," I said, trying to keep from sinking into his touch. I couldn't deny the similarities. He'd known the truth of Verity's death even as I'd raged and grieved, only telling me when there was no other choice. Now I had the answers, and Jenny was the one running into dead ends. I was just as loathe to explain as he had been.

"Same as what?" Jenny asked, eyes darting back and forth.

"Ignore him." I wasn't going to stonewall Jenny completely. She deserved better—Kowalski deserved better, I thought with a pang. He used to sit in this exact booth, dogged and decent, and I wondered if Jenny had chosen this spot on purpose. "My uncle didn't have anything to do with your dad, and trying to prove it is a waste of time. But the rest of it, taking Billy down . . . I'll do what I can to help."

Jenny dropped what remained of the napkin. "You will?"

"On two conditions. One, you leave Colin Donnelly out of it. That file never goes public. No one ever hears about it."

"He's part of the organization. I can't guarantee that."

"Then we're done." I nudged Luc, who obligingly scooted out of the booth. "You can pay at the register."

"Wait. Fine. We bury Colin's file." She glanced out the window. Colin was hunched over a cup of coffee, collar turned up against the wind. He was deliberately keeping his back to The Slice, no doubt to avoid seeing me with Luc. "Guess that clears up what the deal is with you guys."

Standing at the edge of the table, Luc went still. I kept my eyes on Jenny.

"You have no idea what the deal is. But you leave him alone. The second condition is that if I tell you to back off something, you do. If I say something is a dead end, you leave it. It's for your own protection."

"This sounds like a lot of rules. What are you going to do to help?"

I took a breath, an idea forming in my head. If I was very careful, and very, very lucky, I might be able to handle Yuri

Ekomov and Billy at the same time. "I'm working on it. I'll let you know."

She sifted the bits of torn-up napkin through her fingers, considering. "Why are you doing this?"

"Does it matter?"

"Not really." She stood and pulled on a polar fleece hat and jacket, frowning as she studied Luc. "I still don't get you, though."

"Nobody does," he said cheerfully, waving as she left.

I elbowed Luc. "Move."

He did—in the opposite direction, the length of his body pressing up against mine, knee to shoulder. The contact sent a pleasant tremor through me, but I still felt awkward, uncertain how to act after our kiss last night. At least Jenny had provided a buffer.

"Why did you bring her here?"

He shrugged. "Didn't know she was the cop's daughter. What's in the files she's talkin' about?"

"Family stuff."

"And dirt on Cujo?" When I didn't respond, he nodded slowly. "Tell me 'bout the sudden remodel."

"We had a break-in." My voice sounded rusty, and I took a sip of water. "Did anyone see you at my house?"

"Give me some credit," he said. "Wouldn't be half-bad to introduce me to the family. Make it easier for us to spend time together."

"My family is not going to be super enthusiastic about me bringing home new friends right now."

He turned my hand palm up and lightly traced my scar. "You okay?"

"They didn't hurt me."

"Ain't what I asked," he said, and waited. Whatever urge I'd had to lie, to fake brave long enough to *feel* brave, vanished. I shook my head, the tiniest bit, and finally met his eyes.

"Didn't think so." He kissed my forehead, my cheeks, the tip of my nose, disarmingly gentle. I settled back against his chest as his fingers laced with mine. For the first time since the break-in, the ground beneath me felt solid.

"Vee told me about your family," he said. "She knew it made things hard for you. She worried it would be a problem, after she'd gone, and you'd have to deal with them on your own."

"Gone?"

"She wasn't coming back, Mouse. Once she came to New Orleans, to stop the Torrent, take up her place . . . that was it. No more regular life."

I sat up again. "She came back, though. So did Evangeline."

"Temporary. Told you before, there's not a lot of minglin' between the two worlds." He waved a hand, like he was brushing away the words. "This is what got us in trouble last night. Ain't any more fun in daylight."

He was right about that, anyway. "Why were you looking for me this morning?"

"Wanted to see you, mostly."

"Mmn-hmn. What else?"

Just then, the waitress came back and handed me the cordless phone. "Special order," she said. "They asked for you."

"Hello?"

"Mo, it's Edie, at Shady Acres."

My stomach dropped.

"I'm sorry to bother you," she continued. "One of our residents is concerned about an order he placed. Mr. Eckert?"

The only order Mr. Eckert—or Mr. Ekomov, or whatever he expected me to call him—had given was to send armed men to my house in the middle of the night. Cold fury seeped through my veins.

"I don't think we can help."

"Are you sure? He seems to think there was a misunderstanding. He'd be happy to talk to you directly."

"No misunderstanding. We don't have anything for him."

Without waiting for her response, I hung up.

"Problem?" Luc asked.

"All taken care of."

"Want me to take you home?"

"No." I tucked my hand in my pocket and found the directions to the nursing home I'd printed out earlier. "But if you're up for it, there's somewhere else I need to go."

CHAPTER 32

St. Mary of the Angels nursing home smelled exactly like you'd expect—heavy-duty antiseptic and something that had moved past ripening to decay, sickly sweet. The smell of bodies failing. I rubbed at my nose, but the odor remained. In the past few months, every death I'd seen was violent, sudden, unnatural in every sense of the word. But here, it was people gradually fading away from old age and illness and neglect. I wasn't sure which was worse.

Still, they were trying to make it as pleasant as they could. Classical music played softly in the background, and the walls were decorated with soothing impressionist paintings. Aides in cheerily printed scrubs chatted with their elderly patients as they wheeled them around. Occasionally, you'd see someone shuffle down a hallway, leaning heavily on a walker or buzzing past in a motorized wheelchair.

Luc took it all in. "Tell me again what we're up to?"

"There's something here. Someone. It's important." Important enough that I'd asked him to conceal us so we could slip out of The Slice unnoticed, then took a series of CTA buses and trains north. He'd grumbled about the hour-long trip but didn't suggest going Between.

"Why do you need me along? Can't you just ask them?"

"There are privacy rules. They won't give out patient information to just anyone. I need to sneak in."

"Oh, this should be entertainin'."

I rammed my elbow into his gut and he wheezed.

Satisfied, I pasted a smile on my face and approached the front desk. "I'm here visiting my grandma?" I said, tilting the end of every sentence up to make it sound like a question. "She has an appointment tomorrow? With a specialist at Northwestern? And they want us to bring, like, all of her records?"

The woman behind the desk barely looked up from her computer solitaire game. "That's Jeannie's department."

"And her office is . . ."

"Left corridor, first right, second door. Next to the director's office," she said, moving one stack of cards to another. "But the records department is closed on weekends. You'll have to come back tomorrow."

Perfect. "Thanks," I said, and walked back over to Luc. She nodded absently and started a new game.

"Liar," Luc said, impressed. "I kind of like this side of you. Naughty."

I rolled my eyes. "Just make me invisible." The air shimmered and settled as he concealed us.

He kept his hand tight around mine as we moved down the hall. "This place is horrifyin'."

"Arcs don't have nursing homes?"

"We take care of our own," he said as an aide lumbered by, pushing a tiny old woman with clouded eyes in a wheelchair. "Nothin' homey about this place."

"It's not so bad," I said. "I've seen worse ones, on field trips for school."

Luc shuddered.

We stopped outside the records office and peered in the small window. The lock on the door was one of the fancy electronic ones; you needed a key card. "Can you do something about that?" I asked.

He raised an eyebrow. "Won't be subtle."

Ten feet away, the door to the director's office was firmly shut, but a hand-painted wooden sign declared it open. "I'll settle for quiet."

He shrugged and covered the lock with his free hand, lips moving silently. There was a popping sound and the smell of plastic burning, and the device fell away. He handed it to me as the door swung open. "We can discuss how you want to show your gratitude later," he said, shoving me through the doorway.

"I'll send you a thank-you note." After dropping his hand, I tucked the melted card reader inside my bag and headed for the lateral file cabinet.

What had Jenny—or rather, Jenny's source—wanted me to find here? Out of all the people in Colin's past, who could possibly be stashed in a nursing home?

"Gaskill, Raymond," I murmured, flipping through files until I reached the Gs.

"Who's Gaskill?" Luc asked from his post by the doorway.

"A very bad man." I scanned the neatly labeled file folders.

"You seem to know a lot of those."

"I don't know him at all." Nothing. I double-checked, but it wasn't there. I was still missing something. "Damn."

"This is about Cujo, right? You're digging into all the stuff he doesn't want you to?"

My secrets, Colin had said. *Mine.* And Billy, so confident: *It's not only his life he's concerned with.*

"Donnelly," I said softly. "Not Gaskill."

An odd, scuttling sense whispered across my neck, and it had nothing to do with magic.

Luc crossed the room, putting his hand atop mine as I reached for the cabinet labeled A–E. "You ever heard the story of Pandora's box?"

"Of course. She couldn't resist seeing what was inside and let out all the evil in the world. Subtle, Luc."

"Never seen Cujo tell you no, 'less he was trying to protect you. Could be you want to take a minute before you knock the lid off this box. Man's always looking out for you."

"Maybe it's time I looked out for him," I said, yanking open the drawer.

"Dinsmore . . . Donaldson . . . Donnelly." I snatched up the

folder. Along the spine were stickers indicating the year—
eleven of them. I looked at the name again.

"Hello, Tess."

Luc ran a hand through his hair. "You found it?"

I opened the file. "Colin's little sister is a patient here."

"Little sister? How old is she?"

"Seventeen."

"What's a seventeen-year-old girl doing in an old folk's
home?" He sounded appalled.

"Hiding." I paged through the folder, my hands shaky.
Tess Donnelly, seventeen, catatonic for the last eleven years.
According to the staff psychiatrist, her condition was partly
physical, a result of the massive head injuries she'd sustained
as a child, and partly psychological, a defense against the
abuse she'd suffered and the night of Raymond Gaskill's final
attack.

I turned to her intake papers. An eleven-year-old Colin
couldn't have been the one to bring her here, no matter how
desperate he was to protect her. He'd had help. And there,
under "Responsible Party," was the name I'd been expecting
all along.

William Grady.

My uncle had rescued the two remaining Donnellys, and
he'd been providing for Tess ever since.

It wasn't fear keeping Colin loyal. It was love.

I didn't know what to feel. The truth wasn't going to set
anyone free. I couldn't help Tess, and Billy could. It wasn't
even a question of whom Colin would choose. What kind of
person would ask him to?

"Time to go," I said, struggling to keep my voice level.

"Already?" He plucked the file out of my hand and
scanned it. "She's in room 433. Don't you want to see her?"

I'd seen enough for one day.

CHAPTER 33

"You're planning something," Colin said as I set the dinner table that night. I'd managed to avoid him all afternoon, sending him a quick text when Luc and I had returned from the nursing home. He'd stuck around since then, finishing up repairs from the break-in while I hid in my room.

"Why would you say that?" I laid out napkins, adjusting them precisely so I could keep my face turned away.

He ticked his reasons off on his fingers. "One, you and Luc snuck away from The Slice this afternoon, to God only knows where. That's never a good sign. Two, you came home acting like the fight with your mom never happened. You're working an angle and you need her in a good mood. Three . . ." He trailed off, and I finally looked up, curious.

"What?"

"I can practically see the wheels turning in your brain. Does this have to do with the Arcs?"

I skirted the table, lining up silverware, trying to explain without showing my hand. "I set a bunch of things in motion, didn't I? The Russians, Billy trying to prove his loyalty to Marco Forelli? Even Kowalski's death, because people think Billy and the Mob are involved."

"You just need to keep your head down a little longer," he said. "Let it all blow over. We'll get you to New York, get you clear of it."

"I'll never be clear of it. You know that. I wanted the truth, Colin. Now I have to decide what to do with it." I didn't mention that it was his truth I'd discovered today.

Before he could reply, my mom came bustling back into the room. She was going all-out with dinner tonight, which was her standard response to stress: cook, clean, make everything as perfect as possible.

"Did you have a nice time with Lena?" she asked, peering into the oven.

"With Lena?" I asked. Colin nudged me. "Oh. Totally, yeah. Great time."

The realization he'd covered for me while I'd been digging around in his past made my mouth taste stale with shame.

"I imagine she thinks it'll be quite the story to tell at school." My mom shook the salad dressing more vigorously than necessary.

"Lena's not going to tell people. She's my friend."

Mom eased up on the dressing. Her hands were almost steady as she poured it over the salad and threw in croutons. "I'm glad. You need to make a friend or two, like that Jenny girl. There hasn't been anyone since . . ."

Amazing how many things my family was conditioned not to talk about. Freewheeling conversation was not something we did.

"I meant to ask—were you able to fix my computer?"

"Yeah, this afternoon. You should be all set. I didn't have the backup disks, though, so I couldn't restore the files."

She waved a hand. "I'll take care of the backups Monday. They're at the restaurant."

I knew they were, under lock and key. All her finances, and the books for my uncle, too.

"You've been so busy lately."

I thought about the old hard drive, duct-taped to the back of my dresser so she wouldn't find it, the trip to the nursing home, my work with the Quartoren. "I have. But I was thinking . . ." I snuck a quick look at Colin, who held up his hands in a gesture of "leave me out of this." "I want to go see Dad."

The salad tongs slipped from her hands, clattering against the side of the bowl. "See Daddy?"

"I should have gone with you. I feel bad about it now."

Her eyes grew shiny. "What about missing school? What will your teachers say?"

"They'll understand. Like you said, it's family. I can do all my homework tomorrow, after church. If I go down to Terre Haute on Monday morning, I could be back late that night. I'd only miss one day."

Behind me, Colin drummed his fingers. I didn't have to turn around to know he was glowering.

"Honey, I just left The Slice for two days. I can't turn around and leave again, not with all the special orders for Thanksgiving coming up. Maybe we could go Thanksgiving weekend. We'd have more time together, the three of us."

I crossed my arms over my chest. "You said you wanted me to spend time with Dad. Now I'm trying, and you won't let me."

She frowned as she pulled the pan of chicken parmesan out of the oven. "I'm glad you want to see your father, but you haven't thought this through. How will you get down there?"

I paused, like I was actually thinking about it. "I guess . . . Colin could drive me, maybe. If it's not too much trouble."

He set his glass down so hard that water sloshed over the rim. Smiling as innocently as I could, I passed him a towel. He didn't smile back.

"Colin?" My mom wiped her hands on her apron. "It's a big favor to ask. But . . ."

I fixed my eyes on the tablecloth, trying to appear wistful.

"It would mean the world to Mo's father," she said. "She's changed so much since he saw her last."

Um, yeah. I'd been thirteen the last time I went to Terre Haute.

"I'm sure she has," he said grimly. I didn't dare look at him, much less breathe. When he heaved a sigh, I exhaled, too. "Yeah. I can take her."

Mom clasped her hands. "Thank you, Colin. I can't tell you . . . The look on Daddy's face when he sees you," she added, sweeping me up in a hug.

I caught sight of my reflection in the window over the sink, pale and unsmiling. Four years since I'd seen my father. It felt more like four lifetimes.

If my mom had been any more delighted at dinner, she would have burst into song. I was making every effort to seem just as cheerful and excited, like this visit was really triggered by a sudden desire to restore family harmony. Inside, I was trying to figure out the best way to approach my dad. Four years was, admittedly, a long time to go without a visit. Mom could be wrong. He might be so resentful about my absence that he wouldn't want to help me. Or maybe he'd be remorseful and do whatever he could to help. Maybe— and this was the possibility that turned my meal to sawdust in my mouth—maybe he was still loyal to Billy and Marco Forelli.

Colin, meanwhile, tucked away his food and stayed quiet, only speaking when my mom posed a direct question. The rest of the time, he studied me, questions brewing the entire time. I wondered if he'd wait until Monday to ask them, but after I'd cleared the table, he shooed my mom out.

"You cooked," he said firmly. "The least Mo and I can do is wash up."

She patted his cheek. "You are a credit to your mother," she said, and if I hadn't been looking for it, I wouldn't have seen the flash of pain across his features. "I'm going to catch up on some paperwork. Let me know when you're ready for dessert."

I loaded the dishwasher as Colin lounged against the counter, arms crossed, mouth turned down.

"Well?"

"Well, what?" I scrubbed baked-on cheese and tried to sound innocent.

He kept his voice low. "Don't try to tell me you're looking to mend fences with your dad."

I considered lying to him for about a tenth of a second, but it was foolish. Nobody knew me the way Colin did. Besides, he deserved better. "Billy isn't going to tell me the truth. My mom certainly isn't. I'm not sure she even knows what the truth is. My dad's the only one who can tell me everything."

"What makes you think he will?"

"I'm his daughter."

"Yeah, and he committed perjury for you. He went to federal prison to protect you. If you're looking for the cold, hard truth, he's hardly the one to ask."

I faced him full-on, hands on hips. "In the last few months, I have witnessed a murder, been threatened by the Outfit, received flowers from a Russian gangster, and had men with guns break into my house. Whatever protection I got when my dad went to prison is all used up."

"Let's say he tells you the truth—which I don't believe he will—but let's say he does. What are you looking to do with it?"

"It's like you said. Everyone wants something from me: Billy, Forelli, Ekomov. And they'll lie to get it. But my dad . . . he has no reason to lie anymore. He's the only one who can give me the truth, and once he does, I'll know what I need to do."

"Stop. You cannot go up against Forelli. Billy's bad enough, but at least he's family. He can make your life harder, but he won't hurt you. You make trouble, Marco Forelli will have no problem hurting you. The people you love. You've seen how easily he got to your family and friends. Do you think that's changed?"

"No. But I'm done letting other people control my life." Everything was speeding out of control, like a runaway freight train—my family, the Russians, the Covenant—and I was absolutely certain that if I didn't act soon, there'd be no stopping the catastrophe ahead. "You said you wanted me to get clear of this. That's what I'm trying to do."

He laid a hand on my shoulder. "Taking on the Mob was not what I had in mind, and you know it."

"Are you two ready for dessert?" Mom called.

I stepped away from Colin and busied myself putting the last of the pots and pans away.

"I'm going to pass," he said, giving my mom a rueful smile. "Get ready for Monday. Billy's assigned someone to watch the house at night, by the way, but you won't see him unless there's a problem."

"Thank you," my mom said softly. We waited in the kitchen as he set the alarm and stalked to the truck, exchanging a quick word with someone in a nondescript Buick.

"Sit," she said. "Have some dessert."

Warily, I settled in at the table as she fixed tea and brownies. The way she'd forgotten our fight, agreed to let me go . . . I should have known it wouldn't be that simple.

"Last week you were a little girl. Remember how you used to skin your knees all the time? I thought you'd go around with holes in your tights forever." She traced the patterned tabletop with a finger. "And now you're practically grown. Going to see your father, turning things around at school. I know pride's a sin, but I can't help being proud of you."

I tried not to squirm. Next she'd be talking about how great it would be to have my dad home again, and I'd have to play along. She cleared her throat. "Your uncle was worried, you know."

"About what?"

"That you might have a little . . . crush . . . on Colin."

My cheeks went hot, and I pushed the brownie away. "*Please* tell me you and Uncle Billy are not discussing my love life."

"Not your love life," she soothed. "Just Colin."

I covered my face with my hands. "Mom. Stop."

"He's a handsome young man. And he's spent so much

time with us, it would be easy for you to misread his attention. I know he seems exciting, and you haven't had many boyfriends. But he's led a much different life than you."

"Mom . . ." I wanted to curl up in a ball, I was so embarrassed.

"I'm grateful to Colin. He's kept you safe these last few months, and given you someone to talk to. I just don't want you getting your hopes up. Besides, you should focus your energies on school. There'll be plenty of time for boys later."

"Later," I said, thinking of Luc at the dance.

She patted my hand. "I told Billy you were too sensible for that kind of thing, but you know how protective he is. You'd better get ready for Monday. I'll clean up."

CHAPTER 34

My mom stayed late Monday morning to see me off. Normally, she was gone before four-thirty, to open The Slice, but apparently my first solo prison visit was the sort of special occasion that merited a late start.

"I didn't want you to get hungry on the road," she said, handing me a Tupperware container of scones. "Should I fix a thermos of coffee?"

"You baked? Seriously?"

Her smile dimmed. With quick, nervous movements, she smoothed down my hair and brushed nonexistent dust from my coat. Colin's truck pulled up outside the new picture window. "He's here!"

"I can see that." Colin ambled up the walk, hands stuffed in the pockets of his sheepskin-lined jacket. He looked surly—surlier than usual, but it suited him.

"Give him a scone," she said. "And be nice. This is a kind thing he's doing."

"I'm always nice," I pointed out.

"Don't be lippy," she said, and practically shoved me out the door. "Give your father my love! Tell him we'll come out Thanksgiving weekend! I love you!"

"You too," I said, hurrying down the sidewalk to meet Colin halfway.

"She made scones," I explained as he took the container. "She's very excited."

"Great. Billy is not."

"You told him?" I should have expected it, but the news still set me on edge. "What did he say?"

"He's not buying the idea you had a change of heart about your dad, that's for damn sure. I told him you thought the attack Friday had something to do with him, so you were going to give him hell."

"And?"

"He found that slightly more believable. He also doesn't mind the notion of getting you out of town, even if it's just for a day."

"Why is that?"

"I assume because he's not thrilled about Ekomov's guys breaking down your door. There are going to be repercussions, and he doesn't want you around for them."

I didn't ask what he meant by "repercussions."

It was strange to drive south and leave the city behind. The rows of closely nestled bungalows gave way to warehouses, factories, train yards, and then the city retreated, leaving suburban houses in their wake, with sprawling yards and trampolines, upscale malls and big box stores.

"Scone?" I said eventually.

He took one, crumbs sprinkling down the front of his shirt. "You never said why Luc came by."

"To visit, I guess." He'd tracked me down for some reason, I was sure. But once he'd heard about the break-in, he'd seemed reluctant to bring up the Covenant or anything Arc related. Like he didn't want to add to my problems.

"And the two of you . . ."

I curled my hands in my lap and watched as the suburbs gave way to industrial parks and cornfields.

"Right," he said under his breath. "Have they figured out how you can fix the magic?"

"We've got some ideas," I said, not wanting to clarify.

"Dangerous ideas?"

I bit my lip.

"I'm coming with."

"They won't like that," I said quietly.

"I did it before. I can do it again."

"This is different. It's the Quartoren, and they don't like Flats."

"You're Flat."

"They don't like me. They need me." Which made them hate me even more. I wondered why I hadn't seen it before—it wasn't only that I was Flat, or that I'd killed Evangeline and caused all this trouble. It was the fact that the power to save them was tied up inside someone they'd always considered a lesser life form. It was like poker, and the aces were being wasted on someone who didn't know how to play.

The time for sitting back and watching everyone else act was over. It was time to play the game.

"What does Billy want from me?" I asked, trying to turn Colin's attention away from Luc and the Quartoren.

"To stay out of his way," Colin said automatically. "Barring that, he wants you to help him keep his position with Forelli. He thinks you could feed the Russians false information."

I'd refused to lie to the police. Billy must have assumed I'd be less particular about the bad guys. "What did you say?"

"You're too unpredictable. And a lousy liar. They'd see through you in a heartbeat."

For some reason, this was vaguely insulting. "I fooled my mom."

"Your mother is emotionally invested in believing you. Yuri Ekomov would never buy it. It's too dangerous. I want you far away from the whole thing."

I thought about Tess, tucked away in the nursing home, and my mom, working so hard to make everything seem normal. Hiding had appealed to me once, but not anymore.

"Look, I know it's your job, but you can't protect me from everything. It's not even possible."

"I can try," he said. "And I'm not doing it because it's my job."

I didn't know what to say to that. We kept driving, past

cornfields cut down to stubble and acres of yellowing soy-
beans. The land was so empty and open, I felt dizzy, like I
was losing my balance.

My vertigo increased, and I pressed my hands against the
dash. I'd never been carsick in my life, but it seemed like a
distinct possibility now. Just as I was about to say something,
the check engine light came on.

"Damn." He peered farther down the road. "Eight miles
to the next gas station. I think we can make it."

"Do you know what's wrong?" Casually, I leaned against
the window, the cold glass soothing against my cheek.

"No. I just changed the oil, checked everything over last
night when I got home."

He cocked his head to the side, listening to the engine. I
couldn't hear anything except the whir of the wheels on
pavement.

"It sounds fine," he said after a moment. "We'll check it
out at the gas station."

I nodded, biting my lip, trying to envision my life away
from Chicago. It was a trick I'd learned—it was easier to en-
dure Jill McAllister and her snide comments when I was
imagining my life in New York. Right now, though, the picture in my head refused to focus.

"Before Verity died, did you know who I was?"

"Sure. I was at Morgan's a lot. I came to The Slice, too,
sometimes."

"How come I never saw you?"

"I'm good at not being noticed."

Of course he was. He'd spent his childhood trying to escape the notice of Raymond Gaskill. It wasn't shyness, it was
a survival technique. One he was trying to instill in me.

"If I leave," I asked, "if I go to New York . . . do you go,
too?"

"You probably wouldn't need a bodyguard there. If you
did, Billy would assign you a new one."

"Why?"

"I'm not leaving Chicago, Mo. Ever."

I knew why. Tess. I'd known his answer before I'd ever posed the question. What I really wanted was for him to confide in me, to give me the truth freely instead of my ferreting it out from police reports and newspaper clippings. The disappointment made my head ache worse.

"What if I stayed?" The question slipped out before I'd realized it. He'd made it clear we had no future. And whether I accepted my place with the Arcs or struck out on my own, I had no intention of remaining in Chicago. But something—the need to hold on to something steady amid the turbulence, maybe—made me ask.

Whatever the reason, once I'd said the words, they couldn't be taken back. Colin's hand reached for mine, and then he swore, yanking the wheel to the right. We'd nearly missed our exit, and the truck bumped over the shoulder as we veered off the highway.

It was one of those tiny farm towns with a gas station, a McDonald's, and no traffic lights. Down the road, I saw a group of tall silos, a bunch of machinery in front of them. We pulled into the gas station and sat, staring at each other. His hands gripped the wheel, knuckles white. After a minute, I said, "Forget I asked."

He forced a laugh. "Not likely."

I flushed and reached for the door handle. "I'm getting a drink. Do you want something?"

"Water, thanks." He climbed out and popped the hood, glancing around the deserted gas station. The bell above the mini-mart door jingled cheerfully.

"Son of a bitch," Colin muttered, and I peered around the raised hood of the truck.

Luc sauntered across the parking lot, sharp and sleek in a black leather jacket.

"Car trouble?" he asked, mischief lighting his eyes. "Maybe I can lend a hand."

CHAPTER 35

"It's a summons from the Quartoren," Luc said as Colin glowered. "No arguments, no uninvited guests."

Colin slammed the hood down, narrowly missing Luc's fingers. "Either I'm along for the ride or we're getting in the truck and heading straight for Terre Haute."

Luc shook his head. "Look, I respect what you're trying to do. Any other time, you want to play guard dog, I could appreciate it. But this ain't my call."

Colin ignored him. "Get in the truck, Mo."

"How's that working for you?" Luc asked. "Orderin' Mouse around? Had a lot of success?"

"We need to get back on the road or we'll miss visiting hours," Colin said.

Luc scoffed. "That truck won't move 'less I say so. And I don't."

"Enough!" I slapped a hand on each guy's chest and shoved. "Luc, fix the engine. Please."

"Mouse . . ."

"Fix it. Now. Colin is off-limits to you. Understand? Don't mess with the truck, or him . . . leave him alone."

"You're making that demand quite a bit these days," he said. Colin eyed me strangely, but I shot Luc a glare my mom would have been proud of, and he crooked a finger. The truck roared to life. "Happy?"

"Not even close," I said. "Can you please stand there and try not to piss anyone off?"

"Doesn't exactly play to my strengths," he pointed out, slouching against the gas pump.

I turned to Colin. "His delivery could use a little work, but he's right. If the Quartoren are summoning me, I have to go."

"What about your dad?"

"Give me a minute to think." I circled the truck, trying to keep warm while I weighed the options. As I paced, Luc watched me, a half smile playing over his face. Colin watched Luc, not smiling at all. "I'll call my mom. We'll tell her the truck broke down outside Indianapolis, and we can't get to the prison before visiting hours are over. We'll stay overnight and go see my dad in the morning."

"Can I listen in when you tell her we're spending the night together?" Colin asked.

Luc stopped smiling.

"We'll get two rooms," I said. "You will, anyway. I'll be dealing with the Quartoren, and Luc will bring me back to the hotel when it's over."

"That's just about the stupidest plan you've ever come up with," Colin said.

I bristled. "Do you have a better one?"

"I do, as a matter of fact. You tell Luc to fuck off and we go see your dad, like we planned."

"You're not listening. I don't have a choice this time."

"Why?"

I swallowed and said the thing I knew would anger him most. "Because they'll kill me. It's part of the deal I made. If I don't fix the magic, they'll kill me."

He went so still, I wondered if his heart had stopped. I knotted my fingers together, the words falling like stones into the silence. "They put up with me because they have to. They won't tolerate you."

He lunged at Luc, shoving him back a few steps. "You let her do this? What the hell is wrong with you?"

Luc shoved back, but it was the red sparks hovering around his hands that really worried me. "*Let* her? You think she asked permission?" He scoffed. "Maybe you haven't noticed, but that's not really her style these days."

"Stop!" I grabbed the sleeve of Colin's jacket and tried to pull him away. "Colin, come on. It wasn't his call. It was mine. Completely mine."

He turned to stare at me. Then he scrubbed a hand through his hair, the ends sticking up in every direction, and started for the truck.

"Give us a minute," I said to Luc.

"Quartoren won't take kindly to waiting," he warned.

"Too bad." I trailed after Colin. "I have to do this, okay? Please don't make it harder."

"You have to come back," he said, his voice barely audible.

"I will."

He took my hands in his. "You asked what would happen if you stayed, remember?"

I nodded, not trusting myself to speak.

"Come back, and I'll tell you." Still holding my hands, he turned to Luc. "Take care of her. You don't, and I don't care how much magic you have—I'll kill you myself."

Luc's expression was as desolate as the sky above. "Something happens to her, you won't need to."

Luc's arms shielded me as we went Between, but the magic tore through my veins, burning me from the inside, clawing its way out. There was a coppery taste in my mouth and wetness on my face.

"It's getting worse," I mumbled, closing my eyes as we made it through.

Luc's voice was urgent and ragged. "Let me fix it."

"No. You promised," I said, and then I felt myself falling, and the words didn't work anymore.

When I woke, something cool and damp touched my face,

TANGLED   231

smelling faintly resinous, like rosemary. A woman's voice said, "She's waking up."

Marguerite.

My eyes opened, closed, opened again. The effort was monumental, but when I could finally focus, the sight of Luc, frown lines bracketing his mouth, eyes clouded with worry, his concern focused on me like a laser . . . it was worth it. My hand brushed soft grass, and overhead the sky was as blue and beautiful as a late June game at Comiskey Park. I had the impression of a vast green field, trees marching in neat lines on either side of me, and then the world went blurry.

He crouched down, his fingers hovering over me like he was afraid to touch. "I'm sorry," he said. "Wasn't expectin' it to be this bad."

I struggled to sit up, and he slipped his arm around my shoulders. "Did you heal me?" I asked, searching his face for any sign of deceit.

He shook his head. There was no lingering glow of magic, no effervescent warmth tumbling across my skin. "Thank you," I said, meaning it.

"How are you feeling?" Marguerite asked.

"I've been better."

"Luc, fetch her something to drink."

"We don't have a lot of time," he said.

"Time enough," she said, patting my hand. "Go on. And you can tell your father all the pacing in the world won't hurry us along."

When he left, I asked, "Did *you* heal me?" If anyone could find a loophole, it was Luc.

"No. I offered, but Luc felt strongly that you wouldn't like it."

"He was right," I said, surprised and pleased that he'd kept his word.

"He worries about you," Marguerite murmured, gently dabbing at my face with the cloth. I was about to apologize, but she continued, "It's lovely, really. He doesn't often allow himself that sort of luxury."

Worrying about someone was a luxury? I wondered what Marguerite would make of my mom, who'd medal in worrying if it were an Olympic event. But all I said was, "The Covenant's a big deal."

"This is about much more than the Covenant, Mo."

Before I could ask more, Luc returned with a glass of something that tasted like fizzy lemonade. As I finished it, he said, "Hate to rush you, Mouse, but we need to get moving. Can you walk?"

"Luc," chided Marguerite. "You've forgotten her cloak."

"I have to wear a cape?" He was wearing one, I noticed belatedly. Raw silk the color of garnets, fastened at the neck with an intricate clasp.

"It's our custom, to show allegiance to our House." Marguerite's cloak was a twin to Luc's, the heavy material swirling around her feet.

"I don't have a House."

"You belong to all of them," she said. "As the Vessel, you're a member of Air, Earth, and Water, and as you're bound to Luc, you lay claim to ours as well. It's a unique situation, and your cloak reflects it."

"White. The color of the magic," Luc said. "And white light is all the other colors of light combined, right? Makes for a nice symbol."

His words made me uneasy. "I'm not a symbol."

"Of course not," said Marguerite. "But we don't want to give the impression that you favor one House over another."

Luc's brow lowered, a sure sign he wasn't going to bend. "You don't like it, we can go ten rounds after the ceremony. For today, what people see counts as much as what really is. And I didn't forget," he said, addressing Marguerite. "I had other things on my mind."

He reached behind him. I felt a tug in the magic as he opened up a small window to Between, just as I'd seen kids doing at his House. A moment later, he produced a bundle of cloth and shook it out with a flourish.

The material was the color of fresh cream and lustrous.

Along the edges, platinum thread made a pattern of inter-
locking circles, vaguely reminiscent of the links I'd forged
with the Quartoren. Probably not a coincidence. "It's beautiful."

"It is," he said, looking directly at me. With a sweeping
motion, he settled the material around my shoulders, and the
hem brushed the ground. I felt old-fashioned, like an actress
in a costume drama, too aware of the cloak to be comfortable in it. The weight of the fabric slid awkwardly off my
shoulders, and I tried to yank it back into place without
crushing the material.

"This'll fix it," Luc said, gently nudging the robe back into
place, covering the two sides of the golden clasp with his
palm.

With a pulse of light, the halves fused together, four inter-
locking circles that rested against my collarbone.

"Magic?" I said, unable to contain my annoyance. "You
guys made me a special robe and I need magic to wear it? I
can't even dress myself?"

"Nobody's makin' a statement. It's tradition, that's all.
Not exactly common to see your type wearin' one of these."

My type. I'd never asked to be a part of Luc's world, but
there was no escaping it. The binding to Luc, the Covenant
with the Quartoren, my promise to Con, and now the magic,
threatening me from within . . . the more I struggled against
it, the more I was caught, like a wild animal in a snare.

Marguerite looped her arm through mine. "You are more
than they realize, and you wouldn't be here if it wasn't your
place. Carry yourself accordingly, and all will be well."

"You never told me the plan," I said to Luc.

He glanced away. "Evangeline's mourning period ends
today. Quartoren want you to participate, show everyone
how sad you are."

I stared at him, incredulous. "You brought me here to
make nice?" I'd assumed the Quartoren had summoned me
to fix the magic, not put on a show for the Arcs. "I can't
stand up there and mourn for Evangeline."

"Fake it," Luc said firmly, and guided us across the grassy lane. As we walked, bloodred flames sprang up, creating a pathway. They were identical to the ones that had surrounded Dominic and Marguerite at the shack. I twisted my head to watch them blink out, but this time they stayed, a flickering beacon stretching behind us. Ahead stood a large marble dais, the Quartoren gathered at the far edge, talking intently. Dominic raised his head, motioning us forward, and the muscles in Luc's arm tensed. "Whole point is to prove you're on our side."

The Covenant had guaranteed that.

"What is this place, anyway?"

Marguerite answered, "The Allée. It's one of our three sacred spaces. The Binding Temple, of course, and the Assembly, where the Quartoren meets. The Allée is used for ceremonies that require the full Houses to meet. Each side is bounded by a different elemental line, but the space within is completely devoid of lines. It is the original neutral ground."

"The Dauphine was neutral ground. That didn't do me much good."

"It's different now," Luc said. "We're bound. No one is allowed to use magic against you here."

I didn't feel reassured. Bound or not, Arcs considered me an outsider. Niceties like neutral ground or Rivening, going into another Arc's mind, didn't apply to me. And publicly mourning the woman I'd killed seemed like a surefire way to tempt fate, if there really was such a thing.

Luc guided us around a stone rectangle, knee-high off the ground. It looked like a coffin and practically oozed power. I shivered and moved farther away. On the other side were marble steps. Dominic descended and greeted us briefly, then escorted Marguerite back to the stage. Luc paused, taking my hands in his.

"This feels wrong," I said, studying the Quartoren in their jewel-colored robes. My own cloak was stifling, the clasp chafing my skin.

"You'd leave, wouldn't you? If there weren't so much forcing your hand." He shook his head. "We belong together."

"Why? Because some prophecy says so?"

He pressed his fingers against my wrist—not where the binding tingled every time I thought about it, but the soft, inner skin, where my pulse had suddenly kicked up. "That's not the prophecy."

"I know." I touched my mouth to his briefly. "Neither is that. But it's a lot to deal with, Luc. It's confusing sometimes."

"We're a good match. Cujo might keep you safe, but it's 'cause he wants to hide you away. You're more than that. You can be, if you let yourself." He brought my wrist to his lips. "You might not always like me or my methods . . . but at least I'm not trying to keep you small."

Arrayed in a semicircle around the platform were four tree-lined pathways. The other three were identical to the one we'd just walked, down to the unsettling coffinlike box and the marble steps. The flames still burned along the sides of our path, but now they filled the stone rectangle, a blanket of fire. In another lane, water seeped up, creating a vast pool. In the next, the bottom of the rectangle seemed to split and heave, transforming to rich soil, and the scent of freshly turned earth wafted toward me. In the last pathway, there was no visible change, but the blades of grass around the rectangle wavered and bent, and the leaves of the trees began to whip around. A bell tolled, low and dolorous. The vibration carried through the ground and traveled up the soles of my feet, into my core.

"That's the Summoner. No matter where they are, Arcs hear it, know to drop what they're doing and head here."

"And you do this every time somebody dies?"

"No. Evangeline was a Matriarch, so there's more customs to observe."

The bell sounded again. "Showtime. Stay close," he said.

"Where would I go?" People were filing up the lanes now,

their voices hushed. You could hear the sweep of their cloaks along the ground, the air alive with whispers and magic, and my stomach twinged in response. The Water Arcs, Evangeline's people, gathered directly in front of us. I edged behind Luc. Neutral ground, I reminded myself. Safe.

Luc said only the Quartoren and a few others knew the truth about Evangeline's death, and I believed him, mostly. But I knew how people reacted when someone died unexpectedly and you were in the vicinity. If these people had anything in common with Constance or Jenny Kowalski, my presence here was a terrible idea. I was about to tell Luc so when Dominic clapped my shoulder.

"Ready?"

Luc answered for me, his hand finding mine through the slits in our cloaks. "Let's get this over with."

The tension between them simmered unpleasantly, but Dominic seemed to brush it off, speaking with a jovial cadence that didn't fit a funeral. "Quartoren'll take their usual places," he said, nodding toward the front of the dais. "You two will stand to the side, but it's important Maura be visible. Want everyone to see she's a part of this now. Helps deliver the message. Marguerite—" He glanced at his wife, concern flickering across his face. "You'll stay with me."

"I should stand with the House," she protested. "It's protocol."

"I *make* protocol," he said.

"You worry so. My men," she sighed, addressing her words to me. "They do protect what's theirs."

Remarkably, Luc seemed to flush as I studied him, the color on his cheeks deepening.

"What about the Seraphim?" I asked suddenly. "Niobe said they were planning to do something big."

"We've been over this. The Seraphim disbanded in the wake of their defeat," said Orla, annoyed.

"We don't know that," Dominic said. "But even so, they can't act here. It's neutral ground."

But Marguerite said Dominic was trying to protect her. And Luc was nervous—I could tell by the way his gaze darted around the crowd and the way he clutched my hand. If the Seraphim weren't the threat, what was?

There was a sudden quiet—the tolling of the Summoner stopped. Its absence was nearly as startling as its commencement.

"Time to begin," said Dominic, moving to the front of the stage, with Marguerite on his arm. Orla and Pascal flanked them. Luc urged me forward, but in the instant before we reached our position, he hesitated.

And that's when I really began to worry.

CHAPTER 36

Time and again, Luc had told me he'd been brought up as the future leader of his House. He was an essential part of the Torrent Prophecy. Taking his place in an Arc ceremony should be the most natural thing in the world for him.

If he was having doubts, something was very wrong.

I started to pull back, but it was too late—we were center stage. Thousands of people were staring at me, questioning, suspicious. A familiar panic clawed its way up my throat.

Dominic began to speak, praising Evangeline's sacrifice during the Torrent.

The back of my neck grew hot as I listened, disgust churning through me. She'd been a traitor to these people, not a martyr for them. His voice carried across the crowded Allée, praising Evangeline's wisdom and courage, her commitment to strengthening the Arcs and preserving their legacy. He spoke with absolute, unshakeable conviction, either an Oscar-worthy performance or a sign that I'd misread his loyalties completely.

Luc didn't seem interested. His eyes swept the crowd continuously. I tried to see what he did, but I couldn't seem to ignore Dominic's words, my anger swelling as he went on and on.

Finally, mercifully, Dominic stopped. He strode down the steps, his cloak billowing behind him, and cupped his hands over the glassy pool of water. An instant later, my skin began to tingle, faintly, as if a limb had fallen asleep. I rolled my shoulders, trying to dislodge the feeling. He opened his hands, as if he was scattering something across the water, but nothing fell. I heard a sizzling sound, and then plumes of steam rose from the surface, scattering on the breeze.

Luc leaned in. "He's offering a tribute. Rest of them will follow suit."

"Everyone?" I looked at the crowd of Arcs. It was the world's biggest wake. We'd be here forever.

He spoke without moving his lips. "Be glad you wore comfortable shoes."

But as Dominic stepped back and Pascal moved forward, offering his own tribute, the magic crawled over my skin again. I rubbed my arms and Luc edged closer.

Orla took her place in front of the pool, the surface whipping up into tiny whitecaps. I flinched at the new surge of magic, and noticed Pascal watching me closely.

In an instant, I saw the error of the plan.

"It's too much magic," I whispered.

"Just a drop," Luc assured me, but his voice sounded strained. "Almost nothing."

"Look. Count them, Luc. How many drops?" Like the old story about putting a grain of rice on the first square of a chessboard—one grain on the first square, two on the second, four on the third . . . by the last square, the pile of rice is bigger than Mount Everest. Those drops of magic were like grains of rice, and I'd be dead before we got to the second half of the board.

Dominic jerked his head, indicating we were up next, but Luc stayed where he was, looking at his father with utter loathing.

"Your turn, son," Dominic said, the words pleasant on the surface and commanding underneath. The crowd stirred, impatient, and his voice dropped to a hiss. "Make the tribute."

Jaw set, Luc tugged me toward the reflecting pool. "Hang on," he said as we approached. "It'll be okay, I swear."

I wasn't sure he could promise that. My stomach cramped, and I wrapped an arm around my waist.

The pool of water was easily ten feet long but less than three feet across—a narrow rectangle of black, glassy stone—obsidian, maybe, or onyx. The water was so still, our images caught in the surface like a mirror. Luc, all smoldering fury, and me, pale and bewildered. I barely recognized myself, and when I did, I was appalled. I'd worked too hard and seen too much in the last few months to be the frightened girl in the water. With an effort, I tore my gaze away and surveyed the crowd. People were starting to grumble, their faces clouding over with suspicion.

Constance stood a few feet from the front, her silvery hood barely drawn forward. She was trying to look bored, her lower lip jutting out, but her eyes were wide, taking in everything. Next to her, Niobe looked exasperated, unsurprised I was responsible for the delay.

With stiff, jerky movements, Luc held his hands out, waiting for me to follow suit. When I didn't move, he nudged me, expecting I would follow his lead.

I couldn't.

It wasn't the fear stopping me, or my anger over Dominic's words. I couldn't stand up in front of these people and pretend to mourn Evangeline. I couldn't pay a tribute—real or symbolic—to the woman who'd killed my best friend. No amount of logic or reasoning or dirty looks from Dominic was going to make it happen.

The noise from the crowd grew louder.

"Mouse, what's the holdup?" Luc spoke without moving his lips. "You gotta do this."

"I *can't*."

He paused, searching my face, his own expression miserable. "Well, I have to. I'm sorry." He drew a breath and summoned the magic.

The world seemed to go high-def, my vision supersharp and clear, Luc's words sounding as if he was speaking inside my head, the magic hitting the water below with a crackle. I felt the power racing along our bond, being absorbed into the chain rather than striking me. It was our bond that protected me, like it did whenever Luc cast a spell.

I felt buoyant, giddy with relief. If we left before the rest of the Arcs took their turn at the reflecting pool, I'd be safe. And then someone in the crowd shouted, "The Flat didn't pay tribute."

"Hell," Luc muttered, and I couldn't agree more.

The murmurs and grumbles of the crowd increased, more shouts ringing out, some so far back the words were impossible to decipher. Their tone wasn't, though—anger passing from a simmer to a boil. The protests increased: I was an interloper, trespassing on hallowed ground, making a mockery of Evangeline's memorial.

With no warning, a crack echoed over the head of the crowd, sounding like a gunshot. At the far end of the stage stood a cloaked figure, sky blue hood pulled up to hide his face. The crowd quieted instantly. His voice rang out in the silence, smooth and mesmerizing. "The Flat has brought us to ruin," he called. "It's this girl who has corrupted our magic and our leaders. She should pay the price."

I could feel the magic eddying around him, an invisible current, surprisingly strong. The others must have felt it, too, or they would never have allowed the disruption.

For a split-second, Dominic's face contorted, like a child who'd had his favorite toy taken away. And then he was back, full of masterful charm. He crossed the stage, Orla and Pascal falling into step behind him. His voice boomed, the very picture of affronted nobility. "We have gathered here to pay tribute to our lost Matriarch. You dishonor her, and your House, by speaking so. As Verity Grey lay dying, she transmitted some essential part of herself to this girl; through the conduits of blood and sacrifice, a Flat was transformed to the Vessel. We owe her our thanks, and without Evangeline's help, we might never have known. Who are you to come here, spouting wild accusations, defilin' this ceremony?"

The speaker pushed back his hood, revealing an utterly ordinary middle-aged man. He was handsome, in a bland sort of way, like an anchor on the local news. Brown hair combed straight back, deeply set brown eyes, square features. It was the calculating light in his eyes that made you look again.

"Anton Renard. I'm not the one making a mockery of this ceremony." His voice was feverish with righteousness as he spoke to the crowd. "Do you see how powerless they are? How weak? They forged a Covenant with a *Flat*. They are so incapable, their best hope is to place our future in the hands of this girl. Look at the magic, at the harm their stewardship has brought about. Their time has passed."

"What would you have us do?" Dominic's voice managed to be strong and nonchalant at the same time, but I could sense the strain underneath. Out of the corner of my eye, I spotted Pascal and Orla try to copy his stance, and I understood—they couldn't afford to look weak or afraid, not with so many Arcs watching. Why not get rid of the guy? Surely they had the ability to blast him into Between.

"Forego the Covenant. Allow the magic to revert to its natural state. It will restore the Arcs to our former glory and free us from the dictates of the Quartoren."

"That sounds an awful lot like treason, doesn't it?" Dominic said, his words hanging in the air. The crowd stood motionless at the accusation.

"Loyalty to the magic isn't treason."

"You belong to Evangeline's house, yes?" Orla said. "You could be elevated to the Quartoren. Is that what this is about? Seems a little gauche, angling for her seat before her mourning ceremony concludes."

Luc bent his head to mine. "The man's lookin' for a bigger prize than Evangeline's seat. He's one of the Seraphim. Best if we get you out of here."

Anton scoffed at Orla's words, letting the audience see his contempt. They watched the spectacle before them, expressions rapt. "You believe I would aspire to be one of you? That I care about the Houses? They're just another relic."

He flung his arm to the side, hand outstretched, and shouted something in the language of the magic.

A foot away from me, the reflecting pool shattered, water streaming onto the ground. A collective gasp rose up, every Arc in the Allée rearing back in shock.

Beside me, Luc's eyes widened, and he shoved me away from the jagged pieces of rock.

"What's wrong?"

"That stone's imbued with magic. It's unbreakable."

"Not anymore," I said.

Anton looked out over the sea of robes, basking in the looks of fear and grudging respect.

"I propose a new world," he said, "built on the rubble of the old, guided by the Seraphim. We shall cast aside the Quartoren, and with them the Vessel. Her presence among us is offensive, but it is hardly the most grievous of her crimes."

He brought his hands together in a thunderous clap and then flung them outward, palms up, in our direction. The force of the blow knocked us apart, sending Luc headlong into the broken stones. I pitched forward, landing on my knees at the base of the steps. The heavy cloak hampered my movements. Anton hauled me to my feet and gathered hold of the material, twisting it so the clasp pressed against my windpipe. Choking, I clawed at it until the silk finally tore, releasing me.

"You have no right to wear our robes," he hissed. A few feet away, Luc was clambering up, blood trickling down his forehead. Before I could reach him, Anton grabbed my arm and thrust me toward the crowd, shouting, "The girl herself is proof of the Quartoren's betrayal!"

I knew what he was going to say the minute I saw the weird, unholy light in his eyes. I struggled to break free as he announced, "She is a killer. It wasn't the Torrent that took the life of our Matriarch. It was her. The Flat used our magic to murder Evangeline Marais."

CHAPTER 37

The effect was instantaneous—a roar of noise, the crowd beneath us surging forward. Just as quickly, Luc bounded up the stairs, sword drawn and pointing directly at Anton's throat. "I will spill your blood right here if you don't let her go."

"You see?" called Anton. "The Heir chooses her over his own people. Even he is deceived." But he released me. "I've made my point," he said, as Luc took my hand.

We circled around Anton, Luc never dropping his guard. "Down the stairs," he said, gesturing to the rear of the platform. I followed on shaking legs.

The Quartoren moved to intercept us.

"Get her clear," Dominic said to Luc. "I'll handle this."

He strode to the front of the stage, his bulk dwarfing Anton, his manner infinitely more commanding. With a wave of his hand, silence dropped, as if he'd magically muted the crowd. Luc hustled me down the stairs, but I could still hear Dominic's words, halting the ceremony, scorning the Seraphim and their desecration of Evangeline's memorial. It was all spin, but I didn't care. I only wanted to get away.

We hurried along a seashell-covered path, putting as much distance between us and the ceremony as possible. When we stopped, I sank to the ground, spent.

"Well," I said. "That was not what I expected."

Luc sat next to me. "You ain't the only one."

I leaned against him, the sound of his heartbeat calming mine.

"You said the Allée was neutral ground. That no one could use magic against another person there. How was Anton able to hurt us?"

He brushed at a smudge of dirt on my cheek, then helped me to my feet. "Neutral ground is a principle. A rule laid down in ancient times, designed to keep the peace between the Houses. Looks like Anton doesn't have much use for the old rules."

"He was making a statement," Orla said. She and Pascal were walking down the path, their pace slowed by Marguerite. "The Seraphim consider themselves above the rules of our world."

"Nice to see you admit they're real," Luc said.

"I was wrong." She looked appalled at the thought. "They are real, and more important, they are dangerous. People listened to him. They're worried, and his explanation, while ludicrous, gives them a target. It's more important than ever that you repair the magic. Now. Before Anton and his people make another move."

"This isn't the time," Luc said.

"It's not the ideal situation," Pascal admitted, adjusting his glasses. "But we may not find a better one. The magic reacted to Maura during the ceremony; it's in a state of flux. I can't predict what might happen next."

"I can," said Dominic, stalking toward us. "Anton vanished, but he's got the crowd whipped up, calling for your blood. Only thing that's going to keep them from hunting you down is to fix the magic. Prove him wrong and they won't take his word about Evangeline."

Pascal and Orla bobbed their heads in agreement. Luc stared at the ground, misery clear on his face.

Dominic said, "Marguerite predicted a new age would rise up, and that's exactly what happened today. You need to do your part now."

"You don't know that," I said desperately.

" 'Course we do. We've known all along."

There was a shout from the direction of the Allée. Constance stormed down the path, Niobe behind her. "Did you kill her? Did you kill Evangeline? You said you tried to help her, you liar!"

"Constance . . . he's not telling . . ."

She didn't lower her voice as she joined us. "The truth? Why would they say it if it wasn't true?"

"It's complicated."

"Yes or no. Did you do it?"

"She was a really bad person," I said. "You don't know . . ."

"You bitch!" she screamed, and flew at me, shoving me to the ground.

Before Constance could land a single punch, Luc dragged her off me, pushing her toward Niobe. "Get gone, little girl. Mouse, you okay?"

"Yeah." I sat up slowly, picking grass from my hair. My pale blue sweater was covered with grass stains and mud. Wordlessly, Pascal offered me a handkerchief as Niobe restrained Constance.

"Calm down, or your next lesson is restraining spells," she said, her voice like a whip.

"You have to believe me," I said. "Evangeline was really bad. That group, the one that disrupted her memorial . . . they're called the Seraphim."

"I know who they are." Constance's face was white as snow, but her eyes were navy with fury and tears, hair whipping around her face. At the base of my skull, a headache started to pound.

Luc frowned. "Your powers just came through, but you know about the Seraphim? How the hell does that work?"

"They targeted her," Niobe said. "New, naive. Suggestible."

Constance whirled, and a sharp breeze sprang up. "I'm not naive! They're my friends!"

"I had a friend," I said quietly. "The Seraphim killed her. Evangeline was one of them."

"I don't believe you." The hatred was pouring off her. I could almost see the black, crackling lines of it as the magic swelled.

"You should," Luc said, his voice deathly calm. "Verity came down to spend the summer with Evangeline, learn to use her powers right, fulfill the Torrent Prophecy. Evangeline tried to recruit her, same as they've done with you. Only your sister was too smart to bite, so they took her out."

Constance started to cry. "You're lying."

"Not about this," I said, fighting the impulse to ball up on the ground. Constance needed to understand. If I could explain, maybe she'd calm down. "They waited until she came home so she didn't have Luc and the other Arcs around to protect her."

"You're lying," she said again, sobbing, her nose running.

"Once Evangeline figured out I could finish Verity's work, she used me to start the Torrent. Her plan didn't work, and she died."

"But it was an accident, wasn't it? You didn't mean to. You didn't murder her."

I bit my lip. I had done the right thing. But if I couldn't admit what I'd done, then maybe I didn't truly believe it, after all.

"She killed Verity," I said. "She deserved it."

"I hate you! I hate you! They were right about you. You ruined everything!" she screamed, and the magic whipped around, knocking me down.

"Niobe!" Luc snapped. "Take her!"

Niobe nodded and grabbed Constance's arm, pulling the two of them Between. The press of the magic let up, but only slightly. There was no reversing it.

"The lines can't contain the magic," Pascal said. "The girl triggered something. We need to act quickly."

Luc crouched next to me. "It's time."

"I'm scared," I whispered.

He cupped my face in his hands. "Me too."

Dominic shouted. "Now, Maura!"

He, Pascal, and Orla had positioned themselves in a triangle around us.

"Don't fight it. You'll be okay if you don't fight it." Luc pressed his palm into mine, like we had during the Binding Ceremony, and reached out his other hand, the words of the Arc's language pouring off his tongue, the Quartoren's voices chiming in. Around us, the air started to whistle and creak as the lines broke through, suddenly visible to me. Rents in the air and the ground, jagged slashes, power bleeding through. They built quickly, crisscrossing the air around us. My heart pulsed in time with the magic, and each beat pushed it further inside me, like the poster from Biology class—big, round vessels to smaller, spindly ones, diffusing through cell walls, filling up my lungs. I could feel it in my spine and radiating out to every nerve, yearning for connection to the web of lines around me. Steeling myself, I reached out, and the world blurred as the magic threatened to burst free. Luc's hand curled around mine, our connection flaring. Instantly, my vision cleared. "Thanks."

He nodded, sweat beading along his forehead.

Around me, three of the four elements were coalescing as the Quartoren called up their magic. With all four concentrated in one spot, we'd have a nexus, an entry point into the raw magic. Last time, I'd used the pillars of the Binding Temple, but the temple was gone now. There was no place I knew of where all four elemental magics came together.

Except, I didn't need all four types, did I? The lines determined the element; the force inside—unfiltered, straining for release—was raw magic. We'd made it so complicated, but all I needed to do was reach inside the line, past the elemental barriers I'd created, to the power within.

A few feet beyond Luc, one of the lines was buckled and swelled, seconds away from bursting. If I could get there first, I could follow it back to the source. If I couldn't, and the line split open, I'd be dead. "Let go of me."

"What?" His fingers fumbled for mine, but I wriggled away and reached out.

The influx of power shuddered through me. I felt the coolness of it against my hands, smooth and rippling like muscle. I had to do this before Luc could interfere. I dragged in a breath, planted my feet, and dug my fingers into the line until the surface gave way, and raw magic flooded me again.

It was like a dam breaking. One moment, a trickle, and the next I was drowning, swept away by the force of the raw magic. I knew enough not to fight the barrage of chaos and energy, and as my body acclimated, the rest of the world faded away. Now my only tie to the outside world was the silvery thread around my wrist. The familiar sweep of omnipotence was powerful, but I turned away. It no longer held any allure. I'd sought answers on my own and found heartbreak instead of peace.

I'd had enough truth to last a lifetime or three.

The magic seemed to hold back, waiting for direction. In my mind's eye, I saw lines—beautiful and complex and strong, weaving together like a braid. My fingers shaped the raw energy, twisting and coiling to form new lines, guided by instinct. As the magic began to flow true again, I breathed a sigh of relief and began to pull back into myself, leaving the lines behind.

And then something went wrong.

The flow of magic through me slowed, turned, began racing back. Exactly as it had at the country club.

This time, no one shut it down.

The raw magic began to fuse, joining with my bones and muscle and blood. The pain grew inexplicably hotter. It hadn't been like this the last time, like every single cell of my body was turning itself inside out. My vision went black and endless, a night sky without stars. I flashed from hot to cold and back again, like a fever. It was the magic, searing me like a brand, and there was no escape.

No escape but Luc. He'd pulled me back last time, the bond between us a lifeline. Now it was my only road home.

I felt blindly for the glowing thread connecting us. "Where are you?" I wailed, but there was no answering surge of magic, no sensation of him reaching for me.

"Luc," I screamed. "Please!"

The magic was voracious. I was losing myself, and I scrabbled against the nothingness, trying to haul myself away, too weak to do it alone.

And then Luc grabbed for me, yanking me away with a shout.

Something tore—both deep within me and just out of reach, more agonizing than anything that had come before. I tumbled out of the web of lines and into Luc's arms, knocking us both down.

Luc took the brunt of the fall, landing on his back, and I slid away bonelessly. He hunched over me, shouting something.

I couldn't hear him through the rushing in my head. His eyes were the greenest thing I'd ever seen, like the leaves of a crocus poking up through the snow, even as everything else was fading into the grainy black and white of a silent movie. His eyes were fading, too, at the end, and then there wasn't anything to see at all.

CHAPTER 38

Panic fluttered through my chest like a trapped bird. I opened my eyes to see snowy linen stretched out in front of me, a marble-topped table with a glass of water. Through the window, the brightly lit revelry of the French Quarter at night was visible through wavery glass.

And then I was abruptly aware of an arm, draped heavily over me, fingers wrapped snugly against my rib cage, a few centimeters from second base. Luc's body was curled into mine, our knees nestled like puzzle pieces, our feet tangled together. His breath drifted over my shoulder, stirring my hair, but he slept on. The rise and fall of his chest against my back stayed slow and regular, unlike my erratic heartbeat.

The thin veneer of my control started to crack. Any moment, it would vanish completely. Underneath lay bottomless wanting, the knowledge that if I dove in, I'd never find solid ground beneath my feet again. Trying to put some distance between us, I wriggled out from beneath the weight of his arm.

"Keep movin' like that, I'm going to think you're interested in more'n sleep."

I froze. "You're awake."

He shifted, his body aligning with mine again. The hummingbirds in my chest beat faster, and only some of them were afraid. "Been waiting on you. Gettin' pretty good at it."

Lightly, he pressed a kiss to the nape of my neck. "You feeling okay?"

Okay was not the word I would use, especially now. I tried to turn, but his leg anchored me in place and his hand splayed against my chest, directly over my heart.

"What happened?" I asked.

"You lived," he said, pressing even closer. It wasn't only lust driving him, I realized—though with Luc, lust was always a factor—it was relief.

He tucked his face into the space between my neck and shoulder. Without the tiny cues I'd learned to look for in his expression—the movement at the corner of his mouth, the direction of his glance, the lines in his forehead—it was his touch and slow, unsteady breath that told me how badly things had gone.

"It didn't work." I wasn't asking. The real question was how much damage had occurred, but I wasn't ready to hear the answer. "How long have I been out?"

"Awhile. It's midnight. Quartoren'll be here soon." He sighed and released me. I twisted around, startled by his pallor. Normally his skin was a tawny gold, but there was a grayish cast to it, and his eyes were dull.

"You healed me," I said.

"Not going to apologize," he said.

"No. I'm glad. Thank you."

He traced his fingers across my forehead, down my cheekbones, dragging a thumb across my lips. The sadness in his face belied the tenderness of the gesture. There was something he wasn't telling me, something awful. "Why are the Quartoren coming here?"

He slipped out of bed, tugging me after him.

"Strategize, I suppose. Not entirely sure."

I narrowed my eyes at him. "You know everything the Quartoren does. You're practically an honorary member."

"They're closin' ranks," he said, looking down like the admission was shameful. "I pulled you out. When the magic started to take over, I felt you trying to get away. I felt how scared you were, and I couldn't . . . I couldn't leave you there."

"You saved me. Isn't that a good thing?"

"I thought so," he replied. "But they aren't likely to view it the same way."

There was a knock at the door. I finger-combed my hair, a last-ditch effort to look like I hadn't been asleep with Luc five minutes ago. The disdain on Orla's face when the Quartoren filed into Luc's living room indicated I hadn't been successful.

We stood in silence, Dominic and the others on one side of the room, me on another, Luc caught between us.

Orla spoke first. "I think we can all agree that today's events were unexpected."

Dominic's eyes burned holes in me.

"The magic turned," I said, wanting to defend myself against their wordless accusations. I glanced at Pascal. "Like before."

Pascal coughed. "We'd discussed the possibility that bonding with the magic would stabilize it. It was going as planned. Why did you stop?"

"It was too much." I swallowed, remembering the feeling of the magic crowding me out of my own body. "It would have killed me."

"Because you wouldn't commit to it," Orla said. "If you'd stayed—"

"I'd be dead now. We decided that I should make new lines instead, remember? If I'd bonded with the magic, there wouldn't have been any . . . me . . . left."

"You're the Vessel." Dominic spoke, and the warmth he'd always shown me was gone. "If the magic hollows you out and wears you like a hermit crab's shell, so be it. That's what you swore to. And you," he said, turning to face Luc. "This wasn't our agreement."

"What agreement?" I asked.

"She would have died." Luc spoke through gritted teeth.

"You knew what she needed to do. What had to happen. Still does. What did you gain by throwing us over?" Dominic's lip curled with disgust. "A few hours?"

He jerked a head toward the bedroom door, the rumpled sheets clearly visible. "Hope she was worth it."

"Luc?" I backed away, banging into a side table. The hurricane candle sitting atop it tumbled to the ground, but I was the only one who jumped at the crash.

He turned slowly, his expression pleading.

"It was never about making new lines, was it? You wanted me to bond with the magic all along. That's why . . ." My voice cracked. "That's why I couldn't find you. They told you to leave me there, and you did."

"Mouse . . ."

"Don't talk, Luc. All you'll do is lie." I turned to Pascal. Of any of them, I trusted him the most—not to protect me, but to answer my questions. The scientist in him couldn't resist. "After I passed out, what happened?"

He recited the facts with clinical detachment. "Picture the lines as a circulatory system, and the magic is like blood. We had hoped that, once you had bonded with the source of the magic, you would function as the heart, directing power to the lines at a manageable rate. When you failed to complete the bond, you created a tear, very close to the source of the magic, like a rupture in the aorta. Now the magic is leaking out of the system."

I grabbed on to the couch for support. "I started another Torrent?"

"The opposite, actually. The Torrent was deadly because the eruption of raw magic would destroy the weaker Arcs. In this case, the magic is diffusing as it spreads into the world. There, lines can't replenish the power with them, and without lines to draw on, most Arcs will be rendered powerless."

"Most, but not all?"

"Arcs with the strongest talents can use even a minor line to cast a working. They should be able to do the same with a low level of ambient magic. But weaker ones will be stripped of their abilities."

Orla cut in, her expression pained. "They'll have to either live among Flats or rely on the largesse of more powerful Arcs."

"Same result," said Dominic. "Only the strongest will remain. It's exactly what the Seraphim want, to make a new race of Arcs and rule the others."

"You've handed Anton his victory on a silver platter," Orla said.

I'd helped the people who killed Verity. That was what they were saying. My entire body went numb. She'd died trying to stop the Seraphim, and I'd given them exactly what they wanted. My promise to her had meant nothing at all.

Dominic grabbed my arm and shook me. Luc, standing with his back to us, didn't react. "Are you listening? You forged a Covenant. You swore to fix the magic, and all you've done is make it worse. You have to go back."

I marveled that I'd ever thought he seemed nice. "There has to be another way."

"There isn't. The magic is failing. We have a day, perhaps two, before it's gone completely. Either uphold your part of the Covenant and fix it or your life is forfeit. And you," Dominic continued, glaring at Luc's back. "Remember who you are."

Pascal shot me a look of apology as they filed out, stopping next to Luc to exchange a few words. And then it was just Luc and me, alone again, and the world had turned inside out.

A soft breeze blew through the room, carrying the scent of sweet olive.

"I couldn't do it," he said. "That's why Dominic's so angry. I couldn't leave you there, no matter how much it cost."

Despite the warm Louisiana night, I was cold to the marrow. "You were going to."

"But I *didn't*. Shows you just what happens when you try to cheat fate. Disaster. Turned my back on the prophecy, the way you're always after me to, and now everything is falling to bits."

"Would you do it again? Save me but ruin the magic?"'

"Don't ask me that." His eyes were wet. "I'm doing my level best to find a way through. You and I are bound, but we're talkin' about my whole world. How am I supposed to choose?"

"You can't," I said, feeling my heart fall into jagged pieces at my feet. That was when I knew that something between us was broken, irrevocably. I straightened. "Take me home."

CHAPTER 39

Colin had texted me an address and a room number. Luc brought us Between in the hotel parking lot, the ground wet from a icy rain. I bent over, battling nausea.

Luc grabbed my elbow as I started across the parking lot, devastation etched into his face. "Let me explain."

I yanked away, so dizzy I ended up on my hands and knees on the pavement, gravel biting into my skin. "Don't touch me. Ever again. Ever."

"Mouse. *Please.*" He took a step toward me and I scuttled back, gulping down cold air to calm myself. Only when my fingers were numb did I get up, leaning against the concrete base of a light pole.

"Please what? Please overlook the fact you sold me out?" I shook my head. "You didn't have to use Constance. You didn't need the Covenant. The magic is killing me. That's all the incentive I needed. But you kept it a secret. You chased after me, you manipulated me, you made me care about you . . . and it was all a lie."

"No!" he said. "Not the part about us, anyway."

"Really? You mean it? Do you *promise,* Luc? Cross your heart?" I could hear the waspish tone of my words. I tried to tell myself that in saving me today he'd gone against his family, his people, all the traditions he'd been raised with. Maybe he was just as caught as I was, tangled in lines of magic and fate and duty and love, making it impossible to move. I almost felt sympathy for him.

Then I remembered what he'd told me once: *Doesn't matter who you love or what you're scared of. If there's one person in the world you can trust, it's the person you're bound to.* My compassion shriveled up and blew away like old leaves.

"The prophecy said you'd be okay. I believed it. I thought if you could fix the magic, you'd be okay." His voice echoed across the parking lot, broken and lost.

I turned, slowly. The rain was coming down harder now, beading on the leather of his coat. The drops stung my cheeks, and I shook my head. "You think the magic defines me, the way you let it define you. But I'm more than a prophecy. I'm not just the Vessel, even if you can't see it. So I will do what I have to, and then I'll go back to my world. You won't have to choose between us again, Luc. It won't be an option."

"Mouse . . ."

I didn't wait to hear his response.

I pounded on the door, trembling as the rain trickled down my neck. I heard Colin's feet hit the floor, the scrabbling of the chain, and then the door was open. I stepped away from the cold, into the warmth and the light. Colin pulled me inside, kicking the door shut behind me, shutting Luc out.

"Hey," I said stupidly.

"Hey." He steered me toward the lamp, inspecting me in the yellowish light. "You're back."

I pushed past him, shedding my coat, my scarf, my gloves like a trail of breadcrumbs. On the counter stood a familiar green bottle of Jameson, a half inch of whiskey still in the squat motel glass.

"Mo?"

I poured another two fingers, my hands stiff. Before Colin could cross the room and take my prize away, I swallowed half of it, feeling the fire streak through my throat and chest.

"What the hell happened?" He snatched the glass from me.

"Nothing. Everything. I fucked up." My eyes watered. Hard to tell if it was from the whiskey or the admission, and I didn't care. "Give me back my drink."

"Technically, it was my drink."

"Whatever." I spun around and grabbed another glass.

"Ease up." Very gently, he tugged the bottle out of my grip, setting it on the table. "Are you hurt?"

I thumped into the desk chair. "Not anymore."

"Luc healed you."

He healed me and broke me all over again. I wondered if a person could only be mended so many times, if they ever reached a point where they were more cracks and chips than they were wholeness, and what became of them. "I'm fine."

"Yeah. You want to talk about it?"

"Not even remotely."

He took a swallow of whiskey. "Is it over? Are you done with them?"

"I'm not ever going to be done with them. When World War Three comes, the only things left on the planet will be cockroaches and Twinkies and Arcs telling me to save the freaking world."

His eyes were dark and worried, but he let me ramble on.

"How do you manage?" I asked. "How can you stand knowing you're going to spend your entire life tethered to something . . . to someone . . . even if you don't want to? Doesn't it make you mad? Don't you ever want your own life?"

"This is my life. I made the choices that brought me here. Now I do the best I can with what I have. Doesn't stop me from wanting more sometimes." He turned the glass in his hand, looking at the amber liquid like it had the answer. "The Arcs won't let you go?"

"They need me. And they've got the power."

Understanding crossed his face like a shadow. Wordlessly, he passed me the glass.

"So," I said, after the whiskey hit my bloodstream and bolstered my courage, "we had a deal."

"We did?" He sat on the edge of the bed, elbows on knees, casual unless you looked at him closely.

"I promised to come back. Which"—I stood, made a sweeping gesture like I was on display—"I did."

The corner of his mouth twitched. "I see."

He did. He had that slow, hungry look, the one that stripped away all my secrets and defenses, more potent than any alcohol.

I eased across the room, sat across from him on the bed. "Time to pay up."

"You don't want to stay here," he said. "You've wanted New York forever."

"If I stayed," I insisted, "what would happen?"

"Depends." He touched the hem of my sweater.

"On what?"

"If you plan to keep throwing yourself at me."

I shoved at his shoulder and he looked up, eyes full of laughter and desire. "I'm not a saint, you know."

"I am so glad to hear it." I leaned in and kissed him, hard. His hands clenched on my waist, and I sank into the delicious familiar sensation, the taste of whiskey and Colin mingling on my tongue.

When we came up for air, I said, as reasonably as I could, "I have not been throwing myself at you."

He sat back, fighting a smile. "You walked in, downed two shots, offered to stay in Chicago, and kissed me. How else should I interpret that?"

It was a rhetorical question, but I couldn't help answering in my head. Colin was solid, and strong, and I wanted him so much it was devouring me. But I'd done exactly what he said—came into the room hurt and angry and wanting something to make the pain go away.

"I'm not complaining," he said, running his hand from my neck to my fingertips, kissing me carefully.

"You should be."

He studied me. "Should I?"

"Here's the thing," I said. "There's so much in my head right now, and lots of it is bad. And I think if we slept together, you could make the awfulness go away."

He started to speak, and I pressed a finger to his lips. "But I don't want to mix them up, because later, all of the bad stuff will still be there, and whatever we did . . . I couldn't separate them."

"You were thinking we should sleep together."

"But now I don't," I clarified.

He tucked his hands behind his head and stared at the popcorn ceiling. I pulled my knees to my chest and waited.

"I think about you," he said. "About us. I keep looking for a way to make it all work, but it's complicated. More than you realize."

Tess, he meant. I busied my hands tracing the pattern on the comforter as he continued. "I wish I could sleep with you and keep it casual, but I don't have it in me. You matter too much. I don't want it to be something you take lightly, or do because you're angry or feel unsure. I don't want any room for regret."

I flushed. He wasn't stupid. He'd known something was wrong the minute I stepped into the room. "I'm sorry."

"Don't be. I want to be the one to make things better. Just not like that. Not tonight, anyway." He laced his fingers with mine. "Tell me how to make it better."

I stretched out next to him, my head on his chest, sighing as his arms came around me. "This is pretty much perfect."

CHAPTER 40

A harsh, jangling noise woke me a few hours later. Before I could do more than lift my head, Colin rolled over me to reach for his phone, putting a finger to his lips.

The red glow of the clock said 3:30 AM, and no light peeked through the ugly floral drapes. Colin sat up, and I curled myself around him, trying to steal his warmth. Gently, he eased away, shaking his head. I tuned into the conversation, but his one-word responses gave nothing away.

Finally, he ended the call and tossed the phone aside. In the darkness, all I could see was the shape of his back—shoulders slumped, head bowed—and I burrowed back under the covers, as if I could hide from what he was going to say.

"We need to go home," he said. When he flicked the wall lamp on, his expression filled me with a familiar sickening dread. It was the look people got when they were about to cleave your life into "before" and "after." I *hated* that look.

"What happened?"

"Everyone's okay."

I started looking for my shoes. "Tell me."

He found my coat and scarf on the floor and handed them to me. I watched the play of his muscles, sinewy as he pulled on his waffle-knit shirt. He didn't move with Luc's fluid, prowling grace, but he was beautiful nevertheless. I forced myself to pause and savor the moment, because whatever was waiting on the other end of that phone call was going to ruin it. I slipped my feet into my ballet flats and carefully wrapped the scarf around my neck. "Well?"

"Everyone's okay," he said again, watching me with that same inky, steady gaze. "Your mom wanted you to know that."

I exhaled slowly. Not Mom, then. That's what mattered. Not my mom.

"There was a fire," he said. "At The Slice."

"How bad?" The room seemed to tilt, the garish colors of the drapes swirling together. He sat down, drawing me into his lap, and I rested my head against the broad plane of his chest. "It's gone, isn't it?" She'd sacrificed everything for the restaurant—everything—and now it was gone. My throat tightened and I shoved away the sadness, looking for anger instead.

"Morgan's has some smoke and water damage. They'll re-open soon."

"But not The Slice."

He leaned his forehead against mine. "We should go."

"It wasn't an accident, was it? Ekomov did this?"

He lifted a shoulder. "It went up pretty fast."

"Why The Slice?"

"Billy has eyes on the house. If they want to send a message, the restaurant is the next best place."

I stood, and he took my hand. "I guess my dad will have to wait."

"Guess so." He helped me into my coat, packed up the room, and ushered me outside. Overnight, the rain had turned to snow, already an inch deep. The sky was heavy with the promise of more to come, all the stars blotted out. Before and after, I told myself. And the night we'd spent here was a moment suspended out of time.

At Colin's insistence, I tried to sleep, my head on his shoulder as he pointed the truck north.

"This changes things, doesn't it?" I asked, an hour into the drive. The gears in my head were turning. "Billy wants me home for something."

"Probably. My instinct would be to keep you out of town for a while."

Why would you send someone you loved into danger? Luc's face flashed in my mind. Because they had something you needed, something you couldn't take by force. Something they could do that no one else could. What did I have that Billy wanted? That made Marco Forelli take notice of a high school girl?

I pressed closer to Colin, breathing in the scent of him, trying to call up the sense of comfort I'd felt last night. As we approached the city, the snow and rush-hour traffic forced us to inch along. At the turn for my street, I shook my head, touching his sleeve. "The Slice," I said.

"I'm supposed to take you home."

"I have to see it. Please."

The building was a shell—the sour smell of ashes and smoke were thicker than the patchy snow blanketing the rubble. Even now, firefighters were picking their way through the remains, making sure everything was out. Emergency vehicles lined the street, blue and red lights swirling over the jagged holes that used to be our front windows. Cameramen from local TV news jockeyed for the best angle, the one that would show the most damage. They could have saved themselves the effort. There was no way to avoid seeing what had become of The Slice. Even the retro plastic sign over the front was melted to an unrecognizable lump.

I jumped out of the truck before Colin killed the engine, slipping on the dirty, sooty piles of snow, soaking my feet.

"Miss," said one of the officers, "you can't go in there."

"That's my family's restaurant!"

"It's not safe," he said firmly, blocking me as I tried to dart around him.

I scanned the crowd for my uncle and found him surveying

the entire scene, his expression as icy as the wind whipping down the street.

"Uncle Billy?"

"Mo? Donnelly was supposed to take you home."

"I made him bring me here."

He nodded absently, never taking his eyes off the swarm of activity before us.

"How's Mom?" I asked.

"Heartbroken," he snapped. "Her life's work reduced to cinders. How do you think she is?"

"I'm sorry," I said, not certain what I was apologizing for.

He exhaled noisily and turned up the collar of his overcoat. "It's me who should say that, darling girl. I wasn't prepared for this. For things to go quite this far."

"Colin says it was the Russians."

"Who else would do something like this?" He shook his head. "They can't be allowed to get away with it."

I watched the smoldering remains, the way the snow turned to gray slurry as it drifted onto what had been my second home. The counter where I'd done homework, the kitchen where I'd learned to crimp a pie crust, the regulars I'd seen so often growing up that they were extended family. Gone.

Billy turned to me, his thin, wrinkled cheeks reddened by the cold. He must have watched all night. "Now do you believe me? They're dangerous."

"I know."

"Will you help, then? Look at what they've taken from us. Will you help us take it back?"

I nodded, and his smile was like a benediction. "Good girl. Have Donnelly take you home now."

Down the street, Colin leaned against a bus shelter, hands jammed in his pockets, taking it all in. As I picked my way around piles of slush and pools of dirty water, every step seemed harder than the last. My feet were clumsy and half-frozen. I buried my face in his jacket, and the tears I'd been fighting were impossible to hold back.

By the time I stopped crying, my hair was soaked with melting snow and my nose was running like crazy. His jacket was wet, too, the canvas rough against my cheek. "You're shaking," he said. I would have argued, but my teeth were clacking too hard for speech.

We started to walk toward the truck when someone called my name.

"Mo! Hold up!" The voice behind me was familiar. I turned, squinting, and saw Nick Petros, the reporter from my Journalism class. He was wearing a battered blue parka with the hood pulled up against the cold, a steno notebook in his gloved hand. Judging from the ruddy, wind-chapped look of his cheeks, he'd been here as long as my uncle.

"I'd like to ask you a few questions," he said.

"No comment," I said.

He took a step back as Colin plowed past him, keeping me tucked under one arm.

"We'll talk later," he called.

I didn't doubt he meant it.

CHAPTER 41

When we got home, Colin exchanged nods with the guy standing outside the screened porch and followed me in.

"There's one out front, too," he said, anticipating my questions. "For the foreseeable future."

I'd felt trapped by Colin at first, I reminded myself. Then we'd become friends, and what had been claustrophobic turned companionable. Somehow, I didn't see that happening with the new guys.

"Mom?"

The kitchen gleamed. Every light was turned on, and every surface—the faucet, the refrigerator handle, the windowsills, the worn linoleum floor—was obsessively clean, polished beyond perfection. "Shoes," I hissed, and Colin bent to remove his work boots while I toed off my ballet flats, ruined by the snow.

The rest of the house was in the same state. In the living room, the bookshelves were completely dust free, the spines of the books all lined up perfectly. Even the African violets looked like they'd been tidied. My heart twisted at the sight, evidence of how desperately my mom was trying to grab hold of some order. "Mom?"

"Upstairs!" she called. I found her dusting light fixtures in the bathroom.

"Did you see it?" she asked, her eyes red from crying, her hands nearly raw from all the cleaning she'd done.

"I'm so sorry."

She wiped at her eyes. "This wasn't your fault. I just wish you'd been able to see Daddy."

"It's okay." The guilt of lying to her sat uncomfortably in my stomach. I didn't need to see my dad. The fire had revealed everything. Whatever my uncle had done in the past, whatever his dealings with the Forelli family, it had to be better than the Russians. I patted her hand. "We'll go another time."

She smiled weakly. "That would be nice. You look tired, sweetheart. I'll fix cocoa."

"Let me. I'll bring you a cup."

She hugged me again, cupped my face in her hands. "You are such a good girl."

Quickly, I changed out of my damp clothes into pajamas and then toweled off my hair, sighing as it sprang into unruly curls.

"How is she?" Colin asked when I came downstairs, headed for the kitchen.

"You could perform major surgery on any surface of this house." I pulled out a saucepan and a box of cocoa. "It's her coping mechanism. Grab the milk, please."

The familiar way he moved around the kitchen made me feel even more secure. "Does that mean she's coping?"

"I think so. But she wouldn't tell me otherwise. She wants to protect me."

He touched my still-damp hair. "I know the feeling."

I watched as the milk started to steam, then whisked in cocoa and sugar from the canister on the counter. "Did you want some?"

"Sure." He watched me fill the mugs.

"I need to run this upstairs," I said, going up on tiptoe to kiss him. His arms came around my waist, pressing me close before shoving me gently toward the stairs.

I dropped off the cocoa with my mom, convincing her to take a break. As I headed back to see Colin, my phone chimed. I dug it out of my coat pocket, checking the text. It was Jenny Kowalski.

we need 2 talk

I couldn't help my uncle deal with Ekomov if I was working with Jenny. And Billy hadn't killed Kowalski, no matter what she thought. If war was coming, it was time to pick sides—and what kind of person would I be if I didn't choose my family?

sorry, I typed. deal is off

The response was almost immediate.

no comment won't work 4ever

The answer to the mystery of Jenny's source suddenly became clear, the tumblers of a lock lining up with a click. Nick Petros was the one feeding her information. He'd visited my classroom and invited me to his office, any time I wanted to chat. He'd reported on my dad's trial. He'd written a column about Kowalski's death. He'd practically told me, that day—what he knew and what he could prove were two different things. He wanted me to bring him proof.

I put away the phone, weary and resolute. There was nothing more to say.

CHAPTER 42

Lena met me at the front steps of the school Wednesday morning. "I heard! Are you okay?"

"I wasn't even there." I shoved my hair back, my arms heavy with fatigue. "By the time we got to the restaurant, the fire was out."

"Is your mom totally devastated?"

I thought back to the scene in our kitchen an hour ago, the mounds of eggs and sausage and potatoes she'd cooked up for me, Colin, and the two guys on guard duty. "She's losing it a little bit."

It was a clear, cold day, hovering just above freezing, and I dragged in lungfuls of crisp air. Nothing could displace the lingering smell of burned plastic and charred brick.

For once, I was early enough that we didn't have to rush in, but I was in no hurry to face my classmates' questions and stares. Lena seemed to understand, and we paused near the steps, waiting for the bell. Colin probably wasn't thrilled about me staying out in the open, but he had a clear view of the courtyard.

"How was your dad?"

"We never made it. My uncle called about the fire and we came straight home. I got to the restaurant as the firefighters were finishing up. I spent yesterday at home with my mom."

"You left Monday morning, but you came back Tuesday?"

she asked, working it out. "You stayed overnight. With Colin?"

"There was a problem with the truck. By the time it was fixed, visiting hours were over."

Not a lie, I reminded myself. I just didn't mention it was a magical problem, or the disaster that had come after. "We figured we'd go Tuesday, but when my uncle called . . . everything changed."

She smirked. "You spent the night with him? I'm betting things changed."

I felt the traitorous spots of color blooming on my cheeks. "We didn't . . ."

"Oh, please. If you didn't, it wasn't because you didn't want to." She peered over my shoulder, in the direction of the truck. "Him either. What's next?"

I didn't know, so I fell back on the only familiar thing I had going. "First period," I replied, and we made our way inside.

The day went exactly as expected. People offered sympathy, asked not-very-subtle questions, passed around increasingly outrageous stories. By the time the last bell rang, Lena informed me that The Slice had been blown up by IRA gunrunners in league with the Outfit, who were trying to manufacture C-4 in the supply closet. Even Jill McAllister got in on the action during AP Chem, asking sweetly—and loudly—if my mom would be able to afford tuition for St. Brigid's, much less college, now that the restaurant was gone. She'd heard that community college was very affordable, she informed me. I didn't have the energy to trip her.

"No aliens?" I asked Lena as we trudged toward the front doors. "I think the story needs aliens in there somewhere."

"Totally. Extraterrestrial involvement would be the cherry on top."

"If it were a sundae made of suck."

As we came outside, someone cut me off. I skidded on the wet steps and barely managed to stay upright.

"Oops." Jenny Kowalski stood in front of me, wearing a blue plaid skirt that almost—but not quite—matched our uniforms. It was just similar enough that she blended into the crowd of girls. "I heard about the restaurant. Do you guys have insurance?"

I gaped at her.

"Do I know you?" Lena asked.

"No. We should talk," Jenny said to me.

"I don't think so," I said. "Things have changed."

She shook her head. "Not as much as you'd think. Here." She handed me a manila envelope. I tried to shove it back at her, but she refused to take it.

"I'm not interested," I said.

"You will be. Ask yourself who benefits the most from The Slice being gone. It's basic police work." She lifted a hand in farewell, her eyes boring into mine. "I hope they catch the person responsible, Mo. I really do."

She strode away, around the side of the building, and Lena watched her go.

"What was that all about?"

"Families," I said, tightening my grip on the envelope. "I think."

"What's in the envelope?"

"Let's find out." We ducked back inside and found an empty classroom. I opened the envelope, spreading the papers out on a back table.

"It's an arrest report," I said.

Lena pointed at the date stamp. "That's from the night of the break-in. Didn't Colin say no police?"

"We didn't file this." The paper detailed a traffic stop that had turned into a weapons violation—three men, four or five blocks from our house, stopped for speeding. When the cop ran the license of the driver, he'd discovered all three occupants had arrest records, searched the vehicle, and found two guns—unloaded, but still in clear violation of the city's handgun ban.

"They must have been the guys who came to your house."

She leaned over the table. "Look, they were heading the opposite direction, away from the neighborhood. And it was right after the break-in. What are the other pages?"

"Their rap sheets." All three were known associates of Marco Forelli.

"I've heard of him," Lena said. "During the last Family Secrets trial. He's the one who walked. A bunch of the witnesses recanted."

"You pay attention to that stuff?" I asked, surprised. "I always tune it out."

"I pay attention to everything," she said. "If the guys who came to your house work for Marco Forelli, they weren't Russian."

"They were Mafia." I sat down hard, fitting together more and more pieces in my mind.

"Why would your uncle's guys threaten you? They want you on their side. Doesn't this defeat the purpose?"

"Misdirection," I said, and the last few pieces snapped into place. I stuffed the papers in my bag. "I have to go. Lena, please, don't tell anyone about this."

She looked offended. "I never do."

Colin was pacing in the courtyard.

"What was that all about?" he asked. "School's been out for twenty minutes."

"I need to go to The Slice."

"Why?"

I wanted to tell him, but I couldn't bring myself to do it, not without proof. It sounded crazy, that Billy and Forelli were behind the break-in and the fire, that they'd do all this to manipulate me. But Yuri Ekomov had never seen me as a threat, only a potential ally.

To my uncle, I'd been a danger—unpredictable and angry. He needed to keep me in line, so why not try fear, especially if he could use me against his enemies?

"I need some paperwork out of the office, if it's still standing."

He watched me closely. "Everything okay?"

"It's getting there." He didn't know. He couldn't possibly know, or he wouldn't have been so worried the night of the break-in. He'd been just as surprised as I was about the fire. Tess might ensure he was loyal to Billy, but Colin would never lie about something so huge. We were better than that now. Stronger. Billy must have kept it from Colin, too, and the realization sent a chill through me, for reasons I couldn't quite name.

At The Slice, I picked my way through the rubble. There was no logic to what had survived the fire and what hadn't. The big stand mixer my mom used for pie crusts had melted into slag, but a few feet away, a shelf of coffee cups was virtually untouched. The door to the office was blackened, but otherwise okay. I turned the handle tentatively and made my way in. Inside, everything looked almost normal. Water pooled on the floor, the face of the time clock was cracked, and there was an awful smell of stale smoke and wet paper, but the file cabinet seemed fine. I yanked on the top drawer. It stuck, like it always did, before giving way with a screech.

"What are you looking for?" Colin asked.

"Background." My mom kept all the important documents in a safe deposit box at the bank, but there had to be copies of the insurance policy. I rummaged through the drawer, feeling a surge of triumph when my fingers landed on the one labeled "National Insurance Co." I didn't understand most of the policy, but clear enough, The Slice was insured to the hilt—both the building and the business. Everything was covered.

Already, the Dumpsters behind the building were filling up as my uncle's construction company cleared away the debris. Morgan's would be closed for at least a week while they repaired the smoke damage and cleaned up after the firefighters. I was willing to bet Billy had insurance, too. The insurance company would pay my uncle's construction business to repair his bar, no doubt at an inflated rate. He'd make a mint. I felt sick at how easily I'd been manipulated.

"Have the police said who's responsible? Do they have any leads?" I asked Colin.

"Right now, they're looking at Ekomov. Fits his pattern, and it's no secret he's trying to move in."

"They don't think it could be Billy?"

He frowned. "Why would he torch The Slice? He's not hard up for money, and the insurance would go to your mom. I told you, it's an escalation."

"It's a con." I stuffed the insurance papers in my bag. "Billy wants to take the Russians down, right?"'

"Framing them for arson isn't going to do that."

"No. But it would help, same as framing them for Verity's murder. He gets the insurance payout. He launders money through the construction company while he rebuilds. And he gets me, pissed off and willing to help him out with the Russians."

"But to burn down your mom's restaurant . . ." He unfolded himself from the doorway. "That's a big accusation. He'd never hurt you."

"He doesn't need to hurt me. Just scare me." I slammed the drawer shut. "I'm going over there."

His hand clamped on my arm. "Somebody's outside. Stay put."

He slipped out, hand on the holster at his back, and eased the door shut behind him.

Waiting was not my strong suit anymore. After about fifteen seconds, I crept to the door and listened, but the voices were muffled.

I cracked the door a bit farther and squeezed through, tiptoeing to the corner.

"Your timing really sucks, you know that?" Colin said.

"Ain't my timetable," Luc replied.

Determined not to let him shake me, I stepped into view. "What are you doing here?"

"Needed to see you." He surveyed the remains of The Slice. "Wasn't quite what I expected."

"The day's been full of surprises."

He poked at a pile of rubble with his toe. "Pretty bad. Wasn't natural, either."

"I'm aware."

"Set there," he said, pointing to a spot near the front counter. "And there . . ." The cash register. "Back here." The kitchen island, where we did most of the prep.

When I raised my eyebrows, he shrugged. "It's fire, Mouse. Not much I can't read here."

"What else can you tell?" Colin demanded.

"Way they set it, fire ran along the outside walls. Left the shared walls intact. Kept it away from the gas lines, so the rest of the building didn't go. Lot of damage in a short time, but very targeted."

He touched a charred tabletop, rubbed the soot between his fingers. "Speaking of damage, we need to go control some."

"I'm busy."

"You want to be pissed at me? Go right ahead. But the magic is failing. By the end of the day, there'll hardly be any left. If you don't come with now, and fix it, the Quartoren will say you've broken the Covenant. You'll be dead."

I folded my arms and stared at him. "If they kill me, I can't fix the magic."

"You will be dead," he repeated. "And who will help Constance? That is a girl in need of help, whether we succeed or not."

I felt my resolve start to crumble, and glanced at Colin, who glowered, jamming his hands in his pockets.

"You're taking me along," he said.

I sighed. "We've talked about this."

"You told me you were never going to be free of these people. That's what you said. But you can't expect me to sit at home while you risk your life for them." He curled a hand around the back of my neck. "They're not the only ones you can't get free of. Got it?"

"Got it," I whispered, feeling the corners of my mouth tug up the tiniest bit.

Luc scowled. "He'll be underfoot."

Colin shrugged. "You keep her safe, you won't even know I'm there."

"This what you want?" Luc asked, and there was no snark in his voice, only hurt and resignation. "Be sure."

"I am."

He grasped my wrist. "You know the drill." I barely had time to grab hold of Colin before he opened a door to Between and wrenched us through.

Dominic frowned as we came through on the marble stage of the Allée. "Stowaway, son?"

"He's with me," I slurred, fighting off the blackness closing in. I felt a gentle hand on my shoulder. It was Marguerite, encouraging me to breathe.

"Remember the prophecy," she whispered. "The magic seeks you. Join it, and you'll find your path."

I blinked, her face swimming in front of me. For a moment, it seemed as if her eyes had gone milky again, but then everything around me snapped into focus, and her gaze was clear and sightless once again.

"He can't stay," Orla was saying, thumping her cane in outrage. "It's . . . it's . . ."

"It's settled," Luc said.

I leaned heavily on Colin's arm. He looked at the Quartoren. "What's wrong with her?"

Luc answered. "Her body can't handle the magic."

"Damn it, heal her," Colin ordered.

"No." With an effort, I came back to myself. He and Marguerite helped me to my feet. "I'll be okay."

"You knew?" Colin asked. "Why didn't you tell me?"

"What would you have done? I told you before . . . you can't protect me from everything." I wiped a trickle of blood away from my nose and looked around. The edge of the stage was crumbling away. The lush green pathways surrounding it had been churned up, resembling a construction site, and tree branches littered the ground.

"Was this from the magic?"

"The Darklings helped," said Orla. "All of that magic set free, and they swarmed the Allée. They won't come back here, though. The four lines bordering the Allée are weakened, not worthy of their attention."

"Can we use one of them now?" I asked Pascal. "I don't need all four, but I do need a way in."

"They should suffice, yes. Remember to draw on Luc's talent so you're attuned to all four elements," he answered.

Luc approached me. I nodded as Colin escorted Marguerite to the other side of the stage. "This doesn't change anything," I told him.

"Never wanted you to be more wrong," he replied, pressing his palm against mine. "Ready?"

I put on the bravest face I could, for Colin's sake. "Ready."

As the others looked on, Luc called up one of the lines bordering the Allée. Fire, crackling to life, and our bond pulled taut. Closing my eyes, I felt my way toward the keening energy, bracing myself for the shock of contact, expecting to feel Luc's presence supporting me as I dove in. Instead, he brushed past me, blocking my way.

"What are you doing?"

He didn't answer, lip caught between his teeth in concentration as he reached into the blazing line. I felt him drawing on our connection, my energy pouring into him as he took the magic inside himself, body convulsing.

Now I knew what he went through every time I touched raw magic. I watched, terrified, as the magic started breaking him down in order to build him back up.

"Luc! It's not supposed to be this way!"

It was supposed to be me.

I was the one the magic had bonded with. I was the one in the prophecy. He was trying to take my place, in some misguided, chivalrous attempt to let me go.

Sweat poured off him, his skin drawn so tightly against the bones I could see the veins standing out on his temple. The tendons in his neck strained, and I could feel his pulse alongside mine, speeding past the point of endurance, faster and fainter with every second.

"Stop!" He hadn't thought it through. Whenever I dealt with the lines, his powers bolstered me. He'd assumed we could reverse the process, but I had no magic to give him. It would never work.

His eyes rolled back in his head. I yanked on his hand, trying to break his contact with the line, but I lacked the strength. Through our binding, I felt the magic reach out to me, hungrily, and I nearly let go. The magic didn't want Luc. It would burn through him, leaving nothing behind, in order to get to me.

Across the stage, the Quartoren huddled together, Dominic's face betraying his own hunger. Colin stood with Marguerite, talking urgently. He must be describing the scene to her, and she was explaining what he saw.

"Colin! Get Luc out!"

He didn't question me or hesitate. He sprinted toward us, tackling Luc low, the force of the hit ripping both of them away from the flaring line.

They bounced and skidded along the marble stage. Dominic shouted something, grabbing Pascal's arm, but I didn't wait to find out what it was.

I pushed my way into the magic, and they were gone.

CHAPTER 43

Here is what I know:
I know that the truth is a hard and bitter thing. I know that love comes in as many forms as people do, and not all of them are good. I know that secrets are lies that haven't been told yet. I know that for every action there is a cost, and that accepting your fate is only the first step in fulfilling it. I know that people have paid for my life with their own, too many times, and the time had come to return the favor.

And as soon as I stepped into the magic, with no shield except my intentions, I knew one more thing: The magic was *alive*.

It had been alive all along. I just hadn't recognized it. What I'd thought was hunger was loneliness, a craving for connection, and its rage was panic turned violent. It had no one to speak with, to ask for help. And now it had me, which seemed like the cruelest possible joke. The magic needed a voice, and it had chosen a girl who'd spent her whole life afraid to speak.

In biology, you learn how a cell works. You learn about the cell membrane, and cytoplasm, and the nucleolus, all the microscopic interconnected workings that make life possible. But they're only labels on a picture, meaningless, until they've been taken apart, bit by bit, which is exactly what the magic did to me. Last time, when I'd opened myself up to the magic, it had made me omnipotent, at least for a time. I'd known everything, seen the whole world laid out before me like a vast and beautiful map I could traverse at will. I had it again, a flash of understanding that illuminated the universe. But as I struggled to make sense of the magic, it did the same to me—invading every cell wall, every strand of DNA, fusing to me, and I choked as the pressure increased, like there wasn't enough room for both of us inside my body.

Just like in my dream, I slipped under the surface of the magic, drowning on dry land, and then Luc was there, buoying me, the crush of my lungs easing enough to gasp a single lungful of air. His strength joined with what Verity had passed to me in the alley a lifetime ago, and I remembered Marguerite's advice: *listen.* I stopped fighting and finally listened to what the magic had been trying to tell me. I couldn't be the bystander anymore. It wasn't enough to be the conduit, the neutral party. If I wanted to live, I needed to go all in.

So I did. I gave myself over to the magic, letting it tell me what it needed. Pascal had compared it to a circulatory system, so I felt my way back through the lines, looking for the rip at the very heart of the magic. My body was still at the Allée, but my consciousness had expanded out along the lines, going as far as the magic did.

It bled power, a billowing, opalescent glow. My own strength ebbed as I watched, and I drew on Luc to sustain myself, relying equally on his talent and resolve. This deep inside the source, intention was the same as action, so I spoke to the magic, coaxing it back into the pulsating heart, into *my* heart. I sealed the fissure with the words of power that Luc used so easily, foreign and silvery on my tongue, and knew as I did they weren't mine to keep.

Despite the power flowing through me, my body was exhausted. The magic wavered slightly, as the strain of what I'd done hit me full force. I pulled back into myself, feeling the magic thrum through the lines in time with my heartbeat, a perfect connection.

"Mouse?" Luc said as I opened my eyes and blinked at him. "You in there?"

"Mostly," I said, and Colin came running toward us. I only had time to smile at him before I passed out.

CHAPTER 44

Someone was shining a light in my eyes. I batted it away and squinched up my face.

"I think she's recovered," someone said.

"She needs a doctor," said Colin, in a voice that suggested if one didn't appear very quickly, I wouldn't be the only one needing medical attention.

"Did you want to see my medical license?" Pascal asked.

"She ain't hurt," Luc said. "She's tired, that's all."

Colin's fingers threaded through mine. "You're sure?"

The bond with Luc hummed slightly against my skin as he checked. "Guaranteed. Wake up, Sleepin' Beauty, 'less you're looking to be kissed." He fed an extra jolt into our connection, and I opened my eyes.

"Jerk."

"See?" he said to Colin. "Ornery as ever."

Colin ignored him. "You're really all right?"

"Just wiped out. Three or four days of sleep ought to cure it."

His smile didn't reach his eyes, and I knew there was more to talk about, but I didn't want to—not when I was exhausted and exhilarated all at once, and there was still the Quartoren to deal with. They hung back, watching us closely, coming forward only when Colin demanded Luc take us home.

"I fulfilled the Covenant," I said, facing them. They didn't intimidate me anymore. We were on equal footing. "You need to help Constance now, no matter what."

"And we shall," said Dominic. "Tell us what happened, if you don't mind."

"You lied. That's what happened," I said pleasantly. Of the three, Pascal was the only one who looked at me with anything like approval.

"You never wanted me to make new lines. That was just a way to get me to step inside the magic, so it would bond with me. Pascal's test at the country club proved I couldn't stop the process on my own, so yesterday, you told Luc to leave me trapped in the nexus. But it was never necessary for the Covenant. The three of you were trying to hold on to your positions."

Luc's voice was like knives. "What?"

"You must have freaked out when you realized a Flat was the only person who could manipulate the lines. What if you couldn't control me? What if the word got out to the rest of the Arcs? They might believe Anton was right, that the Quartoren's time had passed. If I was locked inside the heart of the magic, you wouldn't have to worry. Everything would go back to the way it was.

"You brought me to the mourning ceremony because you hoped it would trigger a breach—with so many people using their powers, the magic was bound to try for me. When Anton stopped the ceremony, you decided to force me into the magic anyway. No sense abandoning a perfectly good plan. You must have been thrilled when Constance lost it and the raw magic broke loose." God, it made me sick to think of how easily I'd been manipulated. Twice in one day—first Billy, then Dominic.

Never again.

Dominic's face hardened. "Hadn't planned on you turning tail."

"Really? I think you did. That's why you ordered Luc to leave me there. You told him the prophecy showed we'd survive, so it was okay for him to abandon me. You played into his belief in fate because you knew it was the one thing he couldn't argue. Quite a shock for you, when he turned out to be a decent human being."

"You agreed to the Covenant," Dominic said. "Argue all you want, but we were simply assuring you fulfilled the terms."

"The terms of the Covenant were to fix the magic. There was nothing in there about helping you."

He shrugged. "Down here, we call that a *lagniappe*. A little something extra."

"I call it dishonest. The Covenant's over now, Dominic. I don't owe you anything. New game. New rules."

Orla sputtered. "But . . . Anton. The Seraphim. Surely you won't let them succeed!"

Marguerite came forward, clinging to Luc. "Enough. All of you. She's been through plenty and she's right. Leave her be.

"You did a brave thing, Mo. And you saved my son." She lowered her voice. "You've changed, I think."

"Yes."

"I told you once that fate wouldn't call someone who wasn't capable. That's truer now than it ever was."

"Thanks. I think." I looked out over the ruins of the Allée, wondering how much magic it would take to repair the damage. Orla would probably lead that project, I figured, making sure protocol was followed, traditions upheld. At the farthest end of the path, something moved in the trees, and I craned my neck to see better.

Anton. Instead of his robe, he wore a dark suit, hands stuffed carelessly in his pockets. I wondered how much he'd witnessed, and how much he'd understood. He waited until he was sure I'd seen him and then threw a hand in the air, a casual farewell—it was a "see you soon," not "good-bye." I knew the difference.

"Can you please take us home?" I asked Luc.

He did, wordlessly, returning us to the parking lot behind The Slice.

"I'll get the truck," Colin said.

When we were alone, Luc asked tentatively, "You're not sick?"

"No." Now that the magic had found its place in me, going Between didn't wrench me apart. "I'm good. Different, but good."

"Different's a bit of an understatement," he said. "Even my mother could see it."

I glanced at what remained of the restaurant. I might have fixed the magic, but there was plenty left to do. "Another time, Luc."

He looked disappointed, especially when Colin came back and took my hand. And then his eyes met mine, challenging. "Bet on it."

Chapter 45

We didn't say much as Colin let me into his place, the half workshop, half apartment he'd built inside an old warehouse. From the street, it was just run-down enough to be anonymous without attracting squatters or vandals. Inside, it was exactly what I'd come to expect from Colin. Sparse but comfortable. No knickknacks, nothing personal except the shelves of books, which ran to American classics and a lot of short stories. A wood stove in one corner, a weight bench and speed bag in the other. I was careful not to look at the door that led to the bedroom. I'd slept there only once, fitfully, while Colin dozed on the couch. My stomach fluttered at the memory.

"You hungry?" he asked as he stowed his gun in the locked cabinet.

"Not really. Sleepy, though."

He crossed the room again, his feet echoing on the cement floor, and stopped less than a foot away from me. "I should take you home."

"That's the last place I should be. I have to figure out what I'm going to tell my mom."

He frowned a little, and then reached for my scarf, rubbing the red wool between his fingers. My breath caught. The room was so quiet I could hear the rasp of the material against his skin. Slowly, he unwound the scarf from my neck, the knuckles skimming my throat. When he'd tugged the last end free, he set it on the couch and took my gloved hand in his.

I'd never realized before how large his hands were, the square, blunt fingertips dwarfing mine. He peeled my gloves away carefully, refusing to rush. By the time the second one was off, I was dizzy with wanting him, feeling it tingle along the backs of my legs and the length of my spine. He stepped closer, running his hands down the outside of my coat, tucking the gloves into my pockets before returning to the buttons.

I closed my eyes, overwhelmed by the seriousness of his expression. I could feel the tug and slide of the buttons as he unfastened each one, cool air edging underneath my coat, and still I felt feverish. He pushed it off my shoulders, the weight suddenly gone, and it seemed like I might float away in the time it took him to toss it over the couch.

And then he crushed me so close that the air squeezed out of my lungs. I tilted my head back to find him right there, eyes dark gray and intent. The line of his mouth was soft and inviting, and the kiss was like coming home, it felt so right.

We didn't move from that spot for a long time. There was so much I wanted to tell him, but I didn't have the words, and none of them mattered, really. I was still glowing from the magic and my success and his touch. I had done the impossible. It didn't seem crazy to think that a shot with Colin—a real one—was possible, too.

Now that I knew the truth about Billy, the power had shifted. I'd help Nick Petros and Jenny bring him down. Colin would be free. We could find someplace in New York for Tess, bring her with us, and start fresh. I was so pleased with myself, I practically purred.

"Hey," Colin said, his mouth traveling along my jaw. "Where did you go?"

"I'm here. With you."

He pulled back a little, studying me. "You scared the hell out of me tonight."

"Forget about it," I said, going up on tiptoe to taste the hollow of his collarbone. "Everything's okay now."

He ducked away. "But it's not over."

"No. The magic is part of me. Or I'm part of it. Hard to tell which." He didn't seem to share my amusement, and I sighed. "If we're going to talk about this—"

"We are definitely going to talk about this."

"Can we sit down at least?" I sank into the worn blue velvet couch, laying my head on his chest. The sound of his heart filled me with a quiet joy.

"The magic was giving you trouble all along," he said. "That's why Luc wasn't taking you Between."

"My body couldn't process it. But it won't hurt me anymore. We have an understanding." A sense of contentment drifted through me, confirming my words.

"You and the magic." The disbelief was plain in his voice.

I didn't want to get into my theory about the magic being sentient, not when I barely understood it myself.

"You lied," he said. "Which I know from experience you are not a fan of."

"I kept a secret. Not the same."

"You've had a lot of secrets lately."

The peaceful, cozy feeling seemed to leach out of the room. "Like what?"

"Other than the magic? How about your source? The one that's feeding you information?"

I straightened, queasy at the reminder of Colin's file. "You have secrets, too. Are you going to tell me what Billy has on you? Where you got those scars?" *Please*, I willed him silently, *tell me, so I can stop pretending I don't know. So I know you trust me the way I trust you. Please, please, please tell me, and I will make it better.*

But he didn't. Instead, he shifted, just far enough to make sure I understood his past was still off-limits. The gesture hurt, and my instinct was to say something cutting back, but I thought about Tess, how their history clung to their everyday lives like barnacles, and stopped myself.

"I'd be okay with it," I said eventually, slipping my hand into his, loving the way they looked together. "Your past is part of you, right? And I want all of you, Colin, not just the good parts. Everything."

He brought our joined hands to his lips, and I scooted closer. Something in his expression, in the set of his shoulders, eased. He drew a breath, like he was about to speak, and the intercom buzzed.

He dropped my hand and stood so abruptly I toppled over.

"Who is it?" No matter who was on the other side of the door, it wasn't good. Colin made a point of keeping his place a secret. Unexpected visitors meant trouble.

He stalked over to the intercom and jabbed the button with his thumb, peering at the tiny video monitor. "What?"

"Donnelly. Let us in, man. We're freezing our asses off out here."

Chilled without Colin next to me, I wrapped myself in a throw blanket. "Who are they?"

"Billy's guys."

"Did you give them the address?"

He shook his head once. "What do you need?"

"We want to talk to you, that's all." Static burst through the speaker.

He studied the image more closely. "Now's not a great time."

"Billy sent us. We can't leave till we deliver the message."

"Mo," he said, after a moment, his voice strangely hollow. "Go in the bedroom. Don't come out until I say."

"What? No."

The voice crackled over the speaker again, less patient this time. "Dude, let us in. We're trying to be polite. We don't have to."

"Give me a minute," he told them, grabbing my coat and scarf. He pulled me up off the couch, started pushing my arms through the sleeves. "Listen to me. You need to go in the bedroom. There's a cabinet, the big cherrywood one, against the back wall. I want you to get in and lock it from the inside. Do you understand?"

"Billy sent those guys."

"Yes."

"They want to talk. That's what they said, they had a message."

"They're not here to talk. You need to hide. Don't come out until you're sure they've left."

"This is crazy, Colin. Talk to them. Let *me* talk to them. They won't hurt me—"

There was a faint pounding, like someone was hammering on the door, and the buzzer squawked again as he led me into the bedroom. "Donnelly, don't make this worse."

"*Now,* Mo. Somebody saw us. Somebody talked. Billy knows."

"I'll call him." I dug in my pocket for my phone. "I'll straighten it out."

"You didn't want me to watch, with the magic. You couldn't afford to be distracted." I started to shake, and he continued. "I can't get out of this if I'm protecting you, too."

"Can you get out of this at all?"

"I'm going to try. But you need to hide. You can't see this."

"Colin . . ."

"I knew we shouldn't. I knew the risk." He kissed me, whisper soft. "Actions and consequences. And you were worth it. Every single second."

He shoved me toward the armoire, as a muffled crash sounded in the workshop. "Go!" he said, and pulled the door shut behind him.

I climbed in, just like he said to, and closed the door. It smelled like Colin, wood shavings and laundry soap, and I buried my face in the worn flannel of his shirts. Feeling my way toward the back wall, I pressed my hands hard into the satiny wood. He'd made this cabinet himself. I tried, in the darkness, to envision his hands gripping the wood plane, applying the varnish in smooth, unwavering strokes. The only sounds were the rustle of his clothes and my frantic gasps, and I tried to time my breathing to the imagined rhythm of Colin sanding this piece.

He'd told me to lock the door. I reached back for the bolt, but when my fingers brushed against it, they froze. Colin was out there, his life in danger, because of me. Because I'd pushed, even when he'd told me not to. I'd worn him down, like water turning stone to sand, and now everything was crumbling. All my fault, and I was crouched in a piece of furniture, powerless to stop it.

Except I wasn't powerless. I reached inside me for the magic, digging deep, and felt the thrum, already so familiar that I barely noticed it. "Come on," I whispered, trying to call up a line. The magic vibrated a bit in response, but there was no crackling current for me to harness, no wave of energy to use against the guys coming for Colin. "Come on, damn it!"

I could feel the power sliding through my veins, wrapping itself around me like a vine, the bond as strong as the instant it had formed. But no matter how I tried, I couldn't use it. I nearly screamed with the unfairness of it, all that power and no way to help.

The rumble of voices from the living room filtered in. The voices stopped, and there was a thud and grunt from the other room, the sickening sound of a fist striking flesh. I clapped my hands over my mouth a second before the shriek escaped. There was a sound of breaking glass and more thuds, and I sagged back.

The magic wasn't going to save me, and it wasn't going to save Colin. He hadn't even *tried* to run, and for an instant I was furious with him. But where would he go? Tess was here. And Colin was honorable enough to think that he needed to pay for violating Billy's trust.

I didn't have that problem. I didn't trust Billy, and he didn't trust me, and if Colin wasn't going to save himself, I would.

Without magic.

CHAPTER 46

I cracked the cabinet door open and crept out, trying to ignore the sounds in the other room. I needed to be rational. Colin kept his guns in the cabinet out front. But he wouldn't sleep at night without some kind of protection, a weapon he could reach quickly and easily. Where would he hide it?

Scrambling across the room, I yanked open the drawer of the nightstand next to the bed and found nothing. Same for the other nightstand. Under the bed? I dropped to the floor and slithered underneath, but all I found were a few dust bunnies and an old copy of *Walden*.

It had to be somewhere close by. I tried to imagine Colin sleeping here, waking to an intruder. The first thing he'd do would be hit the ground, putting the bed between him and the door. I knelt down, grateful for the area rug cushioning my knees from the cement floor. He'd poured the floors himself, he'd told me once. He'd been so proud, which seemed like a total guy thing to be excited about. I didn't have the heart to tell him they were hard as hell and icy cold.

There was no place to hide anything. Nothing under the mattress, no furniture except the nightstand on this side, which I'd already checked. I scooted back under the bed, trying to see if he'd taped a gun to the underside or the headboard, but there was still nothing. I wriggled out again, dislodging the rug.

And there it was. No wonder he'd been so proud. A square

slab of cement had been cut out and replaced, grooves chiseled into the surface so it was easier to grip. My fingers scrabbled for it, the slab coming away with a grinding sound. Beneath it was a hollowed-out space, holding a gun and several cartridges of bullets.

My hands shook as I lifted it out, the metal oily against my fingertips. I had no idea how to shoot a gun. I didn't even know if it was loaded. I'd nagged Colin about it when we first met, told him I should be able to protect myself. He'd dismissed the idea. You'd think being right would have been more satisfying, but the noises from the other room were sounding worse—I heard Colin moan and cough, a wet sound that couldn't mean anything good.

Maybe it worked like a camera, point and shoot. And maybe I wouldn't have to shoot. I really, *really* hoped I wouldn't have to shoot.

No one noticed when I slipped into the living room. Gripping the gun like I'd seen on TV, I pointed it at the heavier of the two guys—the one kicking Colin in the ribs.

"Leave him alone."

My voice sounded small to me, insubstantial amid the violence, but it was enough to make all three men jerk around and stare. Colin lay sprawled on the floor, his face battered, blood dripping from a cut over his eye. Even so, he still managed to shoot me a furious look.

"Stop right now," I said, and I might not have been able to call up magic, but I leaned on it anyway, to keep my voice strong. Its presence was a reminder I was more than these guys saw, more than anyone saw, and the knowledge steadied my aim.

"Don't touch him again. Go stand over there." I angled my head toward the door. "Stand there and don't move, or I swear to God, I will shoot you."

The bigger guy turned toward me. "You're Billy's niece? Jesus, Donnelly. She doesn't even have a decent set of . . ." He gestured, crudely, to his chest.

I cut him off. "Hey! Don't insult the girl with the gun."

The little one spoke. "Kid, put that down before you hurt yourself."

"I don't think so. Colin, are you okay?"

He groaned, the sound turning into a cough. "Mo . . ."

I knelt next to him. "Do you need a hospital?"

"No hospital," he wheezed. "You were supposed to hide."

"I didn't like that plan."

The heavyset guy took a step toward me, and I trained the barrel on him. "I really will shoot you. I won't even feel bad about it."

He took another step. "Sweetheart, you're not gonna shoot anybody. You don't have it in you."

I locked my elbows, keeping the gun steady while I clambered to my feet. "Really? I am *Billy Grady's niece*, you dumb-ass. You just hurt someone I love." I adjusted my grip and planted my feet, like I'd seen Colin do. "Are you seeing the family resemblance yet?"

He paled. "Right. Sorry. And sorry about the . . . uh . . ." He waved his hands vaguely. "The comment."

"We were just doing what Billy asked," whined the second guy.

"Where is he now? Morgan's?"

They exchanged a look. "Yeah."

I blew out a breath and felt in my coat pocket for my phone. Lena answered on the second ring.

"Hey. I need your help." The gun was too heavy to hold with one hand. I tucked the phone between my ear and shoulder, switching back to a two-handed grip.

"Calc test help or sneaking out of the house help?"

"Colin's hurt, and I have to take care of something. If I give you the address, can you come and take care of him?"

There was a long, long silence. "How hurt?"

"Hurt," I said. "But he doesn't like hospitals."

"Where are you going?"

I gave Billy's thugs my sunniest smile. "To see my uncle."

CHAPTER 47

If there is any upside at all to watching your bodyguard / potential boyfriend get the crap kicked out of him, it is that he is in no condition to stop you when you go charging off to avenge him. Lena probably weighed 115, but Colin was in enough pain that even she could keep him under control.

I didn't try to get him to the bedroom—Lena and I managed to move him to the couch, an awkward process made worse by my unwillingness to put down the gun. I showed her where the shoebox of first-aid supplies was. "If anything seems weird, call me. If he gets worse, call 911. I'll be back soon."

"You're leaving with them?" Lena asked, her voice squeaking. "That's crazy stupid."

"They work for my uncle. I'm pretty sure they won't let anything happen to me."

"What if you get pulled over?" She twirled her ponytail so tightly that it curled back on itself in a glossy black rope.

"Who are the police going to believe? Them or the minor in a school uniform?"

"You are kind of scaring me," she said.

"I know. Thanks for doing this." I bent down and kissed Colin on the forehead. "I'll explain it all later, I swear."

"You totally will," Lena replied. "Finish this, okay? I am feeling very uncomfortable right now."

"Be careful," Colin rasped, gripping my hand. "Billy's playing the long game."

"So am I."

If there'd been another way, I would have taken it, but what other choice did I have? I needed to make sure the thugs didn't come back and hurt Colin once I'd left; I needed to see my uncle; I needed someone I trusted to watch over Colin. It was an imperfect plan, but it was all I had. That and the gun, which I hid inside my coat as we walked out to their car.

It was the longest, quietest car ride of my life. My fingers ached from clenching the handgrip so tightly. When we got to Morgan's, I tucked the gun in my pocket and let Billy's men enter first.

Morgan's still wasn't open for business—not technically, anyway—but a few die-hard regulars clustered around the bar. The repairs were minor, and I didn't doubt that they'd be back up and running in a week, at most. The Slice would be shut indefinitely, and the thought kicked my anger up another notch.

I watched Billy's face as he spotted his thugs. Cold expectation—he had given an order, and he was merely waiting for confirmation. When he saw me, shock wiped his features blank. I let my fury propel me forward, feeling as cold as he looked.

"Mo," he said cautiously. "What are you doing here?"

"Your guys drove me. I don't think they like me very much."

"And why would that be?"

"Well." I set the gun on the table between us. "Probably because I threatened to shoot them."

"Put that away," he hissed, rearing back. "Are you mad, child?"

"I'm not a child, but I am mad. Those two troglodytes beat the hell out of Colin tonight, on your order."

He shot me a look of complete indifference. "He knew what would happen. And I told you not to chase him."

"I'm almost eighteen. You don't get to decide who I love."

"You're in love with him, are you? It's a mistake. He's broken on the inside."

"I'll fix him."

Billy scoffed. "That's what your mother said about Jack Fitzgerald. Didn't that turn out nicely? You don't know what you're dealing with."

"I know about Raymond Gaskill," I said. "Most of it, anyway. He's dead, right? Colin shot him."

"He told you?"

I didn't answer. "What I can't figure out is how you got involved. They grew up in Denver."

He settled back, arms folded, his gaze locked on the gun. "Raymond Gaskill was a small-time enforcer. Periodically, our paths crossed. He would have business in Chicago, I would fly out to Denver. You get to know people, after a while. And I knew he was an evil man."

His eyes cut to me. "I'll wager you thought I was as bad as they get. But Gaskill was much worse. Always wanted to scrub my skin raw after we shook hands. I knew he was using the boys as punching bags, had my suspicions about what he was doing to the little girl. But he was connected, and useful, so the people above him turned the other way."

"Until Child Services took the kids."

"She was new, easily fooled. Any caseworker worth her salt could have proven the man unfit. But when the kids were sent back, he lost his mind. He went after them one last time." He shrugged. "It was easy enough to cover up. No one wanted an investigation into Gaskill—he had ties to a lot of people who valued anonymity. Donnelly was shell-shocked. The girl—Tess—was still in a coma. There was nothing for them in Denver. They would have been split up. So, I brought them back, sent Colin to military school to learn some discipline. Gave the mother and the younger boy a proper burial, and found a place for Tess."

"And Colin decided he owed you for the rest of his life."

"Gratitude." His eyes narrowed. "His attempt to seduce you does not strike me as particularly grateful."

"He's paid his debt to you. He was a kid, and you manipulated him into thinking you saved him."

"I *did* save him. That's what I do, Maura Kathleen. I save people who cannot save themselves, and it's not outrageous to expect some degree of loyalty in return."

"He's grateful. But now he's out."

"Darling girl, I appreciate your moxie. But you're hardly in a position to bargain."

"I think I am."

"What do you have that's worth Donnelly's life? Think carefully before you answer. This is the man you say you love, so you'd do well to price his life accordingly."

I brushed a finger over the gleaming barrel. "I know you were behind the fire at The Slice. And the break-in."

"That was the Russians." But he didn't try to sell it the way he would have even a week ago.

"Yuri Ekomov wanted to work with me, not terrorize me. But if The Slice burned down, you'd get the insurance money. You could use the construction business to rebuild. And best of all, I'd be motivated to help you. I'm guessing you didn't tell Mom about your plan."

"Your mother allows me to handle the complexities of our lives."

"Maybe. But we both know she wouldn't allow you to manipulate me into taking on the Russian Mafia." I felt antsy, anxious to check on Colin. "You're in the protection business, Uncle Billy. So understand this: The Donnellys are under my protection now."

"And what do you give me?"

"Silence. I don't tell Mom."

Billy snorted. "Is that all? You're openly defying me for the second time in as many months, and corrupting one of my best men in the process. I love your mother dearly, but I'm less concerned with pleasing her than you might imagine. As long as she gets her restaurant back, the rest will fade away, especially with your father's return. She'll forgive me, because she's a good person, and we're family, and she appreciates everything I've done." He tsk'd. "You need a better hand to play."

Understanding dawned, and my heart felt heavier than the gun. This was what he'd wanted all along. I'd underestimated Billy. Again. "Ekomov," I said quietly.

He smiled. "He wants to work with you. All you'll have to do is pass along the information we choose."

If this was the price for Colin's life, so be it. But I wanted to be clear on the deal.

"You'll leave the Donnellys alone. Both of them. You pay Tess's bills, and Colin can pick up and go, any time he wants. Anywhere he wants."

"He can. You can't. You're agreeing to stay in Chicago. Give up your silly plans for New York. There are perfectly good colleges here, and a place for you in the business someday."

I couldn't get enough air. It was one thing to stay on my own terms, for a chance with Colin. It was another to shackle myself here as Billy's pawn. "But . . ."

"That's my price for Donnelly's life. What do you say?"

There had to be a way out. I'd find a way out. It just wouldn't be this minute. In this minute, it was Colin's life that mattered most. I'd pay whatever price Billy set.

"Done." There was no waver in my voice, no hesitation. I would never show a weakness in front of him again.

"Excellent." I stood to leave, and he said, "He'll find out, you know."

"Not from me," I said. "And not from you, or our deal is off."

"Truth has a way of worming its way to the surface. He'll

find out what you've done, and you'll lose him. The man lives to protect the people he loves, and you've turned that on its end. He won't be able to forgive you. You'll lose him, Mo."

"Lost is better than dead," I replied, ignoring the icy nugget of fear that lodged itself in my chest.

CHAPTER 48

The door to Colin's workshop had been smashed in, the lock ripped out of the frame, so it was easy to get inside. But in case he and Lena had armed themselves against unexpected visitors, I knocked on the door to the apartment. "It's me."

I heard the dead bolt scrape, and Lena cracked the door. "You're okay?"

"I'm cold. Let me in."

She stepped back, and I went straight to Colin, who was holding a towel full of ice to his cheekbone. The split over his eye sported a butterfly bandage, and there was a glass on the table smelling strongly of Jameson.

"I think they broke your nose," I said.

He touched it gingerly. "Wouldn't be the first time. What happened?"

Before I could answer, Lena stood up, shifting from one foot to the other. "I'm bailing. See you tomorrow. Colin . . ." She trailed off, slightly green. "Let's not do this again."

"Lena . . ." I couldn't find the words to thank her, and she dashed over to give me a quick hug.

"You are so spilling your guts tomorrow," she said, and took off.

I turned back to Colin. "Do you need anything?"

"Tell me."

I tucked the blanket around him more securely. "We talked. It was almost civilized."

"And?" Speaking hurt him. I could see it in the way he tensed up before every sentence, the rasp in his voice.

"The good news is, no one will be showing up at your door again." Before he could ask why, I hurried on. "The bad news is that you're still working for Billy."

It wasn't entirely bad, I told myself. Tess needed medical care. Colin would live on ramen noodles for the rest of his life to provide for her, but his tie to Billy wasn't just financial. No matter how monstrous my uncle seemed to me, he'd still rescued Colin and Tess when the rest of the world had ignored them. It was something Colin wouldn't forget.

"How?"

This is where it got tricky. Billy was right—if Colin found out I'd traded my life for his, he'd never forgive me. He had to believe I'd found some other way to convince my uncle. So I perched on the edge of the couch, looked into eyes as dark and churning as the lake in winter, and lied to the man I loved without a shred of remorse.

"I threatened to tell my mother about the fire. She's given up a lot for Billy over the years, but everyone has a breaking point. It's a stalemate. He doesn't interfere with us, I don't interfere with him."

He dropped his head back on the pillow, exhaustion and pain turning his skin a sickly color. There was one spot on his forehead that didn't seem too bruised, and I kissed it carefully before he drifted into sleep.

"You told Billy's man he'd hurt someone you love," he said, the words drowsy.

"I was angry."

"You're in love with me?" He touched my leg.

I met his eyes. "Would that be a problem?"

"You should have left," he said. "It would have been easier."

"Nothing about this is easy. That's how I know it's right."

*   *   *

I made two phone calls after Colin fell asleep. The first was to Jenny Kowalski. "I have something for you," I said, envisioning the hard drive still hidden behind my dresser. "I don't know how useful it will be, but it's a start."

"You changed your mind? You'll help us?"

The long game, I reminded myself. My only shot at beating my uncle. "The deal still holds. Nothing about Colin, and you back off if I tell you to."

"Whatever you say."

"After school tomorrow, okay? And don't bring Nick. Try to blend in."

"You're doing the right thing," she said. "Even my dad would say so."

Next, I called my house, knowing Mom would be frantic, readying myself for the storm.

It never came.

"Honey! How's Colin feeling?"

"He's . . . resting? How did you . . ."

"Oh, I called your uncle about some insurance questions. He mentioned you'd stopped by and that Colin was sick. Is it the flu? I'll bet he didn't get a flu shot, did he?"

"Probably not."

"Do you want me to bring anything over? I've got some soup already made. He might like that, once he's on the mend."

"Maybe I'll drop some off tomorrow," I said. "After school."

"That sounds nice. It will give you something to do, since The Slice is closed."

"Yeah."

"Your uncle said you could help out at Morgan's until we were up and running again. Isn't that sweet? I was a little worried, at first. I'm not sure a bar is really a suitable place for you to work, but it keeps everything in the family. And you know how hard it is to say no to your uncle."

"I don't want to work at the bar." Already, Billy was maneuvering around me. How was it that my mom was so blind to him?

"I know you're angry with him, but honestly, I think it's safer." She paused. "For everyone."

And for the first time, I heard what she was saying. I don't know why it had taken me so long. It was the same thing she'd been telling me all along. She wasn't blind to Billy's actions. She never had been. She'd been trapped, so she'd built a life she could live with, and learned how to close her eyes to the things she couldn't.

No wonder she'd been so unbelievably calm at the idea of me and Colin. He was familiar and loyal, and he'd lay down his life to keep me safe. If you could overlook the fact he worked for the Outfit—and my mom was very good at overlooking uncomfortable facts—he was a mother's dream.

I glanced at Colin, asleep on the couch, and considered telling her I was going to stay overnight. But even magic couldn't change my mom that much. "I'll only be here a little bit longer," I said. "Then I'll come home."

"I'll have dinner ready," she said. "It will be so nice to have you back, sweetie."

CHAPTER 49

L ena was waiting just inside the doors the next morning. It was too cold to linger in the courtyard, and Colin was still laid up at his place, sending me grumpy texts to check in every hour. We headed over to the cafeteria and grabbed a table, pretending that we were studying.

"How's Colin?"

"Very cranky."

"Back to normal, huh? He was pissed when you left yesterday. I almost had to sit on him to keep him from going after you."

"I figured. Thanks for watching him."

She leaned forward, propping her chin in her hands. "Your family really is as bad as everyone says, aren't they?"

I met her eyes. She already knew the answer. "Worse."

"And your uncle sent those guys after Colin because you two hooked up?"

"He wasn't thrilled." Hard to say which bothered Billy more—my relationship with Colin or that we'd defied him. But the end result was the same.

"In some families, they just, you know, ground people for that kind of thing."

"Must be nice."

"Your uncle set the fire, didn't he?"

I caught my lower lip between my teeth and nodded.

"Why'd he do it?"

"Insurance, mostly. Leverage with me." I didn't mention Ekomov or the hard drive wrapped in newspaper and stuffed inside my messenger bag, waiting to be dropped off with Jenny. "He wants me to work for him."

She made a dismissive motion with her hand. "Like that's ever going to happen."

I stayed silent.

"Are you crazy?"

"You can't say anything. Especially not to Colin."

"You're insane," she said bluntly. "Why the hell would you . . . oh. Colin."

I twisted the metal tab on my Diet Coke.

"So you're going to work for your uncle and he's going to let your boyfriend live. That should make for a fun Christmas."

"You don't seem rattled by any of this," I said. "Why not?"

She looked uncomfortable, eyes sliding away, crumbling her Pop-Tart to bits. "You're my friend," she said after a long silence. "Isn't that what friends do? Stand with you during the bad stuff?"

"I guess it is." I thought of Verity, and how I hadn't been able to stand with her until it was too late. I wondered if I'd ever get to help Lena the way she'd helped me. "Thanks."

"The one thing I don't get is Luc. What's the deal with him? How does he fit into all this?"

"Luc doesn't have anything to do with my family," I said. "It's a job, kind of. Something I'm doing as a favor to Verity. We're not . . ." I waved my hand, because finding the words to describe what Luc and I were or were not was more than I could handle today.

"You guys looked very . . ." She mimicked the hand-wave. "At the dance."

I bit my lip. "That was a mistake."

"Oh." She was about to say more, but stopped abruptly. "So . . . French monarchy."

I blinked at the subject change. "What?"

"Shouldn't you girls be in class?" Niobe asked behind me. "First period has started."

We gathered up our books, mumbling apologies, and Niobe held up a hand. "Actually, Mo, I'd like to see you in my office."

Lena grimaced as she hurried off.

"Let me guess. The Quartoren want to see me."

"I'm sure they do, but that's not why I sought you out."

We walked silently through the office, and she opened the door, unlocking it with a spell instead of a key. I could feel the casting, the exact shape of the magic as it worked. A side effect, I supposed.

Inside, Constance sat on one of the low chairs, nose red, cheeks wet.

"Hey," I said, slipping into the other seat. "Are you okay?"

She wiped her face with her sleeve. "Niobe said you fixed the magic."

"Yeah."

"She said it was really dangerous."

"It wasn't so bad. The important thing is that they have to help you now."

"Only because you forced them, right? They would have abandoned me."

I glanced out the window at the patchy snow still clinging to the bedraggled planters and statues in the courtyard. "I don't know. I don't really understand how they think."

"But you helped them." Her hands clutched the edge of the seat, white-knuckled.

"I wanted to set things right. They needed my help, and I needed theirs." I felt oddly defensive, and that was annoying. I'd nearly died. Was that not enough?

"Constance," Niobe said. "You said you had something to tell Mo?"

She seemed to come back to herself, tucking her hair behind her ears, smoothing her skirt, her chin wobbling. "I wanted to say thanks. For saving me. Even though I was kind of a bitch."

I miss her, too, I wanted to say. *Every day.* I settled for, "You're welcome."

She darted a look at Niobe and took off without another word.

When we were alone, I asked, "Does this mean you're leaving?"

"No. Constance still requires supervision. The Quartoren must uphold their part of the Covenant."

"That reminds me," I said, digging in my bag. "What do I do with these?"

She took the stack of Covenant rings from me. When I'd finally returned home, they were scattered across my nightstand, blackened and unlinked. There was no longer a hum, or any magic, emanating from them.

"Whatever you wish. The instant you fulfilled your oath to the Covenant, they reverted back to their mundane form. You could recycle them, I suppose." She looked doubtfully at the green bin beside her desk.

"It's really done, then."

"Not in the slightest. You did well, but there will be ramifications. More political than anything, I would assume."

"I don't care about the politics."

"You should, considering your position."

"I'm bound to the magic, Niobe, but I'm not looking to get caught up in that sort of thing."

She smiled. "You're bound to the Heir, Mo Fitzgerald. You're caught whether you were looking for it or not."

CHAPTER 50

I was taking out the trash in the alley behind Morgan's when Luc appeared.

"Takin' up a new career, Mouse?" His teasing held a tentative note, like he didn't know if I'd find him funny.

I hefted the bag into the Dumpster. "Hard to make any tips when your restaurant's burned down. Besides . . ." I plucked at the white twill apron. "The uniform's better."

"Don't know about that," he said, examining me. "Always thought the little hat was cute."

"Smurfs are cute," I said. "That thing was a crime against fashion."

He smiled, just a little. "Cujo around? Figured I should thank him."

"For pulling you out? You healed him after the Torrent. Consider yourself even."

"I did that for you," he said softly.

"I know." I paused, toying with the string of my apron. The anger I had expected refused to come. He'd had an impossible choice to make, I realized now. And in the end, he'd chosen me. "Why did you try to step into the magic? That was my job. Why did you risk it?"

He shrugged, looked away. "Was hoping it might work both ways—if you could draw on my talents, I could draw on yours."

"I don't have any talents."

"Smart mouth, big heart, stubborn streak wider than the Mississippi. Seem like talents to me."

"Magic ones. And that's not what the prophecy said. Why would you—"

"I was afraid." He kicked halfheartedly at a stack of wooden pallets.

"That I couldn't do it?"

"That I'd lose you."

I hugged myself against the cold, kept my voice gentle. "I'm not yours to lose."

"You made that pretty clear." Bitterness laced through his words. "You said the only reason I loved you was 'cause I had to. That I cared more about the prophecy than you."

"And risking your life was supposed to prove otherwise?"

He looked up, eyes blazing green and gold. "From the day we met, you've been stark terrified of us, you know that? Thinking it was Vee I wanted. Worrying what I feel for you is because of the prophecy, or our bond, or fate. And so you run the other direction, sayin' you can't trust me."

Pointless to deny it. "You haven't given me much reason to."

He shrugged. "The thing is, what we hate most about other people? That's usually what we hate about ourselves. Makes me wonder if it ain't just my feelings you don't trust. Maybe it's yours, too."

He'd lost his egotistical mind. He was trying to con me. He was absolutely wrong, and if my heart was jackhammering in my chest, it was from outrage, not fear that he was right. "That's crazy."

"Really? I'm thinking it makes perfect sense. You're scared to death what you feel for me is something you're being forced into. There's nothing in the world you hate more than someone telling you what to do, whether it's your mom or the Lord above or fate."

I started to protest, but he lifted an eyebrow, and I shut up.

"I tried to take over so you could get free of the prophecy. So you'd know that what you're feelin' is coming from your heart instead of the magic. You won't trust yourself to be with me, 'less you're convinced of that. Until you choose."

"You can't make me choose you," I said unsteadily.

" 'Course not," he said. "But I sure as hell can try."

"I wish you wouldn't." The words slipped out.

"Aw, Mouse. If wishes were horses . . ."

"I need to get back," I said, tilting my head toward Morgan's.

"You can't walk away from this anymore," he said, his voice carrying through the night. "We're long past that."

The magic curled inside me, my constant companion. "I know."

"The Quartoren are weak. They're still short a member, and they ain't winning any popularity contest these days. The Seraphim aren't giving up, and you're the perfect target."

"What do you mean?"

"You and the magic are part of each other now. If you're hurt, the magic suffers. Anton's people want to do some damage, and you're easy pickings."

A light snow began to fall, tiny white flakes that vanished as they hit the ground. Despite the cold, I made no move to go inside.

"We need you," he said softly. "They'd destroy the magic to bring about their version of the perfect world, and trust me—it won't be perfect for your people or mine. You were meant for this. How else do you explain everything you've been able to do, everything you've survived? You and the magic, your fates are so tangled up together that we couldn't separate 'em if we tried."

I ground my teeth. He was right, and he didn't even know the half of it. "I don't believe in fate."

"Don't call it fate. Call it the cost of free will. You had the chance to walk away the night they killed Vee. She told you to run, and you chose to stay, and every step you've taken since that night has brought you further down this path. There's no going back anymore. You think otherwise, it's the worst lie you've ever told yourself."

I watched him leave, the snow swirling around him. I wasn't lying to myself, but there was no point in chasing after him to say so. We weren't finished, Luc and I—only changed, just as the magic was changing me. Already, I could feel it transforming the pieces of the girl I'd been into the girl I could be. Someone stronger, capable of forging a path that traversed both my worlds.

Luc had been right about one thing. There was no going back, no returning to the life I'd had before. From now on, all I could do was keep moving forward.

FOOD FOR THOUGHT

1. At the beginning of the novel, Mo says that the truth is overrated. Do you agree? Are there situations where dishonesty is the right choice, or is it always better to tell the truth, regardless of the cost? Is it truly possible to lie to yourself?

2. Constance copes with her grief by lashing out at Mo. After her powers emerge, Constance's emotions become physically dangerous to those around her. Is there a point at which she should be held accountable for her actions? How long does grief or depression excuse a person's behavior?

3. Mo spends much of *Tangled* dealing with the consequences of her actions in *Torn*. For example, killing Evangeline during the Torrent inadvertently triggered the magical surges. Also, her refusal to falsely identify the Russian gangsters escalates the problems between her uncle and Yuri Ekomov. If she had known what would happen, do you think she would have chosen differently—allowed Evangeline to live and / or lied for her uncle? Should she have? In a situation where following your principles will cause problems later, how do you choose? Are there times when the cost of following your most deeply held beliefs is too high?

4. Colin tells Mo he knows her, whereas most people only know *about* her. What is the difference? Considering her actions and her agreement with Billy at the end of the book, do you think he's right? How long does it take to know someone really well? Does anyone ever completely know anyone else?

5. Mo agrees to pass information to Jenny about her uncle's criminal activities, but she keeps the Arcs a secret. Is it enough to help with the case against Billy, or does she

have an obligation to tell Jenny how her father really died? Are there any differences between Jenny's quest for vengeance and Mo's?

6. Mo and Luc's relationship is complicated by their opposing views on fate. Does Luc's belief in the prophecy and fate make his feelings for Mo less genuine? Is Mo's fear—that being with Luc means letting fate control her life—reasonable? Who is right? If someone's worldview and beliefs are completely different from yours, is it possible to overcome those differences?

7. Why does Colin keep his past a secret from Mo: to protect her, to put it behind him, or another reason? Should he have been more open, or was Mo wrong to investigate after he asked her not to? Does loving someone mean sharing all your secrets, or is it better to keep some things to yourself?

8. Mo forges the Covenant with the Arcs to help Constance and agrees to work for her uncle to spare Colin's life. Why do you think she repeatedly puts herself second? Is her self-sacrifice a strength or a weakness? At what point should she put herself first? Her mother also sacrificed her own happiness to ensure a stable life for Mo; do you agree with her choice? Is there a difference between Mrs. Fitzgerald's deal with Billy and Mo's?

9. How does Mo's view of her mother change over the course of the novel? Mrs. Fitzgerald is aware of much more than she lets on, particularly about Billy's activities and Mo's relationship with Colin. Is this an effective way to cope with the situation? How does her approach to the family's troubles differ from Mo's? When you're faced with difficult things you can't change, how do you handle it?

10. At the end of the novel, Mo realizes that she will never be free of Luc and the Arcs; her bond with the magic

means she will always be connected to their world. How will this affect her future? Do you agree with Luc that she will eventually have to choose between the Flat world and the Arc one, or is there a way for her to balance the two? What is the appeal of each world for her? How would you make that decision?

Read on for a sneak peek at *Bound*,
the conclusion of Erica O'Rourke's
darkly magical Torn series,
coming in July.

The problem with terrible ideas is that the people who have them don't recognize how truly awful they are until it's too late. After all, nobody deliberately chooses the worst possible course of action. They have great plans and good intentions. They're caught up in the thrill of the moment, seeing the world as they wish it to be, blind to any hint of trouble. You can warn someone that they're running headlong into disaster, beg them to stop, plant yourself in their path. But in the end, people have to make their own choice.

Even if it's a terrible one.

My father's coming home party was a perfect example of good intentions gone awry.

"This is ridiculous," I said to Colin. "Who throws a huge party for someone fresh out of prison?"

My mom, that's who. I'd tried to talk her out of it completely—I felt less than celebratory at the prospect of my dad's return—but she'd insisted. Then I'd argued that a small family gathering at the house might be more appropriate. But for once, my mother wasn't concerned with propriety.

So I was stuck at my uncle's bar with everyone we'd ever known, waiting for my dad to walk in the door for the first time in twelve years.

Around me, the crowd was growing impatient, their small talk taking on an irritable note. I should have been setting out bowls of peanuts and pretzels, but instead I slumped against the back wall and watched a game of darts. "You know she's hoping for one of those big reunion scenes. Like we're all going to hug and cry and be a happy family again."

Colin's hand found mine and squeezed, but his eyes swept across the sea of people, searching even in the dim light of the bar. "Just hang in there a little bit longer."

"I don't know why I even agreed to come," I said.

"Because it's important to your mother," my uncle said, appearing beside us. Irritation flickered across his face at the sight of my fingers linked with Colin's. "Be grateful I told her you had to work, or you'd have been off to Indiana along with her. They'll be arriving any moment, so start practicing your smile."

I bared my teeth. "How's this?"

"I'll not have you spoil her day, Mo. She's waited a long time for this."

"Longer than she needed to, right?"

Billy's eyes narrowed, and beside me, Colin made a low noise of warning. *Don't bait the bear,* he was telling me, and any other day I would have listened. But tonight, my nerves were stretched to breaking.

Ignoring the ripple of tension along Colin's arm, I lifted my chin and stared at my uncle. A moment passed, and finally Billy made a show of looking around the room. "Make sure everyone has something to toast with, and then you're free for the night. I'll need you Monday, though."

With that, he was off to mingle. I leaned my head against Colin's shoulder and he murmured, "The sooner we get The Slice up and running, the better. I don't like you working for Billy."

I wasn't a fan of the arrangement, either, but I had no choice. Or rather, I'd had a choice—my freedom or Colin's life—and I'd taken the latter. As long as I worked for my uncle, Colin was safe. He didn't know about the deal we'd struck, and he definitely wasn't aware my job was more than wiping down tables and carting empties to the recycling bins out back. He assumed, like almost everyone else in my life, that I was working at the bar until my mom's restaurant was rebuilt, at which point life would go back to normal.

I had learned the hard way that normal was not an option anymore.

I went up on tiptoe, brushed a kiss over his cheek. His hand tightened on my waist for an instant before he edged away.

"What? Everyone knows we're together." I sank back down, trying not to feel hurt.

"I'm not crazy about having an audience."

I glanced around. There were a few people eyeing us—not many, but enough to make Colin uncomfortable. "Fine. But we're not staying here all night."

He grinned and ducked his head, his breath warm against my ear. "Wasn't planning on it."

I made the rounds of the bar, my back aching from carrying a full tray back and forth. The whole time I could feel Colin watching me, an anchor in a stormy sea, and I clung to the sensation. But gradually I became aware of another one, a prickling awareness that made me rub my arms to ward off a chill, despite the overheated room.

"They're coming," someone said.

Around me, voices dropped to a hush, somehow as noisy as the earlier chatter. I spun, looking for Colin, but the crowd was surging toward the front, hiding him from view. Within me, the magic stirred—anticipation and stress and dread serving to wake up the force inside me. Something was happening.

Cheerful hands urged me forward, but the magic tugged at me, worried, and I stopped short, trying to hold fast against the tide of people.

Luc? He had a knack for showing up at the worst possible moment, and I couldn't imagine a worse one than tonight. The connection between us had lain dormant for nearly three months, a welcome break while I acclimated to my new life. I'd known he would come back eventually. I'd hoped to have things under control before he turned everything inside out again.

My hands clutched the empty tray to my chest like a shield. I squeezed my eyes shut, feeling along the lines for the vibrating tension that would indicate an Arc was here. But the lines were quiet, their power held in abeyance. There was no sign of Luc or anyone else in the room working a spell—even a concealment. I opened my eyes and searched for a familiar green gaze and sharp cheekbones, but they weren't there. It was better that way.

People stood three deep in front of the oak counter running along the side of the room. Behind them, I could see the hunched backs of the regulars and Charlie, my favorite bartender. He was pulling beers and gauging who'd hit their limit, working his way down the line in a steady rhythm. He seemed to pop in and out of view as the people milled around him.

It was a familiar sight, but something seemed just slightly off-kilter, out of place. I tried to imagine Morgan's like a puzzle in a kid's magazine, where you compared two pictures of the same scene and circled the differences. What was the difference? The bar. Charlie. The customers. The party. What was out of place?

A gap opened in the crowd, giving me a clear view of the bar for only an instant. But it was enough.

The regulars all faced Charlie or the front door. From my spot at the rear of the bar, only the backs of their heads were visible. Except for one guy, facing the opposite direction.

Facing me.

For a split second, I could see him as clearly as if I'd taken his picture—eyebrows raised mockingly, mouth twisted in a caustic smile—and then the shutter closed as the crowd filled the gap again.

Not Luc.

Suddenly, I wished it were.

Anton Renard. Leader of the Seraphim. A renegade Arc who had every reason to want me dead.

The feeling was mutual.

I forced myself to walk toward him, but when I reached the bar stool, he was gone, and the lines were silent.

"Problem?" Colin asked from behind me. He rested his hands on my shoulders, the weight reassuring.

I drew in a shaky breath, turning to him. "I thought I saw Anton. Here."

His expression hardened. "You're sure?"

"No." If it was Anton, I would have felt the spell he'd used to hide himself as it resonated along the lines. Either I was mistaken, or he'd managed to blend convincingly into a Flat bar on the South Side of Chicago. But the Anton I knew was too arrogant for blending.

Something had triggered the magic's fretfulness, but maybe it was my own unhappiness. Over the past few months the connection had strengthened. I'd noticed how it responded to my moods—a pleasant hum beneath my skin when I was content, a tremor every time I crossed the threshold of Morgan's—and assumed it was further proof the magic was alive and intelligent. Proof I wasn't ready to share with anyone.

From the front of Morgan's, someone called, "They're here! Where's Mo?"

Colin took my hand, tugging me toward the narrow front doors as they opened. The crowd drew a collective breath as my mom stepped inside, cheeks flushed with excitement and cold. And I forgot all about half-seen faces, because immediately behind her, blinking at the noise of the crowd's shouts of "surprise" and "welcome home," was my father.

I hadn't seen him in five years.

From behind a wall of people, I studied him carefully. He was still my dad, sharp greenish-brown eyes framed with heavy black glasses. His dark red hair needed a trim, curling at the collar, and his narrow face transformed quickly from shock to pleasure. But there were lines at the corners of his eyes that hadn't been there before, and his hair was streaked with gray. His posture was a little more stooped, like he was trying to withdraw into himself. He looped one arm around my mother, drawing her close as people lined up to pump his hand and welcome him home.

Billy spotted me on the outskirts, trying to fade into the crowd, and grasped my elbow. "Don't you dare ruin this," he muttered, and towed me into the middle of the circle surrounding my parents. His voice suddenly brimmed with warmth and good cheer. "Jack! Welcome home! Look what I've brought you—a sight for sore eyes, don't you think?"

He stepped back, releasing me. I could feel the crowd watching us, waiting for the tearful reunion.

After a moment, my father let go of my mom and took a tentative step toward me, spreading his arms wide. "There's my girl," he said, his voice cracking in the suddenly quiet room. "There's my Mo."

I wanted to turn away, punish him for all the pain he'd caused us. I wasn't going to let him back in, and there was no reason to pretend otherwise.

Until I saw my mom blinking back tears, a wobbly smile on her lips. All her hopes for our family were crystallized in a single moment, and my reaction would either let them grow, or shatter them on the worn oak floorboards. I licked my lips and swallowed the dust clogging my throat.

"Hi, Dad." I stuffed my hands in my apron pockets, dug my nails into my palms. "It's . . . good to have you home."

He was across the room in three strides, wrapping me in the same bear hug he used to give me when I was a little kid, and for a moment I let myself believe my mom was right. Tonight could be a fresh start, a chance for us to be a family again. His return might not be such a terrible thing after all.

And then, still squeezing me tightly, my father whispered one word to me: "Liar."